THE ONE-EYED MAN

LARRY L. KING

with an introduction by the author

and a foreword by Fred Erisman

TCU Press / Fort Worth

Copyright © 1966 by Larry L. King;
copyright ©2001 Texhouse Corporation;
foreword copyright © 2001 by TCU Press.

Library of Congress Cataloging-in-Publication Data

King, Larry L.
The one-eyed man : a novel / by Larry L. King; with an introduction by
the author and a foreword by Fred Erisman
p.cm.—(The Texas tradition series ; no. 31)
ISBN 0-87565-236-0
1. Southern States—Fiction. 2. Race relations—Fiction. 3.
Segregation—Fiction. 4. Governors—Fiction. 5. Elections—Fiction. I.
Title. II. Series.

PS3561.148 O54 2001
813'.54—dc 21
00-062031

Praise for *The One-Eyed Man*

"This is a firecracker of a novel. The talk is profane and alive. The people move. Things happen."—*Houston Post*

"Written with a social satirist's skill, this book is out of *All the King's Men* territory and it's got our vote."—*Virginia Kirkus Readers' Service*

"In the end [King's] novel succeeds because . . . it conveys with incredible impact the difficult truth that men are unmoved by rational arguments and material blandishments when issues are held in the heart."—*Boston Traveler*

"Cullie Blanton comes hauntingly alive, and the atmosphere of the South is so accurate that one can smell the fat-back frying, the collard greens steaming, and feel the clammy heat rising out of the swamplands."—*Louisville Courier-Journal*

"King's first novel is well-handled, sensitively put together and good reading."—*The Cleveland Press*

"Mr. King exhibits an acute sense of hearing. He captures to perfection the tongue of that Southern political hybrid, still flourishing in legislative chambers, whose bloodstream is host to the viruses of colorful Claghorns, the jacknape Snopses and the revered Nathan Bedford Forrest."—*St. Petersburg (Florida) Times*

"The seriousness of King's subject is lightened by his humor and fabulously funny descriptions. King is rare in his ability to combine the vulgar with the humorous in such a manner that the four-letter words don't seem to be what they really are."
—*Beaumont Enterprise*

"A fine novel . . . . Cullie Blanton is a superb characerization."—*Chicago Tribune*

In the land of the blind,
the one-eyed man is king.

—Anonymous

Do you think I am trusty and faithful?
Do you see no further than this façade, this smooth
and tolerant manner of me?
Do you suppose yourself advancing on real ground
toward a real heroic man?
Have you no thought O dreamer
that it may be all
maya, illusion?

—Walt Whitman

This book is for my wife,
   Rosemarie.
   And
   for
   these
   three:
   Cheryl,
   Kerri,
   Bradley.

INTRODUCTION

I WAS ALL BUT certain during the writing of this, my first book, that it would win the highest literary honors, become a runaway bestseller, and cause sleepless nights for Norman Mailer, William Styron, Irwin Shaw, Eudora Welty, and John Steinbeck—among other gifted novelists—as they worried about being displaced by the new kid on the block. I don't suppose, these near-forty-years later, that it's necessary to inform you it didn't happen quite that way.

First-time book writers almost always expect more than shall be granted them. Knowing nothing of the publishing realities, they somehow assume a huge readership that has never heard of them anxiously awaits their initial offering. Clever editors, hoping to encourage the neophyte writer to stay the course and finish the Damned Book, sometimes heap outlandish praise on the writing rookie. And, of course, the rookie is all too eager to believe it. By the time his book is finished he may be confiding to strangers in barrooms that had he been born a few years earlier he almost certainly could have helped this fellow Shakespeare avoid so many clichés.

It is a small miracle that *The One-Eyed Man* ever was written or published. I had wished two earlier malformed novels on the only novelists I personally knew—Billy Lee Brammer, David Halberstam, Warren Miller, and Tristram Coffin—in a fruitless attempt at having them persuade their editors and publishers that I was certain to become the next Hemingway and should be gaffed and hauled aboard. Warren Miller did tell his New York editor, Robert Gutwillig, that I "perhaps" one day might produce something publishable. On a slow day at the office, apparently, Mr. Gutwillig wrote to ask whether I had any fresh prose he might look at. I did not but was not above lying about it.

Within an hour or so I had spun a plot in a three-page letter and had found my title by searching *Bartlett's Familiar Quotations:* "In the land of the blind, the one-eyed man is king." I added the fiction that I had been working on the novel "for about eight months" and that I expected to have finished my manuscript "within a year." Very truly yours. . . .

Three days later Mr. Gutwillig called to say, "If you can write a novel that's as good as your letter, we'll both become rich and famous." He urged me to fly myself and my manuscript to New York at the expense of the McGraw-Hill publishing house. I was more than willing to go but had no manuscript to take with me. One deception breeding another, I told my boss—Congressman Jim Wright of Texas—that I felt a siege of flu coming on and must go home. My "flu" lasted long enough for me to write the novel's first chapter, produce a more complete outline, and sneak off to New York. I was astonished when Editor Gutwillig signed me to a contract and handed me a $1,500 check for an "advance against royalties" almost as soon as he finished reading my thin manuscript. Hell, this was *easy: is that all there is to it?* Little did I know, on that bright and dizzying September afternoon of 1963, what lay ahead. . . .

John F. Kennedy's assassination, for one thing—and in my native place. I had helped advance President Kennedy's fatal trip, had known him personally for some five years, had campaigned with and for him and—more starry-eyed then than now—saw him as a personal hero. Soon there was a new trauma—a split with my wife of thirteen years, an ill-advised attempt at reconciliation, and then as ugly and mean a divorce as poor people can afford. Three children I loved were pawns in the many battles to follow. I came down with writer's block and drank far too much. I solved *those* problems by quitting my paying job and getting married a second time. Stone broke, I freelanced magazine articles for small money to pay the rent and child support. Those jobs, of course, took away time from my novel writing. Book deadlines came, were missed, and new ones set amidst much gnashing of editorial teeth. Though damn little was getting written, I clung hard to my belief that *The One-Eyed Man* was a great book and would, in time, launch a literary career to goggle the eyes of the world. In retrospect, I suppose I *had* to believe that to stay semi-sane and keep slogging.

I wrote the book catch-as-catch-can. On the sly, in Congressman Wright's office, until I quit my job. In two scabby, cheap rooming houses on Capitol Hill. On an old leaky boat owned by wife-to-be and docked at a run-down Maryland marina. In the Austin home of my cousins Lanvil and Glenda Gilbert, where I hid out from bill collectors and the ex-wife's lawyers. In the small efficiency apartment in Washington of my new bride. In the Delaware beach cottage of columnist Robert Novak. In mom-'n'-pop motels as I traveled to write those rent-paying magazine pieces. And all the time, of course, I was writing a book destined to be a "classic." *Sure* I was. . . .

To add nervous spices, Editor Gutwillig moved mid-book from McGraw-Hill to New American Library and complicated life by instructing me how to break the contract he had signed me to, so as to join him at his new publishing house. (This gave me my first clue that publishing might not be the "gentlemanly trade" it advertised itself to be.) The compensatory factor was that NAL would pay back the $1,500 I had taken from McGraw-Hill—and give me $5,000 in "new money" to switch publishers. It is only fair to confess that I would have robbed a bank and shot two tellers for $5,000, broke as I was. Of course, I did lose more writing time wrangling with "gentlemanly" McGraw-Hill executives and lawyers, each of us threatening the other like a gang of racketeers. Eventually, if with some institutional surliness, I was freed.

At long last—in the fall of 1965, about three years after signing my original contract—I actually *finished* my novel. And while I was celebrating myself in numerous cocktail lounges and beer joints (telling all hands, naturally, what an amazing book I had wrought) all the New York newspapers went out on strike. "*Oops!*" said the NAL nabobs and then postponed publication of my novel until the summer of 1966. Well, dammit, okay: but my novel remained a work of genius, so how much harm could a six-month delay cause? Two months before *The One-Eyed Man* was to make its debut, a *Time* magazine cover story treated America's brilliant new first-time novelists and their magnificent new works soon to be released. I broke several fingernails in my haste to open that magazine and read of myself and my fellow Distinguished Artists. The yarn ran on for page after page, generously praising every neophyte novelist in the land and his or her outstanding work. Except for me and mine. Obviously, those *Time* assholes wouldn't recognize a genius if he walked in wearing a label and a red suit, right?

I am astounded, these years later, to discover all the *good* things that actually happened to *The One-Eyed Man*—because, over time, I had persuaded myself it was a miserable flop and a bigger dog than Plato. *The New York Times*, see, had devoted but a few ho-hum paragraphs to my love child. *The New Yorker* snidely said it was "as frantically entertaining as a resort social director on a rainy day." Neither *Time* nor *Newsweek* mentioned my novel in a time when the weekly newsmags were far more influential than they are today. My editor and his top boss had not concealed their opinions that my book had failed them both commercially and critically.

So, until we began combing old records in preparing this new TCU Press edition, I had truly forgotten the numerous nice or good or bracing reviews *The One-Eyed Man* received all those years ago. And that the original publisher's hardback sold about 14,000 copies, quite good for a first novel. And that my novel became a Literary Guild Book Club alternate selection in hardback and was also issued as a Signet paperback. In short, I wonder now why I felt I had been so kicked in the teeth back there in 1966. At the worst, *The One-Eyed Man* launched a career that has not turned out badly—thirteen books and seven produced plays, a few TV documentaries, a couple of screenplays, short stories, and countless nonfiction articles in about 100 magazines. So let me here say a heartfelt—if tardy—"thanks" to the publications, editors, directors, actors, readers, and theatergoers who have kept me in business and more or less off the streets and the welfare rolls. Even a few of you goddamned critics have helped here and there! (Said he, grudgingly.)

I am still not persuaded that *The One-Eyed Man* is as worthy as Dr. Fred Erisman has found it in his remarks for this TCU Press edition. But I am not mad at him for his generosity. Who knows, maybe one day I will re-read this book—a thing I have not been able to bring myself to do in probably thirty years—and come to agree with him. One is never too old to hope.

Larry L. King
Washington, D. C.

FOREWORD

WHEN THE Great American Novel is at last written, it almost certainly will be a political novel. It will not be a tale of white whales or runaway slaves, wealthy bootleggers or impoverished Okies, southern plantations or interminable trail drives. It will be a story of the workings of politics, whether at the local ("All politics is local," a former Speaker of the House has said), state, or national level. It will be about politics as it is practiced within the United States.

Politics, after all, is at the heart of the American experience. Whether expressed in the Pilgrims' 1620 banding together as "a civil body politic" or the writers of the Constitution proclaiming their determination to create "a more perfect Union," the political process has been a part of American life from the outset. And this is as it should be. No other process so vividly captures the peculiar ideals and contradictions of the United States: its mix of idealism and cynicism, altruism and egotism, principle and compromise, good and evil. Study American politics and one studies America.

American writers have long taken this premise to heart. Henry Adams, in *Democracy: An American Novel* (1880), for example, casts a skeptical eye on the workings of power and patronage in the national context of nineteenth-century Washington, D.C. Edwin O'Connor, in *The Last Hurrah* (1956), memorably filmed by John Ford with Spencer Tracy starring as the old pol Frank Skeffington, turns to local politics, following the final campaign of a big-city political boss loosely modeled on Boston's James M. Curley. And Allen Drury, drawing upon his years as a journalist in Washington, uses his Pulitzer-Prize-winning *Advise and Consent* (1959) to examine the public *and* private machinations associated with efforts to confirm the appointment of a controversial Secretary of State.

All three, however, pale alongside the quintessential (so far)

American political novel, Robert Penn Warren's *All the King's Men* (1946). Harking back to Louisiana during the administration of Huey P. Long, Warren establishes for all time the basic characters of the political genre. There is the Idealistic Liberal—Dr. Adam Stanton, surgeon and scientist, whose life is guided by his straightforward and absolutistic view of the dilemmas the world presents. There is the Pragmatic Politician—Willie Stark, governor of an unnamed southern state, who is willing to cut the rawest of deals, so long as he furthers his genuine desire to do good for his people. And there is the Cynical Journalist—here Jack Burden, historian and governor's gofer who narrates the book and understands at last the unsolvable incompatibility of his two friends' ideas. He alone grasps the worthiness of both and the near impossibility of reconciling them and at book's end faces the uncertainty of the future carrying the burden of his knowledge. *All the King's Men* is a peculiarly American story and, within its context, a peculiarly southern one. And therein lies its importance.

Larry L. King's *The One-Eyed Man* is neither *All the King's Men* nor the Great American Novel, but it does for Texas politics of the 1960s what Warren's novel does for southern politics of the 1930s and 1940s. It extends the themes of the exercise of power in a democratic society and the qualities that, for better or for worse, characterize the American South. But, whereas *All the King's Men* deals in myth, symbol, and metaphor (look again at the names of the three principal characters: Adam, Stark, and Burden) to expand its political context to a more philosophical level, King's novel overtly shows the unvarnished, real-world workings of the modern political system, with a pragmatic, practical politician juggling desperately opposing forces at its heart. It builds, perhaps unconsciously, upon Warren's model, and a more local one, as well—*The Gay Place* (1961), by King's friend, William Brammer. Writing about what one writer has called "the flea circus of [Texas] state politics" in the Lyndon Johnson era, Brammer gives a memorable picture of Governor Arthur (Goddam) Fenstemaker, a person of profane goodwill who is echoed in King's own Cullie Blanton.

King's book, however, goes beyond purely state matters to consider the larger practice of politics in the later twentieth century, and it prepares the way for the presence of politics in King's later works. Among these, his journalistic treatments of Nelson Rockefeller, Gerald Ford, and Lyndon B. Johnson and his plays, *The Best Little Whorehouse in Texas* (1978), *The Kingfish* (1979), and *The Dead Presidents' Club* (1996) stand out. These works extend elements of *The One-Eyed Man* as assuredly as King's novel extends elements of *All the King's Men* and *The Gay Place*—and therein lies *its* importance.

Born in Putnam, Texas, in 1929, Larry L. King began his reflections on the political scene in the early 1950s as political reporter for the *Odessa* (Texas) *American* and as a volunteer in the gubernatorial campaigns of Ralph Yarborough. His stories in the *American* attracted the attention of Democratic congressional candidate J.T. Rutherford, and, when Rutherford was elected to the House of Representatives in 1954, he took King to Washington with him as his administrative assistant. King stayed with Rutherford's office until the early 1960s, when he became administrative assistant for Representative Jim Wright (Democrat, Texas), where he worked until May 1964. Then, still shaken by the assassination of John F. Kennedy in the preceding year, he resigned, determined to make his own way as a freelance writer. He began what would become a long association as a regular contributor to the *Texas Observer*, a liberal, Austin-based political journal, and he also began the novel that became *The One-Eyed Man*. He finished the novel in early summer 1965, learned in November of that year that it had been selected for distribution by the Literary Guild Book Club, and saw its publication in May 1966. Initial reviews were not strong, but the book sold well nonetheless and later went into a paperback edition and sold respectably.

Two attributes make *The One-eyed Man* noteworthy. The first is its cast of characters, which, in one respect, closely parallels that of *All the King's Men*. Among the principals, there is Dallas Johnson, state legislator and liberal politician—but politician before he's a liberal, and always ready to be wooed and persuaded as policies take shape. He understands the workings of the system and strives to use it to carry out his vision of what should be, but, like H.L. Mencken's "honest politician," he "stays bought" when he cuts a deal in his search for results. And there is Jim Clayton, the journalist narrator through whose eyes we see the events of the novel. He has an ingrained sense of truth and veracity, but he accepts the reality of the journalistic and political world; as journalist he writes what he is expected to write, and as political aide he does the chores he is ordered to do. At the same time, he knows what he's doing, and, like many others of us in the real world, recognizes the contradictions and hypocrisies forced upon him.

Balancing Dallas and Jim are the figures of the opposition, for the book deals, among other matters, with the ferment and frenzy of an election year. There is the right-wing gubernatorial challenger, "Bayonet Bill" Wooster—an ex-Marine general with no compunctions about appealing to the basest qualities of the electorate. His campaign is based upon fear: fear of racial integration, fear of the Communists, fear of the federal government, and he presents his candidacy as the forefront of a holy war against the incumbent infidel. And there is cagey old Poppa Posey, a former governor who's drawn into the race by Wooster's money so as to split the support for the incumbent governor. Wooster is a demagogue and Posey an opportunist, and neither augurs well for the future of the state.

Towering over them all, as indeed he towers over the entire book, is Governor Cullie Blanton. Altruist and egotist, idealist and pragmatist, sophisticate and vulgarian, Blanton is easily the most intriguing and complex character of the novel. His real-life origins are cloudy; just as Warren vehemently denies patterning Willie Stark after Huey Long, King downplays Blanton's resemblance to Lyndon Johnson, arguing that the character contains at least as much of Huey Long, Herman Talmadge, and Alfalfa Bill Murray—all colorful southern politicians in their own right—as he does of LBJ. But King's portrait belies the protest: Blanton, in his wheeling and dealing, his crudities and profanity, his ruthlessness and his compassion, is a dead-on portrait of LBJ in full cry.

Like LBJ, Blanton is given to conferring with associates at all hours, often wearing only his bathrobe. Like LBJ, Blanton is wedded to the telephone; he is never far from one, and some of his most impassioned erupting is done over the wire. Like LBJ, Blanton is capable of astonishing crudities; Johnson's barnyard metaphors and exhibition of his gall-bladder scar are nothing alongside Blanton's holding a press conference while wallowing naked in a bathtub in the

Hay-Adams Hotel. Like LBJ, Blanton is fond of quoting the Bible, his pronouncements at times taking on the resonance and rhythms of the evangelist.

Like LBJ, Blanton has no reservations about arm-twisting, even coercion, silently reminding readers that Johnson's oft-quoted Scriptural tag, "Come now, and let us reason together" (Isaiah, 1:18), is followed by Isaiah 1:19-20—"If ye be willing and obedient, ye shall eat the good of the land: / But if ye refuse and rebel, ye shall be devoured with the sword: for the mouth of the Lord hath spoken *it.*" Even Jim, no stranger to Blanton's irresistible powers of persuasion, is taken aback when Blanton gives him a list of a dozen dissidents, details the dirt he has on each, and tells Jim to use that dirt to bring the twelve into line. Like LBJ, Blanton is at times massively insecure, swinging wildly from ecstatic visions of himself as *the* mover and shaker among the movers and shakers of the world to self-indulgent moments of piteous "God, how I pity me" lamenting.

And, like LBJ, Blanton is a capable, determined person who in many respects is precisely the wrong person in the wrong place at the wrong time. His state, deeply imbued with the traditions of the Old South, is facing a Supreme Court mandate to integrate the state university. The outcome, as Blanton recognizes, is foreordained; African Americans are going to enter the university regardless of the protestations of the reactionary elements throughout the region. He strives, therefore, to make the transition as painless and as bloodless as possible, and he fails. His efforts to awaken the legislature to the vanishing of the Old South are destroyed by an unguarded moment of profanity. His efforts to rally university student leaders to the cause are crushed by the tragic accidental death of one of the young people. And his desire to bring his state, albeit kicking and screaming, into the mid-twentieth century are thwarted by tradition, inertia, and demagoguery. He is, as he himself concedes, one who has done some good things, but, in the last analysis, has "just got in the way of goddamn history." For every progressive step forward, an enormous burden of tradition and ingrained popular mindset must be challenged, and that burden can at times overwhelm even the most honorable of intentions. Blanton's defeat at the hands of Bayonet Bill, like LBJ's surrender in the face of the growing protests against him and his administration, is ultimately tragic: he knows what ought to be done, but his manner of doing it, in style, substance, and technique, is at odds with the national—in this case, the state—temper.

The second attribute distinguishing *The One-Eyed Man* is King's capturing of a time, a place, and a world-view. The novel is very much a work of the 1960s; it evokes the post-Kennedy *angst* and the racial turmoil that so vividly colored the decade. It resonates with the calls of both sides in the racial dilemma: the integrationists, who argue the cause of equality, access, and human dignity, and the segregationists, who hold to the power of a century and more of common practice, the accepted inferiority of African Americans and the seductive doctrine of state's rights. King demonizes only Bayonet Bill; the other figures he presents accurately if not approvingly, and we see again the emotional, political, and human dilemma that North and South alike faced.

But, still more than its recreation of the American 1960s, *The One-Eyed Man* gains merit because it asks a series of questions as its story unfolds: essential questions, necessary questions, but questions largely unanswered even at the dawn of the twenty-first century. What, for example, separates the demagogue from the leader? At what point do personal desires outweigh public ones? At what point does a desire to do good become overwhelmed by one for self-advancement or self-aggrandizement? What injustices are acceptable in the name of a larger justice? What should the people expect of their chosen leaders? And who, finally, is the person or body, whatever the level—local, state, or national— best equipped to determine the greatest good for the greatest number?

No, *The One-Eyed Man* is not *All the King's Men*, but it does its part in posing haunting questions for American readers. King himself goes on to explore some of these questions in his later works: the fulminating television personality and the spineless governor of *The Best Little Whorehouse in Texas* have their origins here, as do the scheming, two-faced opportunists who populate *The Dead Presidents' Club*. He has, moreover, through his journalism and his political profiles made clear many of his own answers for the questions; a proud Democrat but not an unthinking one, he knows where he stands, and why. While he strives to entertain in his work, he also strives to inform and to challenge, and out of that challenge he offers a similar call to individual insight for each of his readers. If he can achieve even a plurality of such awakenings, Larry L. King will indeed have justified his novel, not to say his existence.

Fred Erisman
Texas Christian University

1

WE CAME SWOOSHING across the fault line of the rock-dotted hills and burst out of the pine thickets into the falling flatlands without slowing down or looking back, like maybe something howling and hairy was gaining on us fast. Soon the black limousine was rolling through the canebrakes where the air was heavy and faintly jasmined, as perfume on a nocturnal lady of the streets. The highway was smooth and flat and broad. Rows of sugar cane mottled by grape-colored blotches marched to the edges of the slab of raised concrete, pressing in God-close on each side.

The Governor slouched in the back seat, wallowing in the feel of good leather, smacking meaty lips over a slice of salted watermelon. His mouth moved up and down as if running the scale on some juice-laden harmonica. The single white line dividing the dazzling pavement rammed straight at the car, boring in from the burnt-orange globe of late-afternoon sun. Bo Steiner, the back of his neck like a sun-blistered tree trunk sticking up from the gingerbread-brown coat of the State Highway Patrol pulled tightly across his bull shoulders, hunched over the wheel.

"Bo," the Governor said suddenly.

The trooper's eyes sought the Governor in the rear-view mirror and he spat his answer like a soldier at roll call: "Hassah!"

"Melon runs through me like shoats through a hog wallow," Cullie Blanton said. "Find a place fit for a good governor to pass water."

Bo Steiner wrinkled his forehead with the rare ache of thinking. His thick lips pursed in an agony of concentration. He cleared his throat and ran his tongue in and out like a frog catching flies.

"Now?" the trooper asked. "Now, Governor?"

"Hell, no," the Governor snorted from around a juicy hunk of watermelon. "A week from Thursday. I just wanted to get on the god-damn waitin' list." He glowered, legs crossed Buddha-like in the wide,

1

plush seat—a great, profane god awaiting the bearer of bad tidings. The trooper opened his mouth a time or two like somebody had pulled his string before he was ready. Finally he choked it past his teeth: "I mean . . . uh . . . right this here second, sir?"

"Godamighty," the Governor said, "why would I want to piddle into the wind at seventy miles an hour? To help the goddamn pants-pressin' industry?"

"Nossah," the trooper said unhappily.

"Sweet Jesus!" the Governor said in supreme disgust. He worked his jaws over the watermelon. "Just hang loose. *I'll* say when."

Bo turned thankfully to the task of driving. And that was something he could do. He could make the big car do everything but card tricks. If you had the heart and the stomach for it, and good kidneys that didn't flush easily, and if you could give up dwelling on how it would be with the car flipping across the canebrakes if ever it broke out of control, and how mere mortal flesh would tangle with ripping hunks of splintering iron and steel and twisting chrome, all you had to do when Bo went lickety-splitting down the highway, finding room enough to caper in the islands of space between the creeping mule-drawn wagons and the whizzing sedans and old pickup trucks, was hang on and whoop silent prayers begging deliverance. And he would get you there.

The Governor must have been thinking of Bo's genius at the wheel. "What the hell," he said abruptly, "all Mozart could do was write music."

Cullie Blanton ate watermelon with a relish. His head was bent into the sweet, pulpy heart of it like maybe he was gnawing through to reach the answer to some woolly riddle. Now and again he pulled his broad face out of the red pulp and blew the black seeds into one hand. The other, cupped so that the dark green rind of the melon rested in his palm, he thrust over toward me. I zeroed in on the pulpy part with a miniature box of Morton's salt and dive-bombed until Cullie Blanton grunted gubernatorial satisfaction, and I wondered what the other members of my graduating class might chance to be doing right at that crossroads junction in Time.

It was food for thought, and I chewed it.

Cullie Blanton had hired me eight years earlier to get a monkey off his back. And I was the monkey.

Yeah, I had been the monkey, and had been well trained and knew my act. Which was to write in *The Morning Star* of the unmatched virtues of a corpulent then-incumbent governor with buttermilk-white skin, deep pockets, and sticky fingers, who never in his life was justly accused of rattling the bushes in the name of the people. But *The Morning Star* was not people. It was a newspaper equally dedicated to elevating profits and to keeping down corporate taxes and new ideas.

The fat boys had grabbed the state a long time before, back when the flop-hat Big Daddies of the plantations called the turn of the wheel. And so the Governor, being the type of high-minded fellow that could barely read or write but could count sufficiently to see that all the brothers of the lodge got a fair split, was crowned with printed laurels and named "statesman." It figured that if the do-nothing Governor was such a grand prize, then only foul fools and crass knaves could oppose him. So the nabobs in the front office decided over whisky highballs and four-bit cigars that Cullie Blanton should be named public fool. And it fell my lot to do the christening.

The nabobs in the front office rigged a little ceremony and commissioned me the ace political writer of *The Morning Star*. They rationed me one of the four-bit cigars and grudgingly poured out a whisky highball, moving their doughy jaws over words like "states' rights" and "creeping Socialism" and "right thinking." And I nodded sagely to show I got the message. I got it, all right. Loud and clear. It said I should compare the incumbent favorably with Jesus Christ and Jeff Davis and jolly old Saint Nick. And I should measure Cullie Blanton against the suspect standards of Genghis Khan, with maybe Judas Iscariot and a little bit of Jack the Ripper tossed in on the side. I was a trained monkey and I did what I had to do in order to earn my peanuts.

Cullie wasn't the governor then, of course, but he was getting there. The race is not always to the swift. Cullie kicked and gouged his way up the ladder from that rung which nestles closest to the common dirt, and the closer he got to the rarefied atmosphere at the top, the more the fat boys felt uneasy in the region of their swollen pocketbooks. For Cullie was an unreasonable man to their way of thinking. He was always wanting to put crooks in jail, and he had a radical notion taxes ought to be returned to the people in manifest ways.

You could have gathered gloom in the plush clubs like it grew on bushes the night Cullie knocked off one of the house men for the office of state commissioner of utilities. Men of sober mien got glass-eye drunk, and the infidel called on God. It was like somebody had let the stealing license get chewed up in the washing machine, and maybe no more would be printed. And sure enough, that turned out to be the case. Within six months he had the moneybag hoarders wailing over the wire at each other through the lonesome hours. He caused the telephone company, who, Cullie held, had knocked the rates up past that point the law said was permissible, to rebate a whole hunk of money to subscribers. A commissioner of utilities who enforced the law was a poor sport indeed. Panic got to galloping through the financial community. They swore the people were up in arms. But out there among the great unwashed, what they were up in was not arms but cashier's checks. Big, lovely, retroactive checks dating back over four solid years of overcharge.

And the people knew where the money came from. Cullie saw to that. He had it fixed so the phone company had to furnish him a list of every manjack who owned a black instrument and how much the fellow would get back. He sent a form letter to each of them, detailing how he fought the good fight for them and won, and in an underscored spot on the letter was typed in the amount of money each particular taxpayer would soon get courtesy of the state commissioner of utilities.

Cullie hit the gas boys on the same ploy, and busted some heads in electric-power circles for conspiring to fix prices against the common good. He stirred up the biggest clamor since the burning of Atlanta and upped and announced for governor after two terms.

I followed Cullie all over the state. I dogged him like he was possum in the brush. I was his shadow and I bayed for his blood. When he leaned into the crowds with his eyes standing on stems and his gums beating promises, it sounded better than the call to eat the barbecued goodness of the golden calf. But I would knock the sharp edge off their appetite by taking to the typewriter to accuse Cullie of tampering with the truth, or else being guilty of very bad arithmetic. Once I wrote that he would have to tax the doorknobs off every building in the state to pick up the tab for his assorted schemes. Later, after I'd switched sides, I told him he couldn't come close to carrying out the programs he'd put upon the tongue of promise.

"I can make a run at it," he said.

"But you can't do it."

"Boy," he said, "do you dispute the state needs all the things I've been whoopin' for?"

"No," I said. "But you just add up the cost of your binge of goodie pledging and see if it won't break the back of reason. It's plain poor mathematics."

"It may be that," he said. "But it is also somethin' else. It is damned excellent politics. It is grade-A, pure, uncut, government-inspected and genuinely certified politics, of the type's been endorsed by everybody from Duncan Hines to the Prince of Peace. They vote for names on that ballot, not a bunch of goddamn numbers."

Once, when I was hounding Cullie for *The Morning Star*, he got careless. We had bounced into this decaying town in the deep boondocks, a collection of antique shacks jammed together at the roots of a red-clay hill, and Cullie had ordered the driver to pull in because he had a hankering for a cold Nehi Cola. I jolted over the dirt road trailing Cullie's car, eating the dust from his wheels, and plaguing him like the past of a repentant scarlet woman. Cullie had coughed up his dime and I was fishing for one before either of us realized we were in as black an order as you could find on the Gold Coast. Cullie began to josh the Negroes and they took up the habit of grinning. He got the cold feel of the Nehi laying good on his tongue, and he got careless. He got careless enough to confide to the awed gawkers that he suspected God of loving all men. Even those with black skins. The way it came out of my typewriter, and the way it read on the front page of *The Morning Star*, was that Cullie had bootlegged a courting visit to the land of the bogeymen, where he had told the ebony natives they were God's chosen children. That was water on our paddle, for you yell "nigger" in the boondocks and all you've got to do is get out of the way of the trampling herd.

That was the bit of chicanery, it turned out, that caused the ball of yarn between me and the nabobs in the front office to unravel. But we didn't know it at the time. It was a week later that our little association fell apart at the seams.

Cullie had come from out of the brush to campaign in King's Port, where *The Morning Star* rolled off the presses in the black hours before dawn. He came for a round of rafter-shaking speeches and baby-kissing, and the requisite number of meetings in smoke-filled rooms. He came like a hill-country circuit rider hell-bent on driving the infidel out of the sinful city, quoting liberally of the Bible, cautiously of Shakespeare, and boldly of Edgar A. Guest. After sitting mesmerized through one of his lung-bursting performances one evening, I took to typewriter and cut him a new one. Cullie must have picked up one of the first papers that hit a door stoop the next morning, for by noon he had sent a lackey around to summon me.

It was late in the evening when I showed at Cullie's hotel room, and it was not one of the best hotels. It was the kind that still had potted plants in the lobby, and no air conditioning, and it was about six blocks too close to the railroad tracks. Cullie was alone in his hotel room except for a bottled friend named Jack Daniel's. After he'd introduced me to that gentleman, he sat on the edge of his bed and watched me a few minutes as if he might be visiting the zoo and had been told my species was fast becoming extinct. He cocked the big mop of white hair over to the right and squinted his eyes at me, grinning like he was in a contest.

"Boy," he said by way of openers, "how you fixed for principles?"

"I reckon I got just barely enough to get by," I said.

"You ain't plumb eat up with high principle, are you? It ain't malignant? It don't gnaw on you like cancer in the dead of the night?"

"It hurts some," I said. "But I never needed transfusions for it."

He nodded and tipped a bit more of his spirited friend into my glass. "It's like the goddamn typhoid fever," he said solemnly. "Some folks carry it and some don't."

"I'm not a carrier. Maybe I never was exposed."

He grunted and gladdened the insides of his own glass. "You hate me?" he asked abruptly. "I ever wrong your stepsister or kick your hound dog . . . anything like that?"

I shook my head.

"Boy," Cullie Blanton said easily, "this here is just between you and me and Almighty God. And me and Him will swear a paralyzed oath this little meetin' never happened if you ever indicate to the contrary."

Cullie walked to a switch on the wall and flicked on an old-fashioned ceiling fan. Its *swish swish swish* sliced the air up in little pieces.

"You're hurtin' me," he said. "You been stickin' me with needles like I was one of them goddamn voodoo dolls. Why, when you hit a sour note on that typewriter of yours I know it if I'm three hundred miles away. For it is like a kick in the goddamn privates. Like that mishmash you wrote the other day about how I went courtin' the black brethren in the bush. I stop and have one little ole pissant Nehi Cola because my tongue's growin' hair, and you make it sound like I appoint two dozen Mau Mau campaign managers."

I didn't say anything. Cullie ambled across the room in a slow lope, sucking at his whisky glass. "Yeah, you got a gift for muckrakin'. You got a natural flair. A regular goddamn knack. And you lay it on the line in three-cent words the woolhats and rednecks and the peckerwoods can get in their heads easy as sniffin' snuff. Boy, you write like your pen's been dipped in bile and boiled in lye water. You are a regular goddamn assassin."

I mumbled thanks for the compliment. Cullie was at the double window at the end of the room. He pulled aside the faded drapes and tugged at his undershorts. He turned around several times like a dog inspecting a potential resting place, and he whistled between his teeth and breathed a neutral "goddamn."

"I got the itch to be governor," he said with his back to me. "I want it like a hog craves slop. You ever want anything till it ached you clean to the bone?"

"No," I said.

"Count your blessin's. With some folks it's whisky and with some it's threshin' around in the bedsheets and with others it's smokin' dope. But with me it's wantin' to be governor. You got any notion why?"

"I reckon," I said, "that you just naturally lack ambition."

He turned from the window to face me, and there was a hazy look fogging up his ice-blue eyes.

"I want to be the winged ram," he said in a hoarse voice. "The winged ram with golden fleece. The political Holy Ghost. I want to walk on the goddamn water. Yeah, and I want to build healin' temples for the sick and give alms to the blind. Put free textbooks in the schools and drive away the dark angels of ignorance. Pave the loblolly roads out in the backwoods. Give the mule-drivin' snuff-dippers a pension. Levy taxes like King Tut. Get reelected and build monuments to dwarf the goddamn Sphinx."

I didn't say anything. I just thought that he carried a burdensome load of ambition for a potential governor in our state. In those days, a progressive in our part of the country favored debtors' prison and wavered on use of the rack. Cullie Blanton cocked the big white head a bit more to the right and studied me like maybe I was the Mona Lisa and he was Leonardo da Vinci trying to decide what was wrong with my smile.

"And you are goin' to help me," he said softly.

"Yeah," I said, "and as soon as I sprout wings I'm going to fly non-stop to the West Coast."

"Boy," he said. And he grinned. "Boy, I see the nubs sproutin' now. How'd you like to go to work for me?"

"Jesus Christ!" I said, and spilled some Jack Daniels.

"Naw," he said. "Wrong fellow. But now you mention it there is a passin' similarity."

"Good God! *I* don't know anything about politics!"

"Yeah," he said, still grinning. "Yeah, and that is a natural fact. But you know about somethin' else. You know about gut-shootin'. You musta been born mean and never outgrowed it. You got the instincts of a goddamn black widder spider. And let's say I'm in the market for poison."

"Hell," I said, "I don't know . . . I hadn't thought about it."

"Well, think about it. You make it on a couple of hundred a week? And expenses?"

"I'm making it on a damn sight less."

"You got a goddamn job," he said. "Congratulations." He reached out and grabbed my hand in one huge paw, giving it three shakes in a pump-handle motion.

I was lost in a fog. "What the hell?" I asked. "I don't even know what I'm supposed to do."

"You got a bright mind," Cullie Blanton said. "You figure it out. Wash my socks. Chant my praises. Make me a statesman. Gut-shoot that goddamn pirate I'm runnin' against."

"I don't even know what it's *like.*"

"It won't be as classy as sellin' reefers to kindergarten kids," he said with a grin slicing his broad face. "Maybe more on a par with playin' backup piano in a Cajun cat house. But we will call the goddamn tunes."

So I had gone to work for him, and that had been long ago as man measures his little demitasse of Time. I had learned to dance to the secret music of politics; Cullie had indeed called the tune, and I'd found that I liked the tempo. Only now and again was there a sour note turned up on the piano. Now and again there was watermelon to be salted . . .

The Governor shoved the watermelon over again and I dive-bombed it dizzy. Cullie was relaxed, almost cherubic. He worked his way down to the light green coating between the red of the meat and the darker green of the rind, took one final bite, and rolled down the window and tossed out the remains. Licking the last sugary traces of juice from his fingers, he looked back at the splatter the melon had made on the highway.

"Broke the state law," he said, as if greatly pleased. "You feel a twitch to do your duty, Bo?"

The trooper tried to smile.

"Hundred-dollar fine for throwin' crap on the highway," the Governor said smugly.

"Hassah," the trooper mumbled.

"Corruption and evil-doin' all around," the Governor boomed. "Half the world in rubble and the other half bound for hell in a paper sack. Heathens in the pulpits and love for sale on sinful streets. Knaves and fools violatin' the sacred temples of public trust. Nation's goin' bankrupt shootin' rocket doodads at the moon. Jaded police officers winkin' at the high crime of litterbuggin' the public's paved primrose path. Shameful, *sinful*, goddamn thang! How long, America? O, how long?"

Cullie Blanton closed his eyes and leaned back in the cool blue leather of the seats. The air conditioner purred like a contented cat breathing across a bowl of ice. The Governor's face began to fold into frowning lines. Little dark pockets of worry bunched up under the eyes and in the shaded hollow of his high cheekbones.

"Talk to me of wondrous goddamn things," he said. "Tell me what you divine. Bend your tongue to knowledge and let wisdom have its way."

"They're not scaring," I said.

"Wrong. Wrong as shortchangin' blind men."

"No," I said, doggedly. "No more scared than Frank Buck would be of a garden snake."

"They're scared," the Governor said, "and that is the unflyblown Gospel. That's the jawbreakin' truth." He opened his eyes and grinned. But it was not a happy grin. It was the kind of cynical grin a man might grow after he has looked too long into the putty faces, midget minds, and tar-black hearts of creatures made in His image, and maybe had wondered and despaired at what in hell He could have had on His celestial mind that He could have botched the job so.

"Pull over, Bo," the Governor ordered. "I got a urgent message from my kidneys."

The trooper eased off the gas and hit the brake in one smooth motion. The Governor, his hand on the door handle, motioned with his head that I should follow. He plunged into the canebrakes fumbling with the zipper of his trousers. Walking a dozen steps behind, hearing the whisper of the wind among the dry stalks, I realized that the box of salt was still in my hand.

The Governor searched the sky as if looking for hostile airplanes and watered the earth with a mighty splash.

"Yeah," he affirmed for the third time. "They're scared. For I have come stalking upon the knowledge of fear. I have found it in the dark bullrushes of Time. And they are afraid, all right. They're so scared they're nothin' but pus and custard."

"Some maybe," I said. "But just the born cowards."

The Governor sighed at the sky. He said, "Jim, you have been off to college and studied how to find X in algebra and maybe learned the name of the doctor discovered a painless cure for clap. You got a diploma with your name on it in writin' so fancy it's hard for an ignorant peckerwood like me to read it. But by God, Jim! Sometimes I wonder if you got sense enough to be coached for a crooked quiz show. Hell, you oughta know by now *all* men are born cowards. And most of 'em don't ever outgrow it."

Cullie Blanton zipped up his trousers. He wiggled massive hips to settle more comfortably in his underwear. Standing ten paces behind the Governor, I was assaulted by the thought that the opposition camp would cough up many gold dollars for a film clip of the Governor rolling his hips and apparently dry-humping the air in a lonesome cane field. Bayonet Bill Wooster would scream to hosts on high about such a vulgar, immoral display. The picture of the former general screening the film for his angry, evangelistic superpatriots in some flag-bedecked hall, touching the blown-up image of the Governor's grinding hips with a Marine-officer's wooden swagger stick itself quaking with righteousness, white mustache snapping in hate and the dark frustrations that seemed to motivate the man, was more than I could conjure up and keep a sober face. I half turned to hide a smile.

When the Governor had finished his chore to the accompaniment of satisfied sounds, he buckled his belt and sniffed the air with raised head. "Smell rain," he said. "Looks like a gully washer comin' up. Put out a press release takin' credit for it."

Bilious thunderclouds boiled low on the horizon. Forked spears of lightning kindled the distant sky, bringing quick touches of color to the cheerless strands of Spanish moss out in the swamps. Soon drops of water would tremble on the yellow leaves in the pine thickets. The earth would smell cool and freshly bathed.

We marched out of the canebrakes. The Governor debouched massively, the great white head inclined as if alert for the drumming hoofbeats of horses. At the highway he paused and stomped his feet on the pavement, responding to some silent signal. Little clouds of dust spiraled from his shoes. The Governor, mired in the deep bogs of private thought, plowed toward the limousine with his head down.

"Scared past the point of passin' water," he mumbled. "Scared like the great woolly mastodon was runnin' after 'em through the shinnery. Jack-rabbit scared."

"Sullen," I said. "They're more sullen than afraid."

The Governor acted as though he hadn't heard. He said, "Take a bunch of rabbits caught in a beam of light. All they can do is freeze and listen to their poundin' hearts throb fit to bust the fur. They're scared. God on a white mule, they're scared! But they don't know what of. You know, Jim?"

I didn't feel the need to play guessing games. I was weary from the day's drive and the series of political pop meetings. By night we would be back in Capitol City and it would be necessary to try to deal again with the personal hairshirt of life. To bring order out of chaos. I decided to take the easy way out.

"No," I said.

"Boy," the Governor said, "sometimes I wonder how you passed anything in school but the Wassermann test. What they're scared of is fear."

We climbed back into the limousine, the Governor lowering his bulk into the seat with the aid of a mighty, hydraulic grunt. Bo pulled the car away smoothly.

"Man," Cullie Blanton breathed. He waited, and there was the deep well of silence. "Man is born into trouble as the sparks fly upward, like it says in the Book of Job. Brought into this mortal coil full of fear and tremblin'. Pulled from the warmth of the womb, hung up by his heels like a side of beef, and smacked on the backside until he takes one shudderin' breath of shock and gaseous surprise. So the first sound he makes and the first sound he hears is the awful sound of fear. And he never gets over it, for there is always so goddamn much to spook him."

The Governor lowered his eyelids as if to shut out both sight and sound, and maybe even to still the rushing train of thought rattling through his mind. It struck me that he looked old, old as the devil's grandfather. The ruddy skin, normally flushed pink with good health like Eisenhower had exuded in his best days, seemed suddenly flabby and sallow. Lines marking the corner of his eyes and running like plowed furrows in the forehead were now etched too deeply into the flesh, as if seared by a branding iron.

"Life is a race against the hairy hounds of horror," the Governor said. "A race run from the swaddling cloth of the cradle to the dark folds of the shroud. Death and war and taxes . . . creditors and vile bossmen and wrathful gods . . . tongues of serpents and cold-hearted lovers and the bu-damn-bonic plague. . . ."

"Falling dandruff," I offered.

". . . and a fiery place called Hell."

The Governor opened his eyes and the sleep went out of them. They were at once hard and bright like round blue marbles. "And around here," he said, "there is something else. The mark of the goddamn beast. The curse of Ham's wife."

He held out a hand and snapped his fingers. I dug into the coat pocket of my wrinkled drip-dry suit for a pack of cigarettes and shook one into his upturned palm. The Governor inserted it between his lips and leaned forward to accept a light. He inhaled and eased back, releasing the smoke with a gusty blow approaching a bellow. Twin streams of smoke poured from his nostrils, and for a moment he was a fire-breathing dragon. Eyes squinted against the wisp of smoke that wafted upward in a slow spiral, he inspected the empty air as if he'd found at long last which shell the pea was under.

"Fear is big and black and wool-headed," he said. "And you wouldn't want your sister to marry one." He stared out of the car window, darkly brooding.

The sun had dropped suddenly behind the flat curve of the horizon, and infant shadows toddled along the cane rows. Cullie bored his eyes into the shadows like he was peeking behind the final veil, glimpsing the Last Secret. The cane fields blurred and bridge abutments faded into vague, ill-defined humps huddled by the highway. Mist lay heavy on the land and cuddled against the edges of the concrete slab, and Bo flicked a switch to mar the completeness of night. Cullie was lost in the steep canyons of the muse. The miles passed and the wheels turned in the Governor's head.

"And that's the shape of the hobgoblin," he said. "That is the craven nature of the spook."

I stirred and blinked my eyes and plotzed back toward the land of the living.

"What do you think the Court's likely to do?" I asked.

"You read the papers," Cullie Blanton said. "I take it you get past Chester Gump once in a while. You know what the courts have done in other places."

"Yeah," I admitted.

"Gonna split this state from hell to breakfast. And the bare bones and tough gristle and most foul innards are goin' to be laid out like somethin' dead on the highway. Gonna order that blackbird admitted to the university and march in a Coxey's Army of Feds to see nobody breaks his wings. And it will be hell among the yearlings."

"Well, if the cookie crumbles that way . . . what then?"

"Boy," the Governor said, "if I had the answer to that one I'd send off for a patent and retire on the profits."

"Hell," I said, "you got to have a plan."

He looked at me like I had something that belonged to him and wouldn't give it back. "You think you're the only one with brains hooked up to figger that out? You think I just got to town on the goddamn Greyhound?"

"No," I said.

"Then quit talkin' like I'm somebody's goofy cousin home for the weekend from the funny farm." He huffed and puffed at his cigarette butt. "*I* know I got to do somethin'. I saw those jake-leg pols today same as you did. Turnin' up their noses like the wind had changed so they sniffed a passin' gut wagon. And I know what that pensioned-off Marine's gonna do. Yeah, with the election waitin' in ambush just around the goddamn bend, Bill Wooster's gonna scream like I'd violated the unsullied maiden aunt of the Virgin Mary. And ever' wool-hat who owns a bedsheet's gonna bust a clavicle rippin' it off the mattress and wrappin' up in it. They'll wave the bloody shirt, hoot the rebel yell, and whistle up the departed ghost of ole Jeff Davis."

"They might not," I said.

"Boy," he said, "it is as certain as sex on a honeymoon. You can't stop the unstopable."

"You might if you put your foot down. You've done it before. You don't hold the indoor record for being bashful."

The Governor birthed a growing sigh. "Boy," he said, "about the time I think you're housebroke and got control of all your marbles, you go spoilin' my illusion by pissin' down your leg. There's a slag heap of difference in squashin' a ladybug and steppin' on a mad rattler. That's just a natural law of physics."

He mashed his cigarette in the ashtray hollowed out in a padded armrest and flicked grains of tobacco from his fingers. He pulled at his nose, cleared his throat, and scowled. In the eerie green light from the dashboard he took on a murderous look.

"All those speeches by Adlai Stevenson up at the U.N.," he said sourly. "All those high-blown words about equality and the eternal brotherhood of man and love ye one another. Red and yellow, black and white. Hell yes, they *sound* good—up at the U.N. But you got to remember I'm governor down here in the fruit-jar-whisky backwoods. In the potlikker and poke-bonnet and pellagra belt. And down here a liberal's somebody don't hold with lynchin' on Sunday. Listen . . . you recollect how I had to go around the goddamn horn to get colored nurses on at the state hospital? You remember that?"

"Yeah," I said.

For I remembered, all right.

And he hadn't done it with high-blown speeches. He had done it in a very different way. Which started with receiving a delegation of hat-in-hand Negroes who had broken the spine of custom by the mere act of calling on the state's biggest political poobah for the purpose of asking for something. They had stalked into Cullie's office joint-locked with unease, mummering their way across new ground, and they had made their pitch. Which in any other league might not have been a high, hard one like Bob Feller used to throw, but which in the magnolia loop where the pitch was made was about as radical as nose bobbing for sharecroppers' daughters. They said how they paid taxes to support the state hospital. They said how they were the last to get a bed and the first to get a bill. They said how the only colored employees were held to the low level of the mop and the pushbroom. They said they didn't want the moon. They didn't ask the favor of black hands poking around the insides of white bodies with the cold steel of surgery. All they asked was a few nurses of their kind. And they stood in a brave little knot, waiting like they had invented waiting, expecting to be turned down.

Cullie had listened them out. He had grunted and nodded and frowned and once in the middle of their pitch he had locked his eyes on an invisible Something, picking his teeth with great sucking sounds. He had toyed with a clay bust of Robert E. Lee and had idly fluttered the folds of a miniature Confederate flag. And when the fellow who'd been tapped finally came down with a tired tongue, Cullie sat as if he'd been stricken with a painful case of lockjaw. Finally, about the time they had begun to figure he had dropped off for a nap, he glanced up from under the forest of frosty eyebrows.

"You want the nurses or you want somethin' to yowl about?"

They had wanted the nurses.

"All right," he promised. "You got 'em. Only don't go out of here hoo-hawin' about a batch of social progress. Any of those newspaper boys go pokin' around askin' questions, lie about it. Say you came to see the goddamn Governor about voter registration for colored folks and I read you the riot act and threw you out."

They nodded and shuffled in confusion.

"You won't like the way I do it," he said, "but it is the only way it can be done. You got to trust my judgment. I'll go out and kill your woolly bear, but don't ask me to do it with a switch. Leave me to my own bear trap . . . Jim, fix these folks somethin' to cool parched throats."

And he had pumped their hands and plunged off on some urgent errand of mystery.

So a week later I hied myself up marble steps leading to the neo-ante-bellum front entrance of the state hospital, which Cullie had sprung out of the barren loins of the clay bogs and hammered out of a reluctant legislature in his first ten months in office, possessed of a clear view of Cullie's buttocks ham-hocking it on the double toward the top. The two of us led a sweating coterie of photographers whose suit pockets bulged with flashbulbs, and a panting swarm of reporters fatally bent on recording the Governor's first eyeball inspection of his prized healing temple. By that time the Capitol correspondents knew that Cullie could make more news at a country goat-roping than most pols could make by breaking wind for a new airport, so we didn't want for daily attention. Everybody had the idea they were trailing around in the indelible tracks of History.

The key hospital staffers were starched to the gills and stiffly smiling, circled back from the door at a distance calculated to give the Great Man room, and the place had been mopped and scrubbed and disinfected until you could drink out of the bedpans. The administrator was a timid soul with the kind of face that must have been made from the mold God Almighty uses when He's behind in His work. It was a mass-production face, with two eyes in the right place and a nose popped out in the middle like a bump on a pickle and a mouth cut into the face about where you'd expect to find it. He owned just two expressions: scared and worried. He alternated between the two as Cullie Blanton padded down on him like a gay grizzly bear, pawing the air and happily pressing flesh, growling some great, practiced glee.

The administrator, propelled along by mobile fear, quivered at the Governor's heels. He squeaked of recovery rooms and blood plasma and out-patient clinics, and for a while it looked like he would get around to quoting a price on salve for bedsores. Cullie nodded and mumbled a great benediction, beaming benign approval of the healing arts. The Governor got his picture made pressing a Snicker bar on a six-year-old boy who had his hips hiked up in traction. The flashbulbs froze him tenderly reading a page of *Chicken Little* to an emaciated little girl in an iron lung, and caught him handing a bouquet of yellow roses to a senile old woman who bared her gums like a chimpanzee, drooled on her nightgown, and announced in a cracked cackle that she had an urgent need to pass water.

When we tooled into the wing where they kept the colored patients, the Governor shook the hand of an old granny and wisecracked at two little giggling girls. He moved across the hall to the colored men's ward and stopped inside, running his eyes over the scene carefully as if inspecting for ticks. He watched a plump blonde nurse take the temperature of an ancient Negro man. He moved over close to me and mumbled in my ear, frowning. He stalked on down the line of beds and put the glim on another nurse, tense and nervous under the all-seeing eye of the Mighty, while she changed the bed linens for an expressionless Negro of indefinite age.

All at once the Governor whirled on the administrator like he hoped to catch him picking his nose, eyes popping.

"What the hell's goin' on here?" he demanded.

The administrator couldn't have jumped higher if he'd been prodded with a pry pole. He clasped his hands in prayer, then he wrung them like a limp dishtowel, and turned the color of Swiss cheese.

"I want to know what the ding-dog devil you think you're *doin'* here," the Governor thundered.

The reporters began to scramble for elbow room, running around in tight little circles and braying the beginning of questions that sounded like barks, acting like they might bite somebody in the leg. The photographers reverted to knee-jerk reaction. They pointed their souped-up Kodaks and caught the paralyzed image of the Governor conjuring up an historic wrath.

"Godamighty," the Governor roared. "You got *white* nurses waitin' on *nigger* men? Carryin' out their bedpans and givin' 'em sponge baths! For Christ sake, you lost your goddamn mind?"

The administrator couldn't believe it was happening to him, after all that scrubbing and scouring of the bedpans. It was simply more disaster than his pea brain could conceive of in one dose. He was be-

yond the form of words. He just made sounds without any recognizable
shape.

"You think this is a charity hospital in New York City?" the Governor shouted. "You some kind of damn trouble-makin' carpetbagger
come to take us in?"

The administrator choked it out that he was from Ospalosso, which
was just a catbird's call down the road, and laid claim to a grandfather
who had ridden with Jeb Stuart.

"Jeb Stuart would spin in his grave," the Governor howled. "They
didn't teach you this down at Ospalosso! They sure-God don't go
around down there teachin' folks to put white women lookin' after the
creature comforts of a passel of field niggers!"

And he was off. He screamed and stomped his foot and if he had
been Shirley Temple he would have ripped loose from his curls. He
walled his eyes like a steer down with the blackleg. He thundered of
the unmatched glories of Southern womanhood and called up obscure
passages of Scripture. He was Jesus driving the money-changers from
the temple and Samson among the thousand swinging the jawbone of
an ass. He scared the nose warts off the administrator by threatening to
fire him on the spot he'd violated.

"Tomorrow mornin' . . . ," he shouted, with his forefinger pinion-
ing the administrator against a wide expanse of guilt, ". . . tomorrow
mornin' I wanta see black nurses in here waitin' on black men. You
don't know where to find any, look in the Yellow Pages."

He wheeled around and moved off down the hall in a running lope,
leaving behind him a sort of instant polio, a quick and sudden paralysis, and it was a while before the news boys could recover enough to
scurry after him, braying questions. And they had splashed it all over
the papers, from the piney woods to the sparkling seashore, in Second
Coming headlines. The woolhats moved their lips over the print out in
the brush and blessed him by name. The professional haters walked
with a spring in their step and started a move to fire the hospital administrator, who, they said with double dead-dog certainty, was from
Perth Amboy, New Jersey, and had nigger blood in his veins. The
magnolia-scented editorial pages across the state for the first time
hauled off and paid Governor Cullie Blanton a sort of cautious hom-
age, and the Daughters of the Confederacy passed a resolution com-
mending him for his vigilant protection of Southern Womanhood.

Nobody seemed to notice that he had sullied the lily-white staff of
the state hospital.

Later on I would tell him that he'd had the luck of the Irish. He never should have been able to pull it off. Because, I said, it was pure corn.

"Boy," he had said with a chortle, "there is corn and then there is corn. You put corn in a can and ship it across the distant miles and it gets the taste of the tin in it and loses a lot in the translation. You open up the can in New York or Chicago and dump it in a servin' dish and the tongue quickly knows it has been tainted by the despoilin' hand of man. You can't taste the warmth of the sun in it, or hear the cool wind singin' among the tall stalks, and the spring-green goodness is gone from the cob."

I waited a while, hoping he would develop the theme. But he just clammed up with a look of rich-man smugness and said no more. "So," I said after a respectable wait, "what does that prove?"

"Somethin' ever' backwoods politician ought to write in his hatband and read as regular as the Ten Commandments," he had said with a pleased grin. "It proves corn tastes better where it grows. . . ."

So now, all these years later, we plunged on into the night and Bo qualified for witchcraft at the wheel. We had outlasted the cane fields and now scooted through a tangled jungle of reedy marshlands where weeping willows bent to whisper to the grass of some vague personal sorrow. Rain tumbled down in the beam of the headlights like strands of clear, wet rope.

Cullie Blanton rummaged in his shirt pocket and found a cigar. He lifted it to his bulbous nose and rationed it one suspicious sniff through the wrapper. "What you got to remember," he said, "is that I don't happen to be Adlai Stevenson and this don't happen to be the U.N. And it ain't New York or California. Hell, it can't even lay claim to bein' *Mars*. It's the deep boondocks. Yeah, and it is the land of the blind. And if Bill Wooster and his mob of nutty hangmen runnin' around with flags stickin' from their bungholes get control of this state . . . well, if they get it, it will be the blind leadin' the blind."

"All I hope," I said, "is that you try to see the full picture. And I'm afraid you're looking at it through just one eye."

"In the land of the blind," he said, "the one-eyed man is king." He leaned forward abruptly. "Haul ass, Bo. You think I want to paint a still life of the scenery?"

So Bo let out the last notch and we screamed through the swamps like caterwauling witches. Cullie looked past the drawn curtain of night and swept the hidden landscape with a strange pride in his eyes like he loved it all.

Cullie stared, and Bo stepped on the horses, and the night flashed by, and I sat in the darkness dwelling among mock shows.

"Boondock country," the Governor snorted in the ear of night. "Coon-ass country, by God. Fit for nothin' but raisin' billy goats and eatin' beans. The land is haunted and the hills are bloody and the wind is full of guilt. . . ."

2

IT HAS BEEN A WHILE since the day when we whooshed through the boondocks, stopping to pump the hands of the back-country jackdaws and feeling the first swift currents of their discontent, with Cullie spraying his waste water among the tall stalks, and bending into the sweet melon, and cheerfully baiting Bo. It has been a while, and tired bones record the passing. The sun has beamed down on rooftops a thousand mornings and the winds have promiscuously changed course, and pious prayers have been shouted over the uncaring forms of the dead. Our mudball has turned among the stars, and beasts have prowled the fields, and time has cracked into the old patterns of split seconds of joy trailed by eons of sorrow.

Later on, the goddamn historians will get hold of it. They will fix the past in the hard glare of twenty-twenty hindsight and go conjuring up visions and assigning motives as though they had a special license for the purpose, when all the time they won't have a clue. They will see the indelible tracks in the endless desert and chart the winding curves of the main path, but miss the subtle signs of struggle on the trackless rocks, and the dead-end cakewalks along the hidden side trails.

History is just a bunch of spooked people hoo-hawing around, straining a gut to stay ahead of those hairy hounds of horror Cullie Blanton used to talk about. Hoping they won't be bayed down and treed. Historians forget the black X of chance. They honk up the notion that everything was planned down to the lobelia herbs, and was willed and done for reason. The old wheel of fortune keeps spinning in worn grooves and the X of chance falls wantonly on the squares, and about all any mother's son can do is ride with the play. Only the historians don't dig it.

So before they rip their meathooks into it, and go slicing it up and labeling it pure grade-A History, and wrap it in the clear cellophane of hindsight, I want to tell it like it was.

And it was all just a bunch of hoo-hawing around.

The Governor slouched behind the big desk in his oval study, faintly perspiring in the morning's promise of heat, bathed and haloed in pale light streaming in from an open full-length window, the light striking silver on the great mane of hair. Behind him, through the window, the dome of the capitol building raised toward a sullen sky as if to finger some obscure guilt. Henry Muggins was there in the oval study, and Stanley Dutton, and I, detecting a decided lack of unbridled cheer among my fellow brethren of the lodge. We were there on short notice, bugled in by the High Caliph.

"We been ambushed lately worse than Custer," the Governor intoned mournfully. "That loan-shark bill oughta whooped through the House like the Lord's Prayer set to music. But the way that bunch of pirates is actin', you'd think it proposed to set aside the third Sunday for the public stonin' of sainted mothers."

Mr. Muggins and Mr. Dutton faced the Governor from two green leather chairs fronting his desk. I leaned against a mahogany bookcase off to the side, modest as befitted the circumstance of a hired hand among three empowered with the public mandate. It was the morning after I had come back with Cullie from out in the canebrakes and the mist-kissed swamps. Cullie looked polished and refurbished as he dawdled over his coffee, faintly scowling.

The Governor grunted into his cup, making a threatening face at the contents, his eyes peeping across the rim at Henry Muggins. The Speaker of the House owned a title that outstripped by a measured mile the mortal clay used by the Great Molder to fashion him. He was fringe-bald and wizened, and if he had ever owned a suit of clothes that fit him properly, he wore it in secret. He had false teeth that didn't fit him either, and a look of faint bewilderment as if maybe he'd just got to town on the day coach with a shoe box full of cold fried chicken and didn't know exactly how to go about leaving the depot. The only thing that seemed to fit him was the name Henry Muggins—a rumpled scarecrow of a short-weight body from the dirt-dauber town of Sand Springs. He reeked of the butt end of smutty stories about traveling salesmen and the eternal farmer's daughter. He was so much plain old Henry Muggins from Sand Springs, with seedy clothes and imperfect bogus molars, that it was too good to be true.

And it wasn't true.

For Henry Muggins was tough and sharp beyond the measure of his puny pounds. He was part mule skinner and a bit sly fox and a right smart magician. He was altogether a sour little ball of dough, and Cullie Blanton liked him.

The Governor brought his cup down and clanged it in the china saucer like the village blacksmith whamming an anvil.

"What's goin' on over in that House, Henry?" he boomed. "What's got into that bunch of cutthroats? Somebody been feedin' 'em ornery pills?"

"Damfino," the Speaker said.

And that was Henry Muggins, too. He hoarded words as though he had to give up a ration stamp with every syllable, and his voice came out reedy, full of the back-country twang.

"Goddamn," the Governor breathed. "Consort with beggars and do business with bandits! They puttin' the screws *most foul* on my loan-shark bill. What they tryin' to do, Henry? Get on record four-square for usury?"

"Siggy Sears won't move the bill," the Speaker said, in what for him was an uncommonly long speech.

"Siggy Sears!" The Governor spat the name like it was worm of the apple. "What in the name of the most precious perfumed Allah does Siggy Sears know? Can't you pinch him where he's tender? Grab him by the shorthairs!"

The Speaker acted like he was in a thoughtful study of the proposition. Cullie drummed one hand on the table top and whistled a tuneless dirge. He dug in his ear with a pink toothpick, pulling out what he had mined, turning the toothpick in front of his eyes to assay the value of the new treasure.

I cleared my throat by way of announcing the embryonic stages of thought. Cullie swung his eyes around at me, awaiting the pronouncement.

"Siggy's in a good spot to squat on the bill," I said.

"Siggy's too damn bloated to squat on anything," Cullie Blanton grumbled. "Especially one my pet bills."

"Well," I said, "he *is* chairman of the Finance Committee."

"Boy," the Governor said, "you are just full of useful information. You are as loaded with it as the Encyclo-goddamn-pedia Britannica." He snorted, sucking at the coffee cup again, and from the corner of my eye I caught Speaker Muggins celebrating my discomfort with a sour-apples smile. Cullie came out of the coffee cup. "Siggy Sears don't have any more spine than a sissy jellyfish taken down with a bad case of *angst*. So he can't be opposin' the bill on backbone and bilious principle. A man wants to hoot and screech against that loan-shark bill, he's got to have some the wise ole owl in him. He's got to know somethin' about fractions and decimal points. Hell, Siggy's still cowed by the thunderin' mysteries of long division."

The Lieutenant Governor signified an approaching spasm of wisdom by uncrossing long legs and shuffling his feet. Cullie turned to him.

"What you think, Stanley?"

Cullie had asked, all right. When the moon was right and the rivers lay straight in their beds, the Governor tried to pay occasional faint deference to his lieutenant governor. When Cullie did that, I knew he was thinking of the particular role Stanley Dutton could play in the drama. Once I had asked Cullie about that role. I had asked why he'd consented to let Dutton run on the Blanton ticket.

"Boy," Cullie had said, "Stanley Dutton's got that precious thing necessary to the life of second-banana politicians and high-wire walkers. And that is a delicate balance. He's the missin' link in my evolution of public life. He's the spiny bridge that makes the connection with that part of the body politic containing the better-folk bone. Besides which, he can bring me the sacred keys to money chests stuffed with many gold dollars. He can feed the campaign kitty 'til it purrs."

Stanley had married a delectable cush who was like a ripe Georgia peach—ready to burst with ripe goodness and covered with tight golden skin—who brought to their union even more oil money than Dutton had bored out of the bowels of the earth. Oh, he had it all except for two minor ingredients: good sense and boundless ambition. But Cullie had enough in both those departments, and he didn't have to spend any bug-eyed nights tossing among the bedsheets, wondering if the number-two boy would tire of his number and get the itch to reduce it by exactly half of the whole.

Stanley Dutton muttered parliamentary mumbo jumbo over the state Senate by day, and by night he cavorted with the fat cats, for that was a big part of his job. But it wasn't part of his job to come under the eyeballs of the unwashed rabble. Cullie had laid it on the line about that. "Looks like he quotes poetry," the Governor had objected when somebody submitted Stanley's name for an excursion deep into the boondocks. "Looks like he quotes poetry, sleeps in silk pajamas, and wouldn't have the belly to string a bloodworm on a fishhook." So Cullie kept him out of the boondocks like the woods were posted and Stanley was always in season.

"The talk I hear on the Senate side," Stanley Dutton said in a smooth bass roll of words, "is that Siggy is working very, very hard against that bill. Yes, Governor, and he can be most influential in certain circles. *Most* influential." The Lieutenant Governor nodded agreement with his own sagacity.

"Stanley," the Governor said, and his face was full of patient pain, "Stanley, you don't know a goddamn thing! You sit there lookin' like a combination of Warren G. Harding and Jay Gould, and then you open your mouth and you don't know a goddamn thing! Listen . . . Siggy Sears don't have the influence to ratify the Ten Commandments in the House. Word got out he was the sponsor of 'em, they couldn't get a simple majority on at least eight. So he's gettin' help bottlin' up that bill in committee, and I got it in me to know who's givin' him that help."

The Governor shifted his eyes back to the Speaker. Muggins rested low in the leather chair, scrootched down on the back of his neck, arms flung out like an abandoned rag doll.

"You find out who the robber is, Henry. And what he wants. Unless he wants too much ransom, promise to pay it. He tries to hold us up at gunpoint, we'll threaten to take away somethin' he's already got."

"Dallas Johnson," the Speaker said.

"What about him? What about that pirate?"

"He's the one."

"For Christ sakes, Henry! You got lockjaw? He's the one *what?*"

"The one," the Speaker said, "put Siggy up to bottlin' up the loan-shark bill. And is helpin' him do it."

"You been smokin' funny cigarettes, Henry?"

"Don't smoke."

"A little bird tells me Dallas Johnson's strong for my loan-shark bill," the Governor said.

"Must be a coo-coo bird."

"Well, Jesus Christ! Why? He's supposed to be such a red-hot liberal. Why would Dallas Johnson be fightin' that bill?"

"Damfino," the Speaker said.

"He been around with his hand out?"

"No," the Speaker said, "and that's a pure puzzlement."

The Governor turned the deep, rich-purple hue of canned beets at the point where his shirt collar nestled against the thick neck, and it flushed up his face like a clear bottle being filled from the bottom. Cullie turned wrathful eyes on me.

"Boy," he said. "Boy, didn't you tell me Dallas Johnson was stout for my loan-shark bill? Didn't you take a holy oath to that effect?"

"Yeah," I said. Then I quickly amended my petition. "He said last week he was. He told me personally."

"Now tell me the goddamn earth's flat and Goldwater has founded a labor union," the Governor snorted, "for it will be about as accurate as your little gem of intelligence about Dallas Johnson."

"Last week. . . ."

"Last week! I don't give a rat's ass about last week! Last week the Pope might have thought of turnin' foot-washin' Baptist, but he's in the Vatican today and seems pleased with his callin'."

Cullie jumped from his desk to pad toward the window looking on the wad of green lawn between the Mansion and the domed capitol building. He gave us an uninterrupted study of his back, muttering low curses and pulling at his nose, leaving me to dwell on the fickle nature of man.

Then he whirled from the window, his eyes focusing on the Speaker. "Find out what's itchin' Dallas Johnson and tell him we'll scratch it. I need him, and I need that band of Young Turks and red-hots thinks Dallas Johnson hung the goddamn moon without benefit of a stepladder."

"Can't find he wants anything."

"He wants somethin'," the Governor said flatly. "You ever run across somebody in this business that don't, call a taxidermist and get the sonofabitch stuffed and we'll open us up a museum and get rich chargin' six bits to look at him."

Cullie flung his girth into the swivel chair behind his desk, tipped the chair back, and made a series of rubber faces at the ceiling.

"Yawl been up long enough to read that mad dog's speech from last night?" he asked suddenly. "Yawl read that tin soldier's foamin' chin music?"

"He fingered you for everything but the Crucifixion," I said. "He accused you of everything but common sense."

"Goddamn and hell," the Governor breathed. "I walk among the hissin' serpents." He cocked his head, monitoring the sounds of the city. Sunlight spilled through the window behind the Governor and tracked across the hardwood floor. Cullie's voice rose and fell in a dreamy chant: "My young men see no visions, and the old belch sour dreams . . . flawed cities decay in the dust and grass grows in the streets . . . there is a great famine in the land. . . ." He trailed off and let his eyes make a detailed survey of the ceiling. The stillness gathered around us and gave the clock something to tick in.

Stanley Dutton puzzled over the Governor's words with a look of abashed astonishment mingled with vague embarrassment. He appeared to harbor the private conviction that Cullie Blanton was lip-flipping crazy and shouldn't be allowed to run loose. But he knew enough to keep such thoughts safely anchored. Stanley didn't know much, but it doesn't take a Rhodes Scholar to figure not to crack a grizzly bear across the snout when the bear has easy access to your person.

"Impeach the Chief Justice!" Cullie exploded at the height of his lung power.

Stanley Dutton leaped halfway to the Governor's desk, clattering into a tray of coffee cups and a silver pot. Speaker Muggins sprawled with a wry smile on his wrinkled face, enjoying the free show.

The Governor lifted his voice into a shrill, reedy imitation of Bayonet Bill Wooster frothing on the stump. "Repeal the Marxist income tax and beware miscegenation!" he howled. "They're tryin' to integrate you plumb up to the bedstead and Reds lurk under ever' rock. Sellin' you out for a mess of poor pottage and draggin' your grandchildren toward a Soviet America!"

He abandoned the parody. "Sweet Jesus . . . how they *get* that way?" He sulked over his empty coffee cup, glum to the shoelaces.

"Wooster's good," I admitted. "He's three giant steps to the right of King George, but in a very terrible way he's good."

"He's good and crazy," the Governor said. "He's so goony I wouldn't be surprised if he favors chastity belts. He's a first-class s.o.b., and that ain't second-hand information and it ain't confidential, as ole Huey Long said about somebody once."

"Puts on a good show," the Speaker said.

"All that business of rolling drums," I added. "All that marching up the aisle in spotlights."

"He walls his eyes, and bristles that mustache until you'd think it was wired for electricity," the Governor said. "He trots out the flag like he was the one commissioned Betsy Ross to stitch it. It's like runnin' against Uncle Sam. I keep thinkin' he's liable to have me deported. Henry, what the hell's that madman tryin' to prove?"

"He wants to take a turn walking on the water."

"Well, he ain't got the feet for it. That jarhead gets to be governor, this state would go back to three-cent cotton and slave tradin'." The Governor unwrapped a sugar cube and popped it into his mouth. Twin indentions like deep dimples appeared in his cheeks as he sucked at it. "May he roast in the eternal pit," Cullie Blanton said, with feeling.

"Wait'll he heats up next week," I said. "That giant Save America rally he's throwing. They're comin' in from all over for that one."

"It will be the greatest collection of kooks and nuts since that bunch of flyin'-saucer fans convened out on the desert and talked to a little green Martian landed on a flat rock." Cullie shifted the sugar cube.

"Not just the rabble," the Speaker said.

"Don't speak to me in parables," the Governor said. "What's the tender message you got on your heart?"

"Wooster's got some folks ought to know better clacking like he was the Messiah come," the Speaker said. "Some the boys over in the House, now. I think that's their trouble." The Speaker sighed, spent after so long a verbal discourse.

"God on the mountain!" Cullie bellowed in whole exasperation. "What right those Simple Simons got to get lathered up over Bill Wooster's chin music? *I'm* governor. I'm the keeper of the goddamn keys. I'm the one can bestow favors most kind or drop their privates in the dirt."

"You know how they are about mail from the folks," the Speaker said. "They're getting mail about how things are headed for the hot place in a gunny sack."

"One half-literate jackanapes writes a postcard, and the ass falls out of the whole democratic system. Sometimes I think we ought to appoint a goddamn king."

"If we do, we better appoint somebody mean," the Speaker said. "Somebody eats nails."

The Governor put fire to a cigar and puffed as a mighty furnace. He looked at Henry Muggins through the balling clouds of smoke.

"You sayin' you see a soft spot, Henry? You sayin' I've crawfished?"

They had been friends too long for the Speaker to say it. They had come to public office at almost the same point in time thirty years before, a time when legislators almost to the very last in number were bought and paid for by the Interests, or at least rented to perform little deeds of dirt. In those days, any firm that didn't hold title to a state senator and a half-dozen House members was held guilty of shoddy business practices. They had fought together, railed at the system, and howled at blood on the moon; and they had lost a lot together before they finally started to win. So the Speaker just shrugged. "Well," he said, "seems to me you been letting 'em up a little easy, Cullie."

"A man gets tired," Cullie Blanton said, after a long pause. He spoke so softly we had to lean in to hear him. "A man sits alone in the night and knows his days have certain numbers, and the wind blows lonesome in the trees. He hears the water in the brook and the cry of birds, and he knows they will be there long after he's gone the same as they got there before him. And the man asks why in the name of the fiery furnace and the Hebrew children he stays with the sideshow. Why he dwells in the fake tents of politics when he knows the shell game's crooked and has seen the bearded lady pass water from a standin' start. He thinks of the nuts he's cracked and the lung-bustin' whoopin', and how goddamn hard it is just to get a little ole pissant bill passed to give the snuff dippers a few pieces of silver to rattle in the pockets of their raggedy britches and a hunk of pork to fry, and a man gets tired.

"He thinks how he has to strain until he gets the dry-gut rumble just to do the nit-pickingest *little* thing. How he has to fight bandits and burglars and smoke peace pipes with punks to get somethin' done ought to have been done twenty years ago. All at once he feels the long miles of the road and the hard months of the calendar burrowin' deep in the bones. And a man gets tired. He thinks of sittin' on the porch and washin' his feet and lookin' at the moon and talkin' with the Great Architect, to see if he can divine some understandin' of the master plan. He wants to listen to the wind sing in the buffalo grass and sit puny in the presence of mountains."

Cullie turned to the Speaker and fixed him with a cloudy gaze. Henry Muggins sprawled in the chair, a distant look in his own eyes, as if recalling debris floating in the corroded brass spittoon of Time. Stanley Dutton wiped at his coffee-stained trousers, beyond all understanding. Cullie smiled, shaking his head slowly from side to side.

"I got tired, Henry. I thought maybe I could take off the brass knucks. Hang up the gloves. Thought maybe I could honey-fugle those pirates by soft talkin' instead of head knockin'. I decided to test that old saw about how you can catch more flies with honey than vinegar. But it turns out the best way to deal with a fly is swat him, for he'll eat all your honey and crap in the jar."

The Governor sat in the swivel chair and suddenly it seemed his body had been dipped in starch. He stiffened along the spine. His head came up. His voice got a ring in it, a ring I had heard before, and the ring always meant the Charge of the Light Brigade and Saturday Night at the Bloody Bucket and Joshua at the walls of Jericho, all rolled into one.

"I been goin' against my better nature, Henry. I been betrayin' what's buried deep in the genes. I tried to be nice. I have said 'please.' I even said 'pretty please with sugar on it.' And all that happened was I got the bloody shaft. I got my teachers'-pay bill beat like it was a dusty rug, and they clobbered my bill to soak the timber boys who don't restore the land after they rape it of the yellow pines. And now they're hangin' up my bill to crack the unfeelin' nuts of the loan sharks. Yeah, Henry, I been nice, and it didn't work."

"The boys been restless," the Speaker said, in a classic example of understatement.

"Well, they better be. They sure-God had. For you take 'em a message for me. You tell 'em I'm through playin' wet nurse and offerin' 'em a sugar tit to suck, and I'm through sayin' please. From now on I'm a fly-swatter-and-vinegar man. From here on in I am the crotchety God of vengeance. I'm the somebody eats nails. I'm the king of kings."

"First thing," the Speaker said, "is to let the boys know you got the kid gloves off."

"Goddamn right. Give 'em the mail and the spike. You get me a list of what's closest to the hearts of the leaders of the cabal. What they want *and* what they don't want. We'll start us a series of political prayer meetin's will show who wants to see the blindin' light. Can you get that list together and come over here to the Big House for supper?"

The Speaker nodded that he could.

"Stanley," the Governor said, "you forget goin' to anybody's fancy-dress ball tonight. I want you to get with Jim here and do the same thing on the Senate slobs. You think you're up to it?"

The Lieutenant Governor cleared his throat and worried up a dark frown.

"I suppose so," he said. "Only. . . ."

"Only what, Stanley?"

"Well . . . my wife . . . she has her heart set on the Crowells' dance tonight."

"She want that worse than she wants you to be lieutenant governor?"

"Well . . . hardly that bad."

"Then, it seems like that settles it," the Governor said. "What you got to remember, Stanley, is that all things are relative."

"One other thing," the Speaker said. "It might help, Cullie, if the boys knew what you figure to do about this Court thing."

"It might help if I knew, too," Cullie said. "Only I don't. Right now that subject is a thoroughbred mystery."

"Some of the boys think—"

"Listen," the Governor cut in, "it is a matter of supreme indifference to me *what* the boys think."

"I was just thinking of how Wooster's courting the rabble-rousers," the Speaker said. "I sure would hate to see him out-seg you."

"Henry," the Governor said, "I can scream 'nigger' loud as the next man."

"You know how everybody's got a tight bunghole waiting to see what the Court's gonna do," the Speaker said.

"Yeah," the Governor said, "I know all right. I been out among the heathen infidel."

And I had been out among them, too. I thought back on the sullen cornpone Buddhas we'd seen in our rush through the back country. The coolness had balled up in their eyes, leaving them with that flat glare usually reserved for strangers from the outlands who show no more gumption than to wear neckties in the middle of the week. Oh, they had smiled with their cheek muscles, but nothing danced in the eyes.

The mean-mouthed sheriffs, who ran their counties like they'd come by them through the grace of bloodline, had scurried away to serve bench warrants, lock up stray niggers, and shake down moonshiners. The dough-faced camp followers of the grass roots, the creeping Jesuses of backwater politics, who normally tumbled backside-over-elbow to pull out a chair for the Great Man, or whinnied in the middle of his jokes, had been slower on the draw.

Not at first, they hadn't. At first they'd come running with chairs and whinnies at the ready, and it took them a while to snag on to the fact that something was up. They just sensed that something was out of place. They had gazed around and they had seen the dead smiles of their local sultans, and they saw the sheriffs hiking off, and something slow happened in their heads and sent out a dull, throbbing signal. And what the signal said was: play it safe. So they scrambled to the outer fringe of the group, competing for the right to seek the safety of each other's sheltering backsides.

Cullie knew. He knew right off. And I should have known. Your old Aunt Ida would have seen. But not me. Oh, no. I was so used to making the scene I didn't even watch the action any more. I'd seen the play and knew all the lines and how it was supposed to come out, so I hadn't worried about where the laugh lines were, or noticed the absence of prolonged applause.

They had treated Cullie like he was carrying the pox, and he had pegged it for what it was. He had seen the Great Sign. He had even tried to read it to me when he whooshed back through the canebrakes and the swamps, but the Governor's not-so-bright and not-so-young man had come down with galloping political myopia.

But Cullie had seen. And so he said, "Yeah, I know all right. I have been out among the heathen infidel." And he said, "I have gazed into the lake of fire." And he said, "I have seen the hairy hounds of horror."

The Governor bounced from his chair to escort the Speaker and the Lieutenant Governor to the door, mouthing closing pleasantries, beaming false cheer, pressing the flesh. "Come over about seven o'clock," he boomed to the Speaker. "We'll drink bourbon and branch water and swap big lies, and eat when we get the gut-rumbles." To the Lieutenant Governor he said, "Jim'll call you about tonight."

When they had trooped from the study, the mirth left the Governor's face. I locked a look on space, studying it like I was boning up for final exams.

"Boy," the Governor said, "it is fourth down with a minute to play and we are protectin' a suspect lead. You go back to punt and fumble the goddamn ball."

I found space most interesting. It had all my attention.

"You can't win 'em all," the Governor said. "That is beyond the reaches of dispute. But lately, Bucko, we ain't won any. We ain't even got a tie to show. Hell, we barely scored!"

He prowled like a bear, growling. "What's happened to our lines of communication with that bunch of cutthroats? You been over to the House or Senate chambers lately? You recollect where the goddamn capitol building is?"

"I recollect."

"Goddamn if it shows," he said. "We been sneaked up on worse than Pearl Harbor."

"Well, there's not any gypsy blood in my family that I know about. I don't come from any long line of mind readers."

"In this business," the Governor said, "you not only got to be able to read minds, you got to be able to change 'em. You reckon you can change Dallas Johnson's mind?"

"I can try."

The Governor snorted. He said, "Tryin' don't count. Folks in Hell been *tryin'* to get ice water piped in." He plopped down in the swivel chair and stared across the desk, inspecting me down to the skin pores.

"Which was it?" he demanded.

"Ah . . . hah?"

"Booze or woolly bugger? Gazin' on the wine or wallowin' in the carnal clover? You help close up all the bars, or wear yourself out ridin' bareback in the shortrows?"

"My strength is as the strength of ten," I said. "I reckon you know the rest of it about how that's because my heart is pure."

"Boy," the Governor said, "you are about as pure as what the cats drug up and the dogs wouldn't eat." He stared me down, unsmiling. I made nervous patterns of guilt on the top of his desk, tracing them with the eraser of a pencil.

"It's just I have this great thirst," I said, vaguely.

"And the flesh is weak. How about that part of it? How about that little songbird lady? That Roxie?"

"No," I said, and winced.

The Governor saw it, and knew it for what it was. "Boy," he said, "what is this kicked-dog streak in you? Why you all time gettin' tangled up with some gal don't care if a goddamn bomb drops on you?"

"That's a question for medical science," I said. "I think it has something to do with the metabolism."

"You must be one of them goddamn masochists," the Governor brooded. "You'd be better off if you fell in love with some clean-cut young man of your own faith."

"Can't break the sex law of politics," I said. "You know the rules: don't get caught in bed with a live man or a dead woman."

"I got a great weariness," the Governor said, by way of dismissing the subject. "I knew this would be a bad day before I put a foot to the floor. Woke up feelin' like the goddamn sun had come up from the west. Like somebody had grabbed all the ancient Talmuds and turned 'em around. Like treys routed aces and canaries sing bass."

"Water runs uphill," I suggested.

"The lion fleeth and the lamb runneth in pursuit," the Governor said mournfully. "And the old, proven faiths dally in the vile presence of mockery.

"Haul ass," the Governor said. "Get outta the chute with spurs on. Come out on the movin' jump and bulldog that goddamn Dallas Johnson. Bring me that red-hot's head on a platter."

I'm no lawyer, but I had picked up enough law to know who signed my pay check. So I hauled out of there on the moving jump.

Liberals sleep late. It's the conservatives who get up in time to milk a dairy herd, and stuff their gullets with a dog's bait of eggs and sausages at an hour when any self-respecting sun would be ashamed to show its round face over the eastern rim. Look around the restaurants at that hour when the waitresses are stretching their jaws with flaccid yawns and scratching the itch of sleep out of swollen eyes. Look around, and you'll see the gullet-stuffers all wear bow ties, and maybe some of them a belt and suspenders at the same time, and look like they're on the way to early Rotary. That's the bedrock conservatives, friend. They're the boys who want to go back to high-button shoes.

Possessed of all that wisdom, I left the Mansion to head for Dallas Johnson's cottage, miles out of the city, by the big bend in the river. He was a liberal, and he would be there, asleep with the country sun spilling across his pillow. There was another reason I figured to find Dallas Johnson dawdling among the bedsheets. Her name was Tanya. She was willowy and about twenty-three, and was always squeezing odd-looking objects out of clay and giving them names like "Thermopylae at Rest." Only she must not have spent all of her time sculpting clay, because she had a living arrangement with Dallas Johnson that didn't call for her to pay any of the rent.

That ought to clue you about Dallas Johnson. I don't know another pol that could have openly played house with some sloe-eyed chick and not had little old ladies in tennis shoes screeching Scripture at him as a mounted posse, led by a Baptist preacher riding as God's grim ranger to hunt the man down. But Dallas had a special talent at causing folks to forgive him his trespasses. He was young, shy of thirty by a couple of years, and handsome in that indolent, insolent way teenagers with crew cuts and that slow, go-to-hell way of lazily working their tanned jaws over chewing gum are handsome.

He was bright, too, and his family had money. He looked like he'd gone to Harvard over the bitter protests of Yale and Princeton, though he'd wisely stayed at home to dig his native roots deeper and to be a big wheel on the campus of State University. He had a safe district, city enough to wink at his helling around and country enough to get a vicarious thrill out of it. Since he wasn't married, he could take his pleasures where he found them without exciting the blood pressure of the electorate past the point of no return.

So I crawled into the dusty convertible in which I owned a minority interest along with the First National Bank. Moving by under the big capitol dome, taking the snappy salute of the state cop who manned a small booth at the main entrance to the capitol grounds, I turned the convertible left up University Drive and rolled past the campus.

I could have been hacking out copy on *The Morning Star*. I could have been squatted squarely in the misery of skid row, or running a combination ice house and filling station down in the little fleabag town where Jim Clayton first drooled and gurgled in the cradle. I could have been doing any of a dozen things instead of what I was doing, but they had called my number on the bingo card, so now I was tooling down University Drive, a big man going on a mission for the Governor.

When I was just a kid in a flyspeck town roaming the piney woods and gawking at the new coat of paint on the old water tower, dreaming of getting rich and famous without pausing to consider how it could be brought off, Cullie had come whooping and hollering out of the boondocks. I knew how he had stepped up the political ladder a rung at a time to hold a sackful of state offices, but I didn't really know Cullie Blanton. So I went to what newspapers aptly dub "the morgue," where all the old dead stories are buried and the yellowed clippings are stacked like brittle bones on a cold slab, and rummaged around for a week catching up with the past. And I learned about Cullie Blanton.

Who started very like the cracker that he was. Who was the patch-seated son of a dirt farmer stuck with mean-poor land and six-cent cotton, and the uninspiring daily view of a mule's bunghole slowly on the move down a plowed furrow. There wasn't a speck on the stars then to portend that Cullie wouldn't follow in his poppa's tedious footsteps among the chunky clods. Cullie was just another boy plodding along behind a plow; a boy whose mama made lye soap the color of light molasses in an old black washpot and washed sweat-salted blue denim overalls by hand on a corrugated rub board, and whose poppa had an equal weakness for corn whisky and the New Testament.

God can take an honorable oath that Cullie wasn't unique in those

days. Hell, if you went back in the deep sticks today, you'd see they still
turn them out like there was an assembly line set up somewhere with
tools and dies for the purpose of mass producing sharecroppers' boys.

He might have stayed there in the big thickets and never have come
out, except to get drunk at a barn dance on Saturday night and whittle
on a spirited neighbor with a Barlow, and he might have died old in
his cornshuck bed. Only something reached out and got ahold of Cullie. Exactly what it was can never be tabbed for sure, but it travels
under the name of Ambition. Maybe it was born in him, burrowed
deep beneath the skin, somewhere in the genes, and little by little it
burned its way out to the surface. Maybe somewhere back down the
family line, a hundred years or more before, some bull-headed egotist
popped a woman whose pretty head was set on reaching for the stars,
who wanted the whole galaxy, Big Dipper and all, and all that ego and
those puffed dreams jumped into their mingled juices and fermented
in the bloodline until it got down to Cullie. It ached his bones until it
had to burn its way out. And when it popped out, he broke out all
over. It flat ate him up.

It might have been something like that, but Cullie had an explanation that wasn't high blown or theoretical. Cullie thought it started
with something he saw once. He told me about it, sitting with his sock
feet propped on a hotel bed in one of those hill-country towns where he
was going about the business of curing his bone-ache to be governor
that first time. It was late at night, or what local opinion decreed late
in that jerkwater town. Silence streamed into the room like a solid
swarm of locust, and one rowdy cricket could have terrorized a whole
county of quiet.

A little earlier there had been folks in the square, lots of folks, wearing calico dresses and wrinkled khaki work clothes, slurring the warm
air with soft R's and dropping G's in the coalbin of night. They were
there to hear Cullie, who had come to bring the flaming Word. He had
bugged his eyes and shouted at them, railing against the pie-eating
politicians and pot-bellied jackanapes defiling the governor's office,
branding the legislators as a collection of hand-picked satraps who
didn't love their sweet mothers and who hadn't had fathers to love. It
was the kind of thing he could do best and he was on his stride that
night, leaning at them and popping the eyes. Oh, he was Washed in
the Blood. And they loved it. They had cheered him to the reaches of
the pale hunter's moon and had climbed in their flivvers and pickup
trucks and had gone home. Now the square was empty and our Jack

Daniels bottle was fast getting that way. Cullie had reared back in his chair, contemplating his sock feet and pulling at the glass of J.D. and tap water. I had asked him what started the big ache.

He said, "The tsetse fly bit me. Bit me when I was about ten years old and Poppa took me to a sheriff's sale. You ever see a sheriff's sale?"

I said I had led a sheltered life and had missed that particular pleasure.

"Well," he said, "I saw just one, but one was enough. The poor bugger havin' his place sold had gone bust and his creditors had foreclosed. And there stood this woolhat dirt farmer with a six-day stubble of whiskers, and his whiskers full of snuff juice, and he was beggin'. *Beggin'!* Like a goddamn blind man rattlin' a cup. The sheriff unlimbered by readin' off the whereases and the therefores and the sobeits, and all the curious gawked around in a morbid little knot. And the fat-bellied bastard who'd forced the sale stood there wheezin' prosperity and rollin' a big cigar around on his tongue."

Cullie had gazed into the past, rubbing one sock foot against the other as if to give it comfort against the crush of memory, juggling the whisky in his glass, moving back over the years to be with the bug-eyed ten-year-old kid in front of the sandstone steps of the courthouse.

"So when the sheriff got through all that shyster rigmarole, this poor bugger faced 'em with snuff on his chops and held out his hands. And he fair begged. He said, 'Don't take hit away from me. Hit's all I got.' And he said, 'Lookie thar, them's my kids over thar by the wagon. Whur am I gonna raise them kids? Whur they gonna lay their heads?' And he said, 'Hit was my daddy's lan' and his daddy's lan' a-fore that, and I got hit in me to hang on.' Oh, he begged 'em all right. He said, 'I'd be much obliged if you didn't take hit. And my woman, she'd be most obliged. And them kids over thar by the wagon.' Oh how that bugger begged! He ate humble pie like it was good to the taste buds. He gave it down like a sinner at the mourners' bench.

"And you know what good it did him? It did him *shit!* He had just as well been recitin' the multiplication tables in a mixture of French and Greek for all the mind they paid. The fat buzzard with the cigar and the mortgage bid the amount he was owed right down to the copper penny, and the sheriff recited some mumbo jumbo and banged his hawg laig on a hitchin' post and took away that poor bugger's land. And all that snuff dipper said was, 'Whur I'll go?' Just like that. He said, 'Whur I'll go?' Then he slumped his shoulders and drug off to-

ward the wagon and clucked at his two skinny-ribbed mules and rode
off with his backside bouncin' on the seatboard."

Cullie's eyes had gone cloudy and he talked to his slowly twitching
big toes. "Sometimes I still wake up in the dark and wonder where that
poor sumbitch went for the night."

"Well," I said, "I don't guess it was the first time it happened. Or the
last, for that matter."

"No," Cullie said flatly. "No, it God-sure wasn't. And that's a flyspecked fact. But it put somethin' in this man's gizzard. It stuck
somethin' in my craw that scratched like cornbread and wouldn't go
down. On the way home, and I'll never forget it, Poppa plodded along
the dirt road cussin' and kickin' at rocks like they'd registered Republican. And finally he said, 'Cullie, there wants to be a revolution.
When rich men's womenfolks don't even get off their backsides to comb
their own hair and a poor bugger's kids got to live in an open wagon
and sleep bareback on the ground and eat wild berries off the bush,
there wants to be a mighty change.' And you know what, Boy? The ole
man was right. He didn't know much and his breath smelled like a
goat's ass most of the time, and he couldn't have picked up a dime if
he'd dropped it in his pants cuff. But by God, my old man was right!"

So the boy Cullie Blanton had gone home gripped by vague visions,
and had stretched out on his cornshuck mattress with a pounding fever
in the blood. And it burned him in the dark.

"I was on fire to do somethin' about it," Cullie said. "I didn't know
what, you understand. I didn't have the foggiest notion." Cullie tipped
his glass and guzzled like the drinking gong had sounded and he'd
missed hearing it the first time. He brought the glass down and wiped
at an amber trickle on his chin. "But I found out," he said, with quiet
satisfaction. "Oh, yes! By the three-toed tracks of the granddaddy bear,
I sure found out."

That's how it started. Only the One Jehovah knows what kept it
going. Dirt roads turned into gummy loblollies by spring rains maybe,
and years when the land didn't produce even enough for the next
year's seed crop, and meals without so much as a slice of sowbelly. The
awful boredom and the great loneliness, and maybe a few tattered
books read in a lean-to schoolhouse, and a few gut-issue remarks by the
grizzled old man. I'm not saying Cullie was motivated by an overriding
need to do good among the snuff dippers, though that was, no doubt, a
part of it. I figure a sour dissatisfaction with his own common lot

played a role, and the burning something in the genes that barked at
him to be the top dog rather than the kicked cur had something to do
with it, too.

He got an education of sorts, and he had to want it to get it. He
picked cotton when the dew of fall was cool on the bolls, and he
sweated in the canebrakes, and he went by wagging thumb across the
state to follow the first oil boom. He was away from home, living in
tents full of rowdy men and in tin-roofed hotels where a man could get
his ashes hauled for the better part of a dollar; but dollars came hard
and Cullie Blanton, even in the full agony of youth, hoarded them like
Silas Marner. For he was hot on the tracks of the Big Dream, and he
bayed hard on the scent.

With a little bit of luck he inched through high school and picked
up almost two years of book-grinding study at a little cow college long
on a Neanderthal type of theology and short on creature comforts. He
might have got more, but his poppa died. He had to bid the cow college farewell and go back to the hard soil to scratch out a living for his
mama. And then Cullie got lucky.

She died, too. But before Cullie could get back in school something
stirred in his loins and he got the urge to replenish the earth like the
Bible exhorted all men to do. He married a square-jawed blonde country librarian with solid, healthy legs and the stout handsomeness of
brood stock.

That shot school. But it didn't snipe down the learning process. Cullie got his hands on a set of dog-eared law books when the oldest of two
town barristers passed behind the Final Curtain, and he went on the
road with a sample case and the law books. He sold anything and everything he could put a price to. He sold crop insurance and *The Silver
Books of Learning,* and Watkins' products. He sold can openers, and
he sold Bibles with all the words of Jesus printed in red letters to set
Him apart from the black lines of the supporting cast. He sold magazine subscriptions and a purple salve said to cure the acne and to
soothe the piles.

That's where he first got his foot in the door when it comes to politics. Oh, he didn't look like any politician. He looked like a thick-
shouldered, muscle-bound, bulb-nosed country preacher who was pad-
ding out the Sunday collection plate's take by selling door to door. He
wasn't one of those flashy drummers with slicked-down hair that put
folks in mind of oily dance instructors or poolhall sharpies. He didn't
hang around the verandas of small hotels at night, swapping smutty

jokes with the other drummers, dotting the night with waves of big cigars like a covey of moving fireflies. He took to the hills.

Cullie would drive out of town along the winding dirt roads in a high-topped old Model T late in the afternoon and work the country folks. And when the shadows began to lengthen he would arrange to put up for the night at the house of some lonesome farm family palpitating to hear the sound of a strange human voice. He was the perfect guest. He would brag on the womenfolks' cooking and tell fanciful tales chock-full of pithy morals to round-eyed kids, and ask the farmer about his crops. Before long it would be like he was a lost brother dredged up from the sea and restored undripping to the family fold. All that was in the days when a penny postcard gave honest weight. So Cullie would write the folks and thank the billy-goat horns off them for their hospitality, and inquire whether the mare had foaled yet, and how was the cotton stand on the south forty, and had little Ellie Mae or Rosemary or Abner finished that theme on the life of Robert E. Lee?

Later on, he would tell me about that, too.

"Boy," he said with a chortle at the green memory, "you couldn't beat it with a stick. When I packed up ever' mornin' I'd try to pay for my bed and board, but of course the farmer wouldn't set a price on his hospitality. That would have violated the code. But I would shout thanks to the far horizons and press a dollar in his hand on the sly, hand-shakin' my way out to the old Model T. And don't think he wouldn't be gut-bustin' glad to get it, for back then you could hear ever'thing in those woods but the sound of money rattlin' and good meat fryin' on the flame. We'd both be happy, for it would have cost me twice that green dollar in town.

"Then I'd send the postcard in a few days, and the man would get to thinkin' about the friendly stranger he took in. He'd remember that cold-cash dollar, and the way I'd bragged on his family, and think back on how we'd set on the front porch together and washed our feet in the same washpan, and had used the same moon while we drew close to a common God. And not a thing on the green earth could knock that man aloose from me from that day forward. He would be like the turtle won't let go until it thunders."

After the moon gazing and the foot washing, there were the long hours in the yellow blob of light from a flickering coal-oil lamp and the grinding at the law books. Hell, he didn't have any secret formula. It was just dogged determination and mind over matter, and the thing that burned him in the night. God knows he didn't lay claim to discovering it. Huey Long did the same thing, and to some extent his brother Earl, and Lyndon Johnson taught at a peckerwood country school in Texas and swept up the floors to boot. Ole Gene Talmadge in Georgia wasn't born to the silver spoon, and Alfalfa Bill Murray came boiling out of the red clay hills of Oklahoma possessed of the same driving demon.

So Cullie went through the brush a friend to all who crossed his wandering path, and about that time Fate reached out and tapped him on the shoulder. Fate asked for the next waltz, and took Cullie Blanton on a whirl of the dance floor.

The county commissioner in Cullie's home precinct was young and reasonably bright, and he should have held his office until he died. Which, in fact, he did. He just happened to die a long time earlier than he had planned. He just happened to play kiss-on-the-mouth and attendant games of passion with the wife of a man who lived by hard work and harder praying, and who took all ten of the Commandments to heart. The fellow's tender sensibilities were offended by cuckoldom to the extent that the Shalt Not about killing lost its meaning to him, so he sent the county commissioner to a place of eternal rest by one quick squeeze of the blunderbuss.

They didn't have the dearly departed firmly planted under grass before just about everybody out of work declared for the deceased's old office. Including Cullie. There wasn't much to choose among the candidates. They all came out of the same thicket and feared the same Deity, and had close to the same number of kinfolks. The rest of the would-be statesmen went to extreme lengths to wear raggedy overalls and chew a vile brand of tobacco, as evidence they could lay just claim to pedigree among the unwashed rabble. But not Cullie.

"I wanted 'em to believe I was somebody come," he told me. "I wanted 'em to think I was somethin' special on a stick."

So he garbed up in a white linen suit and two-tone brown and white shoes with factory-punched airholes on top of the toe slots. He bought a floppy white hat you could see coming down the road in a blue fog, and he kept his old Model-T Ford washed as clean of road dust as a mere mortal could. He wore a necktie and a white shirt and smoked ready-roll cigarettes. Under the circumstances, he drew more attention than a drunk Presiding Elder at a quarterly conference of Methodists. He quoted the Bible like he'd ghost-written most of the books, and he had all those foot washings and postcards going for him.

When they counted the votes he was so far ahead the others gnashed their teeth about how the fix was on. But it wasn't crooked. It was just that Cullie had planned for his chance, and took it when he saw it. He was waiting for somebody to get shot, or drown in the creek, or go home to Jesus by whatever chariot happened to swing low. He had planned and was ready for anything up to an earthquake.

Cullie was a good commissioner. Or so I've heard many times since. He was the kind of man who raised a considerable number of quizzical eyebrows, and some influential blood pressures, by holding fast to a quaint theory that contracts for county hospitals and roads and schools ought to go to the lowest bidder. He stuck with this alien position even when it caused embarrassing complications for beloved relatives and generous friends of the other three commissioners, who happened to bid right frequently on county jobs, and who had never before played the ball game under Cullie's handicapping rules.

Before Cullie, the brothers of the blood had operated the county business under a private equation where X marked the spot for payoffs and kickbacks. Cullie's approach was as foreign to them as the papal oath, and was held by some to be as dangerous as wing walking. He was not a favorite son in the musty halls of the courthouse.

Public opinion began to crystallize in Cullie's favor when he proved up a forty-six-thousand-dollar bank account on the presiding officer of the Commissioner's Court. Then he worked out a mathematical exercise that left people wanting to know the answer in the back of the book. It went like this: If a presiding officer of the Commissioner's Court saved every cent of his twenty-four-hundred-dollar salary, how long would it take him to get forty-six thousand green bills ahead of the bill collector? Answer: Ten years longer than this particular presiding officer had been in office. And part two of the same problem: If this same presiding officer had no visible means of support, and could not be justly accused of ever having been gainfully employed except on a worn-out pea-patch farm before he was elected to the twenty-four-hundred-buck bonanza, did the Good Fairy bring him the money? And did the Good Fairy bring him the new car and the diamond stickpin for his hand-painted neckties, and the new brick house built on the pea-patch farm? Answer: Not likely, unless you have overpowering confidence in the Good Fairy's goodness.

Cullie didn't have that kind of faith in the Good Fairy. He poked around and found a more acceptable answer. He said the money and the car and the diamond stickpin and the new brick house came on dirty wings in the night from a certain construction company that had the bad habit of building blacktop roads that cracked under the first hot scowl of the summer sun and melted away in little black rivers every time it rained enough to fill a modest frog puddle. The wealthy presiding gentleman was sent off for five years to board at state expense and was assigned to a room with southern exposure that had the scenic view slightly marred by crossbars.

So the cheat from the pea-patch farm went to the big house, and Cullie went down to the state capitol and passed his bar exams. The next time the people went to the polls they promoted Cullie Blanton to the exalted post of district attorney. Now he wore the high crown of officialdom in nine counties instead of just one.

Cullie showed uncommonly plain gumption and horse sense as district attorney. He didn't get himself standing in the way of a certain high sheriff's bootleg operations. He didn't do it for two very valid reasons, the first of which was that the sheriff was said to boil and peddle a brand of sour mash pleasing to the tastebuds and senses of a clear-cut majority of the male voters in at least five counties. And the second reason was that the distaff element in the community held the sheriff to have the nicest smile in the boondocks, and to be the best baritone in the history of the First Baptist Church choir. So Cullie did not bug the sheriff and the sheriff had no reason to bug Cullie. It was live and let live at its best. It was very cozy.

The new district attorney didn't bring any troublesome murder charges against anybody for fatally frog-sticking somebody else in the spirited dances that highlighted Saturday night along the creek bottoms, so long as it looked like a fair fight and so long as the survivors of the deceased were not overly well thought of in the community. Anybody could have a little bad luck, the folks felt.

The D.A. did crack down on a timber combine that tried to bilk a few good gray widows. He cracked down hard, and he shouted about it until the echoes lingered in the woods. He locked up one distinguished skinflint banker who kept taking work home with him and forgetting to bring it back. And, of course, he padded out his conviction percentage by laying the stinging whip of Justice on a passel of Negroes charged with theft and murder and making bad moonshine whisky. So ultimately, because of good judgment and an understanding heart, Cullie was elected state representative. He went off to Capitol City on the Greyhound in a bright blue suit with the funky smell of the store still in it, wearing slick-soled new shoes the color of molasses cookies that pinched his feet some. But not to be taken, friends. Oh, no. He did not go down to Capitol City to be taken. The rube went down to take the city slickers.

And he did it, too.

Cullie had hardly got the shine off and the scuff on his new shoes before he trapped a lobbyist trying to buy his vote in favor of a land giveaway bill. Saying Cullie trapped the fellow makes it sound a lot grander than it was. Trapping him was really kinda like dynamiting little fish. Anybody who couldn't have trapped him probably couldn't have trapped a grizzly bear hung up in a phone booth.

It was easy. The lobbyist had approached Cullie as the new legislator left the House floor one afternoon, volunteering the information that he would be obliged to drop by that evening bearing gifts. Cullie called out a room number at his fleabag hotel. It turned out not to be the lobbyist's lucky number. When the poor lobbyist went walking into Cullie's cubbyhole room in stalk of his prey, carrying a small bundle of neatly wrapped new bills fresh out of the vaults, he didn't know he was flushing out the political game warden. Nobody had told him he was hunting out of season or poaching a posted reserve. He just had tough luck. He had forgotten it was against the law to bribe public officials, because it had been so long since anybody brought the subject up.

So he walked in and forked over the tainted baksheesh, carelessly admitting it was for the kind of commerce he specialized in. Cullie counted it out and got the fellow fatally on record, and then he turned toward a clothes closet to say in a dead, weary voice, "Okay, come out and get the sonofabitch." Out walked the state attorney general and one of his investigators armed with a filled-out warrant for the lobbyist.

The lobbyist was packed off to jail for a stretch, which was itself something like the Second Coming in the middle of washday without any advance blowing of Gabriel's horn. But the people heard Cullie's horn. He blew it on the lobbyist and on crooked games in high places, and used that to leg up to the state Senate.

Where he became the hog-calling voice of the People. Where he became the gadfly, the hair shirt, the Devil's advocate, in the halls of the legislature. And couldn't get any help. But he kept howling like a stuck pig and finally the people began to howl with him. All at once Cullie was roaring across the state bringing the flaming Word, bugging his eyes and damning the Interests to the outer reaches of the lake of fire, and he beat the house man for commissioner of utilities. The next thing anybody knew, the telephone poles around the state blossomed with his picture and seemed to endorse him by acclamation for the exalted gubernatorial roost.

Then I came along with my sour disposition and poison pen, and Cullie talked with me about whether high principle ate on me like cancer in the dark of the night, and he won.

So all that had happened, and there had been eight years in between. And now, on this fine morning, the sun was shining down on the boy who was heading out to see Dallas Johnson and to bring back his bloody head on a platter.

Or thought he was.

3

MY HIGH-BLOWN THEORY about how only conservatives got up early was knocked a-kicking by the delicious eye-feast of Tanya. She met me at the door of what Dallas Johnson liked to call "mah little white cottage" (though it rivaled Mount Vernon for size), in black leotards clinging to her like they were in danger of going down for the third time, and a gold-thread blouse. My eyes took a restful walk among the little peaks and valleys of her form, and she tipped her head over a bit, hands resting on slim hips, grinning.

"Verdict?"

" 'Male and female He created them,' " I said. "Only now and then He lost His head and got carried away with His work. Praise His name."

The interior of the living room was awash with sunlight. Through a tremendous expanse of glass the big bend in the river lay nakedly exposed. The room was a monument to that happy union of informal good living and healthy financial condition, the chairs and sofa glowing in bright warm hues and Tanya's modern-art objects presiding over teakwood tables. A few impressionistic paintings were like cheery islands of color on the muted walls, and the whole effect was underscored by a thick, white rug.

Tanya tossed her ripe goodness on a low, scarlet sofa and bounced among the off-white pillows.

"Come," I said, extending my hands, "let me take you away from all this."

"When Dallas gets fat." She grinned. "And old. And loses all his beautiful black hair and his beautiful green money."

"Christ," I said, with a glance at my wrist watch, "I'd better rush home and pack."

"You wouldn't go even if I bought the tickets. You'd want to take a certain canary along to chirp to you," she teased.

Or I think she teased, though maybe I'm just naturally low-minded. Maybe the lady really needed to stretch at that particular moment, and with those particular muscles and tendons.

"I don't think Roxie's your type," she said. "Or you're not hers or something."

"Early returns indicate a definite trend in that direction," I admitted.

"How is she?"

"She's great," I said. "Terrific. She's dead in a ditch someplace . . . who the hell knows? Christ, I haven't seen her in almost a week!"

We burrowed into one of those throbbing silences.

"Bigmouth," she muttered to herself. "I'm sorry, Jim."

"No . . . forget it . . . hell. . . ."

She bounced up from the scarlet sofa. "You didn't come to purloin me away," she said, lightly. "You came to see Dallie."

"I come bearing gifts of gold and frankincense and myrrh," I said. "We're a couple of wise men short at the Mansion today, so I came to worship the Infant Jesus alone."

Tanya flashed gold across the floor and banged with vigor on the closed door of the bedroom she shared with Dallas Johnson.

After ten minutes of water splashing, gasping, and gurgling, Dallas Johnson stood revealed in the doorway, dark and warmly tousled in a bright yellow terry-cloth bathrobe, blinking.

" 'Lo,' " I said, in imitation of Cullie, " 'he comes trailin' vapors of misty glory . . . who walketh upon the wings of the wind?' "

" 'Thorns and thistles,' " he said huskily. " 'Thorns and thistles it shall bring forth to you'." He frowned, thinking hard. " 'And you . . . shall you eat of' . . . well, I'm too sleepy."

" 'And you shall eat,' " I supplied, " 'the plants of the field.' "

Dallas Johnson tasted his tongue and shuddered. "Way my mouth feels," he said, "I ate of the bad plants. The very worse parts." He lurched toward the scarlet sofa and pitched forward. "Christ, I feel better since I quit drinking."

"And when did that terrible jolt hit the booze industry?"

"About four o'clock this morning. To what do we owe the pleasure, et cetra?"

"Happened to be in the neighborhood, et cetra."

"Balls," he said, delicately. "Only three things could stir you at this hour. Money, girls, and the Governor's pleasure."

"He's the one holds the deadwood."

Tanya was back with the coffee.

"Got to remember Scripture better," the young state representative said, suddenly. "You don't remember it in this business, you'd just as well get out and open a poolhall."

"If you want to arouse the folks in this state," I said, "you can be short on gray matter but you got to be mighty long on Jesus."

"Look at Cullie," Dallas said. "He knows all the Scripture there is to know."

"Cullie knows something else, too."

"Cullie knows all knowledge."

"Cullie knows you're fighting his loan-shark bill," I said, dropping it on him.

Dallas Johnson even smiled. "Well, hell. As the pregnant gal said, 'I didn't think I could hide it forever' . . . but it took him almost a week to find out. The old 'possum is slipping."

"The old 'possum," I said, "has a different notion about who's doing all the slipping. The old 'possum dwells among dark thoughts that your friend Jim Clayton's taking the downward plunge."

"Ahhhh. . . ."

"Look, I caught unbuttered hell."

"Cullie couldn't wash his socks without you. And he knows it."

"Or salt his watermelon. But he can damn well function as the political High Priest without this altar boy. And he knows that, too."

"With or without you," Dallas Johnson said, "he'd better start functioning better than he has lately."

"Let's get down to the lick-log. Why have you got your tail over the dashboard about the loan-shark bill?"

"Bad bill," he said, automatically. "Too restrictive. Obscure language."

"You're talking what makes the grass grow green. Any other time, you'd be raising a hybrid variety of cain about how it didn't tie up sharks tight enough."

He had no ready answer, so he hid behind the bottom of his coffee cup. Tanya sat with her chin framed in the open V of her hands, taking it in as though expected to transcribe it in shorthand.

"Cullie says find out what you've got itching," I said. "And what it takes to scratch it."

"You bastards think everybody's got a hand out," he said.

"Dallas, what is it about you red-hot liberals that makes you want to call everything a buy? It's just that the good Governor figures when somebody steps out of character to fight a bill, then that somebody wants to do a little horse trading."

Dallas Johnson said, "He has no earthly possession I covet."

I sighed. I said, "All right, dammit, what *will* it take to scratch the itch? What do you want?"

He looked surprised, thinking about it. "I don't know," he said. "I truly don't."

"Tanya," I said, "you are a sweet and wonderful child, while I am an old man and full of years. Vile words are about to pass my ancient lips. Words you shouldn't hear. Go play with your dolls."

"Aw, let me stay. I might learn something that would come in handy."

"The first thing you learn," Dallas Johnson said, without looking at her, "is to do as you're told. Beat it, Baby."

I waited until she had slammed the bedroom door.

"You're mean," I said.

"Damn whistling."

"The Governor's mean, too."

"Mean as hell," he agreed. "Born mean."

"And will die that way. Dallas, I'm begging you. *Ask* for something. Take something. And give up the fight on the bill."

"Can't think of anything I want."

I got up and walked to the window. Weeping willows on the banks bent low to kiss the water, and an old man and a boy lazed on the banks soaking up the slow pleasures of pole fishing. It was peaceful and bucolic, and altogether another world.

"I've got two ways to approach this," I said. "The first is to give you whatever you want . . . within reason. The other one is to bring your bloody head on a platter, and those are Cullie's words, not mine. Me, I'm a gentle soul and love my mother. I'd rather do it the first way."

"If you can't do it that way," he said, "you can't do it at all."

"I think I can. But I'd rather not."

I turned away from the peaceful world outside the glass wall. Dallas Johnson wasn't lounging in stupor on the sofa any more. He was rigid on the edge of it, knotting into a powerful anger. Cullie Blanton must have been like that in his youth. True, they came from different planets, but they had migrated toward a common denominator: the public service.

"Dallas," I said, "this isn't going to be any more fun for me than the lung cancer. I'd just as soon get mixed up in the tong wars. Do us both a favor and call off the dogs. You know what it's like when a governor calls some of a member's key constituents and says 'Hold this boy's feet to the goddamn fire.' Due bills are called, and campaign funds dry up like milk cows eating bitterweeds, and everybody gets to treating the poor fellow like he's toting around a load of the leprosy. Bills are vetoed, and state agencies are moved to places where the local representative is a more reasonable fellow, and it gets sticky as hell down there in the legislative halls. A sensitive soul could get to feeling like a cross between an invisible man and a lonesome polecat."

"Let him turn the screws," Dallas Johnson said. "I don't have to depend on his charity. I don't have to worry about bank notes being called or where I'll get my next campaign dollar."

"No," I said, "you don't. But there are some other things to worry about."

"Name me one."

"You ever hear of Ken Reigel?"

He puffed on his cigarette, frowning. "The name calls up a flicker," he said, "but I can't do much with it."

"Let me freshen your memory. Ken Reigel was a while before your time down here in the hallowed halls. Ken was some like you. Young and fairly bright and a pretty good man. He wasn't rich like you, and he wasn't blessed by bachelorhood. He was married to a sweet girl and he was a mighty pillar in the church. But the serpent beguiled him, and he did eat. He took to bundling with his secretary, who had good legs and was a long way from home, and who got bit by the lonely bug. And about the same time Ken Reigel started knocking the edge off her loneliness, he unwisely took up the burden of fighting the Governor's reorganization bill."

"I'd have fought it, too," Dallas Johnson said. "It gave him the power to put his stoolies and spies and cronies in every goddamn office has a door."

"The Governor looked at it a different way," I said. "The way the Governor saw it, he relieved the heads of state agencies from the worrisome task of acting as an employment agency. And it allowed the Governor to pass on the qualifications of potential public servants. With, of course, the aid of a commission appointed to assist the Governor with the chore."

"Commission! Bunch of rubber-stamp yokels who jump from here to

Mobile when Cullie yells 'frog.' Half of 'em can't read or write. Dammit, Jim! That's what I'm talking about. Cullie runs this state like it was a wind-up toy left for him under the Christmas tree."

"You think it was run any better before he took over? You know damn well it wasn't. And that's what I tried to tell Ken Reigel."

"So did you buy him?"

"I couldn't even rent him."

"Good for him," he said.

" 'Rest his soul' would be more appropriate."

Dallas Johnson jerked his head.

"Relax," I said. "I didn't shoot him. The point is, Ken Reigel was stubborn. So he got the treatment. Somehow word got around in his district about the lonesome secretary. It was shouted from under brush arbors and wailed from the stump. It was the subject of gossip at quilting parties and bemoaned on the banks of baptismal rivers. There was a recall petition that just missed, and an election that didn't miss at all. He lost the election, and he lost his letter in the church, and he lost his pretty, sweet wife. He even lost the secretary, who high-tailed it home to mama and maybe entered a nunnery. And finally he lost the most precious gift. He went quail hunting and didn't come back. They found his body near a barbed-wire fence."

Dallas Johnson said, "That fellow Reigel should have been more careful."

"He was careful," I said. "I've been quail hunting with Ken Reigel, and he was the most old-maidish sonofabitch with a gun you ever saw."

Dallas Johnson didn't say anything. He stood and walked to the window, his hands thrust deep in the pockets of his robe.

"Dallas, you're rich and you're clean-cut enough to be elected president of the Jaycees, and you've got a devoted grass-roots following that believes you designed the Pyramids. But there are enough peckerwoods and rednecks and meddling preachers and plain jealous wives in your district to excite some commotion about that lovely unit there in the bedroom. If a man just was forced to walk that route."

"Jim," he said. And he shook his head slowly, a sorrowful grin on his face. "Jim, I don't know if I should laugh or pitch you out on your ass. You're a hell of a fine one to talk about that kind of thing," he said. "You think it's any secret about you and Roxie? You think you got special dispensation from the Pope? I imagine she uses hers pretty much like the rest of 'em do. They've all got it in the same place."

"Look," I said, "you go to raising hell among the Christians about

Roxie, and the Governor will just announce he's shocked beyond any measure of it. He'll quote the Bible with a tear in his voice and stage a public stoning to run me out of state. He'll just get himself another boy and percolate along like always."

"All right," Dallas Johnson said. "You've shown me the fallacy of my thinking. Now let me poke a few holes in yours. I don't have a sweet wife to lose or a letter in the church. I don't even own a shotgun. And I don't scare. I lead a lot easier than I drive."

"Pride," I said, "goeth before a mighty fall."

"Who the hell you trying to snow? Cullie's got more troubles out in the brush now than there are redbugs in the tall grass. And here in this cracker-box legislature, too. The Governor's program is in more trouble than a knocked-up nun. The only time Cullie's pushed anything through this session has been when I've humped up like a dog passing persimmon seeds and shoved it through for him. *He* needs me a hell of a lot worse than I need him. The boys are on the verge of mutiny. They're looking for somebody to rally around. I'll draw them unto me. Liberals and conservatives and the ones who walk in the middle of the road. I'll have me the screechingest, pissingest, howlingest, hell-raisingest bunch of greenwood sonsofbitches who ever clamored together under a common roof. And by God, I will lead like Moses."

Dallas meant it, too. He slammed down against the back rest of the sofa, breathing hard, full of beans and spoiling with fight.

"Just please tell me one thing," I said. "Why all this sudden compulsion to fight Cullie? And especially on the loan-shark bill."

"It just happened to be the bill that was up," he said, with an impatient wave of his hand. "Hell, it could just as easily have been a bill to bell cats. I'm trying to prove a point. I'm trying to show Cullie Blanton and you and everybody else up there that a coalition of my so-called liberals and moderates can get together with the Neanderthal pols and whistle any tune we call, including 'Dixie.' Only you guys in the catbird's seat can't see it because you're still blinded by the shining glories of the past. You think you can go along cramming whatever bitter pill you've got down the throats of this legislature without anybody gagging. But everybody in the legislature can read and write a little now, and maybe that makes their stomachs a little more sensitive. If we can get a coalition strong enough to kill the loan-shark bill, then we can do about anything else we want."

"What the hell *do* you want?"

"I want Cullie to quit putting the hide-skinning whip to anybody who crosses him. And I want him to give up the bad habit of drifting. Hell, Jim! Lately he's reacting instead of acting."

"You're not winning any gold cups for consistency," I said. "First you say Cullie pulls the reins so tight the bit makes the mouth bleed and then you turn around and say he doesn't even have his hand on the reins."

"Jim, open your eyes! It's *happening* that way. On the little nit-picking, coon-ass things he's still the same driving, mean, go-for-the-throat sonofabitch. You cross him on the appointment of some hick he wants to name tick inspector and he'll come yowling and swinging the meat ax. But when it gets down to the place where the boils are sore, like all this mess brewing in the courts, he fades out."

"Cullie's done all right."

"He *has,* sure. But you're talking in the past tense, Jim. Let's talk about the present. Level with me. Has the Governor got even a frag-mentary plan to meet whatever crisis comes up when the Court rules on this university lawsuit?"

"I'm sure he's got something in mind."

"Dammit, has he or not?"

"Christ, yes. Okay?"

"But you don't know what it is," he shouted, jabbing his forefinger at me. "You sit at the Right Hand and don't know! Jesus, how you think it is with the rest of us. *We* don't know what the hell's happen-ing. All we know is a little history, and history says the Court will order the university integrated. So what the hell happens next? Does any-body know?"

"Not anybody in this room," I said.

"You're wrong. I know. At least I know the rabble will start to rouse. And I know something more. I know there's only a handful of us who've got the guts or the pazzaz to help still the madness when it starts. Cullie ought to be courting me, for when there's blood on the moon he's gonna need somebody down on the floor of that legislature who'll climb to his feet and shout something besides 'nigger, nigger, nigger.' "

"You're not going to be asked in to break bread by fighting the Governor's loan-shark bill," I said. "You don't kick a man in the most precious spots and then ask for his daughter's hand in marriage."

"No," Dallas Johnson said, "and apparently you don't get asked into the inner circle and told the family secrets even by grunting the

Governor's bills through the legislature until you get a hernia. I've tried that route and I don't know whether the Governor's going to call out the troopers to comply with the Court's order or stand screeching in the mob and throw stones. So I am going to get me that little coalition together and knock his loan-shark bill from here to next Christmas. Maybe then he'll put his mind to work on problem number one and clue his friends about the answer."

I got up and headed for the door.

"Is that what you want me to tell him, Dallas?"

"Yeah," he said. "And tell him one other thing."

"What?"

"Tell him there's blood on the moon."

The sun was riding higher in the anemic blue sky, climbing, getting a better angle on the world, and I tooled along the sweeping highway that stretched by the river, the top down on the convertible, wind rushing at me. There was a time when the highway had been pitted and potholed, washboardy and jagged with crumbling hunks of blacktop. But Cullie came along and built a modern highway that would do for a test track at Salt Flats. Thundering down it, I dwelled on Dallas Johnson and how he had accused Cullie of running the state like a wind-up toy left under the Christmas tree.

Well, I guess he had, at that.

There was the time late in his first term when the Governor got it into his gray head to make an old crony who had fallen on evil times superintendent of state hospitals. The Boss ran up a test flag on that one, dropping a hint of his intentions to a few favored newspaper boys queued up at the Mansion one night for some deadly serious whisky quaffing and card shuffling. I didn't know anything about it, because Cullie had me out trying to find a state senator who had incurred his displeasure over some obscure sin, and I was poking among the gin mills and the harlot houses that masqueraded as motels, for that was the type of relaxation this particular senator favored. But I learned about it the next morning when trembling hands reached for black coffee and the newspaper. I took one horrified glance and burst into Cullie's private office like a bear was breathing on my neck. He was shuffling through some mail stacked on his desk, mouth set in an expression of vile distaste.

I had paused just short of ramming into the Governor's cluttered desk, croaking what the hell was this unfettered crap about naming Pat Hodges superintendent of state hospitals. The Governor pursed his lips and studied his mail with a baleful eye.

"Goddamn and hell," he said, "how you reckon all these pecker-woods' letters get to soundin' alike? They got a school somewhere teaches folks how to write letters gives a good governor heartburn of the blow hole?"

I said I didn't know. And how about this Pat Hodges business?

Cullie Blanton pushed his reading glasses firmly against the bridge of his nose with one thick forefinger and cleared his throat. "Make a man favor illiteracy," he said gloomily. "Make a man wonder at the wisdom of exposin' little minds to big words. I got a sumbitch here accuses me of havin' the moral shrinks for favorin' a veterans' bonus, and one says he wouldn't help elect me tick and hide inspector just on general revolvin' principle, and a poor bastard implorin' me to keep him from gettin' killed in the tornado's gonna strike his house next August. *August*, for God's sakes! How the hell you reckon a statesman goes about stoppin' a goddamn tornado?"

"Look," I said, "I'm not exactly expert on the tornado schedule for next August. But you can stop the ill wind that's blowing up about this Pat Hodges foolishness. Tell the news boys it's a misunderstanding or a very bad joke or something."

"I remember when this state had an eighty per cent illiteracy rate," the Governor mourned. "I remember when eight peckerwoods in ten couldn't make their mark. Oh, for the good ole days. . . ."

"Dammit," I said, "will you talk sense to me about this thing?"

"I will send rain upon the earth," the Governor mumbled absently, stroking his chin and peering at the letters.

"Okay," I said. "Dummy up, then. But at least keep your ears open. You might be interested in knowing what the law says about the quali-fications of the superintendent of state hospitals."

"What you got against ole Pat Hodges?" the Governor snapped, suddenly.

"Not a rig-widdling thing," I said. "He may be the greatest humani-tarian since Albert Schweitzer. But the law says he's got to be a medical man. And I don't care how many shopping centers he's built. The con-struction business isn't exactly the place to intern for medical knowl-edge."

"Pat Hodges is as honest as they turn 'em out," the Governor said. "If he wasn't, he wouldn't of gone bust in the buildin' business with me here in the sweet seat of power. Pat Hodges could've called his personal friendship with the Governor to the undivided attention of the state contractin' officer and got a deal to maybe pave over the Mississippi River with concrete and paint it green with pink polka dots. But he stayed honest and so he went broke. And I got it in my bones to help him."

"I don't necessarily hook up honesty and failure together."

"Then you don't know much," he said.

"I know the law says the superintendent of hospitals gotta be a medical man."

The Governor pushed back from his desk and sighed. He shook his head slowly from side to side. "Boy," he said, "you are like all the other nut-boy liberals. You go around presumin' that if a law's on the books it's firmed up tighter than the lockjaw. *I* have read the goddamn law about what qualifications Pat Hodges has to have. And it don't say word one about bein' a medical man. It says, and I quote it from memory and from the goddamn heart, that the superintendent of hospitals has got to be 'a recognized doctor.'" The Governor sat back, smiling.

"Pat Hodges isn't a doctor of *anything*. He wouldn't know salve from saliva."

"Pick up the black instrument there and get me that Whitlow fellow runs the state university," the Governor said. "He's gonna make Pat Hodges a recognized doctor. He's gonna whistle up a big ceremony. He's gonna dress ole country-bumpkin Pat Hodges in one of those flowing gowns and the mortarboard hat with the little swingin' tassel, and haul off and lay a doctor's degree of some kind on him. I don't give a goddamn if it's Doctor of Divinity or Doctor of Letters or Doctor of Unlearned Hokum. But it will be somethin', and it will qualify the empyreal piss out of Pat Hodges under the law."

"You can't do that!"

"I am the mother of All Living," the Governor said. "I can do anything."

"What the hell makes you presume Whitlow will do it? Hell, he's the president of the state university. He's a *professional* man!"

"Yes," Cullie Blanton said softly. "Yes, by God, he is. And he wants to stay president of the state university, for he is old and tired and dreams of pensions more than of glory. Professional men got to eat the same as us mortals. And under another law you may not have read, he serves at the pleasure of the governor. Who happens to be me."

So that's how Doctor Pat Hodges got to be superintendent of state hospitals, and astounded the bejeebers out of a lot of folks by doing a whale of a good administrative job; maybe the best in the whole damn administration. But he could have done the worst. The point is, Cullie Blanton ran the state exactly like Dallas Johnson had claimed. Like a wind-up toy left under the Christmas tree.

I tooled along the highway, the wind blowing sweet and easy in my face, thinking of the unlimited exercise of raw power. I wondered at what point the use of power quits being good and starts going bad, and if anyone could say. You take a governor burning to change that part of the universe he thinks of as his, and give him the mandate to work his will. He will make some improvements: he will heal the sick and put free textbooks in the schools; he will pick up the little man from the prone position where he's been kicked and stomped by the long-dollar boys, and he will build superhighways to get some folks clipping freely down the road and get some others killed on the hairpin turns. So what is good and what is evil?

I thought about that, and I thought about other things.

Fate, for instance.

And Roxann Winston, for another.

You sit in the grape-colored shadows of a humming cocktail lounge, applying liquid medication, and a woman swings soft and pliant across the floor, moving with that easy rolling motion the good ones have, coming through the shadows, her face wearing a pensive look. You forget your miseries for a moment, and give the eyes free rein to wander over the form soft and supple, the form swaying with the rhythm of womanly locomotion, and you take rapid stock of what you see. And something clicks. A good thing has happened. Contact has been made.

That's the way it was when I met Roxie.

Don't think I'm one of those guys who goes out of his skull about every babe he sees driving down the street in a Mercedes-Benz with her skirt pulled up to a point exposing a little something just above the knee. My style is wedded to caution. I have struggled with one very bad marriage that died of clustered apathy. The experience unsettled me a bit. It made me snuggle up to caution. I moved around in the thorny rose garden of love on tiptoe for fear something might jump out of the bushes and sink a quick, poisonous fang in my leg.

This little cocktail spot was huddled in the shadow of the capitol dome, a place of darkness at noon, the hangout of Capitol Hill folks, with uneasy caricatures of the state's bejeweled political figures frozen in foolish exaggeration on muraled walls. The place was full of the usual drone and hum and cackle of secretaries to legislators, impressed with walking on the outer fringes of what they thought was History, and smug lobbyists who wore out their pocket flaps tugging at billfolds for to spread corporate cheer, and some of the great preening tin gods themselves striking poses for posterity. Everybody was talking learnedly of consent calendars and closed rules and mail from the folks, and about who got smashed at Senator Wingwoah's bash and why the goddamn Governor was such a sumbitch.

I sat gazing into the clear bottom of a vodka martini glass, taking long looks at the innermost self of Jim Clayton, in the historic tradition of folks who fear they have a bottle problem. What I saw was Jim Clayton slogging along in his mid-thirties with nothing much good happening to him—the swamper, the lackey, the pale shadow of a slightly mad governor who wanted to do good and build monuments to dwarf the goddamn Sphinx.

You take a poor boy like me from a jerkwater town, who's never been more than a half-step ahead of the bill collector and who has made his uneasy peace with Failure a long time before, and give him a state to run. You hand him a piss-elm club and whisper in his ear to get in there and lay 'round him a little, and never mind the stomped feet or the cracked heads. You give him a salary he equates with the presidency of U.S. Steel and a high-falutin' title, and tell him he is at once the Father and the Son and the Holy Ghost, and the Lord High Executor, and it will run to his head like strong wine.

That's what happened to me, and for a while I was the meanest, cussedest, swingingest, lay-on-McDuff sonofabitch. I was reshaping the destiny of a hunk of mankind and changing the curvation of the earth. I was God breathing on clay. Or thought I was. But when I paused to look around me, all I saw was Jim Clayton, a hired hand, doing the Governor's precious bidding. So I was gazing on dark blood when this geranium swayed across the floor among purple shadows.

The woman who would turn out to be Roxie was in the company of a girl with a vaguely familiar face, whom I pegged as secretary to a legislator of widespread obscurity. She was my only visible means of immediate rapport with Roxie-to-be, so I turned on my best-wattage smile and shouted a warm greeting. I had stood, motioning them to my table, and while Roxie hesitated with a look of faint annoyance creasing her forehead, the Hill gal gushed her way into a chair.

I told jokes and invented improbable stories, and grinned until the cheek muscles ached. Oh, I knocked the secretary out of it. She flipped, but that didn't count. She was throwing down liquid until about the time I decided she must be wearing a urinal bottle strapped to the inside thigh, like the state senators do when they're bent on all-night filibusters, she proved to be human by excusing herself.

"Roxie," I said with an easy familiarity I didn't feel, "what do you do?"

"I sing," she said.

"What?"

"Songs."

"Well," I said, after giving it some study, "I reckon that beats Moslem prayer chants."

I got a tired, patient smile for a reward.

"I want to tell you something," I said, recklessly, desperately. She looked at me with those brown eyes, waiting, curiosity jumping from them. It was the first time she'd indicated I was any more interesting than the average doorknob. "I want to tell you something and I want you to keep your lovely red mouth shut until I finish. What I want to say is that you've turned me around. I don't know your story and you don't know mine, and if I didn't have this thing that's a cross between the world's worst hangover and a brand new buzz I probably wouldn't have the guts or the lack of judgment to say it. I want to know you better."

"My God," she said, "an hour ago you didn't know I was alive."

"An hour ago," I said, "I didn't know *I* was alive."

"I'm very hung up," she said. "I'm half married and half not, and I'm bugged by so many things you simply wouldn't believe it. So drink your drink and go pass laws or something."

"No," I said, "and that's a warning."

"Look, I don't need this kind of aggravation. You don't want to get mixed up with me."

"Lady," I said, "will you please hush and let Jesse rob this train like he wants to?"

It was an old gag line and everybody knows it, but she poured her vocal amber over ice, laughing, and lightly squeezed my hand. Just for an instant, a frozen speck in time, but it was enough.

"Let's cut out," I said. "Let's fly away from here."

She grinned, shaking her head from side to side, her face moving in wonderful patterns of animation. "I knew musicians were crazy," she said, "but nobody told me about politicians."

"Let me tell you. I've got all the time in the world."

"I haven't," she said with a darting look at her watch. "I've got to get out of here and get some dinner and go to work."

"Let me buy dinner," I said. "Let me buy dinner and tell you all about those crazy politicians. Just for tonight."

"No. Not tonight or any other night. And besides, I don't think I want to be disillusioned about politicians. Anyway," she said, "I would drive you right out of your mind. I would make you a basket case inside of a month."

"Sounds ominous."

"I don't mean it to be," she said. "But somehow that's the way it usually works out."

The no-name secretary returned from the little girls' room, and soon Roxie swayed away through the shadows, taking something of me with her.

4

THE GOVERNOR loomed over the marble-topped breakfast table, mournfully sucking at his second ration of morning coffee. He rattled his cup in a china saucer and tugged at the crotch of kelly-green silk pajamas. "Sweet Jesus," he said, and bent to peer suspiciously at the Great Seal of State, half-buried under neglected remains of curdling egg yolk.

Slices of sunlight spilled through the screened porch at the rear of the Mansion. Behind us the capitol dome caught the brunt of the day's early light.

"Hen fruit!" Cullie Blanton snorted. "We raise up cities out of the bleached desert floor and hoot of leadin' the Free World to a time of endless glory. But goddammit, we still eat *rooster semen!*"

The Governor pointed an accusing finger at the morning newspaper spread open by his plate.

"Who's in charge of the goddamn good news?" he demanded.

"He must be on vacation."

"Well, call him back. The world needs him. You don't kidnap a movie star or start a cholera plague or call somebody a card-carryin' Communist, you can't grab a headline any more. What this country needs," the Governor said, "is a good five-cent newspaper. I'd like to meet one goddamn publisher didn't believe in a flat earth and werewolves."

A chocolate houseboy slipped up behind Cullie with the stealth of an Apache, threatening his coffee cup with a silver pot. Cullie instinctively sprang to defense, throwing one hand across the opening. The young Negro struggled to maintain control of his silver burden and maybe his rectal muscles. He had come within kindergarten fractions of giving the Governor's hand an unscheduled baptism, and he pulled back shaken to the lobes, scurrying halfway to the door leading from the sun porch.

"Melacadies," the Governor called, twisting in his chair. "We got any cantaloupe?"

"Yessuh. I thinks so. . . ."

"Get me some," the Governor ordered. "And ice cream. Pack some that strawberry ice cream in half a cantaloupe. And tell Nettie don't go sendin' me any more goddamn eggs up here for a while. I eat any more eggs, I'll have to *crow* my next inaugural address. Way she pushes eggs she must own a chicken farm. I think Nettie's gone and got herself involved in one of those conflict-of-goddamn-interest thangs."

"She read a book," Melacadies volunteered.

"Couldn't been a cookbook," the Governor said. "All the evidence is against it . . . you want some, Jim?"

"At the risk," I said, "of losing the dairy vote, I stand four-square against the proposition."

Melacadies soft-shoed it into the Mansion.

A bird cried in the rose garden below and sunlight washed the surface of the marble table. Cullie tugged at his nose and stuffed his tongue in the space between lower teeth and bottom lip, creating a mighty bulge of flesh.

"I guess you know about that little song and dance our distinguished junior Senator went into up there in Sodom-on-the-Potomac," I said.

"That's some the bad news I was talkin' about," the Governor said, nodding toward the newspaper.

"Well, he's hollering before he's hurt. The Court hasn't even ruled and he's blessing out the judicial system retroactive to Gladstone. It's not exactly helpful to the situation."

"That's what I told the Hollywood bastard," Cullie said, sloshing cold coffee in the bottom of his cup.

Surprised, I said, "You've talked to the Senator?"

"It won't rank with the dialogues of Plato," the Governor said, "but we made sounds at one another."

"When was all this?"

"Early," the Governor said. "Before the young Senator got out of bed." He grinned a great satisfaction at the memory. "I caught him with his brain immersed in the lullin' fog of sleep. And I quoted the prophet Isaiah and shouted snatches of Shakespeare and I said, '*Dammit, Sentuh,* all the other great statesmen in Washington been runnin' around for two hours gettin' *gunny sacks full* of Federal aid for their folks and leavin' their bejeweled footprints on the face of goddamn

history! And you still threshin' around in perfumed bedsheets while
our factories stand idle and our children grow up ignorant enough to
serve in the United States Senate.' Got him in a god*awful* uproar."

"I don't like Price Collins any better than you do," I said, "but I
hope you didn't needle him too much. We don't need another one of
those bawling speeches of his about Federal troops marching into our
midst and making our children use a bayonet for a bookmark. We
need us a batch of unity," I said. "And a whole mess of harmony."

"Boy," the Governor said, "tryin' to keep Price Collins from making
goat-blattin' speeches is about as rewardin' as tryin' to change the flow
of the goddamn Nile. He's gonna stand up there in Washington and
yell coon-in-your-cafés and scream pickaninnies-in-your-schools until
the very day God quits makin' little green apples."

"I guess there's some excuse to be found in his youth," I said. "Only
we don't have time to wait for him to grow older and wiser. I wish I
knew what to do about him."

"We could have him shot," the Governor said. "Only that might get
to be an issue in an election year."

Melacadies slipped up to place the cantaloupe and ice cream on the
marble table.

"How you and the Speaker comin' along convertin' infidels?" the
Governor asked.

"We think we've got fifty-two votes in the House."

"That's cuttin' it a little too near the hamstrings." The Governor
frowned. "That gives the other side forty-eight."

"I figure 'em for forty-one firm," I said. "About seven are playing it
cozy. Straddling the fence."

"Name me some," the Governor ordered. He attacked the vile deli-
cacy before him. While I named the seven uncommitteds, the Governor
grunted, calling up mumbled, obscure facts about the seven prize sheep
from a vast store of memory. Now and again he fired a quick question.

"This is one I got to win," he said suddenly. "It is a by-God must. A
politician's record's the same as a small-town girl's reputation for chastity. Word gets out he can be had, everybody lines up to take a turn
screwin' him. So give those seven peckerwoods whatever they want. I
don't care if it's the disjointed thigh bone of the great woolly mastodon
or a life-sized statue of Jesus Christ that glows in the dark. Somethin'
else. We got to jar that bill out of Siggy Sears' committee. You got any
bright ideas how?"

"It's as good as done," I said. "I think we've got Siggy beat seven to five." I sat, feigning elaborate casualness.

The Governor goggle-eyed me over the cantaloupe. "Boy," he said, "unless you can explain yourself I got to bring prompt charges of witchcraft. The Speaker thinks the committee's knotted at six and six."

"I know the heart's desire of a certain representative from Calhoun County," I said, "who just happens to serve on that Finance Committee."

"Freeman? R. E. Lee *Freeman?*"

"One and the same."

"Can't give him the time of day," Cullie Blanton said. "That pirate hasn't supported one of my bills since he's been down here. He's a stumblin' block in the path of the blind."

"He'll support you on this one," I said. "High principle not withstanding, R. E. Lee Freeman has decided to enter into vulgar commerce. All you've got to do is appoint him to the Board of Pardons and Paroles."

The Governor halted his spoon in mid-air, mouth agape. A gob of strawberry ice cream plopped back into the cantaloupe. "Boy," he said, "I have got a lot on my conscience, and no doubt when I see my Maker we will have many things to iron out. But I am *not* going to my eternal reward with that particular stain on my soul. R. E. Lee Freeman wouldn't know a habitual criminal from a writ of mandamus. I cannot and will not appoint him."

"You don't have to," I said. "I gave him my certified Confederate oath. But you didn't."

The Governor favored me with a look of frank amazement. "Sometimes," he said, slowly, "I wonder if the tutor taught the pupil too well."

Cullie poked absently at the cantaloupe, lifting a spoonful of ice cream and then putting it back without taking any. He pushed back from the table and prowled the sun porch, blinking down at the rose garden, rubbing the back of his neck in somber reflection.

"One thing I've always done," he said, after a spell, "is honor a promise. Oh, I am mortal and reasonably mean and maybe have more or less *misled* my colleagues in the public service when the price was right. But you make a political promise, you by God *keep* it."

"You didn't give Lee Freeman any promise."

"You did," he said. "And that's the same thing."

"No. It's almost the same thing. But almost doesn't count."

The Governor judged the distant roses. After a while he turned slowly, shoulders hunched against some vague menace, squinting across the sun porch. "I never cottoned to losin'," he said. "Somethin' in me always shouted for the blue ribbon. Losin' is just not of my breed. But in this particular instance it's more than that. It's more than ego or just wantin' to bust nuts. This legislature's been showin' an uncharacteristic streak of independence. They've squatted on their hands and howled toward the stars, and if they get the notion they can get away with it they'll be wantin' to bite me in the leg."

"Then it seems," I said, "the decision dictates itself."

" 'Now the men of Sodom were wicked,' " the Governor muttered, " 'and great sinners against the Lord. . . .' " He pulled at his nose, blinking. He alternately lifted his arms, scratching under one armpit and then the other. "Why the gooseberry hell does Lee Freeman want such a nit-pickin' little ole job?"

I could have said how R. E. Lee Freeman had come to the legislature a few years before, hunting the ancient truths, anxious to make some kind of mark for mankind, leaning toward Main Street conservatism but not yet wholly grabbed by the Babbitt mind, possessed of an obscure half-conviction that a public man ought to have some beliefs of his own and, moreover, vote them on occasion. I could have said how in his blissful ignorance he voted for the working man by standing against a sales tax on bread and work gloves, and for his pains got resoluted against by the chamber of commerce, and leper-shunned by the country-club set and bawled out at Rotary Club. How he recanted, voting with the chamber gang and the country clubbers and the Rotarians on the next vote, only to be set upon by labor leaders and cracked across the political groin by a vengeful governor, and strung up in absentia by the Farmers' Union.

I could have said how the chamber of commerce favored him for a series of backward votes by throwing an appreciation dinner, giving him a brass plaque speaking of Good Government and Honesty and Integrity in High Places, and how a week later the same man who had presented the brass plaque, and who just happened to own a major construction company, shook his fist in R. E. Lee Freeman's face and said, "Goddammit, there was nothin' wrong with my bid. It was a perfectly good goddamn bid and don't hand me that cheap crap about saving the state a half-million dollars, for the frigging Governor will just waste it on the rednecks. You go see that highway commissioner and get me that goddamn road job or I will ruin you quick."

I could have said how R. E. Lee Freeman grew to recognize (but could not bring himself to understand) the age-old double standard: a businessman with money is respected, a politician with money is suspected; a businessman driving a hard bargain is wonderfully shrewd, a politician driving the same bargain is abysmally crooked; a plain citizen in church is cleansing his soul, a politician in the same circumstance is grandstanding for votes. Oh, I could have railed on about how the folks elect ordinary men and then expect of them extraordinary conduct. And I could have said how R. E. Lee Freeman had wearied of the sport, how he had finally reached a prayerful decision to look out after old Number One.

As to specifics, I could have pointed out how Freeman's law partner specialized in criminal law, and did as well as could be expected. Only you can't expect to represent clients who have played loosely with the commandments of God and man without their having to pay the tab for their follies now and again. The clients of this particular firm had got the bad habit of being singularly unbelieved by juries, even under solemn oath. R. E. Lee Freeman had stumbled upon the fact that if word got out his partner's clients got sprung from the jug in jig time, business was bound to show a sharp upswing.

I could have said all that. But what I said was, "Well, let's just say R. E. Lee Freeman is eat up with the urge to do good among the wicked."

"He's been right successful at concealing it up to this point," the Governor said sourly. "I never even suspected him."

"Folks change," I said easily.

"Not some folks. Now tell me the straight of it."

So I told him. When I had finished, the Governor furrowed his brow with thought lines. "Jesus!" he said. "I wonder if ole Diogenes ever found that honest man?"

"If he did," I said, "it wasn't in this state."

"What it boils down to," the Governor mused, "is that I either break my word or appoint that jackanapes to a job he'll foul with stench most high."

"No," I said. "It's one of those multiple-choice things. The other choice is to call up Lee Freeman and denounce me as a stranger to the truth. You could renege on the whole deal." I waited a few seconds, letting him mull it over. "And," I said, softly, "you could lose his vote."

"Boy," the Governor said, "they can't say you don't give a man enough rope. All right," he said, abruptly. "I reckon it's the lesser of evils. I will lie to a thief and hope it don't keep me awake nights. Tell Freeman I've bought the deal. But tell him for Christ sake to button up about it."

I nodded total understanding. Freed of his burden of decision, the Governor plowed back into his cantaloupe.

"Now we've got the skids greased," he said, waving his spoon, "don't waste precious time. Get that bill out of committee and do it in forty-eight hours. I want us hootin' and hollerin' and lightin' up the green board on that House floor in seven days."

"That's not much time," I said.

"God made the world in seven days," Cullie Blanton said, "and the moon and the stars and the universe. And He wasn't as fortunate as you. He didn't have me to help Him."

There was an old chandelier hanging from the ceiling, one that would have been incongruous in almost any room and that was stupifyingly out of place in the cluttered cubicle established for my suspect deeds of perfidy and sorcery deep in the catacombs of the capitol building. It was the morning the Governor's loan-shark bill was coming to the floor. I was hunched down on my shoulder blades, blood-flecked eyes glued on the hideous chandelier.

About that time two things happened at once, and it was not the type of day where I could best cope with twin evil. The first thing that happened was to the telephone, which started ringing. The second thing that happened, which happened just a hair behind the first thing, was the appearance in my doorway of the fellow who was on Cullie's payroll under the label of administrative aide. Only he didn't look as impressive as the title. He was gaunt and his eyes burned bright, and though he normally moved like slow molasses, he was often taken for a religious fanatic because he looked as if he might press on you one of those little tracts predicting immediate doomsday and insist you join him in shouting the Lord's Prayer.

Zero Phillips stumbled through the door in a tangle of feet and a bugging of myopic eyes, and this made me forget the ringing telephone. He'd got tagged with his nickname because it was said to reflect his blood-pressure reading. Zero probably wouldn't have paid a nickel to see a good earthquake or have ambled across the street to watch the Chicago fire. He had the kind of metabolism that allowed him to look full on the ravaged face of Disaster and give it a slow wink. So when I saw Zero gazing on dark blood, eyes bulging alarm, my brain churned slow and grappled with visions of unmatched disasters.

"You heard the news?" he gasped.

I had not heard any real news since the Japs surrendered.

"The Court," Zero croaked. "The goddamn Court."

I knew what he meant. He meant the earth was cracking open, and the ice age setting in.

So I sat gaping at Zero and he stood gaping at me. After a while, it looked like neither of us would ever break the tie. Then Zero made a fuzzy gesture and croaked, "The phone."

"Jim," the Governor boomed in my ear, "Hell has popped."

"I know," I said. "I just heard."

"Well then, what you waitin' around over there for? To grow tits?"

I denied that particular ambition.

"Get over to the House chamber," he said. "Get over there and help the Speaker calm those baboons down. It's like the Tower of Babel. I think some of 'em may have the foamin' rabies."

"What are they saying?"

"They ain't exactly comparin' the Court justices to the Lord's sainted Apostles."

"I mean what are they saying about you?"

"Right now," he said, "the consensus of opinion seems to be that I am an *entire* sonofabitch. Get on over there and change their minds some."

Before I could hang up and do his bidding, he stopped me with another outburst. "Hell of a day," he said. "*Hell* of a goddamn day for that loan-shark bill to be up. Looks like ole Earl Warren could of at least give me that much."

"You think there's any chance to pass the bill?"

"Boy," he said, "the only thing those pirates might pass today is their breakfast food. Get on over there."

I pushed by Zero, who had started to look as if he might live provided somebody got the emergency oxygen supply wheeled in on time, cantering out through Statuary Hall under the stone gazes of the ersatz statesmen of the past who were all circled up like Indians whooping around a wagon train: long-dead governors with mutton-chop whiskers, a sprinkling of Confederate generals, a war-bonneted Indian chief wearing a frozen expression of puzzled pain, as if wondering what had happened to his people.

Galloping down the hall, I darted off on a quick side journey, bent on checking the wire-service ticker in the press room just off the House floor. The newspaper boys had bolted when the news came in and had deserted their chewed cigars, half-cups of black coffee, and their poker hands. The ticker told how Hamilton Davenport was a twenty-nine-year-old Army veteran and the father of two small children, and how he would be the first Negro to enter State University. It traced all the tedious legal skirmishes dating from the moment Davenport had filed his petition of admittance with the board of regents.

The fossilized old frauds who served on the board of regents had issued a statement revolving around States' Rights and The Southern Way of Life, somehow working in mention of some sinister international conspiracy said to be bossed from Moscow. The Supreme Court, which for a sackful of months had been mulling over a final decision in *Davenport* v. *The State,* had thundered up a decision. Now all the beard tugging and judicial grunting was over, and the high tribunal up there on the banks of the Potomac had worried up a ruling.

The House floor had all the dignity and decorum of a bawdy house on payday with the full fleet in. The members ankled around in full tremble, anxious to get on record with the working press about what a dark day in history it was.

A state representative with the fetching handle of Hardtimes Hansen was braying tested nonsense to a circle of reporters scribbling as if they were transcribing the original version of the Holy Writ. Hardtimes broke away and lumbered down on me, extending an obese forefinger quaking in righteousness.

"You theah," he hailed. "I just tole these gentlemuns of the press how Joe Stalin is dancin' in his grave today. Dancin' in his *grave.* What have you done about it?" Hardtimes demanded. "What've you and the Governor *done?*"

"I don't know what the Governor's done," I said. "But I telephoned Earl Warren up there in Washington to thank him."

"You *whut?*" Hardtimes shouted.

"Anybody gives you something, you thank him. That's the way us Southern gentlemen get raised. It's part of being of the landed gentry."

Hardtimes offered up choking sounds.

"I called, and I said, 'Earl, Mama says I should thank you for the nigger. And wants to know can you come to Sunday dinner and maybe make us one of those nice brotherhood speeches.' "

Leaving Hardtimes in the throes of the blue sputters, I moved among the knotted clusters of legislators thinking how my conduct was not exactly conducive to the baboon-calming mission the Governor had laid on me.

I pushed toward the podium where Speaker Muggins jerked and twitched, his hands worrying a small wooden gavel. The Speaker frowned at the collection of buzzing satraps trooping about the chamber, spoke in quick asides to a couple of legislators clamoring for his attention, and beckoned me to the podium. Page boys scurried about filling inkwells, bearing messages, dropping the Finance Committee's report on the loan-shark bill on the polished surface of an elongated table near the front of the chamber, predicting through their nasal twangs how niggers would have their jobs by next session.

I hailed the Speaker and he grunted vague acknowledgment, worrying a series of gravy spots tracking a course across his tie.

"Not too good a day," I opined.

"Seen better."

"You think we can salvage the loan-shark bill, Henry?"

"No," the Speaker said. "Our asses belong to the gypsies. As of this date." He brooded a while, eyes locked on far horizons.

"Dammit," I said. "We had 'em, too. We had Dallas Johnson beat. That wing-ding Cullie tossed at the Big House bewitched those prehensile bastards out of their socks."

"Waste of perfectly good whisky."

While the Speaker fretted over the waste of taxpayers' whisky, I watched a technician in striped overalls down on the House floor plod from desk to desk, punching buttons that cheered the tally board in festoons of color. He flashed the lights alternately red and green, then struck them down, clearing the machines for action.

"No green board today," the Speaker mumbled.

"Afraid not," I said. "The mood seems pretty black down there."

The Speaker nodded. "Wouldn't be surprised if some the boys want to conscript an army and march north."

"I might volunteer," I said. "It might be easier soldier-boying in the chigger grass than calming those baboons down. And that's what I've got explicit orders from the Governor to do."

The Speaker grunted, fingering his tie. He said, "While you're workin' miracles you might move Christmas closer to the Fourth of July."

Dallas Johnson materialized in center aisle at the rear of the chamber and was immediately overrun by howling hordes. He stood as the center of a revolving ring, darkly handsome, slick-dressed to the shin-bones, hair carefully tousled, crackling with that vitality that makes leaders of men.

I reckon the Speaker must have been following the same line of thought. " 'And on the third day,' " Henry Muggins grumpily breathed, " 'He arose from the dead.' "

We had left him for dead, all right. When Cullie gave me the seven days to work a wonder, I gave up sleep like the pious make concessions to Lent. I bribed bellboys and wheedled newsmen and rousted out the harnessed and buckled state cops to help rattle the bushes. With perseverance and conniving and the mean presence of hard-faced cops, the boys were flushed out of their holes and marched into the Mansion in lock step, slack-jawed and atremble, to face the all-seeing Governor.

Who fixed them with eye most evil and roared a mighty wrath.

Who threatened some of the more illustrious members of the august assembly with a limited future. Who leaned toward the soft putty blobs, with his eyes standing on sticks and veins cording like reptiles in his thick neck, and said, "Goddammit, what ever put you in possession of the two-bit notion a pettifoggin' punk like you could play Mickey Mouse games with *me*? Don't you know I figgered out the answers before you even thought of the goddamn *questions*?"

Who would clench his teeth and speak from knotted jaws, saying, "Listen, I could break your goddamn back, and the sound of your crooked bones crackin' would set off a state-wide celebration."

And who would say, his voice deceptively soft and crooning the dires, "He who touches pitch shall be defiled. And you got it smeared halfway up to the armpits."

Oh, he intimidated them down to their honorable pared toenails. He preached power in the blood. Looking on the legislators squirming in their chairs, defiance fading to fluttering uncertainty, which in turn hardened into historic fright, it was easy to see the Governor had impressed the polka-dot bejeebers out of all those clay gods.

The night before the loan-shark bill was due to hit the House floor Cullie gave up vinegar for honey. He dolled up in Sunday-go-to-meeting best and put on the dog some, serving up trays of frothy tidbits that looked uncommonly out of place in the plowboy hands of the country bumpkins come to hold up the torch of democracy, and offered up ample fermented spirits so the tidbits wouldn't stick in sensitive throats. He made public love to the legislators, flattering them by word and deed. He draped his arms around shoulders he had set to heaving with the dry sobs only scant hours before, and gave brotherly pressings to hands that had trembled upon knees taken by the quick shakes. He beamed bogus cheer and shouted ribald humor at the holdout handful of the members of the militant opposition ("Goddammit, Spears, you keep on screwin' me regular as you have, and you either got to buy me some groceries or at least give me a goddamn *kiss*"). He led a few of the budding statesmen off to secret trysts in the deep bowels of the Mansion, guiding them by fleeting pats on the elbows, lighting their way with flashing smiles, and they returned taken by the fool grins.

But the stone had been rolled away from the tomb. The most dead cause of the enemy had risen from the final dust possessed of new ghost.

The Speaker nodded toward the buzzing bees down on the floor. "I guess," he said, "we'd better see if we can do a little business behind the door."

Henry Muggins almost nubbed a favored digit putting the finger on recalcitrant legislators he bid march down center aisle and approach him for frantic whispered conferences at podium side. He called in due bills and cashed in old political chits dating back to the Ark. Meanwhile, I moved among the growling baboons, promising earthly kingdoms, pledging charms of vestal virgins, but our cause was down with the boils. Cullie didn't honor us with his esteemed presence, but from the way the page boys kept hauling the members off to a battery of telephones lined up in the cloakroom I knew the Governor wasn't investing time in studying the wallpaper patterns in his office. While I was crooning saccharined nothings in the ear of a little tyrant from down-state who kept howling he had admissible evidence God was the Original Segregationist, a page boy danced nervously at my elbow until he finally blurted the intelligence that it was my turn at the telephone.

All I had to do was breathe "hello," and that kicked off the verbal squalls. After the Governor had exhausted his vituperative vocabulary, he took a deep breath and got down to business at hand.

"Haul down the goddamn flag," he puffed.

"You mean give up?"

"Unless you got information it was Lee asked Grant for his sword at Appomattox Courthouse," the Governor said, "that is the precise meaning of my communiqué."

"We could ask the Speaker to get somebody to move for adjournment," I suggested. "That'll keep us from getting trounced on the record." I fell silent, awaiting faint praise.

"Boy," he said with a tired sigh, "sometimes I wonder if I got you durin' hire-the-handicapped week. Dammit, you think those pirates are gonna agree to adjournment *before* they've got speeches on record recommendin' the Supreme Court to the thorniest parts of Purgatory? You think you could get six among 'em to close up shop before they've had a chance to put the public knock on every black from Martin Luther King to Haile-by-God-Selassie? Recommit the goddamn bill," the Governor ordered. "Tell the Speaker to get Buel Rapp or somebody else identified as a Blanton man to move to send the bill back to committee. Tell him to hoke up some reason. Say I'm in dark mournin' for the late Wylie Post. Anything."

"We could say you'd decided to postpone action in order to, uh . . . deal with the present crisis."

I listened to the Governor breathe over the wires while he thought about it. "Deal with the present crisis," he said, with grudging approval. "I must be gettin' old . . . all right, you've found the magic words. They won't fool anybody but men of low gifts, but it's the best we can do."

"Okay. I think we can swing it."

"Listen . . . tell Dallas Johnson I quit. But tell him to line his bunch up behind that recommittal motion. Tell him I got to devote my time to the present goddamn *crisis!*"

"He may want to make a deal."

"Well, seems like he picked a good day for it."

"He may want some assurance of how you're going to meet this Court-decision mess."

"In that case," the Governor said, "he is foredoomed to disappointment."

"Well," I said, "it might help if you had something to tell *me*. The news boys are eating me up for comment, and it's pretty hard just to look wise and say nothing."

"You want a statement?" the Governor boomed. "All right, here's my goddamn statement. Forthwith, which is to say right now, I am goin' to deal with the *present crisis* by eatin' me some apple pie. With goddamn ice cream. And then I am goin' to lock up in my paneled study and gaze on all those books with the big words of wisdom, and dwell on which tome holds the mystic secret. And then I will proceed by the most direct route to get knee-walkin', grass-grabbin', belly-crawlin' drunk."

Cullie didn't do it, of course. Within an hour after Henry Muggins had trotted out all his wiles to extract us as delicately as possible from the graceless entanglements of the loan-shark bill, Cullie had whistled me to his office to hold the hog while he sawed at the big vein. Zero Phillips had recovered his aplomb. He sat disjointedly behind an over-sized desk, calmly surveying the end of his cigarette, as if smoking in the nature of scientific experiment.

"What's he doing?" I asked. And nodded toward the inner office of Cullie Blanton.

"Making A.T.&T. richer," Zero said.

"Who's he calling?"

"Bible scholars and Senators and bootleggers," Zero said. "College professors and labor leaders and maybe a few circus clowns."

Cullie was hunched in his chair, telephone receiver pressed against his ear in familiar pose. His eyes recorded my presence and he waved me toward a chair.

"Goddammit," he said, "I'm not askin' you to stand up at a nigger weddin'. All I'm askin' is one little ole pissant statement to the press. All you've got to say is how the trade unions of this state are made up of reasonable men who don't intend to pull on bedsheets and howl in mobs. All you got to do is come out for law and order. That don't give you the deep bends, does it?"

The Governor listened a while, imploringly rolling his eyes toward the heavens, making exaggerated faces, squinting, grimacing. Finally he broke into the other fellow's drone. "Joe," he said, "when I got to be governor the first time you labor boys didn't rate much above rat droppin's. Hell, you didn't have any more rights than a chattel slave. I got in behind you, and we knocked some heads, and we got you an industrial safety law and workmen's compensation. We even got you a goddamn minimum-wage law, which is equal to a legless man kickin' a football."

There was an interval while Joe-the-labor-leader filled and back-tracked, giving out with *yes buts* and *yes howevers*.

"Joe," Cullie Blanton cut in, "I didn't want to make it personal but you force me against the wall. So be it. You know how you hungered to be president of the State Labor Council. And an honest brain will deliver the message that you didn't have the chance of a teetotaler at an Elks' convention until I got behind you. All those other labor bosses opposin' your election came to me mouthing pleas how I had to push repeal of that goddamn right-to-work law thing, and I said, 'You folks elect my friend Joe Snyder president the goddamn labor council and I'll push until the breath leaves me.' And they did and I did.

"And for three years you've tooled around in a shiny new automobile and gummed good beefsteak off the expense account and had more good whisky than Mister Schenley himself. Maybe you even got bed-mounted by a sweet woman or two, and that's all right because I like to see a poor boy get ahead and take his worldly pleasures. But goddammit, Joe, there comes a time to pay due bills. I never asked you for a plagued thing. Until now. Well, by God I *am* askin' as of this moment, and if you turn me down I'll let the whole trade-union movement wash down the drain. I may even be the one turns on the goddamn spiggot."

And with that the Governor placed the receiver down with a decided lack of gentleness. "That's the only language those labor looneys understand," the Governor rumbled. He swiveled in his padded chair, fumbling with a myriad of buttons on an intercom box. A syrupy drawl from the box said, "Yassah?"

"Honey," the Governor bellowed, "get me that nutty professor next. That Lambert fellow." He released the talk button and swung back to face me. "I've chinned with preachers and bankers and so-called civic leaders of the first stripe," he said, "and all I've got to show for it is telephone ear. I've never seen so goddamn many elastic consciences in my life. Everybody's around to yell 'gimme gimme' and grab for the goodie bag, but just by God tote up the due bills and watch 'em scramble. You can't find 'em."

"You said anything to the press yet?"

"Little as possible," the Governor said. "I figure the less said right now the better."

"The legislature's not exactly following that theory."

"It is the nature of wild creatures to prowl the darkness," the Governor said, "and the nature of pols to babble. You can't think of any mutes in this business, can you?" The intercom box hummed and squawked. The gal with the molasses voice announced the presence of Professor Lambert on line one.

"Professor," the Governor boomed into the phone, "hah yew? Yawl still teachin' little innocents how man sprang full blown from apes?" He winked, grinning at me. "Well, any time the Methodist bishops start screamin' for a new Scopes trial all you got to do is bring the jury

up here and let 'em eyeball my goddamn legislature. Make the best case
for your side of anything I can think of. I can point out at least seventy-
five certified Neanderthal politicians. Listen, you wanta do me a favor?
I want you to round up a half-dozen your fuzzy-minded colleagues and
issue a statement about this Court thing. How it's founded on good law
and steeped in moral justice. Somethin' like that."

A frown began to worry his forehead. "Don't worry about the
goddamn regents," he said, "or the university president, either. Hell,
I'm the big cheese appointed most of 'em. 'The Lord giveth and the
Lord taketh away. Blessed be the name of the Lord'. . . ."

The professor turned out to be a man of considerable verbal discourse. Cullie listened with growing impatience, turning in his chair,
pulling at his undershorts.

"Listen," he said, "you teacher types always whoopin' about academic freedom and buggin' me to resolute about the wonders of same.
So show me some that freedom now. I need a few folks on record sayin'
in effect how the Court decision won't necessarily bring Thaddeus
Stevens back from the grave before Saturday night. I don't mean promise 'em the *Millennium*. You been such a red-hot liberal, it seems you
wouldn't have any trouble dredging up some your colleagues to put
their John Hancocks on such a simple statement as that."

The professor took the longest time to rebut the Governor's statement. Cullie's face gave over to wild scowls.

"Damn right it'll do some good," he said. "I can't say how *much*
good. But a little bit beats a pure blank."

The Governor invested in more impatient listening. Outside light
slanting across his features touched up spots of silver in his hair,
illuminating shadows under the high cheekbones.

"Professor," he said, "I am just beginnin' to get a glimmer of what
you might call my *liberal* education. I am just commencin' to recognize
certain unfumigated facts about you red-hots. You get reputations as
charitable men bent on rightin' ancient wrongs, and run off to make
speeches to bleedin' hearts in New Jersey and California and other
faraway places where they clap hands for your courage and cluck
tongues over the backward mudbogs where you hold sway. Once a year
you pick out one perfumed and scrubbed-down black boy who has
been up North to college and maybe speaks with a fake British accent,
and you set him up to fancy drinks in your parlor and talk condescend-
ingly about *the problem* and how peckerwoods like me don't understand the blowin' winds of change because we won't take a nigger to

lunch. And that's supposed to make you somethin' special on a stick. Well, the test of a man is what happens when he hulls down to the lick-log. And any time you red-hots have a chance to get off your bazoos and show me somethin' that would be of practical help *here*—not in Maine or by-God Oregon but *here*—you get taken by constipation of the mind and paralysis of the tongue."

The Governor stopped to blow, eyes alight with honest anger. After gulping oxygen into his lungs he waved his hand impatiently, breaking in on the other fellow's indignant response. "I have heard much of academic theory," Cullie Blanton said, "but have seen precious little of its practical application. Goddammit, you condemn me to the bottomless reaches because I won't parade across the state with one arm around Thurgood Marshall and the other tossed across the collarbone of some visitin' African king. But what the hell have *you* done?"

The Governor had reached room-throbbing volume. "You think about it," he said. "You get out some those lectures you give before the bleedin' hearts in the East and the North and read 'em over tonight. Talk it over with your conscience and listen to your heart."

And with that the Governor most abruptly banged down the receiver.

"Well," I said, "in a variety of ways we seem to be purging ourselves of friends."

The Governor shot a malevolent look, pushing up from his chair. He stood over me, finger boring a path toward my chest, only the big desk between us. "Friends!" he snorted. "Listen . . . didn't I put truth on my tongue?"

"Or a reasonable facsimile," I said.

"Truth pure, plain, and unvarnished," the Governor said. "Have those red-hots busted a gut pushin' bills through a cantankerous legislature to more than by-God *double* money for Negro education in this state? Have they pulled strings and outwitted real live reprobates in order to get the colored man a few jobs in state government? Have they called the pussel-gutted bankers and twisted rich nuts to get some poor darky money for a seed crop when his field's lying fallow? Have they seen to it the State Welfare Department doesn't turn a poor ragged bugger away from the door just because his hair happens to be kinky? Have they?"

"Not that I know of."

"Not that anybody knows of," the Governor said. "But *I* have. Oh, I don't want a medal and you can keep your membership card in the

Brotherhood League. I personally prefer mine plain vanilla, just as my daddy did and his daddy before him. But by God, I have done more upliftin' works than all those parlor liberals put together and got their sneers for my pains."

"I'm not faulting you on that score," I said. "I'm just a little worried you're handling these folks with a heavy thumb. We lose the labor boys and the few knee-jerk liberals, who else have we got left?"

"Boy," the Governor said, "at this late date you are findin' whole fault with power politics?"

"This thing runs mighty deep—back to the taproots of hysteria. It beckons up old ghosts. The success of a power play is based on fear of reprisal. And fear of this racial thing may run deeper than any fear of what Cullie Blanton might be able to do to anybody who incurs his displeasure."

"That is a very impressive lecture," the Governor said. "Or would be, to a freshman class in civics. But the fact is, power is where power goes. Power is what the user makes of it. It beats the beleaguered hades out of anything else yet invented and it shouts louder than the soft voice of reason."

The Governor seated himself in his chair, took a cigar from his coat pocket, crinkling the wrapping in one huge paw. "All I got to do," he said, "is spook those spineless bastards worse than anybody else can. And I am not exactly a novice in the field."

He beckoned for a match, and I moved forward to supply it. Cullie Blanton looked at me from under his bushy eyebrows, gazing across the flame. "And speakin' of lectures, I got a couple to divest myself of. You reckon you can stand 'em?"

"I generally cry under torture," I said, "but I'll do my best."

"Number one. Don't go makin' any more bad jokes about callin' Earl Warren and thankin' him for the nigger. Oh, I see your eyebrows raisin'. The story's already gettin' around and is bein' improved on, which is always the way. The latest version has *me* doin' the callin'."

"You can't seriously think folks will believe that?"

"Boy," the Governor said, "this is the age of suspicion and mankind stands atremble. People will latch on to damn near anything but the truth. Why, the Sainted Virgin Mother could get elected to high office and it wouldn't be six weeks before the word was out she'd deserted her baby and skipped with one of the three Wise Men."

I nodded agreement with the Governor's summation of man's base nature.

"Now the second thing may be a little delicate," the Governor said, "so I will try to state it with utmost care." He twirled the cigar in his fingers, pondering the right approach. "Understand," he said carefully, "I am no great moralist and I reckon I have a reasonably healthy respect for your private life. But we've got to face the cold, clinched fact that we live in a goldfish bowl. Pols really don't *have* a private life that can be separated from their public one. You see where I'm leadin'?"

"I see," I said. "But I can't say I like the view."

The Governor nodded. "And I can't say I blame you. But that won't change the facts. And the facts are these: the talk about you and that little songbird lady wouldn't do to put in the Sunbeams' bulletin. The lady happens to be married, at least to some extent. And if all my legions of opponents want to howl foully about the matter, that makes her as married as the Mother of the Year, for all intents and purposes."

"All right," I said. I got up from the chair and started the long walk to the door.

"Dammit," the Governor thundered. "Who you think you are? The Russian delegate to the U.N.?"

"No," I said. And kept on walking.

"Then quit actin' like it," the Governor said. "I got enough troubles without havin' to wet-nurse you through a private melodrama. Simmer down and let's talk it over."

I had stopped at the door and looked back across the wide room. The Governor regarded me balefully from behind his desk, massive and looming, lines of worry creasing his face.

"Cullie," I said, "I won't go into any song and dance about how long I've labored in your personal vineyards. Though it is true. Let's say it's been good fun, but it's just one of those things."

"Boy," the Governor said, "you are desertin' in the face of the enemy. I need you now worse than I ever have. Don't walk out that door. But if you do, don't come back."

"In this job," I said, "I've had to be consort of rebels and companion of thieves. I've kissed keesters, broken heads and supped with swine. When it reaches the point I've got to ask the unqualified blessing of every crackpot hatchet man in this state to live my private life, they can have their goddamn badge back."

The Governor sighed. His shoulders rounded with weariness and he lolled his head back on the padded chair. He closed his eyes and I listened to him breathe a while. Finally he said, "Jim, nobody's tryin' to dictate to you, and I'm not passin' any harsh judgments. You got your tail over the dashboard before I could make the point. All I'm askin' is that you watch your step, and I say that for your good as much as for mine. The point is, before this thing's over it'll be as dirty as an orphan's face. There'll be more folks ready to celebrate my comeuppance than turned out for V-J Day. And they'll go through you or anybody close to me to bring me down. So I just wanted to drop a word to the wise."

The intercom buzzer sounded, and Cullie paused with his hand on the switch. "I sure hope it's not more bad news," he said. "I'm at the point now where I'm just hopin' to get through the day without a snake bite."

The honeyed voice from the squawk box revealed the presence on line two of a radio Gospel minister of some notoriety, possessed of a vast audience out in the brush. The Governor wrinkled his nose at the news. "Talkin' to that pious sumbitch," he said, "can be classified at the very best as one of life's minor ecstasies." He picked up the telephone, his glooms dropping away, features lighted by practiced cheer.

"Brother Sturges," he boomed into the phone, "may the light of the Lord shine in your eyes. . . ."

5

It was a slattern-like day, gray and misshapen, the sky bloated and full of tears, gutters untidy with floating debris. I lolled abed, blinking, just inched out of exhausted slumber, hearing the sound of rain slanting against the windowpanes, drumming as if God had angered and broken His covenant. The disorder of bachelorhood lay round me in cheerless abandon: tangles of clothes in scattered chairs, ashtrays overflowing, here a half-empty beer can, there the curling peels of a consumed orange, stacks of jazz records shorn of their shucks, piles of books, magazines, and newspapers.

A form spurted across the room and jumped with a yowl onto that vicinity of the body known to the poolhall Lotharios as the family jewel case. My knees came up by reflex action. "Goddamn you, cat," I said. "Goddamn you, Poontang." Poontang purred and stretched, molasses-colored hair rising in hackles, arching her back until she looked like all the Halloween posters in the world. "You want breakfast, you crazy cat?" Poontang bared a row of barracuda-like teeth.

Mustering up maximum courage, I put reluctant feet to the floor, thus officially breaking the maidenhead of day at six-thirteen in the p.m. Slipping into scuffed leather house slippers and an old silk robe of hideous purple hues, faded and spotted by time and dry-cleaning fluid, I padded into the kitchenette where only the strongest stomach could stand the sight of unwashed dishes and gummy glasses afloat in the sink. I went about setting out a bowl of milk and a dish of fishy canned cat food. Poontang sniffed suspiciously at the cat food and started to lap at the milk. "The trouble with you, cat," I said, "is you think you're a goddamn *people*."

Back in the combination bedroom-living room, gazing on the political Grinning Guses who, framed and autographed with tender greetings, smirked from pea-green walls, I took stock of Self. Self was in bad shape. Self had imbibed copiously in the previous evening of the grape that pleases, to the extent that when Self came hard upon bed at the milkman's hour ole Self lacked timing and balance. Self was bruised of spirit and wearied of mind, not altogether certain how equitably joys and sorrows would be divvied up and parceled out to the stockholders by the Great Broker.

It had been a week since the Supreme Court had laid on heavy club by ruling that the state university had come to the shank end of segregation. A week that had sent editorial writers hopping to their typewriters to peck out shrill warnings of the dire threat now poised over fragrant Southern Womanhood and of impure blood soon to foul the veins of children yet to be begat. The air had been full of political ack-ack, with every banana-head possessed of tongue running it across sounds of folly.

Forty-eight hours ago, I had trod into Cullie Blanton's office to find the Governor's massive head cocked toward the intercom system, as he followed what passed for debate among the slew-foots and buffle-gabs of our great elective body. Cullie nodded toward the squawking sounds and beckoned me to a chair.

"God's own agent," he said, "is bad-mouthin' me some."

The agent of Deity was a state senator from prime bogs in the red-clay country, who got himself listed on official ballots as Preacher J. C. Hodding, and handed out campaign cards branding himself as "God's Own Agent in Our Senate." That might make you doubt the depth of Preacher's modesty, but considering his initials, he might be said to have exercised admirable restraint in failing to claim celestial kinships and succession to the Heavenly throne by right of bloodline. If Preacher Hodding had ever darkened the door of any institution of higher learning, he got away before dangerous knowledge could spoil his simple visions. He was wholly unencumbered by weight of formal degree from even one of the diploma mills that dotted the state to the deepest stumps of the backwoods, where would-be priests of foot-washing fundamental persuasion learned how to foam at the mouth, bay like dog packs, and pound pulpits fit to crack stout oak.

The state did not suffer for lack of such Jesus-whooping schools, where the only possible way to bust a course was by becoming inquisitive about biological details of the Virgin Birth. But Preacher Hodding had got to be God's agent by proclaiming himself so on the basis of a nocturnal conversation (to which there were no other known witnesses) in his very own bedroom with no less a personage than the Lord Himself. The Lord, it seems, came to chastise him gently for slothful

ways of the soul and the flesh, hinting he should put down Evil and
take up the Cross. Now J. C. Hodding was not one to offend honored
guests and was always susceptible to suggestion. So he right away surrendered to the Lord without undue fuss.

Before long, it seems, the Lord had advised Preacher Hodding in
myriad ways. He advised the chosen J. C. Hodding about matters of
business and even of state. God had diligently carved out a career for
His agent. He wanted him to be honored by high offices and gifted
with riches. Say for the Lord He was a responsible citizen. He didn't
just haul off and push Preacher Hodding in the Senate race and then
leave him to his own devices once elected, a poor ignorant son of the
soil lost among base souls. Oh, no. He consulted, He did, with Preacher
Hodding on each and every vote. We had the Preacher's word for it.
Which gave our state Senate, as far as I could tell by limited research,
the unique distinction of being the only legislative body in the world
where Deity seldom missed a roll-call vote.

Preacher Hodding was now saying how the President of the United
States, the lion's share of Congress, Governor Blanton, and the Supreme
Court in its vexing entirety, vied foully with each other in a below-the-
belt scramble for votes. He said *Amuricay* had turned into a land of
booze bottles and beer cans, cigarette snipes and nigger coddlers, and
folks who accepted delivery of newspapers on the Sabbath.

No doubt, he said a lot more, but Cullie Blanton fatigued of the
game. He jumped from his chair and gave a mighty twist to a button
on the intercom so that it fell quick upon silence. Then he said something too ugly to be repeated in this space. He prowled about the
room, growling deep, and turned toward me hand-patting his pockets
as if to assure that he was not in possession of lethal weaponry. I carried him a cigarette and put fire to it.

"Jim," the Governor said between puffs, "say something to me.
Quick."

"What you want me to say?"

"That'll do fine," he said. "I've heard so much shit spoken the last
few days I had near about forgot how English sounded. You been over
to the hallowed chambers lately?"

"A couple of times," I said, "when it couldn't honorably be
avoided."

"They got a net under 'em over there?"

"Uh . . . *net?*"

"From the sounds they been making," the Governor grumbled, "I had a feelin' they must be swingin' from high wires."

The Governor tugged at his cigarette, worrying up a mature frown. He licked his lips experimentally. "Well," he sighed, "I reckon we can thank Christ they're just *talkin'*. Soon's they come on a shortage of crappy things to say against me and ole Earl Warren, somebody'll get the brilliant notion to offer up a brace of new seg laws. One thing," Cullie Blanton prophesied, "they won't be laws future historians will look to for guidance. They'll be so goddamn tough a poor darky won't be allowed to take a pee in his own hog trough."

"It won't help the situation any," I said. "We don't need to agitate the natural conflict between state and Federal power."

"Maybe we can stall," the Governor said. "Maybe we can call up a whole spate of little ole toilet-paper-and-ice-water bills that won't mean a damn thing."

"We can't do it," I said. "We're more in the minority than the poor Turks on Cyprus."

"Don't sell the Speaker short," the Governor said. "Henry Muggins has dismissed more parliamentary tricks from his mind than the rest of those peckerwoods can hope to know." The Governor suddenly shot me a dartlike look. "Can't you do somethin' to get some these goddamn newspaper boys off my neck? Ain't they supposed to be your pals?"

"That's not so easy," I said, "pals or not."

"Spread a little somethin' around. Give 'em some the three B's. Lay on beefsteak, bourbon, and blondes."

"It's not that simple," I said. "It's not the working press giving us fits so much. It's the editors and publishers. They're harder to reach."

The Governor snorted. He said, "You'll forgive me if I never noticed how uncorruptible they are."

"No," I said. "It's not a matter of morals. It's just that editors and publishers have got enough money to buy their own simple pleasures of the flesh. Reporters are too poor to be honest."

"We got to do somethin'," the Governor grumbled. "I been blasted by everybody owns a flat-bed press. Except maybe *The Bicycle Journal* and *The Flower Seed Review*." He brooded, sucking at the fleshy insides of his cheeks. Then he reached into a desk drawer and pulled out a slip of paper with maybe a dozen names scrawled on it, tossing it flutteringly my way. I stooped and picked it from the floor, putting the names under my eyes. None of the names struck me as strangers.

"What's this?" I asked. For want of anything better to say.

"You hold in your hand," the Governor said, "the honor roll of maybe the most certified, genuine, uncut, motliest bunch of four-flushin' sonsofbitches ever drew free air in this state. In one way or another."

"Well . . . what've they done?"

"Nothin' for me," he said. "And that's the problem. They are in their sundry ways men of rare influence and high gifts. I need 'em. Get 'em for me," he said, nodding. As if that explained all life's mysteries and freed the universe of guilt.

"Get 'em for what?"

"For Christmas-tree decorations. Whatta you think?" The Governor flushed, stripped of all patience. "Number one boy there," he said with heavy emphasis, "does a lot of contractin' business with the state and has been lax about expressin' his appreciation. I need some his gold dollars for the campaign kitty. Otherwise, state inspectors might get harder to please than Duncan Hines. Go see him and leave him a wiser and lighter man."

Cullie Blanton screwed around in his chair, craning to see the list. "Number two man," he said, "is pious to a fault, and his fellow deacons think maybe he is the Messiah come and God no more than his front man. Only I know his secret shame for I got him out of a jam once."

"What sort of jam?"

"A very sticky kind of jam," the Governor said. "The poor man exercised bad judgment in the company of a red-haired lass who liked to take spicy Polaroid-camera pictures and was not particular who saw 'em. Captain of the state troopers called on her and discouraged the exhibition. I need this fellow's Christian influence among the faithful of his creed.

"Number three," he said, "owns a bank specializes in carryin' valuable papers of a financial nature. And he holds the deadwood over number four. Who has foolishly gone and bootlegged long dollars to the campaign of that goddamn Marine general. I want number three to crack number four across the tenderest of parts. Threaten to call in his note."

"What about number three?" I asked. "What have we got for leverage?"

"Boy," the Governor said, "we have got the ultimate weapon. We have got the power to chop his bank off from all those beautiful tax greenbacks in the general fund the state shifts around to deservin' and enlightened members of the financial community. And which the moneylenders loan to folks at compounded interest rates. It is like pickin' money up off the ground."

He went over the entire list, man for man, uncovering past perfidies. When he had finished he leaned forward, reaching across the corner of the desk to tap one thick forefinger against my knee.

"Spook 'em up some," he said. "Go to 'em unannounced in the dark of night, for that's the hour ghosts walk and man's spirit shrivels small. Threaten 'em with floods and fires and pestilence. And threaten 'em with that horror all men fear most."

"It might help some," I said, "if I knew the nomenclature of that particular horror."

The Governor took on a benign look. His eyes rounded in innocence. "Why, Jim," he said, "I don't see how a man got to be grown without knowin' that. What man fears most is the public revelation of his private self. . . . How about a cup of goddamn coffee?"

"So that," I said to the milk-lapping cat, "is the reason why breakfast and dinner have gone and got all balled up in the awful scheme of time." Poontang seemed singularly unimpressed. She hid her face in the milk bowl.

The telephone jangled.

"Lo," said a trilling voice.

"Lo yew own sef," I said.

"What's shaking?"

"Jello," I said, "and Santa Claus' belly. Jelly Roll Morton."

"Yukety-yuk," Tanya said, "and ho, ho, ho. You trying to work up a night-club act? Are you in circulation, or official mourning or what?"

"Right now," I said, "I am thinking how if niggers would stay in their assigned place and men of low gifts would cease bugging my favorite Governor, I could be engaged in wanton pursuit of lustful pleasures."

"Funny you should ask. For I called to put to you a proposition."

"Bearing in mind that I am a poor boy," I said, "without shoes to wear or enough to eat and am of the highest morals besides, I accept."

"The proposition," she said, "is to wit and as follows: Mr. Dallas

Johnson and his lady friend name of Tanya request the pleasure of
your company at home. Tonight."

"Dallas Johnson is a blatherskite in no wise to be trusted and is the
very scum of the earth. But he does mix a good drink and when the
moon is right has high gift for funny sayings. I think maybe I accept."

"We are charmed," Tanya said. "Delighted. The moat will be raised
to the blaring of trumpets."

"Who'll be there?"

"Everybody," she said. "Just avar-goddamn-badhy. Weird folks."

"Assuming no immediate race riots," I said, "or governors gone
mad, deal me in."

"It's getting sticky, isn't it?" she said.

"Stickier than flypaper," I said. "All those outside agitators! All
those insidious Northern and Eastern el-e-*ments* comin' down here
puttin' in whur they ain't wanted and arousin' our contented weather-
beaten slaves. All because the President's got nigger blood. And maybe
served time in Joliet for armed robbery."

"You've been watching local television," she said.

"Hell," I said, "you hear that kind of talk in the streets. Out of the
mouths of babes. From little old ladies in tennis shoes. Everywhere."

"About tonight. . . ."

"Yes," I said. "About tonight. Indeed."

"Well . . . Roxie will be here."

"I have tried and tried," I said, "and I can't think of any germane
objections."

There was a silence. After a while I cleared my throat to signify
continued presence and sustaining interest. "There's something else
you ought to know," Tanya said. "Her husband. He'll be here, too."

"Oh," I said, choking on a speech as long as that.

The thin Mexican bent over his guitar, grinning foolishly, strumming up sounds lost in the worst din since they popped the big one at
Yucca Flats. Beside him on the sofa a grossly fat lady wearing purple
lipstick bounced up and down, drink sloshing over the rim of her glass,
periodically whooping, "*Olé!*" A girl possessed of one of those shaggy
haircuts and wearing eyeshade green enough to spook an old house at
high noon plucked at the arm of a pop-eyed man precariously perched
on an arm of the scarlet sofa. A State Senator from the downstate
coastal area approached a padded chair, addressed it with careful dig-

nity, then climbed unsteadily into it. He pulled up to full height, feet sinking into the cushion, tossed back his head and yowled a coyote-like series of *yip yip yips*. Then he clambered down, flushed face shining, and wandered into the crowd, vastly pleased. "Hell of a party," somebody shouted in the uproar. *"Hail of a party, man!"* There was so much smoke in the room I had the feeling somebody had put out smudge pots to save the citrus groves. The room crashed with the high haw-haw of camaraderie. From out back, under trees hard by the riverbank, an impromptu jazz band wailed high notes that occasionally floated through the jumble of noise in Dallas Johnson's living room.

Tanya, glittering in a gold blouse and dark peasant skirt, stood encircled by goggling admirers. She spotted me through the smoke, blew a smiling kiss. Dallas Johnson swayed in his own oval of followers, hair rumpled in his patented way, teeth flashing as he engaged in lengthy discourse. *"Olé!"* the fat woman shouted again from the sofa.

Zero Phillips sat on the floor in a far corner, reposing under one of Tanya's grotesque objects of art that appeared to be a wrought-iron hatrack with prongs bent beyond common usage. The Governor's administrative aide idly turned a whisky glass in his hands, but otherwise seemed in a trance. I ambled over his way.

"Hello, white folks," I said.

Zero cocked his head in painful effort to peer up through the smoke and gloom, his eyes floating with drink. "Hava zeet," he said. I squatted beside him. Zero blinked at me vaguely. His eyes searched my face for familiar landmarks and began to clear slowly, transmitting a fuzzy picture to the brain. The brain grappled with it, sorting out bits and pieces of information stored in fogged crevices.

"Jim," he said thickly. "By God. Ole Jim. How yew?"

"The question is, how are you?"

"Fahn," Zero said. He squared his shoulders and groped for dignity. "Ah'm jes' fahn."

"You look peaked," I said.

"Ought not be dronk," Zero said. "Worl' in flames and Governor got the red-ass at me."

"You need some air, buddy," I said. "Here, give me your hand." I stood, took Zero's stiff hand, and pulled. It was like trying to budge a giant redwood.

"You got to help me some," I said.

"Do anything in the worl'. You best fren ah ever have had."

"Okay, good buddy. Start by putting that whisky glass down. Then take your free hand and push up from the floor." Zero obediently followed instructions, frowning, concentrating mightily.

We negotiated through living-room traffic, my left hand gripping Zero's right elbow. We passed through the kitchen unmourned by a couple necking in the lemon-yellow breakfast nook. One of the Neanderthal types from the legislature was standing over the oblivious couple, waving a beer bottle, spouting hot stuff against the Pope.

"Wanna hear music," Zero said. "Wanta find the Lost Chord. They gotta jazz band out there."

Zero broke from my grip and lunged into an oak tree. He backed up against it, his feet doing a slow, uncertain box step in search of steady anchor, and then with spine against the tree trunk slid down in slow motion until he had firm earth under his seat.

"You all right, Zero?"

"Wanta rest," he said. He yawned at the pale moon.

"Don't flake out," I said.

"Never hoppen. . . ."

"Maybe you ought to get on your feet, Zero."

"Never hoppen, either." Zero blinked at the moon as if he'd just discovered its position and was studying it for navigational error. He shook his head. "Goddamn, Jim . . . Cullie," he said definitively.

"How'd he put you down?"

"Lotsa ways. Raised hell about letters. Wants more hockey in 'em. You know?"

I knew, all right. For I had been on the scene once when Cullie Blanton had dog-trotted through his outer office, pausing at a number of desks to scoop up letters awaiting his signature. He'd read them over, scowling.

"Goddamn!" the Governor had exploded with feeling, and turned to me. "Get all my brilliant young brain-trusters together," he had ordered, "and don't squander time doin' it, either." Three minutes later, with everybody streaming in the door taken by tongue-pants, Cullie had rared back in his padded chair with feet elevated and crossed on his desk top.

"Those are nice goddamn *businezz* letters you're writin' out there for me," he said. "All that 'yours of the fourteenth instant noted and hereby acknowledged.' That might grab 'em some at the Hunt-and-Peck School of Business Letters." He plopped his feet on the floor quickly, leaning forward with one elbow on the desk, shaking an angry forefinger. "But goddammit," he said, "I don't happen to be loanin' money or peddlin' road machinery. I ain't *in* businezz. I don't want any letters goin' out of here sounds like I'm tryin' to sell John Deere tractors.

"I want letters the peckerwoods will fold up and carry in their pockets and will pull out to show to folks 'til the goddamn crease wears out. I want folks thinkin', 'Ole Cullie, he's up there in the capitol tossin' in a restless bed worryin' up ways to get me a pension, and no doubt talkin' it over this minute with the Lord Jesus Christ.'

"When some sumbitch passes to his just deserts and we write the grievin' widow, I want real tears runnin' down the page. And when some jackanapes writes in goony suggestions about how we can bring prosperity to all hands by crankin' out new bales of greenbacks on the printin' press, I want my answerin' letter to sound like he has stumbled upon the final truth and I have ordered reams of new paper and oceans of green ink.

"Talk to the folks. *Communicate!* Don't be afraid to put *love* in those letters. Show the folks some heart! Some you city boys, you won't live until you've felt what makes the grass grow green squashed between your toes. So don't be afraid to shuck off your shoes and wade in barnyard juices. Now get back out there and show me some hockey."

So I knew what Zero had meant, all right.

"Mean," Zero said sadly. "He's turned *mean*."

"Well, you got to remember Cullie has a lot on his mind."

"Cullie's not thinkin' straight. It's like he was . . . goin' through the menopause. Can't solve the nigger thing just bein' a sumbitch about ever'thang else."

Suddenly, Zero's eyes were bright and clear. He seemed to have achieved instant sobriety. "I see the brightest visions," he reported. "I am possessed of ancient wisdom. I think I will go home."

Then he toppled forward and mashed his nose into the damp, spongy grass, out like a cripple trying to take second against Bill Dickey. I sighed, straightened Zero out to full length. I leaned down, loosened his tie, and folded his arms into a neat X over the chest.

"I'm short of lilies," a voice said softly behind me, "but I think I can come up with a couple of pennies for his eyelids."

"Hello, Roxie," I said. It hadn't been necessary for me to turn around.

She moved beside me, gazing down on Zero's earthly remains. A peaceful expression had claimed his features.

"He's out of it," she judged.

"His senses dwell in restful places," I said.

"So how've you been?" Roxie asked. Her brown eyes caught silver glints from the moon.

"Except for poison ivy and chigger bites," I said, "I can't complain. But I have this terrible personal problem. The type thing poor wretches in cold-water flats write on lined tablet paper to the lovelorn columns. You know: 'I got weird hair and premature ejaculations and my wife has run off with a gotch-eyed zoo keep.' There is more. 'There is this young lady. . . .' "

"Ah."

" '. . . to whom I take a kind of personal shine, you know? And the last time I saw her, say like ten days ago, everything was coming up roses. Till, all at once, she quit answering the telephone and returned my many gifts unopened.' "

Roxie wrinkled her nose in concentration. "The telephone part sounds familiar," she said, "but I don't remember that part about the gifts."

"Figure of speech," I said. "Anyway, she probably *would* have returned them if I'd sent any."

"Then she lacks sensitivity and curiosity," Roxie said.

"You have certainly been a big help," I told her, "and I shall be forever grateful for having chanced upon your person on this night."

We were heading into a bad scene and couldn't find the exit. We avoided the final locking of eyes, turning our gazes across the dark lawn as if expecting a ghostly apparition to materialize out of the night and with shrieks and mad flappings spook away the strangeness between us.

"I take it," I said, after a long dry spell, "that you have gone and effected one of those reconciliation things with Pete." She didn't answer. After a bit, I said, "Gods above know, I ought to sense it. I've had enough practice."

Roxie turned to face me, our eyes meeting for the first time that evening. Hers were soft and troubled in the muted light. "Let's not get on that kind of time, Jim."

"Goddammit," I said, "why stay hung up in something you've had your fill of?"

"It's not that . . . simple. How can I tell you about a dozen years?"

"Are you trying to tell me you still *love* him?"

"Yes," she said. "No. Sometimes . . . Oh, hell! *I* don't know. He's my husband!"

It was my turn to sigh, and the sound I offered up came from a very weary place. "I'd give my turn at the shovel on the coal pits of Hell," I said, "to understand how that mind of yours works."

"I told you long ago," she said, "not to expect anything from me. I warned you in front."

"Yeah," I said, "but don't expect the croix de guerre for it."

"In just about ten seconds," Roxie said, "I am going to walk away from here."

"Before you go," I said, "give me a couple of minutes to ask Pete what my reaction ought to be. I'm sure he's had enough experience being walked out on so that—"

"Good-bye," she said abruptly. She walked rapidly into the darkness under the trees toward the musicians. I stood numbly under the hovering oak, staring down at Zero's prostrate form.

There was enough smoke in the living room to flush the jungle of wild game, and a pick-up jazz combo wailed up noise strong enough to disturb the deep sleep of Helen Keller. The fat lady no longer shouted *olés*. She was prone on the floor, mouth open, snoring hugely, a wet towel covering her forehead.

Tanya gamely danced in the middle of the floor with a puffing Farmers' Union lobbyist, who stared in grim unbelief at the wooden motions of his feet, as if they had somehow betrayed him. The girl who had been playing kiss-face in the breakfast nook pursued the same delights with a new partner.

Dallas pushed his face to my ear and shouted something about the library phone. I weaved down a carpeted hall. A couple locked in close quarters against a beige wall, nuzzling noses, paused to nod and smile pleasantly and I returned the small courtesy. After I'd closed the library door to mute the whoop of the jazz combo, I fell into a leather chair and picked up the phone.

"Jim?" the Governor thundered. "That you, Jim?"

"It's me, Governor."

"Goddamn, boy. Don't you ever sleep?"

"I reckon," I said, "that could be taken as a two-way question."

"You sober enough to have your wits about you?" the Governor asked. "You reckon you could pour piss out of a boot with instructions printed on the heel?"

"It seems like an odd assignment. But I ask not what my country can do for me. . . ."

"Any time," the Governor said heavily, "you are through crackin' little funnies. . . . When you sober up enough to focus your eyes, take a look at the headlines in the mornin' papers. Maybe that'll curtail your sense of humor some."

"What's happened?"

"That goddamn general's stirred up a real witches' brew," Cullie said. "He's braying how he'll bar the door to the university with his very own spit-and-polish patriotic body when the black boy tries for admittance. They shall not pass."

"Sweet Jesus," I breathed.

"He has gone and stumbled on a powerful scheme," the Governor mourned. "I got a feel for that kind of thing."

"We can jump him for inciting a riot," I said. "Encouraging violence."

"Boy," the Governor said, "do you truly think we can knock down a stunt like he's come up with just by talkin' plain *sense?* He's got me in a bear trap. Think how to get me out."

We had come jaw-to-jaw with a most hairy dilemma. If the Governor hauled off and called General Wooster the kind of fool we knew him to be, it would give the opposition a leg up at out-segging us. Wooster would be in the happy position of taking up solitary cause for the Caucasian race, and the redbones would down Cullie Blanton for a lover of blacks.

"I can't think of any way to attack him," I said, "without getting you tagged as Earl Warren Junior."

The Governor grunted over the wire. "On the other hand," he said, "I can't stand mute. If I get the verbal lockjaw he'll beat me to death with this breast-beatin' stunt."

"You reached any conclusions?"

"Only," the Governor said, "that I don't intend to stand around bumpin' bellies with U.S. marshals. It's a shoddy way to do business and it won't show a profit."

"Well," I said, "if you cotton to living in that big white house and eating all that peach ice cream and sleeping on silk sheets and having a passel of folks look after your creature comforts, we'd better come up with something."

"That unfeathered fanatic stole a long march on us," the Governor grumbled. "I could take a blood oath personally to snatch that burr-head bald in the middle of University Avenue and it wouldn't impress folks much *now*. Why'd the good Lord send such pests as that god-damn general to plague me?"

"It's a test of your faith," I said.

"He lacks the human juices," the Governor pronounced. "He'd sell his own sweet mother for glue." He paused, thinking of how low-born a fellow was his opponent. "Get some rest," the Governor said. "Put down your booze bottle and go on home. Be in my office about noon and have your thinkin' cap on. You got me?"

I said I had him.

"Goddamn," the Governor gloomed, "whatta way to make a livin'. Why couldn't I of been born rich instead of so smart and so goddamn good-lookin'?"

He had slouched back on the purple silk of the bedspread, tugging at ear lobes, stretching his fleshy nose from the end outward, the big hand flicking up to brush back a cowlick existing only in the reflex memory of the gesture. The roving hand verified the presence of his Adam's apple. It checked the two frosty patches of eyebrows and sneaked a furtive pinch at his lower lip. The Governor reminded me of a coach poised along the third-base line, flashing signals to squint-eyed runners whose muscular minds grabbed slow at instructions.

After he had inventoried all his equipment Cullie Blanton said, "Your ole mama. She teach you to tell the truth?"

I said she wasn't what you'd call a fanatic on the subject, but she didn't see it did any harm if the truth came handy.

"Judicious woman," the Governor nodded. One arm snaked out to claim a jigger of bourbon, catching dark glimmers from a mahogany night stand. After he'd tossed it off neat, the Governor mastered the breathing processes and, divesting himself of a small shudder, said, "How you feel about it?" The bite of the whisky sounded fuzzily from his throat.

"Lukewarm, if it's the other fella's truth. Red hot if it's mine."

The Governor's impatient gesture brushed aside my answer. "No," he said. "All this Nigra business. How you feel about that? Down where your guts coil, I mean?" He settled back in a great shifting of flesh, one elbow poking at pillows in search of hidden fluff.

"In the blood," I said, "I reckon something shouts a few Rebel yells. Maybe I hear an echo from Grandpappy's grave. But up where I suspect the brain is . . . well, up there it sounds different. It must be what tiptoes around under the name of reason."

Cullie Blanton snorted. He said, "Try me again. Only this time don't pick around the thing like somebody's dropped his chewin' gum under the chicken roost."

"Well, I don't guess I'd want my sister to marry one. But," I said. "*But*. I always had a weak stomach when it comes to lynching."

"Sensitive boy," the Governor said, nodding. "Overeducated, too. Bad combination. Simply *turrible!*" He stood, abandoning the pillows, blinking and tugging his nose. "Me," he said, "I wish the cup would pass. I'd trade whatever chance I got of bein' immortalized in bronze just for gettin' outta this thing with mah political hide."

"You've got a chance to be a great force for good."

"So'd Jesus," the Governor said.

I rustled up another drink, and the Governor communed with himself amidst the pillows and mystic grunts. "Yeah. I got a chance to do good, all right. But you know what, Jimbo? I'm thinkin' maybe I've *done* my share the goddamn good. I built 'em schools and roads and hospitals till feces looked like fruitbowls, and by God I made the fat boys pop for the bill! So why can't I be left idle and happy and on the road to many riches in mah old goddamn *age?* Why can't they just let me take root-rot in mah tired ole brain and die right here in this high office and this soft bed? And in silk pajamas? And with the budget balanced and peach ice-goddamn-*cream* on mah saintly lips?

"Never had a chance to get mine," the Governor mourned. "So busy rootin' for the folks, I forgot to root for *my* share the good apples." The Governor sucked at his whisky. "Folks'll think I didn't have any ambition."

After he had washed away more of his bereavement Cullie Blanton said, "If I quote you correctly, you said somethin' about how you're red-hot for *your* truth but lukewarm on the other fella's. It's sonsofbitches like you got this old globe in the *shape* she's in. You don't feel that ever-gnawin' inner doubt gives a man what passes for compassion. Yeah, and it's you birds caused all the spilled blood from Jesus Christ through Adolf Hitler. Hell, this state's runnin' over with sonsofbitches like you. Some of you've got college degrees enough to spook ole John

Harvard. And some of you couldn't fill out a crossword puzzle required a five-letter word meanin' piss."

I said, "Boss, did you call me up here for anything besides pure sport?"

The Governor's eyes searched his bedroom as if for hidden microphones. He said, "But what you and I think's Gospel truth don't necessarily make it so. I got to know where the *real* truth lies. The majority truth. I got to figger how much I can stand on mah haunches and demagogue against this blackbird's tryin' to enter the university without incitin' a riot in the process. Know when to push and when to pull. And you are goin' to find out for me."

"Any notion how I pull off the miracle?"

"Grow you a cover of face whiskers," the Governor said. "Climb in some old clothes. Use the eyes and ears the Good Lord gave you." He pulled at the whisky. "Dog that Wooster person. Attend his goddamn rallies. Spy on who he talks to. Tell me how the folks react."

I said, "Can't somebody else play cloak and dagger?"

"No," the Governor said. "This job happens to be cut to your peculiar specifications. You know all the pols. You know the folks, and what makes 'em slobber. And you got the habit of tellin' me the truth even when it hurts."

"I admit to many virtues. It's just possible I may be worth more money."

Cullie Blanton raised his glance in a toast. He said, "You get yourself caught, we may have to reckon your worth in Confederate coin. You know what they do to goddamn *spies*, don't you? They by-God *shoot* 'em." The Governor flashed a dazzling campaign grin, apparently much cheered by the thought.

Bayonet Bill Wooster might have made a hell of a businessman, football coach, oil-company executive—even a boxer. And no doubt he *had* made a hell of a general, of the kind who win battles—not because of any masterful grasp of grand strategy—but by being able to arouse his warriors to fever pitch so they'd willingly die alone, cold in the mud, and hard. Wooster had the killer instinct. He knew the advantage of throwing your very best punch when the other fella figures it's time to fall back and blow. And he was stubborn. He liked to say when the going got tough the tough got going.

Wooster made a good Marine. He had no fertile imagination to get in his way. It wasn't long until he was spotted as natural officer material. After his commission he served peacetime tours stateside, in Panama and the Philippines. When the Japs bombed Pearl Harbor he was assigned a company to command. His company helped take one of the first islands in the Allied comeback in the South Pacific, and soon he had new rank and a battalion.

The war in the Pacific was his kind of war. It didn't require much finesse to dig Japs out of rock. All you needed was grenades, flame throwers, rifles, and guts. Washington issued the first three items, and Wooster instilled the fourth. He came out of the war much decorated, and a full colonel. In Korea, when the Marines were encircled and retreating during the cold winter of 1950 that was their darkest hour, Wooster's forces at his orders fixed bayonets and scrapped their way out. That got Colonel Wooster promoted to general—and it also got him the revered nickname "Bayonet Bill."

He came home to a hero's reception with ticker-tape parades, keys to the city, and one of the Corps' best public-relations men assigned to him forever after. He began to make speeches before "patriotic groups," and before long his associates were the moneyed men who finance far-right-wing causes. In the service, Bill Wooster had learned some absolutes. They were: there is a ruling class (officers) which by Divine Will and Act of Congress rule the lesser classes (enlisted men); too much education makes a bad Marine; and Communists are no damn good.

These beliefs were not in conflict with the Talmuds of his new associates, who taught the general that since 1932 America had been ruled by fuzzy-brained intellectuals or physical or mental cripples who coddled the trash of society and who were in some dark league with the hated Communists. They taught him that all the cherished values of the Old America were being drowned in a filthy backwash of labor goons, racial agitators, sex perverts, and nuts who wanted the rabble to vote. Bill Wooster heard the call.

When he turned in his stars for mufti and a cushy pension he set out to end the welfare state where, as he saw it, in exchange for personal freedoms men were housed, clothed, fed, and given guaranteed wages for the balance of their lives. Not once did the nagging thought that this imperfect welfare state was reflected almost perfectly in his beloved Marine Corps enter the general's mind, and so, untroubled by the devil doubt, he began to ride the peas-and-carrots circuit.

General Wooster's politics could be summed up this way: he admired MacArthur as a fighting man, but personally felt him soft on

Communism. Little by little, Bill Wooster had gravitated back to the land of his birth—which happened to be the state of pinebogs, hillbillys, new money, and teeming industrial plants over which Cullie Blanton held sway. It wasn't long until Wooster became the White Hope of that wing of the Democratic Party convinced that Calvin Coolidge was the last great President. Inevitably, he became their candidate against the Blanton regime. And when he did, he became a concern of mine.

Promptly at seven o'clock the Sons of Uncle Sam—four young men in striped pants, star-spangled coats, and white chin whiskers—stood under tall hats to lead us in "America" and "God Bless America." Then in case anybody had been about to make the error of connecting the Wooster movement with the national union, the Rebel-Aires offered us "Dixie," the official state song, and a hand-clapping little ditty somebody had dreamed up in the misguided notion it somehow honored the candidate:

> Bayonet Bill,
> The man who will
> Get the Communists off our backs!
>
> Bayonet Bill,
> The man who will
> Repeal the Marxist income tax!
>
> Bayonet Bill,
> The man who will
> Win this race for sure!
>
> Bayonet Bill,
> Whose strength is ten
> Because his heart is pure!

Before you could get through blushing, some hillbilly type glorified Wooster through guitar and nasal passages in a little selection called "God's General in the Trenches," while the ten-dollar-per-plate diners below us on the coliseum floor surreptitiously mopped up their ice cream. Around me in the bleacher seats, men who worked with their hands on sick autos, delivered bakery goods, or climbed telephone poles—and the lumpish women who cooked their gray meals and bore their children—swayed and clapped hands. A bevy of preachers scolded

God about the latter-day Roosevelt, labor goons, race mixing, and the erosion of states' rights, then took the edge off by thanking Him for the Crusading Soldier he had sent in to clear up His earlier mistakes. A lady with top-heavy breastworks mangled the national anthem.

Suddenly, drums rolled. Multicolored spotlights played about the hall, and the house lights dimmed. The spotlights caught the general marching up the center aisle, and the cry that went up from the assembled was a gleefully angry roar.

One of the poobahs on the platform bawled an introduction lost in the hubbub, and the general stood stiffly in the spotlights, the white mustache seeming to bristle, until adulation had run its course.

"I was raised a warrior," the general said. "And a warrior always comes to fight!"

Bedlam again. He hadn't named the enemy, but he didn't have to. The crowd *knew* the enemy. The enemy was change, and new if unknown threats. They had come wishing blood, hoping to see the enemy slain. These were the people (you knew) who on another day had burned books at Heidelberg, cheered Mussolini's jutted jaw on the balcony, fired witches at the stake in Salem.

"No soldier," the general said, "was ever called to more sacred ground to do battle—nor to a higher duty. In the long march of crusaders, no army ever had more to win than those of you who have joined me in *this* holy war.

"And it *is* a holy war. For we defend anew the precious thing this country was founded to offer mankind: *freedom!*" He waited out the wave of angry applause, his hawk-eyes flitting over the scene, taking in the contorted faces and frenzied whoops. "For many years this nation—and this state—had its defenders of freedom. I know, for I have led them into battle. But our freedom is being eroded away by a centralized, depersonalized, pressurized, all-powerful Federal government in Washington, by Godless Communism throughout the world, and by men whose patriotism has paled in the evil vacuum of the welfare state!

"You don't want opportunity, they told us. You want security. And they told us again, and again, and again." The general gave the phrase the old Roosevelt cadence, holding his head cocked to the side and the jaw thrust out in exaggerated manner, while the crowd hooted its angry delight at the parody.

"So they took away the farmer's right to raise crops—and paid him blood money to murder little pigs!

"They took away the working man's right to contract freely the sweat of his labor—and made him pay alms to union goons.

"They took away the businessman's right to run his own affairs—and made him pay his hard-earned profits to Big Brother in Washington.

"They took your tax dollar and sent it across the water to promote alien isms—and when we got in a war with those alien isms we'd helped, Washington tied our hands. I know—*I was there*."

The sharp, angry, frantic hootings and stompings shook the coliseum. The folks were getting their money's worth.

"And you know what we did—we Americans born to freedom and defenders of it? *We took it!*

"But now they've gone too far. Now they tell us not only what we must join, or who we must pay blackmail, or how we'll run our businesses—but they tell us who our neighbors will be—" (the roar, starting) "who we'll sit by in our restaurants—" (the roar, building) "who our children will go to *school* with—" (the roar, exploding) "and I will fight it to the end!"

Pandemonium. A fat woman in a print dress near me jumped her gross body up and down, eyes wide and wild, screaming, *"Kill 'em, kill 'em, kill 'em!"* Men pounded each other on the back and whooped Rebel yells.

Well, I had seen enough. So I pushed and shoved my way through the zealots, feeling them close in on me, feeling I was their rabbit and the hounds had me trapped. Outside the coliseum, I could hear the harsh, strident beat of Bayonet Bill Wooster's oratory as he flayed Cullie Blanton, and the periodic animal roars swelling until the old structure seemed fit to burst. I turned and walked away toward the parking lot, my eyes taking inventory of the number and types of cars. Though the night was warm, with a soft, gentle breeze, I felt chilled to the marrow.

We traipsed up the ramp to the aircraft glistening with the first timid touches of the day's sun, possessed of morning melancholy. The Governor led the parade. Speaker Muggins reluctantly single-footed behind him as if going to some grossly undeserved punishment. Then came three National Guardsmen in olive-drab fatigues, moving bovinely, banging alone under the burden of assorted grips and cases owned by the two important personages. I followed the Guardsmen, toting my own bags as befitted my common station, and Zero Phillips clopped along in my wake. Zero looked maybe as if he had spent the night at a roadside park during a sandstorm. His hair was dry and blowy and his clothes so rumpled he was about as svelte as a sack full of doorknobs. Dallas Johnson floated behind Zero. He had for some moments given himself unto rendering a suspect tenor version of "The Blue-Tailed Fly."

Cullie Blanton stopped suddenly at the top of the ramp. He pulled up so short I had to use air brakes to avoid ramming knees into a Guardsman. Behind me, Zero did a little shuffle step to avoid nipping my heels and then lurched into the ramp rail as Dallas Johnson plowed into him. Dallas and Zero exchanged routine insults bearing largely on the marital status of their respective mothers.

The Governor turned on the steps and sourfaced it down at Stanley Dutton, examining the impeccably dressed Lieutenant Governor as if he belonged under thick glass. "Stanley," he boomed, "I reckon any advice I give you will most likely go to waste. Just remember to engage your brain before puttin' your mouth in motion. Look wise and say nothin'." He paused, blinking as if stepping from a dark theater onto one of the brighter stars. "You unnerstan', Stanley?"

Stanley mumbled that yes, he understood. The Lieutenant Governor stiff-spined it at the foot of the ramp leading into the old twin-engine C-47 operated for the Governor's pleasure by the National Guard. He preened self-importantly, possessed of sweet knowledge that as soon as the plane had climbed into the pale sky and had winged across miles of mudbogs, stands of loblolly pines, and rocky, red-clay hills to cross the state line, he would be acting governor until Cullie Blanton returned. As befitted his new eminence, Stanley Dutton wore a frown of dignified deliberation. "I'll do my best, Governor. I truly will give it my best."

"I reckon," the Governor said, mournfully, "that's meant to give me some small comfort." Cullie Blanton grimaced, faintly agonized in the mind. "Don't make any pronouncements," the Governor said, looking down on his running mate. "And don't even sign a goddamn postcard to your mama. Don't go throwin' any wild parties in the capitol building, and for sweet Jesus' sakes don't open your mouth about politics, for the field just ain't your specialty. Anybody asks you about weighty matters of state, you just opine how our Foundin' Fathers got it by the balls the first time they grabbed at it, and it was a wonderful thing they caught."

The Lieutenant Governor marched in place step, tugging at his tie.

He smoothed back the lacquered sides of his hair, and cleared his throat.

"There *is* one thing, Cullie," he said. "There's this businessman down at Shelbyville who wants to come up to the capitol and ask me about—"

"Goddammit," the Governor snapped, "didn't you just hear me say look wise and say *nothin'?*"

The Lieutenant Governor flushed about the head and face. "It's J. B. McGiffin," he said. And hesitated. "From," he said after a bit, "down at Shelbyville."

"From down at Shelbyville," the Governor echoed flatly.

"He wants to ask about some state land he's interested in leasing. He wants to drill it for oil."

"He wants," the Governor said in that same flat tone, as dead as an undertaker's business, "to drill it for oil."

"I thought he might make a contribution to our campaign," Stanley Dutton said, his head angled up to view the bulk of the Governor framed against the aircraft. "I thought he might put something sweet in the kitty." His smile begged approval.

"In the first goddamn place," the Governor said evenly, "if you'd paid me a dime's worth of attention when I was talkin' to you a minute ago, you'd know it's not your function to go around havin' goddamn thoughts, and it's certainly against your nature. In the second place, nobody's got any business askin' you *anything* because you stand stripped of the primary answer. And in the third goddamn place, I'll run you in for smokin' dope if you insist on your pipe dream about that downstate libertine comin' with somethin' for the kitty. Damn it, don't you know if J. B. McGiffin had been in charge of the Crucifixion he'd of asked Jesus Christ to cross his feet so he could save on nails? Don't you know if he got you hemmed up in a smoke-filled room and flattered you some and fawned a little he'd screw you right out of those state lands and wouldn't even hug you as he left?"

The Lieutenant Governor couldn't decide whether to wag his head, or if he did, which way it ought to be wagged.

"Jesus!" the Governor said in disgust.

"Have a good trip," the Lieutenant Governor said, abruptly. He ducked his head, abashed.

The Governor said, "Do *nothin'* 'til you hear from me. And remember to keep your ambition in delicate balance with your limited judgment. If I see your name in the newspapers one goddamn *time* unless it's to announce your death by natural causes, I'll consider you've grossly failed me."

The Lieutenant Governor scuffed well-shod feet on the edge of the blacktopped runway, smiling rather pitiful ersatz cheer, ratifying his public humiliation by rapid nods. He shot a quick, cautious glance toward the milling collection of sullen newsmen and photographers pushing against a wire fence less than a hundred yards from the aircraft. It didn't take a practiced seer to know what was on the Lieutenant Governor's mind. He was wondering whether the Governor's harsh words would carry to the group and discombobulate his dignity. Four bulky state troopers kept the news boys at bay behind the wire fence, intimidating them with hard eyes.

"Goddamn," the Governor said, dispiritedly. He paused again. "We shall never surrender," he said idly, borrowing a line from Winston Churchill. The Lieutenant Governor seemed on the verge of breaking into applause. "I commit you to the deep," Cullie Blanton said. He plunged into the yawning door of the plane and our little safari took up the slack behind him.

The Governor flopped into a wide, two-man seat and motioned the Speaker to sit opposite him in a single-person container. Zero and Dallas joined me across the narrow aisle.

Cullie Blanton threw me a look slightly tinged with malevolence. "I keep rememberin' what used to be printed on those wartime gasoline stickers," he said. "I keep wonderin' is this trip *really necessary?*" I didn't say anything. The trip didn't sound as inspired as it had on the noonday following Cullie's predawn telephone call to me at Dallas Johnson's cottage. When I had ambled into his spacious office, jumpy in the gut and blue of outlook, the Governor was tipped back in his chair passing sour judgment on all he surveyed.

"I hope," he said by way of greeting, "you got some magic grunted up for me."

"You remember the presidential election of 1952?"

"Boy," the Governor said, "I remember back before men flew like birds in the sky and swam like fishes beneath the sea."

"Then I reckon you remember," I said, "General Eisenhower stirring up the folks by announcing how when elected he'd go to Korea and end that war nobody wanted."

The Governor nodded. He said, "Folks saw visions of Ike wavin' his arms like the good fairy godmother and stillin' the boomin' of the guns. Whatever slim chance poor ole intelligent Adlai Stevenson *might* have had was shot in the ass. I take it," he said, "you recommend I do some travelin'."

"Yep," I said. "Washington."

"Washington," the Governor repeated. He sat and thought about going to Washington.

"Haul off," I said, "and announce how you're going to beard 'em in their den. Say you're fatally bent on seeing everybody from the President down to the lowest wage-board janitor at the Botanical Gardens. Tell 'em you'll see anybody with lungs or eyeballs who might help solve this integration mess."

"It might take some play away from that fool Bayonet Bill person. It might tarnish his bright scheme to skulk around schoolhouses screaming 'nigger,' " the Governor said. I remained silent and let him debate the proposition internally. During the debate he made a prolonged study of the ceiling plaster. After a while he stirred, and said, "What assurance we got those red-hots up in Washington will go along with us?"

"Less than none," I admitted. "But at least you get credit for effort. At least you grab your share of the headlines. You make the grand gesture."

"Illusion," the Governor said. "All is goddamn *illusion*. Pretty girls wearin' fake titties and bald merchants getting rich sellin' men's hairpieces. Everybody riggin' quiz shows, and movie stars havin' their cavities capped. Politicians rushin' off fifteen hundred miles to strike cardboard poses. Everything perfumed and corseted and dirt swept under the rug. God*damn*, what went wrong with our daddies' old faiths . . . ?" He gave himself to deep thought, whistling without melody, turning the scheme over in his mind. Suddenly he reached over and flicked the intercom button. "Honey," he rasped into the black box, "get me the White House on the phone. And don't go puttin' some palace guard tutti-frutti on the phone who'll want to sing to me from light opera and tell me about Keynesington economics. I want to chin with the head-goddamn-knocker. . . ."

Five days after Cullie Blanton had talked to the head-goddamn-knocker, drums duly banged and the message gone out, we climbed for altitude above the spires and towers of Capitol City. The C-47 groaned and shrieked witch cries against resisting air currents. We roughly followed slow meanderings of the river toward a rendezvous with our flight pattern.

Henry Muggins peered nervously out a side window, half concealing his face behind a brown curtain, as if fearful the clouds might catch him at spying. His features were not altogether radiating delight, for the Speaker had long suspected flight by mechanical means. It had taken every ounce of Cullie Blanton's famed wiles and all his storied guile to persuade the Speaker aboard our flight.

"I hope," the Speaker muttered, "you told 'em to fly this thing low and slow."

"Relax," the Governor grinned. "We're prepared for any emergency. Pilot's a Protestant and the copilot's Catholic and we got a Hebrew crew chief. Anything goes wrong, we can offer final rites in three tongues. You'll find copies the Lord's Prayer printed on those little upchuck bags."

"Sure is a weight off my mind," the Speaker said.

"You'd look *good* lyin' in state in that capitol rotunda, Henry. Think of all those bronze statues of dead statesmen circled up guardin' your bier. You'd likely get a stone likeness raised to your memory right smack dab in Capitol Plaza, with maybe a big clock stashed in your belly button to tell folks the time of day. Bands would blow sweet music, flags would snap in the breeze. Why, I wouldn't be surprised if they turned out school."

The Speaker didn't seem exactly enchanted by visions of the festive occasion. He tore his orbs away from the awful fascination of the city, spread out toylike and misty far, far below us, and eased them closed. The pallid vulgarity he breathed was a concession to the ears of gods in close proximity.

"It ain't the *fall* that gets you," the Governor said learnedly. "It's that sudden goddamn *stop*. We got scientists can say the multiplication tables in Roman numerals workin' on the problem right now." He paused, a wayward smile lurking at the corners of his mouth.

Cullie abandoned the Speaker to his private fears. He turned to regard the three of us sprawled across the aisle from him.

"I been thinkin' about it," he said, "and we got us a tough nut to crack. That fellow in the White House, now . . . I can sympathize with the sticky position he finds himself in. If the President eases off and gives me the delay I'm gonna ask for, he'll be fair game for ever' hyphenated American, bleedin'-heart liberal, and Yankee politician known to the confines of our national borders. And there's no earthly reason why the President oughta get his own hands burned pullin' Cullie Blanton's chestnuts outta the fire."

"How'd the President act when you talked on the phone?" Dallas asked.

"Correct as Emily Post. He's a right cool customer." The Governor sat and tried to analyze the President of the United States on the basis of a three-minute telephone chat. After a while he said, "Dallas, you're gonna come in mighty handy when we get to Washington. You gonna be a real big man! Gonna get your handsome likeness plastered all over television screens until people will wonder if maybe you're in the Miss Rheingold contest. You'll probably get quoted verbatim on the very front page of *The New York Times,* and maybe invited to one those fancy garden parties at Perle Mesta's place. Boy, this could be where you cross over the marginal line." The Governor beamed at the legislator, rejoicing for his great luck.

Dallas Johnson fidgeted in his seat, considerably more dubious about what kind of luck he owned.

"You're in the mainstream of goddamn history," the Governor declared. He looked smug, fishing in his shirt pocket for a cigar. Dallas Johnson was glum witness to the ritual lighting of the stogie.

"There are men of dark purpose waitin' to ambush me in the sinful city," the Governor said. "But I have sniffed their deceit and am prepared to meet it. Times change, and men must change with 'em or be left alone to old memories." He waved his cigar in great circles. "All us politicians," he said, "got new warts to worry with. It's not enough any more just to referee the sweaty dogfall between selfish spirits or to fight schemes against mankind. Nowadays, that public-image thing throws a long shadow.

"We got to fret over our postures and the bob of our noses. And what shade of face powder suits us best for TV. We got to masquerade our moles and bust a hump tryin' to look like Gary Cooper and dance like Fred goddamn Astaire. We got to worry about what folks tell Sam Lubell, and how much we're loved by shoeless dictators of banana republics."

The Governor's face registered gloom over the plight of politicians as a breed. "All mah lost glory," he mumbled on the surface of his breath. "All mah spilled tears. . . .

"Those Feds, they think I'm a throwback to that dark age when all life crawled and wiggled. They stand habitually convinced I just barely made it out of primeval oozes, and was playing in luck when I reached solid ground. They don't know me, but I was born in horse-blinder climes and got elevated by mudbog jackals, so they down me for a demagogue and figure maybe I bomb the church of my choice each Sunday."

We waited for the Governor to make the point at his own sweet leisure. When the waiting had reached the cracking point he cut his eyes toward Dallas Johnson, and he said, "But you're gonna help me get my poor ole public image back on its feet. Brush the mud off its coat and spruce up its shine and comb its hair, maybe."

"I would truly admire," Dallas Johnson said, "to know what the deuce you are talking about."

"I am talkin'," the Governor said, "about your many talents. You got special qualifications for a certain job." He beamed, reaching across the aisle to pat Dallas Johnson on the knee the way you calm a spooked mount. "You *look* good," Cullie Blanton said. "You got that Rock Hudson pretty on your face and got the proper bearin' of Henry Cabot Lodge without turnin' your nose up like you're sniffin' bad garbage. And sometimes you say things makes more sense than a politician's got any right to make."

Dallas thought on the sweet compliments and glanced nervously at the Governor's hand on his knee, not knowing whether to brace for a physical assault or a proposal of marriage.

"You gonna be my showpiece," the Governor grinned. "You gonna make all those Feds and hostile Yankees associate our state with good groomin' and gentle charm. Boy, you have been chosen as my official, enlightened, sincere, ar-god-ticu-damn-latin' liberal spokesman. You are proof positive we have heard tell of the twentieth century."

"Wait a minute," Dallas Johnson protested. "I got my *own* image to be thinkin' about. I spend more'n half my time now trying to *sound* reactionary so I can get away with voting liberal on gut issues. I'd just as soon my constituents think I wear lipstick as think I'm liberal."

"All you got to do," the Governor said soothingly, "is croon soft and nice to those reporters. They'll be lookin' to nail my pelt to the wall, and no matter what I say they'll make it sound like I hit town tremblin' in a bedsheet. So I got it figured how I will walk around in prayerful attitudes weighed by burdensome decisions while you as my official spokesman mouth words of a gentle persuasion."

"Look here," Dallas said in some agitation. "I didn't bargain for all this."

"You were in no wise a party to the arrangements," the Governor agreed. "I made all the decisions myself."

"I just made one, too," Dallas Johnson said, peevishly. "And my decision is, I won't do it."

The Governor put on a mask of sorrow. "You mean," he asked in injured tones, "you won't help solve this terrible crisis you been howlin' about?"

"Governor, you think you can shove me out in the spotlight and let the folks at the grass roots identify *me* with all this unpopular hoo-hawing while you skulk in the wings. In position, of course, to come running front and center with appropriate breast-beating in case we get up there in Washington and accidentally perform some kind of miracle."

"Boy," the Governor lamented with a sad shake of his head, "you sure must of sprung from a long line of suspicious people. You're one among the many. When it gets down to hard diggin' you are just like ever'-goddamn-body else."

Dallas tried a new tack. He said, "I don't know why I owe you anything special. I don't know why you should get this sudden urge to be pals."

"Boy," the Governor said, "if I didn't need you I'd just as soon sic the hound dogs ᴜn you. But I *do* need you. Our common state needs us both, and so we come together in uneasy bond. Right now we'll cuddle up in the same bed without fightin' over the blanket. Until, that is, we can get this goddamn vexation laid by the best way that's in our power. And then we will settle that old score between us."

Dallas Johnson was genuinely puzzled. "What old score?" he asked. "I don't have any old score to settle."

"No," the Governor said, "but I do. *I* lost. And that makes a heap of difference in your outlook about old scores."

"Are you referring," Dallas asked incredulously, "to that little ole loan-shark thing?"

"That little old loan-shark thing," the Governor nodded, unsmiling, "is just *exactly* what I refer to."

Dallas looked to me for understanding. All he got was an exhibition of shoulder shrugs with matching upturned palms. "My God," he said to Cullie, "I didn't know you still had a mad on about that."

"Boy," the Governor said, and his eyes sparkled with the grim, vibrant joy of jousting, "you have misread my hand. I'm not mad, for to get mad would discredit my philosophy. I got a motto I owe boatloads of allegiance. And it goes: 'Don't get mad . . . get *even!*' "

6

CULLIE BLANTON prowled the hotel suite like a house detective in love with his work. He peeked in closets, inspected the shower stall, thrust a finger under the ice-water tap, bounced his bulk on the bed he had chosen under a wide window overlooking LaFayette Park. He pulled a cord, freeing the window of green drapes, gazing across the park toward the White House, perched on a grassy plain almost within hailing distance of our diggings at the Hay-Adams Hotel.

"Mecca," the Governor said, simply. He stood most uncharacteristically motionless, straining to study contours of the famed building glimpsed over the tops of trees festooned with the mature bloom of summer. Traffic adopted a lazy gait on the street below, sunlight dazzling the tops of cars. Three little Negro boys played happily around the feet of Andrew Jackson's rearing horse in the park. Their mouths opened to emit joyous whoops unheard through the closed hotel windows. Cullie remained at his lofty outpost, lost in reverie. "Boys," he said, with a wave toward the White House, "over yonder's the end of the line. It's like sleepin' with the latest Hollywood sex symbol and havin' her beg you for seconds. Where the billy-goat-hell do you go after you've had the best?" He stood in reverent witness of power symbols close at hand.

"Herbert Hoover stayed in this hotel," Dallas Johnson volunteered. He sat on a round footstool, reading from a house organ extolling the unmatched virtues of the Hay-Adams' hostelry.

"Then I reckon," the Governor said, "that makes two of us great men who've graced these portals." He turned away from the window, rummaging in his inside coat pocket. From a crumpled collection of papers bulky enough to stuff a small briefcase Cullie ultimately fished out a typewritten card bearing sundry Washington telephone numbers. He slumped into an easy chair, shucking his coat on the way down and letting it fall free to the floor, and elevated crossed sock feet on the edge of the bed. Frowning at the list of numbers, mumbling in his throat, he nestled his good ear against the telephone receiver.

"God's sakes, Jim," he said, "you favor a man havin' sunstroke? Get a boy to pissant some ice and fixin's up here. And twist those doodads on that air cooler some. Surely to Jesus it'll put out more'n this."

I ambled toward the sitting room to order the fixings, and Zero approached the cooling unit to begin a tentative rotation of knobs and dials.

Cullie Blanton spent much of that first humid day in Washington holed up in a hotel room, phone propped against his ear and jawbone in motion, playing politics by the very same rules he played in grass-root latitudes. There is this great legend about Washington. Only like all legends, you peel it down and look at it under the skin, and Washington has got varicose veins. On top, it glitters with glamour and trembles a high-voltage current of excitement, and everybody ankles around wearing rich frowns and shuffling mysterious papers while growing ulcers as the price for propagating history. But, underneath, the city is ruled by parochial transients who use her like a woman in whom they have no interest beyond the immediate passion. They bed her and rise to return to older loves. They wallow in her warm spring embrace, and when a purple haze hangs on distant woodlands they take her crisp days of Indian summer in pleasure void of praise. They are miserly with schools for her children and money for her purse. They are summer lovers of the first water, taking without giving. And when the city brings them the first touch of winter, they dash off newsletters to the folks back home naming her a cold witch from whom all men graced with sanity would flee to native habitats if the fearful press of public business would allow.

Cullie understood all that. So Dallas Johnson watched him eyeball the list of numbers, and asked what the Governor was about.

"I am about," the Governor said, "to hull down here and play me some old-fashioned politics. Stump-water variety. 'Lasses-and-hoecakes kind of politics."

Dallas wrinkled up a frown. "Do you think that'll sell up here in the big leagues?"

"Boy," the Governor said, "there is one simple fact about Washington you gotta remember and it is this: everybody is from Pocatello and has got a ware to hawk."

The bellboy arrived bearing trays laden with ice, setups, and harsher mixtures. Cullie glanced up from the telephone to motion me

toward the supplies. Dallas Johnson heaved himself from the footstool
and happily advanced on the liquor. The Governor put his hand over
the mouthpiece. He said, "Dallas, you need another drink like a
rooster needs socks. Order you up some black coffee strong enough to
shudder a mule and maybe somethin' to eat that will stick to your ribs.
I need you possessed of all possible wit and grace."

Dallas set his mouth along lines of protest. "I just want one little ole
scotch and water," he said. "I'll barely color it."

"You don't seem to have much requirement for it," the Governor
said. "You tossed down everything on that plane but Lucky Tiger."

"You make it sound like I've got a problem," Dallas said, nettled.

"Why, Governor," Zero said in mock surprise, "don't you know
Representative Johnson don't drink?"

"He don't drink formaldehyde," the Governor said, dismissing the
subject.

Dallas Johnson sulked in the corner a while but soon stalked into
the sitting room to ask room service to dispatch a pot of black coffee,
scrambled eggs, and country sausage.

Cullie Blanton wasn't hitting his numbers on the telephone. His
first call to a Congressman from his home state, with whom he had
served in the legislature many moons ago, elicited information that
Congressman Ed Gobert was lunching but would return the Governor's call. Next he invested five fruitless minutes in trying to raise a
young Congressman from the down-coastal area. The drawling receptionist at first blush imparted the intelligence that yes, the Congressman *was* in, and then having heard the Governor's identity allowed
maybe she had better check just to be sure. She returned in a couple of
minutes to say sure enough the Congressman had departed for unknown regions without her being privy to the fact.

The Governor turned to display wrinkled brow, his highball glass
hidden in the folds of one outsized hand. "That young Congressman
from the coast," he complained, "heard I was on the phone and fled to
Burning Tree. Mah reputation has preceded me." He made connection
with a Senator from South Carolina, whom he had met when the fellow was himself a governor, and exchanged banter of a banal sort. He
got in touch with a Republican Senator from New Jersey, of all un-
likely places, with whom he had once spent a long weekend hunting
quail at the Southern estate of a favored Eisenhower Cabinet member.
They sparred over the racial question, both admitting to grave problems, and terminated the conversation when it quickly became ap-

parent it wasn't going anyplace. He passed the time of day with an acquaintance on the Court of Military Appeals and a chum from his cow-college days who had inched high in the bureaucracy of the Veterans' Administration. He called a Washington public relations man whose typewriter was perpetually for hire and who would for the right number of dollars bring forth from it words espousing any political philosophy known to the mind of man, but the flak turned out to be drinking a late lunch at the Metropolitan Club.

He shrugged, dialed the Capitol again, and asked for the office of crotchety old Baker Pool, the state's mossbacked senior Senator known to his intimates as Muley, who'd got to Washington two years ahead of the New Deal and showed no signs of releasing his grip on the public teat.

Baker Pool was not exactly my kind of folks. Or Cullie's either, for that matter. He was almost a too-perfect caricature of the old Southern patriarch. He owned black bottom lands so vast the eyes teared trying to see their far horizons, and he owned turpentine mills, and at least one cotton gin, and he graced the officialdom charts of three banks. He was in sulphur and oil and timber, and if he'd ever had an original thought he had managed to wrestle it back before it could get exposed to public scrutiny. Muley Pool considered Harry Byrd and James Eastland the two most reliable men in the Senate, next to himself, though he privately confessed wavering faith in Senator Byrd because the Virginian was rumored to have voted for a WPA project in the early nineteen thirties.

By advent of recurrent election to his Senate seat, Baker Pool in due erosion of years was elevated to the chairmanship of the Committee on Farm Problems, where he diligently sought high price supports for crops of types grown on his family acres. Each spring he sent under Senatorial frank an autographed document bearing the best of wishes and the worst of poetry to every high-school graduate in his state. Muley Pool was wealthy, entrusted with high position, and enjoyed playing his public role. But the Senator wasn't about to give Cullie Blanton the smallest measure of aid and comfort in the present circumstance. So while the Governor waited for the Capitol operators to get confused enough to ring the proper extension by mistake, I put a question to him.

"Boss," I said, "why do you waste time calling the likes of Muley Pool?"

"Protocol," the Governor said, shortly.

"Playing the game," Dallas Johnson put in laconically.

"Well," I said, "it's a poor contest when you've got to play it with jackals like Muley Pool. Can you think of one good thing about him, Governor?"

The Governor rolled his lips thoughtfully. "Well," he said, "I never knew him to rape a cripple."

"To quote what I think is from the Bible," the Governor said, "it might be to my political advantage to adopt the posture that when it comes to racial segregation 'none shall walk before him.' "

The white-haired man across the desk nodded, his hands folded in neat pup-tent fashion before him. Alert ice-blue eyes encased in a ruddy face looked unblinkingly at the Governor. "It would be my hope," the owner of the bright blue eyes said in a flat Midwestern twang, "that we could avoid vituperation or an aimless contest of personal wills."

Cullie Blanton returned the unblinking gaze, a dead cigar jutting from his mouth. He wallowed it on his tongue loosely and then extracted it with a quick motion, as if realizing his whereabouts. "I didn't come here," Cullie Blanton said, "to try to take the skin off with the fur. But I didn't come *lookin'* for a painful skinnin', either. I got problems, Mister President."

The President of the United States reached for a cigarette. He took it from an oval receptacle of California redwood resting on his desk among souvenirs of history he had helped make: a gold-framed telegram from his presidential opponent conceding defeat at the polls, a hunk of jagged shrapnel from the Battle of the Bulge that had come to the desk by way of being first removed from his leg and fitted to a bronze plaque subsequently presented by survivors of his old infantry outfit, a replica of the Liberty Bell given by the Premier of France to celebrate signing of an international treaty, a gold pen with which six months earlier the President had affixed his signature to a bill fulfilling one of his pet domestic dreams. The President rolled the cigarette between thumb and forefinger, forming his thoughts with the care of a craftsman.

"You realize," he said, cautiously, "my limitations in conciliation. I have a job to do. My concern is in doing that job with a minimum of difficulty."

"In my own bush-league way," the Governor said, "I harbor deep respect for your position. Hell, Mister President, just tryin' to administer *one* little ole peckerwood state sometimes gets me down to the level of a midget's shinbone." The President allowed a fleeting smile to cross his lips. Cullie waved his cigar like a baton used to direct martial music and plunged on. "Bein' a public official has all the parallel horrors of war and little of the glory . . . trying to deal with highbinder legislators . . . mollycoddlin' main-street merchants who can't see beyond the immediate jingle of the cash register . . . newspapers bustin' you open on page one because you can't always move mountains, and when you *do* gird up your loins and grunt a mountain out of the path, the news gets printed in agate type over near the goddamn *truss ads!*"

The President chuckled, good-humor lines appearing around his eyes. He said, "Governor, I've never heard it better put. Hardly a day passes that I fail to wonder why everyone in the United States seems to feel better qualified than the next man to be President."

"Some damn fellow goin' broke runnin' a jewelry store in Ohio," Cullie offered, "stands in flat-footed ignorance convinced to the toenails he can operate the government in a more businesslike fashion than any President since George Washington."

"Yes," the President nodded, "and no doubt a sheep rancher in some lonely corner of Texas will think himself in a better position than I to determine foreign policy." He lost his grin for a moment, his eyes staring as if looking on a private scene of personal grief. "And sometimes," he said, "I wish I could *let* him make foreign policy."

"It's funny," the Governor said. "A man takes his car to a professional mechanic and casts about for men of special skills to repair his television set, and wouldn't *think* of tryin' to perform his own brain surgery. But when it comes to government, everybody gets to be a goddamn do-it-yourself expert."

"True, true," the President said.

"It reminds me," the Governor grinned, "of somethin' Father Divine once said. Some of his 'angels' got to fightin' among themselves at his little man-made Heaven up there in Detroit. A reporter called on him and found him robed in silk and settin' on a big throne. He asked for comment on the trouble. Father Divine rared back and frowned, and he said, 'Bein' God ain't no bed of roses.' "

The President tossed his head and howled mirthfully at a crystal chandelier. It was a good belly laugh, boiling up deep from inside, and it helped to ease some of the tension our country-boy delegation felt in being in the presence of such high company. When the whooping laughter stilled, the President's famed grin traveled after it. The grin gave his face the look of a very wholesome cherub who had just performed a saintly act. "That fellow," the President said, "certainly put his finger on the truth." He reached for a desk lighter shaped like a miniature Statue of Liberty and angled his cigarette into the upheld torch. "And whatever we do here today, Governor, somebody will be quick to criticize."

"Some folks," the Governor said, "cast a handy brick."

"Would you include your senior Senator in that group?" the President asked, grinning again.

The Governor snorted. He said, "Muley Pool will be the first sonofabitch to reach for the rock pile. He's about as useful to my purpose as tits on a boar, and I personally doubt he could pass the entrance test at a home for backward children. But he's got a goddamn *cult* back home, and if Muley told his disciples their ghosts would eternally walk the earth they'd all insist on bein' buried with extra shoes. We need to work out somethin' here will keep him from shoutin' foul."

"I served with Muley in the Senate," the President said. "He's sometimes a difficult man. I'm afraid I can't hold out much hope of gaining his blessing."

"We don't have any more chance of gettin' his blessin'," the Governor said, "than I do of addressing a joint session of your Congress in Mandarin Chinese. I just hope we can keep Muley from bombardin' us with dead cats."

"Have you tested his temper on the situation, Governor?"

"Tried to," Cullie Blanton said. "But he found it convenient to be unavailable. He found other dangers to pursue. Same as our junior Senator, Price Collins. They're a hell of a pair to draw to."

The President puffed his cigarette, nodding. "Congressman Gobert told me of your helpful gestures in calling the members of your state delegation," he said. "I'm grateful to you and to the Congressman for your good efforts."

Congressman Ed Gobert, poised on the edge of a chair pulled into the semicircle facing the President, smiled his vast pleasure. The Governor's old friend from bygone days in the state Legislature had literally taken political life in hand to act as the go-between for Cullie Blanton, the President, and the less rational men in our state's Congressional claque. To a man the Congressmen had considered the Governor's trip to Washington as something of a Munich operation and made it obvious they wanted no part of the action. Ed Gobert seemed almost pitiably pleasured by the verbal scraps of kindness the President had tossed his way.

"Ah don't suppose it's any secret," the Congressman said, "that some mah colleagues don't saddle too easy and they ride even harder. Ah don't think we did much good with 'em."

"Well," the President said, "at least your efforts didn't go unnoticed. I'm truly appreciative."

Cullie Blanton shuffled in his chair and toyed with the cigar. "Mister President," he said. "Let's get down to the lick-log. What can we work out?"

"I don't know," the President said, "and that's my honest answer. Willing to hear you out. I consider our talk exploratory in nature."

The Governor turned his head down the row of chairs to read the face of Speaker Muggins. Which was not exactly easy reading material. Henry Muggins sat primly in his chair, scarecrow body stretched to its maximum height, his expression blank enough to summon up questions about his native mentality. Dallas Johnson occupied the seat beside the Speaker, listening intently, bright and alert. By contrast, Zero Phillips sprawled like he might be hammocked in his own back yard. Zero's boney features reposed in such bliss and contentment it was hard not to suspect him of having gone back on Dallas's Lucky Tiger. I was next to Zero, straining not to miss a word, conscious of the walking feet of History all around, possessed of a vague feeling that the whole scene was somehow unreal.

The President's entourage was on hand, too. Mickey McGuire, his roly-poly press secretary, rivaled Zero for unmatched serenity to the extent that neither could dare doze off in a morgue. McGuire was shucked down to his shirt sleeves the way you always saw him on television, and a cascade of ashes periodically spilled from the pipe that had become his trademark to mingle in the folds of his rumpled shirt. Two assistants to the Attorney General, as alike as peas in a common pod down to crew cuts and dark suits with subdued ties, looked on deadpan from choice vantage points. A balding member of the President's Commission on Civil Rights leaned over now and again to whisper to a rather horse-faced young male stenographer who frantically transcribed the mysterious messages on a note pad.

The Governor failed to divine any great wisdom from Speaker Muggins' face. He turned back to the President, forehead creased with thought, holding the dead cigar loosely in his hand. "Mister President," he said, "it's my understandin' our comments here are off the record."

"There will be no official transcript," the President said. "Only rough notes. No statements shall be released other than the one we agree upon at the conclusion of our discussion."

"Then I take it," the Governor said, "I can hull down and talk to you like a Dutch uncle?"

The President's smile favored all present witnesses. He said, "Governor, I've been given the Dutch-uncle treatment before. Feel free to proceed."

Cullie Blanton started to move from his chair to prowl the Presidential office as he was wont to do in his own official diggings. At the last moment, he remembered his manners and reluctantly dropped back into the seat. He cocked his head to the right and let his eyes measure the President in some vague judgment.

"I'm not a Ku-Kluxer," he said. "I never cry 'lynch.' I don't go out of my way to shout 'nigger' even in election years, and you got to understand that in my part of the country it's a mighty temptation to do just that. Especially *this* year, followin' that Court decision. But I didn't come up here to preach the doctrines of reigning clowns. I come in good faith."

"I accept you in good faith, Mr. Blanton."

"Thank you, Mister President. That's more'n I can say for some of your politicians and newspaper boys up here. They got it in their heads all governors south of New Jersey go around with snuff stainin' their shirt fronts and maybe peddle snake oil." The Governor bent forward, resting one heavy hand on the edge of the President's desk. "Understand," he said, "I don't figure to change the course of history. I don't know the words or own the magic can change the fact my university's gonna be integrated whether I like it or not."

"That's right," the balding member of the Civil Rights Commission chimed in bluntly.

Cullie Blanton turned the color of glazed bricks just out of the kiln. The President's blue eyes iced over and he turned a look on the offending fellow of the type calculated to wither fresh roses. "Mister Yeager," the President said in biting tones, "perhaps the Governor prefers to proceed without interruption." It was Yeager's turn to color up with the blush of blood, and he promptly obliged. The President turned back to Cullie Blanton. "Go ahead, Governor."

"So," the Governor said, bringing his temper under control, mollified some by the President's words, "it's goin' to happen whether I like it or not." He paused for effect, puffing his cheeks. "And," he said softly, "I don't pretend to like it."

"I sympathize with your difficult position," the President said.

Cullie Blanton had remained in the chair as long as his nature would allow. He stood and began to roam the vast carpeted acreage of the President's oval study, careful to keep turned toward the Chief Executive. "Yeah," he said, "it's difficult, all right. And that's the Gospel accordin' to Saint Matthew. I'm caught between a rock and a hard place. If I go along with a minimum of hoo-hawin' and don't show much blood in my eye, that crazy damn fellow runnin' against me's gonna eat my lunch and keep the sack it came in. If I bow my neck and force you to run the Federal steamroller over me, I might shore myself up some politically. But in the process my state gets gored in tender places. My folks wind up in the yonder fork of Hell with their backs broke. And either way, I get a black eye and dirty britches."

"Governor Blanton, I am not unmindful of your difficulty. But as a politician you must know that I have to run for office, too. Even the President of the United States isn't exempt from certain considerations."

The Governor held up his hand in protest. "Oh, I'm not askin' you to worry about *my* political chestnuts," he said. "A man from Missouri who once occupied that same chair you grace now, Mister President, he said, 'If you can't stand the heat get out of the kitchen.' Politics ain't the craft for folks who fry easy. I'm feelin' the heat, all right. But I won't leave the kitchen because I'm chief cook and bottle washer, and it's my job to hang around until the job's done. I didn't come to the most powerful man on earth to make any selfish plea just so Cullie Blanton can win a nit-pickin' little ole election down in mudbog precincts. There's more at stake than that."

"Then what," the President asked levelly, "do you suggest?"

"Time," the Governor said. "Mister President, I need time!"

"How much time, Governor?"

"All I can get," Cullie said. "A minimum of five months."

"You understand," the President said, "that I'm in no position to pledge you as much as thirty minutes. The decision isn't mine to make. The petitioner—what's his name?"

"Davenport," McGuire supplied.

"Yes. The petitioner, Davenport, asked the Court to admit him this

September. The Court found in his favor. I can't willfully order the petitioner to postpone something he's fought for over a lengthy and rugged course."

"If I don't get some help," Cullie Blanton said, "we're *all* goin' to fight over a lengthy and rugged course. Mister President, I don't think you realize just how far-reachin' this thing *is* down there. It goes back to the genes of dead generations. We got men and women would take a petrified oath they're Christian souls in every way you can name, but you go to talkin' about mixin' the races and they blanch and tremble and grow cold. We got folks down there who'll swear on their mother's precious memory how they won't sit still for integration so long as they can walk with the aid of sticks, and they're dead set on provin' it. We got ecclesiastical boobs who'll be in their pulpits Sunday mornin' to sob and bellow and fill the livers of their parishioners with black hosannahs promisin' God they won't let mortal man interfere with His plan for separate races. We got rednecks and rounders and white trash and more rabble to rouse than a dog has got fleas. We're settin' on a dynamite keg down there, Mister President. I need some time to put a long fuse on it."

The President listened attentively to the Governor, almost as if under a spell, his eyes following Cullie Blanton's prowling movements.

"It would seem to me," he said, "that your civic leaders could help in the situation. I dislike using the words 'better element,' but for want of handier terms I must. I would think those people should be able to rally for the purpose of preventing any explosive actions."

The Governor stopped in mid-stride. He looked very pained. He shook his head slowly. "Mister President," he said, "there are two things wrong with your suggestion. First, I'm not fully trusted by men with money in the bank. They think I'm tryin' to cause a bigger social revolution than Fidel Castro. Your so-called better element will buy me a nice funeral any day I will agree to oblige them by givin' up the ghost, so don't expect them to rally around me. And the *better element,* as you call 'em, they're just as wild and woolly on this issue as the ole boy who has long greasy sideburns and drives a dump truck. We've got bank presidents and school superintendents elbowin' for choice seats at White Citizens' Council meetin's. We've got state representatives and city judges and oil millionaires can't wait for Saturday night to come so they can pull on their bedsheets and go dashin' off to play spook. And all because the Court ruled like it did." Cullie Blanton had approached the President's desk. He leaned forward and gripped the edges with both hands as if getting set for a marathon workout on a speaker's lectern. "Mister President," he said softly, "have you ever seen a mob at work?"

"No," the President said in a muted tone.

"Well, I have. And it's not the kind of sight you'd want to point out to visitin' dignitaries or show your grandchildren."

"Governor," the President said in a flat monotone, "there will be no mob rule in this instance. It would be intolerable. If you can't assure the public peace, then I'll commit whatever troops might be necessary to maintain law and order."

Cullie Blanton straightened up with a tired sigh. He said, "Mister President, I'm here to *prevent* mob rule. That's why I need a little time. That nutty fellow runnin' against me is so far out I keep waitin' for him to break into a goosestep, or deny the Kaiser caused the First World War. If that black boy gets admitted to my university in the heat of this campaign, Wooster's gonna work up a first-class riot even if you send in all the troops you've got and maybe borrow two divisions from the United Nations."

"I have every confidence," the President said coolly, "in our ability to maintain control."

"Like at Little Rock?"

The President flushed and his eyes flashed hostility for a brief moment. He opened his mouth to speak, thought better of it, and when he'd brought his temper under control spoke with deliberate care. "Little Rock," he said, "never should have happened. The situation was allowed to get too much out of control before any meaningful action was taken. I won't make that mistake."

"Are you sayin' that when this boy Davenport shows up you'll march him to class by gun-totin' troops?"

"If necessary," the President said, his voice firm. "I would *hope* it could be avoided. We're all Americans. We can't tolerate varied standards of conduct because of geographical differences."

"We're talkin' about different worlds," Governor Blanton said, sadly. "You come from out there in the heart of the wheat country where a man can drive for four hours without seein' anybody a shade darker than I am. But down in *my* country—down there in fat-back and potlikker latitudes—damn near sixty per cent of the folks are *black*. It's just a different continent! My people look around and get the feelin' they're in the middle of Haiti. You add that to the old customs and the old fears and it's just naturally got to spook you. Don't forget, my people still cringe with remembrance of those sad years of Reconstruction followin' the War Between the States. Don't forget how the black man ruled supreme down there with the sufferance of Washington."

"And don't you forget," the President said a trifle sharply, "that I have a duty to assure the sixty per cent their basic rights. In admitting to minority rule, you're making my case."

"You're talkin' about a dandelion field and I'm talkin' about a bramble patch," the Governor said, dispiritedly. "I'm tryin' to gain precious time so we can get our ducks in a row."

"When you talk to me of time," the President said, "I must remind you that the South has had a hundred years."

"Then five or six more months," the Governor said, "ought not to harelip the nation. That little gob of time can't make that much difference to you. But it means everything to me."

The President stood from his desk and walked to a window. He studied the smooth green lawn behind the White House and looked up toward the erect Washington Monument. The President turned from the window.

"Governor," he said after a lengthy wait, "I don't want to be harsh or unfeeling. But there's no way I may order Mr. Davenport to postpone his entry. Even if I had the power, I wouldn't do it. This thing must be eventually resolved and delay doesn't help resolve it. And there is a very practical consideration. Our party is committed to a strong program in the field of human rights. I simply can't do anything contrary to that position." The President absently fingered a tasseled drape cord and adopted an expression of faint grief. "A few minutes ago," he said, "you referred to me as the most powerful man on earth. That's flattering enough and many people hold that view. But it simply isn't true. The President of the United States has power, certainly. But it's not absolute. It springs from many sources and is dissipated by circumstance. There are people by the tens of thousands with whom I must maintain careful relationships. Congressmen . . . Senators . . . party leaders in fifty states. Representatives of business, labor, farmers. And, of course, the clairvoyant gentlemen of the press. Sometimes it seems there's no end to it. If, as has been said, the White House is a prison, it certainly doesn't lack for turnkeys."

The President stood with head slightly bowed, a man weighted by cares. I saw a man who had started low in the councils of his party, and who had lent his talents to mundane tasks designed to cause great gobs of the electorate to make their franchised cross marks for a given slate of candidates. No doubt, he had wearied of the low buffooneries of organizational politics as had many a man before him, and soon had his fill of the boozy dreamers and ignoramuses and sniveling poltroons and gaping clowns indigenous to the craft. But he stuck with it, for the dream was larger than the man, and he started a slow ascent in the party.

He was nominated for district judge and won the office, but eight years later he still marked time on the same low rung, and bitter gall must have sloshed deep in his viscera. Then all at once he got a break. A Federal judge accommodatingly died, and the President appointed a Congressman to fill the vacancy, which threw open a seat in Congress from his native prairie state.

He won, and came to Washington wearing the bleached chemise of idealism, and although it got spotted with tattletale gray as time and men conspired to soil it, he hung on to some portions of his shining dream. He quit Congress in the face of Pearl Harbor and went off to war, where he won some medals; and when he came home to peace, the House seemed a smaller place. So he took on an aging Senator whose contributions to the national defense effort had largely been confined to profiteering on slum housing in the District of Columbia. The old Senator got shellacked in the election and died sour in his bed, leaving unspent riches, and the new Senator heaved onto the national scene just in time to say appropriately harsh things about Russia during the birth pangs of the Cold War.

The Senator proved to be a man of considerable ability, and, no doubt, played his share of good luck. He chanced to be in Berlin with a small Congressional task force investigating servicemen's morale, which was an assignment of chintzy prospects—until the Reds picked that moment to throw up their blockade. The young Senator recognized the knock of opportunity, and he rushed to let it in. With the world goggling Berlin, he stepped into the spotlight and claimed the position of spokesman for the United States, which made salty old Harry Truman invent new cuss words, but which also got the Solon on the cover of *Time* and *Newsweek*.

He became an overnight expert on foreign affairs and wrangled a semiofficial assignment to the United Nations, where he grew learned and wise. Visiting strong men from alien shores sought out his presence. The Senator's star spiraled to astronomical heights. He met success, all right, but always somebody had to extract the proverbial pound of flesh. When he jammed the foreign-policy plank he had written through his party's national convention, he had to fight off wild assaults from braying isolationists. When he branded the President's notions as ill-conceived and likely to plunge the country into war, the Chief Executive cut him to ribbons by artful application of tart ridicule at his next press conference. Joe McCarthy took the Senate floor to sidle up against calling him a Communist, and Wayne Morse consumed one entire afternoon in a slumbering Senate to dub him a windjamming artist in tedious ways.

He got a bright notion, and the notion was that if he could be President and control all the unbridled power of that august office, then he could work large wonders among nations. So he launched his campaign in the best tradition. He gave out a loud burble of words and a series of whoops. He hired marching bands and dancing girls, and he put bunions on his feet crisscrossing the nation to take part in that special torture peculiar to American politics: the presidential primaries. He stuffed himself on cheese in Wisconsin, grimaced joyfully from beneath Indian war bonnets in Oregon, posed with big-bosomed bathing beauties in Florida, and in Indiana he chewed on a blade of grass and dished up philosophy straight from the cracker barrel. He observed all the rituals and he won the primaries and also the nomination. In due course of time, he won the Presidency.

And then hard reality set in. The crown had hardly settled over his ears before he realized the Presidency wasn't the raw ball of power he had thought, but was a mysterious cream puff stuffed to its spongy core with vexations. Party bosses besieged him for partisan favor and cried bitter tears in demand of his precious hours. His old colleagues from Capitol Hill would breakfast in the historic White House dining room, all chuckles and fellowship and friendly smiles, but before digestive juices could dissolve his culinary hospitality they would shock him by vicious attacks upon his well-intended policies from public halls.

Solutions to problems from Cambodia to Brazil, seemingly so elemental when he had been in the Senate, grew horns and thorns and eventually jumped off the bluff. Old truths became blowzy, vague delusions. Bureaucrats vied for his ear to cry of perfidies among their subordinates. His own ʻpalace guards engaged in never-ending back stabbing among their number. The opposition party meanly balked him at every turn. Labor blew as high as buzzards fly over his bringing about compulsory arbitration in a railroad strike. Big business jumped him with wild cries for opposing steel-price increases. Preachers wailed

evangelical dithyrambs against his name because he wouldn't do some
vague something about a Supreme Court ruling touching on prayer
in the schools. Two Cabinet members quit in a huff, and it became
painfully necessary to recall three ambassadors. He received letters
from crackpots ranging in affection from mild hopes that he would
soon expire of heartburn to black threats about dynamiting his person.

He grow lonely and tired and his nights passed without sleep, for he
had come to an exalted place to prance before his lieges in triumph at
the making of large miracles, but in time he came instead upon abys-
mal truth. And the truth was this: in a free society the tail often wags
the dog.

So the President stood idly fondling the tasseled drape cord,
haunted by the selfish schemes and parochial pleasures of the same old
clowns and bosses and mountebanks among whom he had labored in
vineyards of lower station. And he spoke his piece, with maybe a little
bit of apology in the manner, but in the end his answer was not the
answer Cullie Blanton had crossed the Potomac to hear. He gave the
word. And the word was "No."

Cullie Blanton took the verdict unflinchingly. He nodded as if to
ratify an unspoken bet he had made with himself, and he lolled the
dead cigar on his tongue.

"Mister President," he said, after a spell, "about this statement
we're gonna work out. I sure hope we can put some kind of respectable
façade on it. I got to go home with somethin' I can live with."

The President cleared his throat. "Mickey McGuire has drafted a
statement we would like to submit to your people," he said. "Let me
suggest that our respective aides withdraw to his office and attempt to
formulate something we can agree upon. Once we're in agreement, the
statement might be issued over our joint signatures."

Cullie Blanton smiled wryly. "Well," he said, "you seemed confident enough how this little visitation would come out."

The President flushed. He made an upturned palm motion with his
hands. "I'm sorry," he said, not unkindly.

"It's just like a poker game," the Governor responded, with an airy
wave. "Some days you get nothin' but flushes and other days you can't
pair up a trey even with your own marked deck."

We began to move around in a shuffle of chairs, falling in behind
Mickey McGuire. "You stay here, Henry," the Governor said. Speaker
Muggins sank back into his chair. The President suggested a drink
while awaiting preparation of the official statement.

"What would you prefer, Governor? Scotch . . . bourbon . . . vodka. . . ?"

"I had a feelin'," the Governor said wryly, "that maybe you had laid me in a choice supply of hemlock."

"Bring 'em on in," the Governor said.

Hairy body immersed in sudsy water, he splashed joyfully in the huge oval bathtub in the manner of a seal at play, grunting and snorting a great satisfaction, periodically taking deep measures of a bourbon highball. Between swigs the highball rested in a sweating glass that Cullie Blanton placed on the thick rim of the pink tub. A sticky heat permeated the Hay-Adams Hotel bathroom. Mirrors fogged over with steam, and the Governor's skin reddened like lobster coming to a boil.

"Here?" Zero Phillips asked. "You want me to bring 'em in *here?*"

"I reckon," the Governor said as he splashed merrily, "they've seen folks in the altogether before."

"Maybe not any nude governors, though."

"In that case," the Governor said, "I'm givin' 'em a rare treat, ain't I? Jim, pour some more that bath salt in here with me. I like the way it smells."

I moved to get the bath salts, thinking how lucky I was to have a college education. Zero shuffled uncertainly in the doorway. "Boss," I said, pouring bath salts, "it's no skin off my rear. But I don't believe I'd receive those newsmen frolicking in the bathtub."

Cullie Blanton scrubbed vigorously at his face with a purple washcloth, spluttering and grunting. "Boy, you got a whole lot to learn about human nature. Those Yankee reporters," he said, the manipulated washcloth muting his words, "are gonna write me up like the prize freak in Mister Barnum's tentshow. And they'd do it even if I got interviewed in white tie and tails with maybe the National Symphony Orchestra softly playin' 'Clair de Lune' in the background. This way I at least get credit for bein' clean." He grinned wickedly, tapping a finger to his head. "Besides, I got another high purpose in mind."

Zero adjusted his features to acceptance of wild reality. I started to follow him out the bathroom door.

"Jim, you stay here," the Governor said. "You're one my main props for this little scene." It occurred to me that at long last Cullie Blanton had tripped over the last line of sanity and had plunged headlong into the chasm of lunacy never to return. The Governor shoved his highball glass into my hand. "You hang on to this," he said. "I don't want anything gettin' on the news wires about how I was wallowin' dead drunk in the bathtub. Take a few sips from it so they'll know it's yours. And hide that goddamn box perfumed bath salts."

I hardly had time to pop the bath salts into the medicine cabinet before Zero ambled to the door displaying all the ease of a fellow stopping by the corner drugstore for his daily cigar, trailed by three very perplexed newspaper reporters. The news boys gaped at the Governor as if the brain couldn't quite pick up the message their eyes insisted was true. Zero stepped discreetly aside and said with the type of dignity unmatched by anybody since Dean Acheson was big on the diplomatic circuit, "Gentlemen, meet Governor Blanton."

Cullie Blanton turned a hideous parody of a smile on the three men favored by what had to be one of the most intimate views offered of any governor in history. He extended one thick, soapy arm in a gesture reminiscent of the old Nazi salute, the grin growing until it seemed his face might split from the strain. "Howdy," he boomed, "sure glad to make you boys' acquaintance. Y'all like a little somethin' spiritous to drink?"

The stunned reporters huddled together as if seeking protection from a common danger, exchanging the kind of glances you can hardly get any more.

Cullie Blanton splashed water on his chest and spluttered. "Ah don't touch the stuff myself," he said. "Had a sweet mother didn't hold with drinkin'. 'Honor thy father and mother in the days of thy youth,' the Good Book says. Yessir, and ah have tried to do just that." The Governor flashed his professional smile again. "You boys might wanta make a note of that," he said helpfully.

The three mesmerized reporters accommodatingly scribbled on their notepads.

"Daddy, now," the Governor said, "*he* took a swig from the jug now and again. But he never let ole John Barleycorn interfere with his plowin' or his prayin'. And he died old in his own bed and no doubt reached the Pearly Gates to find many gold stars by his name, for he sweated in honest toil and paid his just debts and kept his word to a fault. And ah've tried to be the son of the father."

The reporters continued to gawk as if training for the Olympics in that particular category.

"Jim," the Governor said loudly, "if you can put down that evilsmellin' booze you got there, you might scrub my back some." He nodded toward a long-handled brush on the rim of the tub, leaned forward in the water, and gripped his knees with both hands, awaiting my favor.

The reporters watched me scrub the Governor's back like maybe I was a visiting surgeon from foreign shores displaying some new and experimental technique.

"Jim here," the Governor said, "used to be a newspaper man. But the booze got to him in the worst way. I found him dog-drunk in a bar ditch with waste matter on his britches and dried him out in a sanitarium and gave him a job. He can't do much, but he's faithful." The Governor dropped his voice to a stage whisper and peered from beneath bushy eyebrows, taking the reporters in his confidence. "I'd appreciate you boys not printin' anything about that. He's a sensitive fellow and God didn't bless him with abundant gifts. Got a bad speech impediment."

The reporters shifted their eyes toward me nervously. "Oh," the Governor said, "don't worry about him hearin' me. He's deaf as a hitchin' post. You gotta be lookin' him smack-dab in the face so he can read your lips." I scrubbed the Governor's back with more vigor than the job called for. He twisted under the harsh rub of the brush, trying not to give me the satisfaction of showing pain, and as soon as pride would decently allow it he swung the gray head around until he looked me flush in the face. Exaggerating his lip movements, he mouthed, "That's fine, Jim-Boy. You done *real* good."

I favored Cullie Blanton with a hound-dog look of pure devotion, letting my jaws go slack, adopting the ecstatic blank look of the truly demented. The reporters turned their eyes away, abashed, not wanting to stare at so obvious an affliction.

"A shame," Cullie clucked sadly. "He comes from good stock, too. Oh, the wages of sin. . . ."

One of the reporters rooted his tongue around in his mouth and eventually decided to chance its use.

"Uh . . . Governor," he stammered, "your . . . ah . . . trip here. We'd like—"

"Fahn city," the Governor beamed. "Just *fahn!* Real inspiration! Nothin' like Washington anyplace else on God's green earth. Show me a man can look on those lights playin' on that Capitol dome at night without gettin' a lump in his throat, and I'll show you a man don't possess the first grain of wisdom about this *wunnerful* country of ours. Such a fellow has my deepest sympathy."

"About your talk with the President," the same reporter said doggedly. "Could you tell us—"

The Governor held up a restraining hand. "Now, now," he said, chuckling in high good humor, "don't you city boys start takin' advantage of an ole country cousin like me. You boys know it ain't proper for a White House visitor to quote conversations with the President. That's *his* dunghill down there, and he calls the shots."

"We thought perhaps—"

"Boys," the Governor said, still beaming friendship, his voice tinged with sorrowful rebuke. *"Boys!* Now I'd love to help you out, I truly would. I know you got a job to do, and my heart goes out to you. But I'm a rank stranger in town and I got to observe local customs and *mores*. Protocol, ain't that what they call it?"

"The joint statement issued by the White House," the reporter said, "doesn't give much information." He hauled a folded paper from his pocket, wiped beads of perspiration from his brow, and gazed on the short statement authorized from the White House. It said only that the President and Governor Blanton had met "in exploratory talks" to discuss matters of mutual interest and concern bearing on the Supreme Court's decision. *A frank and full exchange of views,* the release revealed deadpan, *served to convince the President and the Governor that existing problems are not insurmountable. Both the President and the Governor expressed hope that men of good will might bring about a harmonious resolving of differences prior to the beginning of the approaching academic year. The President has instructed the Attorney General to show all possible consideration in carrying out the law of the land.* The lead reporter bravely plowed through a vocal rendition of the statement, stuttering over words as the Governor distracted him with happy splashing. Cullie Blanton glowed with health, grunted approval, ratified the reading by rapid bobs of the head.

"Doesn't say much," the reporter said cryptically, folding the release and jamming it back in his pocket.

"Sure don't," Cullie admitted cheerfully. "And that's a fact. Jim, fill that pitcher and do the honors." He nodded toward the lavatory taps. I filled the pitcher with water while the reporters stood petrified in anticipation. "Souse me," the Governor said. "Souse me good." I poured the water on the Governor's head and he gave great, shuddering gasps

of joy as it cascaded down his body. When he had conquered his spasms
the Governor jerked his head up and smiled at the reporters. "Nothin'
like it," he said with enthusiasm. "Opens up the pores and sets the
blood runnin' free. I wouldn't be surprised if it cured ever'thing from
dandruff to chilblains."

One of the reporters edged skittishly toward the door as if to flee
danger. The fellow who had assumed the role of spokesman struggled
with himself and with difficulty got back on the subject at hand.

"Governor," he said, "the last sentence of the statement refers to
'the law of the land.' Isn't that in conflict with the Southern position?
Doesn't the Southern position hold that Congress and not the Supreme
Court makes 'the law of the land'?"

"Boy," the Governor said, "on that subject we got more positions
than you'll find in one those old-time Roman sex orgies. How about
handin' me that towel?"

The spokesman took a clean towel from a rack and shuffled two steps
toward the bathtub, extending it cautiously as if maybe he had precar-
ious grip on the business end of a mad rattler.

Cullie Blanton stood in the tub, revealed for a moment in full glory.
He wrapped the towel around strategic parts. "Boys," he said, "you are
gonna have to excuse me now, for I am a shy and modest man. . . ."

There are some things you just don't do. Curse the Pope in the
confessional booth. Make love to the tax collector's wife. Speak heresy
of J. Edgar Hoover in Rotary Club society. Use the flag for a buffing
cloth.

And you don't beard the President of the United States in his own
den.

Which, applying the rules of best evidence, the President had great
reason to presume Cullie Blanton had done. And which I got the primary inkling of in the worst possible way when the telephone rang
early agonies in my room at the Hay-Adams Hotel just a hop, skip,
and jump down the hall from the Governor's suite. When Cullie's
voice boomed in my ear, I heard he had greeted the dawn wearing a
new set of fangs.

"Jim," he boomed, *"goddammit,* Jim! Let go your cock and grab
your socks. Ever'body up."

"Wha'?" I said. "Huh . . . wha' . . . ?"

"Get your britches on and get in here."

"Uh . . . wha'sa mat—"

"Christ on the mountain," Cullie Blanton exploded. "I got a crisis on my hands would make an earthquake seem like the purest pleasure, and you got to turn up without enough wits to tie your shoestrings."

"What's happened?"

"Boy," the Governor said, "I will mercifully withhold the sad facts until you get down here. Which better be within two minutes at the out-goddamn-side."

The Governor was fit to be tied with the strongest rope. He stirred the air, flailing his arms expertly, the terminals of his silk robe flapping around and about, as he measured the sitting room of his suite with agitated steps. Speaker Muggins huddled dejectedly in a corner chair, a consumptive elfin, wan of face, skinny ribs and limbs poking from underwear so old-fashioned it must have come down to him as his family legacy.

Cullie Blanton whirled on me, eyes popping. "That *sumbitch!*" he snorted. "That goddamn, Simple Simon, rotatin', revolvin', perpetual, son-of-a-dog of a mental cipher!"

I stood pulling at my disarrayed clothing.

"That pigheaded, addlebrained, abysmally ignorant, reptilian, hallucinary prize of a fool."

"I don't know exactly who it is," I croaked in my morning voice, "but I take it he finds no immediate favor in your sight."

"He is a priest of idiot beliefs," the Governor thundered. "He has got two left feet and is shorn of all graces. He has crap for brains and water on the knee. He ought not to be trusted with any position higher than towel boy in a Korean cat house."

"It might help," I said, "if you would care to identify the gentleman."

"That goddamn wisp of evaporatin' intelligence," Cullie Blanton roared, "who presumes to be mah Lieu-goddamn-tenant Governor. Stanley Dutton." He spat poor Stanley's name like it fouled the roof of his mouth.

"In time," I said, "I reckon you will specify your charges."

"I'll throw him in the deepest dungeon," the Governor ranted. "I'll grind up his bones and sell 'em for feed mix. I'll pluck him bald a hair at a time. I'll use his gastric juices to pickle his liver." He went on to embellish the theme, expurgating his soul, educing new venom. When he had drained himself he hurled his body down with a plop on the couch, running hands through tousled hair. "What in the name of Satan could have possessed even *that* witless popinjay to have made such a foolish goddamn statement?"

"Not knowing the statement," I said, "I'm working at a slight disadvantage."

The Governor sighed and slumped against the sofa, his head lolling on broad shoulders. "Henry," he said, "you tell him. I don't think I can bear to repeat it."

"Quoted the Governor," Henry Muggins said. "Or *mis*quoted him. Said Cullie pledged a fight to the death. Said he'd never surrender. It's big in the papers this morning."

"It's ruined me," the Governor gloomed. "Press secretary for the President called me up before I got any coffee in my gizzard and threatened to draw and quarter me on the spot and judge the wisdom of the action at a later date. Said the President's gotta issue a statement pickin' up my challenge. Said the President had no choice, and the liberals in Congress already stormin' White House gates demanding mah blood! I begged like a Buddhist monk, but my plea fell on deaf ears. They're drivin' me to the wall, and it's gonna do the *very* goddamn thing I came all this way to avoid. It's gonna set the rabble to howlin' at the moon and scalpin' in the streets. Christ the Savior, what was Stanley Dutton thinkin' about? Presumin' he *can* get a brain twitch now and then."

"Damfino," the Speaker said, washing his hands of the vexation.

"Well," I said, "what's Stanley say?"

"Stanley," the Governor said heavily, "is what you might call unavailable for comment. He must not of come in from his latest social obligation. But I got more folks huntin' him than tromped through the underbrush lookin' for Dr. Livingston."

"What exactly did he say?"

The Governor plunged up from the couch and beat a path to a telephone table. He looked on a notepad possessed of his personal scrawls, squinting, and translated. "He quoted me as sayin' 'I will never surrender.' You recollect anything like that?"

I indulged in cogitation. The scene came back to me. *Stanley Dutton stood at the foot of the ramp leading to the aircraft, fielding the Governor's abuse, ratifying his humiliation by agreeable nods, throwing surreptitious glances at the newsmen fenced off at the edge of the runway. "Goddamn," the Governor had said dispiritedly. He paused again. "We shall never surrender," he said idly, borrowing a line from*

Winston Churchill. The Lieutenant Governor seemed on the verge of breaking into applause. "I commit you to the deep," Cullie Blanton had said, plunging into the yawning door of the plane. . . .

"Yeah," I said. "I recollect it, all right."

"Huh?" the Governor exploded.

"Do?" the Speaker said, coming up off his shoulder blades.

"He got it a little wrong," I said. "He slightly misquoted Winston Churchill."

"Boy," Cullie said, "I think we have reached a point where you have got to haul off and explain yourself to a great but thoroughly muddled governor."

So I explained.

"Goddamn," the Governor said, "don't you know I didn't mean anything by that? Hell, you know how I mumble to myself. I quote Shakespeare and the holy prophets and Winston Churchill, and it wouldn't surprise me much if I've quoted Ezzard Charles on some appropriate occasion. But it don't *mean* nothin'."

The telephone rang.

"Maybe," the Governor said, "I will have the rare privilege of speaking with His Eminence now." He picked up the telephone, listened briefly, and said, "You got 'im, Operator." He placed his hand over the mouthpiece. "Jim," he said, "get on that extension phone in the bedroom. I might have a stroke in the middle of this. And if I do, you pick up the cussin' and carry on in the noblest tradition. Hold the torch high. . . ."

On the extension, I heard the Lieutenant Governor shouting repeated hellos.

"Stanley," the Governor said after a bit, "I hope you got wax-free ears. I got some wisdom to impart."

"Have you seen my statement?" the Lieutenant Governor asked, poised for praise.

"Stanley," the Governor said, "as a matter of fact I called you about that exact subject."

"It got a big play in the press down here," Stanley Dutton said, oozing confidence. "It's on the front page of *all* the papers."

"I think I can tell you without revealin' any classified information," the Governor said, "that it was noticed here in Washington, too."

"Honest?" the Lieutenant Governor gushed. "Honest Injun?"

"Honest-goddamn-Injun," the Governor said. "The White House called me about it personally. . . ."

"Sure enough?" Stanley Dutton said in quizzical delight.

"I wouldn't lie to you," the Governor said. "The President saw your statement first thing this mornin' and thought enough of it to see I got a telephone call from the White House even before I'd had my coffee."

Stanley Dutton went to his shambles unaware. "Can you *imagine* that? Can you imagine the President taking note of *my* statement and thinking enough of it to call you?"

"Your Excellency." The Governor paused for a pregnant instant. "Since you're actin' governor," he said, "you don't mind if I call you Your Excellency?"

"Oh no," the number two man said grandly. "I consider it a very high honor, Cullie. One of which I may be unworthy, actually."

"Modesty," the Governor said, "is one the most becomin' traits in a public man. And you got plenty, Stanley, to be modest about."

"Ah . . . beg pardon?"

"There ought to be a monument built to your modesty," the Governor said, "with maybe an inscription attestin' to your gross stupidity."

"Hah?" Stanley Dutton said as the sands shifted under his feet. "Wha'?"

"The President," Cullie Blanton said tightly, "is takin' the pains to wipe the floor up with me today, and all thanks go to you. You have gone and let the cat out. You have done the very goddamn thing I expressly told you *not* to do. Didn't I put you under penalty of goddamn *death* if you opened your yap while I was gone? Didn't I?"

The Lieutenant Governor made choking sounds.

"Dammit, *didn't* I?"

The poor fellow on the other end of the wire coughed up a strangled admission.

"I am flyin' back today," the Governor said, "for you have seen gratuitously fit to make my presence here an evil thing in the eyes of duly constituted authorities. And in the meantime, you keep your lip buttoned until folks think maybe you've lost the power of speech. You got it?"

Stanley Dutton wheezed and spluttered.

"Goddamn you," the Governor shouted, "say 'I got it.' "

That poor unfortunate said he had it.

"And while I'm returnin'," the Governor said, grinding his teeth, "you better figure out a way to grow muttonchop whiskers and cultivate a limp. You better take on protective coloration. You better make yourself a small thing before my eyes. You got that?"

"Yessir," Stanley said, faintly.

"And give your heart to God," the Governor said, "and your eyes to an eye bank. But save your ass, Stanley. Don't commit it to anybody. For your ass belongs to *me*."

7

BY PREARRANGEMENT not exactly long on ceremony, the Lieutenant Governor was by special invitation at Cullie Blanton's disposal when we arrived back in Capitol City. He sat at heel in the Governor's outer office, hat in hand, his expression as readable as a red-letter quarantine notice and just about as cheerful. Cullie stalked by his running mate like maybe the fellow was a fence post, turning his head the barest fraction and speaking just one harsh word: "Inside." Speaker Muggins and your present hero presumed to hang back, but the Governor changed our collective minds with one jerking motion of his head. We trailed the victim to his carnage.

The Governor plucked a set of reading glasses from his desk and adjusted them with all the care of a British judge robing himself for court. Stanley Dutton shuffled his feet in a jittery little jig step. The Governor lowered his head a trifle and peeked over the rim of the spectacles, puckering lips in a soundless whistle, his eyes crawling slowly over the wretched hunk of humanity who looked like a well-dressed store-window mannequin. Stanley Dutton, who when our state's most enlightened legislature appropriated more money for the old winos' home than it provided for promoting the fine arts, had managed to get quoted to the effect that our state had more winos than artists anyway. Now that is not a contention I would dispute with vigor, because it has the ring of whole truth. But Stanley had a lot to learn about human nature and politics, and the biggest lesson he could never get down by rote was how truth is sometimes a burdensome commodity and is better left unremoved.

So the Governor looked at Stanley Dutton and no doubt he thought how his Lieutenant Governor had once made a speech to the Jewish War Veterans during which he called on Jew and Arab to get together and settle their differences in a *Christian* manner, for the love of Jesus.

And who, with the woods full of raggedy-assed rednecks so hungry their guts growled at their backbones, rednecks who had not laid lips over a leg of fried chicken in so long they couldn't remember if fowls crept, crawled, or sprouted wings, had allowed himself to be photographed at his plush country mansion preening with his fighting gamecocks.

Maybe Cullie should have directed his ire at the system that demanded a geographic balance on the state ticket, a pretty boy to offset one with rough-hewn features, and somebody palatable to the gizzards of reactionaries when the other fellow on the slate happened to be thought of as a screaming liberal. But the system was intangible and hard to get boots to, while Stanley Dutton was very real and within handy kicking distance.

After the Governor had thought his thoughts, he got his eyes in focus and leaned across the desk, speaking in that soft calm-before-the-storm voice that could bring tremors to the limbs of the earlier-initiated. "Stanley," he cooed, "you may be a very bright man and have just got exceptional ability at hidin' the fact. Maybe as a businessman you are the soup and nuts. You can find oil in the ground and pick up money off the street. And if you had turned your talents in that direction, why you might of turned out to be the world's very best goddamn piccolo player." The Governor mused on the vagrant thought, sniffing suspiciously at a cigar extracted from his coat pocket. "But as a politician," he said in foreboding tones, "you are about as adroit as a spastic shootin' billiards."

Stanley Dutton sent a dry tongue over parched lips, and it must have been like rollerskates on sandpaper. Poor Stanley had tried to play at God and had got caught short of firmament, and now the day of reckoning was at hand.

All at once the Governor shouted like a redneck addressing a stubborn span of mules. He brought his clenched fist banging down on the desk top, causing a spasm of the Lieutenant Governor's eyelids and Lord knows what other moveable parts hidden from view. "Goddammit! You have any *notion* what's happened since you made that statement to the press?" Without waiting for the response which seemed beyond the call of Stanley's abilities of the moment, the Governor said, "Tell him, Jim. And use three-cent words. For I want the demented sonofabitch to get the hang of it."

So I read the indictment. "Number one," I said, as I ticked the specifications off on my fingers, "it's caused every loose nut group term-bling wildly on the fringe to come yowling out of the woodwork, pledging bucketfuls of blood to the unyielding position the Governor is reported to have taken."

"Which position," the Governor said, ominously, "I most decidedly did not take."

"Number two. The President followed up with a statement muscled enough to shame Samson. He's practically threatened to invade us. And may be thinking of using the Bomb."

"Which was not," the Governor growled, "exactly how I had planned it."

"Number three. The President's statement caused our little friend General Wooster to jump through his one-hundred-per-cent American bunghole. And he is wildly calling the countryside to illicit arms."

"And it's bearin' sour fruit," the Governor added. "Tell him, Jim."

"Number four," I said, "concerns the first rotten apple. In a typically dismal village down in the red-clay country, a group of pedigreed patriots fell with rocks, clubs, and tarpots last night upon the person of their local Negro man of medicine."

Dutton flicked his tongue out like a lizard and used it to push forth a few more stammered words. "Wha' . . . what had . . . had he done?"

"He aroused base feelings in the community," I said, "by subscribing to *Ebony* magazine and always taking his vacation up North someplace. And he wasn't in the habit of getting off the sidewalk and down in the gutter when he saw some white peckerwood come slouching along with cow dung on his shoes and snuff spittle dried on his whiskers. And accordingly, he was thought by the natives to lack appropriate humility for one of his cast."

"Number five," the Governor said, "I had to send troopers in there to put the lid on what could get to be a brewin' vat of very bad business."

"Which," I reported, "brings us to number six. And that is all those Christ Returns headlines in the newspapers this morning frothing over the arrival of martial law. Courtesy of our Governor."

"A courtesy for which I had just as soon not receive due credit," said the Governor.

"Number seven," I intoned. "The Grand Kleagle or All-Seeing Cyclops or whatever he is of the Klan has called on all loyal Southerners possessed of bedsheets to put 'em on and gather around the fiery crosses no later than tomorrow night. For the purpose of electing delegates to a state-wide conclave to be held one week hence, and I leave it to your imagination how *that* little scene could turn out. Which brings us to number eight, the Attorney General's statement from Washington saying how he'll send in Federal marshals with gas and guns to police the meetings. And won't, I got the notion, put up with a shovelful of the kind of crap the Klan will try to spread by the wagonload." Stanley made vague jaw motions, but I stopped him with a wave of the hand. "And *that* in turn gave the N.A.A.C.P. and CORE and all the dusky outfits courage enough to call on their own few members down here in the potlikker belt to stage demonstrations. They said make it peaceful. But down here that's like giving Machine Gun Kelly the prime tool of his trade and asking him to break jail by merely using his wits."

"I wish the N-Double-A-Cee-Pee would attack me some," the Governor muttered.

"So to sum up," I said to Stanley Dutton, "something has hit the fan."

"And what has hit the fan," Cullie Blanton chimed in, "is not lemon meringue. I went all the way up there to Funland-on-the-Potomac to pour oil on troubled waters. But thanks to you sayin' I'll fight 'til the last dog is dead, Stanley, we seem to have succeeded in kickin' off a state-sponsored riot. You got any bright suggestions how we can improve the situation?"

"You might issue a statement. That I was ah . . . mistaken. Mistaken in what I said. I wouldn't mind, Governor."

"You," the Governor said flatly, "wouldn't mind." He watched the fellow across the desk, his round eyes visited a moment by something akin to pity, and he shook his head in some negative sorrow. "Joseph, Mary, and Baby Jesus," he said in prayerful tones. "I should have had better gumption than to ask." He jumped from the chair behind the desk, jabbed the unlighted cigar in his mouth, and paced off distance across the carpet. He walked and he thought, and the more he thought the less he liked what he thought about. The high flush started to take him, coming up from neck to full face and disappearing in the gray, tangled convolutions just above the hairline. "Talk about lockin' the barn door after the horse got out," he grumbled. "Dammit, you mean to stand there with your bare face danglin' and claim I can undo your considerable damage by sayin' you just happened to be goddamn *mistaken?*"

Stanley Dutton reached deep down inside himself and got hold of something he must have thought a long time dead. And what he got his hand on was spunk. Oh, not much. Just a tiny glob, a little corner of it, and he held it uncertainly in his grasp the way you would a wiggling eel. But he hung on and conquered his foul fear, choking it back, and after a while he coughed up his response. Which was: "Yes. I can't see it would do any harm."

The Governor ceased his pacing and whirled in huge agitation. "You can't see it'd do any *harm?*" His voice said he wouldn't be any more incredulous if his number two man had just announced the opening of a beet-canning factory on a distant planet. "You got the President of the United States threatenin' me with physical violence, kindergarten kids writin' my name alongside dirty words on outhouse walls, and the whole state quakin' like a dog in a thunderstorm. And your idea is for me to say it's all just a terrible misunder-goddamn-standin'. Just a mistake. Because it can't do any *harm!*" Cullie Blanton moved to stand nose-to-nose with Stanley Dutton. All at once the Lieutenant Governor seemed just another wilted fellow who had looked upon his own pale ghost.

"I," the Governor said in heavyweight tones, "am about to lay down certain decrees. Which you had better by-God commit to memory and keep in faith. From the present goddamn instant you are expressly denied the pleasure of givin' out a mumblin' word to the gentlemen of the press. With the *sole* exception of statements reduced to writing and cleared by me. The Press Club Bar is off-limits to you, and if they should happen to lose their minds down there and throw you some kind of testimonial dinner with free drinks, you will send sorrowful regrets and a deaf-and-dumb representative. And from this minute on you have got a bodyguard."

"A . . . what?"

"A bodyguard. I am goin' to pick out the meanest, toughest, foulest, bullyingest mother lover I can find among my cadre of cops, and that gentleman will be under orders to stay so close you'll have to brush your teeth in handcuffs." The Governor gulped air after his discourse and cut his eyes toward me. "Jim," he said, "who's the meanest trooper we got?"

"Shivers," I said. "And the name fits. I get 'em any time I have the ill luck to run across him."

The Governor creased his forehead in thought. "Big fellow? Butch haircut? Thick lips?"

"No," I said. "Little fellow. Red hair and knotty arms like string-beans. Got eyes like a snake. He'd rather pistol whip a cripple than eat when he's hungry, and he's got a good appetite."

The Governor nodded, satisfied with the choice. "Get on the phone and track him down. I want him here by the time this left-footed lout takes his leave."

He turned back to the Lieutenant Governor and prodded him in the chest with one thick forefinger. "And about the campaign," he said softly. "You are to be seldom seen and *never* heard. You ain't even to make a goddamn telephone call without it's monitored and what you say has been put down with chalk on a slate. You got it?"

Stanley Dutton croaked and spluttered and quivered in his joints.

"Goddammit," the Governor snarled, "it's not a debatable question. It's like the gonorrhea, you either got it or you ain't. *Have . . . you . . . got . . . it?*"

Maybe if Stanley hadn't just copped a small feel of his long-lost spunk, or if the Governor hadn't hissed the last four words from between his teeth, that would have been the end of it. But something pushed Stanley Dutton, who didn't have the intestines of a humming-bird (and what's more, knew it), over the line. He gulped and dredged the bottom of his small soul, and this time he got his spunk in a little tighter grip.

"No," he said. "No. I won't do it."

But if Stanley had surprised himself, then we've got to invent new language for what he did to the rest of us. The Speaker, who had been hunkered down in a big leather chair apparently grabbing forty winks during Cullie Blanton's histrionics, came scrambling up like a tornado was blowing and he was hell-bent on the storm cellar. I literally dropped the telephone I had been fiddling with preparatory to calling in Red Shivers, and the Governor. . . .

Hell, I don't own words to describe the Governor at that point. If he ever goes all-the-way crazy I will know I caught him at the world pre-mière of it. His eyes jumped out like twin yo-yos and his jaw dropped as if somebody had tripped a trap door hooked to his wisdom teeth. He plopped down in his tracks, and if the edge of his desk hadn't been there as a bracer, Cullie Blanton would have been down for a rare count.

"You won't do what?" he asked. Like he was shell-shocked.

"Any of it. I won't have the bodyguard. I won't be told where I can go. Or who I can talk to." Now, Stanley's tone wasn't anywhere near as impressive as the words. His voice was full of treble clefs and his hands jerked like somebody was giving him powerful juice. But he had got the words out; I had to give him that.

The Governor had difficulty adjusting to the mutiny. "Hell and god-damn," Cullie Blanton said, absently. He pulled himself together and bunched up his jaws. "I don't know," he said gruffly, "just what the hell you think you can do about it."

"I know," Stanley Dutton said. And it was plain he was starting to enjoy the feel of being a free man. "I know," he repeated, savoring the words like a kid might linger over a lollipop. "I'll resign."

Cullie blinked eyes to clear his vision. "You'll *what?*"

"Quit the ticket. I won't run again." Stanley Dutton said the magic words with the strange, shining joy of new discovery in his own orbs. "You've kicked me around the way you might kick a dog," he said. "Well, I'm not taking it any more. You can have the job. I quit." For the moment he was absolute monarch of himself.

Cullie Blanton swapped popeyed looks with the Speaker and yours truly. He placed his hands flat on the desk, propelling his bulk away from its stolid support, and he rummaged in a glass container in search of a lemon drop. Finding one among the collection of peppermints and licorice sticks, he wandered to his chair, lowered into it gently, and indented his cheeks suckling at pleasure. After a bit he cocked his head to the right and his eyes turned indolent.

He said, "Stanley, I have lived long and gazed on miracles and had just come to the point of thinkin' the world holds no mysteries unfath-omable in nature. Yeah, I had reached the point where I fancied I could tell a shyster from an honest man through fifteen feet of pig iron. But now. . . ." The Governor shook his graying head, smiling rue-fully, as if about to divulge a private joke of which he was the butt. For the first time his eyes recognized Stanley Dutton as human. As something with a heart and sensibilities of a sort, and a brain in which something stirred now and again. "But now," the Governor repeated. "Now, you go and shake my faith in the old rules. By suddenly decidin' to grow a little backbone." He smiled sweetly at the other fellow, who seemed unnerved anew at the exhibition. "Too bad it had to go to waste, Stanley. Too bad I can't allow you to get away with it."

The Lieutenant Governor betrayed panic lurking just under the surface of his tumbling emotions by clearing his throat in a ragged little concert of sounds. "I told you," he managed to say. "I won't be your kicked dog any more."

"You told me, all right. For the first time since you drooled and kicked in the cradle, you screwed up your courage and made noises like you might sometime grow up to be a man. I can't let you get away with it. You know why, don't you?"

Stanley Dutton's tongue flirted with his dry lips. After a moment's pause his head wagged some uncertain signal.

"Not because I love you so much," Cullie Blanton said. "Not because it would deprive the world of any greatness. But because, Stanley, if I let one bounder get out of hand then the mutiny spreads. Yeah, if I rested on my duff and let you walk out of here beatin' your breast about how you had deserted my ticket, why . . . well, it just wouldn't do. Naw, by the time you had told the story a few times and built it up some until you got to thinkin' it truly happened the way you told it, and the newspaper boys twisted it the way they can, the word would go out how a lightweight like Stanley Dutton had got Cullie Blanton on the ropes and pounded him unmercifully about the body politic."

The Governor shook his head against the prospect. "I can look ahead and see the vision. Stanley Dutton, standin' on the platform lookin' as sincere as ole Eisenhower and as righteous as John the Baptist. With that goddamn mad general bristlin' his mustache like God passin' out the final judgments. And you bleatin' about how my administration is so full of loose morals it would shame a goat. And how finally God Almighty himself shouted loud to you, callin' you by your full name, and said '*Stanley Moncrief Dutton, go forth and sin no more.*' And how you came to do battle on the side of the angels. Yessir, Stanley. It's as predictable as wads in a henhouse, and I am not in the market right now for that sticky kind of mess. So you had just better forget all about sproutin' a spine this late in life."

"No," Stanley said, doggedly.

"Then I will break you," the Governor said. The friendly look had gone aglimmering and Cullie's jaw lines hardened until little pulses throbbed along their rugged paths. "What I will do is make you a walkin' felony. And I can do it, too. You ever take the time to read the constitution of this sovereign state?"

"As much," Stanley said in a quaver, "as some others I might name."

For a flash it looked as if Cullie might reach and get him. The Governor's hands knotted and his body tensed. But then reason restored itself in the Governor's mind. He struggled with his temper and won a victory, and sat shuddering. Thinking, no doubt, what a sweet-smelling mess it all would have made in the papers had he followed his instincts and slapped his number two boy kicking. When he had got his breath blows under control, the Governor thought of Abe Lincoln. "'A house divided . . .'" he mumbled. Then he whipped around toward the Speaker as if hoping to catch that worthy off base. "Henry, who is it charged with administerin' the Veterans' Land Program?"

"He is," the Speaker said, laconically. And nodded toward Stanley Dutton. Who, all at once, got robbed of his small store of confidence.

"And who has the *legal* responsibility of administerin' the General Tax Fund?"

"Same fellow," the Speaker obliged.

"That clear enough for you?" the Governor asked the tall fellow across the desk.

Stanley wallowed his tongue in a mouthful of cotton. "I didn't . . . I hadn't. . . ."

The Governor rose and jabbed his forefinger in the air, very much in command again, sure of his footing. "This is whole truth. The *constitution* says the Lieutenant Governor of this state has got *legal* responsibility for administerin' a whole passel of various tax funds. The details of which I have never burdened your limited mentality with. But that don't mean you can escape the consequences. For it has been put down black on white. The money involved is enough to pop the eyes out of a stone Buddha, and whosoever mismanageth or misuseth it for his *own* gain shall be quick consigned to a place of limited freedom. You got any notion what I mean?"

"I didn't steal anything," Stanley Dutton said, quickly.

The Governor ignored the denial of record. He locked his gaze on space, peering into some misty vale, and mused. "History," he said idly. "Wunnerful goddamn thing, history. You'd think man would learn more from it. Yeah, you'd think he could look back on the recorded mistakes of ancient kings and pharaohs, and see where they made the wrong turns, and use all that knowledge to his own end. To avoid wars and plagues and famines. But each man, he's so sure the finger of destiny has poked *him* in the puny ribs and whispered in his ear how *he* should go out and make goddamn history that he . . . well, he just forgets. You ever read much history, Stanley?"

"Some."

"Not enough, most likely. But *I* read it. Yeah, I am evermore a history-readin' sonofabitch. It is all there for us. Take you, for instance. Yessir, I even read about *you* in history books."

Stanley Dutton looked wildly about as if to flee madness. The Governor calmed his frazzled nerves by dropping into a soft singsong.

"Yeah, Stanley. You are a character right out of the pages. Huey Long's gang, they wanted somebody tame for governor. So they put poor ole O.K. Allen in the governor's chair and pulled his string and told him when to yelp, and in what key. And it worked. For he did like they told him. He signed anything they put in front of him. Ole Earl Long, he once said a leaf blew in the window and Governor Allen signed it." The Governor gave over to mirth, a bubbly little series of chuckles rising deep from his chest.

"Well, Stanley, when the pussel-guts came to me bearin' their bloated faces and fingerin' their long dollars and pleadin' to get you on my ticket that first time, they talked about how good you'd look on tellyvision. How you'd charm the ladies young and old, and appeal to the better folk. They said how your heart was pure as Ivory soap and how you were such an all-fired smart businessman you could probably make cheese out of buzzard earp. So I beamed and nodded and gave you my blessin'. And those pussel-guts swaggered out of my room blowin' cigar smoke in each other's faces. They thought they'd put you over on me."

The Governor gave his head a little more incline to the right, grinning. "But I didn't take you because of pretty dimples or because I detected any superior intelligence. Nosir, I took you because I had read *history!* Because you would sign a goddamn leaf if it blew in the window."

Cullie Blanton let the grin go off his face. The mirth in his eyes got replaced by the icy coldness of a blue norther' freeze. "And you have signed the goddamn leaf," he said. "Which means, reduced to its lowest common denominator, I can send your earthly remains to the big house for the high crimes of embezzlement, malfeasance, and nonfeasance in office."

"All I did," Stanley Dutton said, defensively, "was sign a few papers."

"All you did," the Governor said, "was get careless. You signed a few too many documents without checkin' on what the words said above that fancy signature. You get excellent on penmanship, but you flunked the examination."

"I . . . they told me the papers were just . . . just routine."

"They told you," Cullie Blanton said, "what I told 'em to tell you.

Who the hell you think hires and fires around here?" Turning his neck the barest fraction, but keeping the Lieutenant Governor in his cold glare, he said, "Jim, go ahead and call that mean trooper."

Stanley Dutton fired one last shot in the skirmish. "Suppose," he blurted, "I don't believe it."

"Goddammit," the Governor said, "you reckon you'd have any trouble takin' it to heart after you'd had about fifteen solitary years to ponder it?" When his number-two boy remained tight-lipped, sweat popping out in ovals on his brow, the Governor said, "Anybody from your family ever been in the hoosegow, Stanley?" And when he got no response, said, "Don't you know that pretty young wife of yours would be pleasured to announce at the next high-fashion charity ball how you had been elevated to assistant librarian at the state pen?"

The Governor permitted Stanley Dutton to stand stiffly thinking on all the notoriety of the thing, and the shame of it. Then he nailed it down with the kicker. "She's a mighty purty little lady, Stanley. Man couldn't expect her to wait forever. Ten, fifteen years could seem eternity to a purty little thing like that." Agony passed over the tanned, handsome face of the Lieutenant Governor and his body gave over to convulsive shudders. Two big tears formed puddles at the corners of his eyes and started a slow descent.

"Goddammit," the Governor said, pressing. "Goddammit, you tame again?"

"Yes," Stanley blubbered.

Cullie looked at the Speaker. "Get him out of here, Henry. Get him out before I throw up. And stay with him until that mean trooper takes over."

Stanley Dutton heard the Governor hand him his hat. He turned and shambled off, and I thought he would weary himself groping for the doorknob. Henry Muggins trailed solemnly behind.

When the door had closed behind the funeral procession, I said, "Would you really send that poor bastard up the river?"

"You could give him a penny for his thoughts and suffer considerable loss on the transaction," the Governor said as he eyed the door through which the victim had so recently fled.

"Would you?"

"Not," he said, lightly, "until after the election."

"Would you do it?" I pressed.

"Goddammit," he said. "There is somethin' in his eyes that won't let you stop kickin' him. It's like you're doin' him a favor. It's like the Lord *meant* for him to suffer. Like the wanderin' Jews."

"Would you go through with it?" I asked.

The Governor snapped his head up and glared at me, going tight around the mouth, and I figured my time had come. All at once I put myself in Stanley's sorry shoes. All at once I had to consider the suspect shape I might be in if the Governor decided to take vengeance on me. I started to mull over in my mind at a rapid clip whether I had signed any documents without reading them. But it was a vain and foolish notion, an idle thought. For who the hell was I? The constitution didn't charge me with responsibility for anything, except maybe keeping out of locked shops. So I relaxed. And said again, "Would you? Would you do it?"

The Governor split his face with a grin. "Boy," he said, "if we're lucky, we won't ever have to find out, will we?"

Crawling in the convertible to move off the capitol grounds and tool homeward, I was startled to hear myself whistling a merry little tune. On key, yet. It had to be a message from Roxie asking me to call. I'd had no more contact with her than with a colony of lepers since that bad scene at Dallas Johnson's party when she had appropriately rewarded my boorishness by cutting out, for there was nothing else to shout huzzahs about.

No, there sure-to-God-in-Glory wasn't.

For there was Bayonet Bill Wooster, trooping across the hinterlands like Caesar come to conquer, a slightly mad Pied Piper trailed by his legions of war-whoopers chanting discord and bloated hate. He saw large conspiracies and revealed them with wild shouts, and he sang of low deeds in high places. His angry bellows ran toward the direction of how Cullie Blanton had gone hat-in-hand to Washington for the foul purpose of selling out the birthright of every breathing protoplasm in coon-dog meridians, and he stood before the upturned country faces jerking like a marionette, possessed of some joyful ugliness. He would come upon the villages and hamlets bearing his own locusts, leaving all things barren and fruitless and stripped of grace.

Yeah, there was Bayonet Bill and there was all the subsidiary phenomena in his wake. The hoodlums and bully boys and penny-a-peck punks spilled from domino parlors and quitting poolhalls reeking of old piss and new beer to bask in the white heat of his public anger, wearing their oily sideburns and skin-tight dungarees like the mufti of evil angels hovering darkly over some seedy hillbilly paradise. He planted bad seeds and moved off to let them germinate until they brought forth strange blossoms. And when his fearful sideshow moved to the next circuit stop to dispense dire Gospel, the poolhall vigilantes left behind nurtured new rebellion and moved among the shadows in search of dark mischief.

And they found it, too.

The woods abounded with rumors of crosses burned and lean-to shanties peppered with buckshot in rural precincts, and of an occasional gang-bang turned in upon the reluctant person of some dusky miss who happened along lonely back roads at, for her, an inopportune moment. The warm nights hosted chill echoes of shrill blasphemies preached against the state by hooded priests gathered for unholy communions under the whispering pines; and the pig-eyed sheriffs and their deputies got to making free use of blackjacks and nightsticks in nocturnal chats with bootblacks suddenly jerked in for ancient crimes of pimpery and bootleggery. Which sins had been winked at before, God knows, so long as the right palms got crossed. Some of the old hand-lettered signs came back, wedged in the ground on the edges of dusty crossroad hamlets, and the message was direct and to the point: *Nigger, this is White Man's country. Don't let the sun set on your head.*

So by this time the pattern of the tugging match was clear. Cullie Blanton was locked in a dogfall, and it was the kind of contest where nobody was going to be particular about gouging thumbs or elbows in the groin. We were in political limbo, beset by haunting uncertainties, fair game for disaster. There had to be troublesome detours ahead down the highway, and attacks from ambush coming.

Which meant we would have to take up the cross. Go on the road like gypsy princes. Traverse long miles in the shank of night when aching muscles cried for feather mattresses, hear the catcalls from the crowd and partake of all the insane, grinning, savage joy of political gut-fighting. Follow all the prescribed mad rituals and patented whoopla: parades and placards and twitching drum majorettes and seventy-six trombones come marching by, and endless sojourns into towns so dead the only amusement open was a stool at the corner drugstore to hear the limitless wisdom of a freshman just home from college. All the boring colloquies from local prophets who would tediously bend the sore ear of the Governor and all in his party. The torchlight rallies and pie suppers and fish frys. All the cheeky smiling and keester kissing, and bootlicking that went with the trade. The bug-infested hotel beds and countless dinners of rubberized chicken and lumpy mashed potatoes with peas reposing bilge-green and cold in little paper cups on the side. Charge and counter-charge. Bluff and blisters, rage and tears, con men and fakirs. Bargains suspect enough to make the doublecross seem singular, and deals shadier than a forest full of oaks.

Jockeying for position on the crowded streets, squinting into the afternoon sun, whipping the convertible in and out of traffic in competition for road space, I thought of the great similarity between political campaigns and war: the marshaling of troops, the sounding of bugles, the tedious logistics and crammed command posts, the strategy sessions, and all the mean sniping. The casualties and the fear of loss.

A stop light caused me to stand the convertible on end, and broke up the little reverie. "A scramble and a rat race," I boomed in mockery of Cullie Blanton. "Yessir, by the great pale ghost . . . a hissin' and a horror . . . a bed of coals and a crown of thorns . . . ah weep foah mah people."

Groaning an honest groan for the future, I caught an old farm couple regarding me with suspicion and mounting fear from a pickup truck of ancient vintage in the adjoining lane. I winked and leered at the washed-out old woman, who tugged at her husband's elbow and wildly reported the offense. The old boy struggled with his sense ot outraged honor as against concrete trepidations, and before he could resolve the conflict I revved up the motor and cut in front of them at that exact instant when the light gave permission to proceed. Hell yes, my conduct was juvenile. But worse would happen in the days ahead, and it would happen to me. For folks like the old couple banging along behind me in the pickup truck, anxious over heavy traffic and city morals, would be courted to the nosewales and could do no wrong come time to hit the road. So I had to get my feeble licks in when and where I could.

I was asleep when the telephone rang. Almost in a state of hibernation, brought on by an acute shortage of bed rest complicated by three giant water glasses brimful of Jack Daniels. So I got off to a flat-footed start in the comprehending department. Somebody was talking to me.

"Jim," the voice was saying when I finally began to sort out words from the sound. "Jim, are you all right?"

"Fine. Just . . . fine."

"Are you drunk?"

"Oh, no. No. Not drunk. Was asleep."

"Did you hear what I said? Earlier, I mean?"

"Hum? Oh. Ah. . . ."

"You didn't hear a word," Roxie said in some exasperation.

". . . I've left Pete."

That woke me up. So she had left Pete. Well, it wasn't the first time. Nor was it her maiden voyage in heralding such tidings to your present hero. I sat and pulled on a cigarette, trying to judge how I felt about the lady of my affection having left Pete.

Roxie's husband, Pete Winston by name, had once been big in show biz. He was through and knew it. And knowing it, he hung around the bandstand where Roxie did her turn, as if hoping that some night the M.C. might come down with laryngitis, and he could vault to the rescue. Roxie was understandably less than enthusiastic about our trio joining hands in a friendship circle at The Sailfish. Maybe I knew (and maybe she knew, too, somewhere in that dark Pandora's box of guilt that is the subconscious), that at some sweet time and at some gay place we would make it.

So I had kept on pursuing. I telephoned repeatedly and wrote silly notes and dispatched flowers. I anted up trinkets and frilly doodads and petitions of unconditional surrender. All of which got me the sum total of three dinner dates, and two cagey handshakes at her doorstep, plus one little lip-brushing thing that to some callow sophomore might have qualified as a kiss.

So that was the background one night when the moon was high on its own beauty and I stumbled into The Sailfish to dwell among the paying saps while the management made a fuss over the Governor's personal aide, and Roxie gave out her last brace of songs for the evening. Fates are said to be fickle, and gods snap men like matchsticks, and just to prove it I can chronicle right here that Roxie and Pete had just come off a breach in domestic tranquility which had left them both stirred up and full of malicious fluids. Perhaps that's why, after her final stint on the bandstand, she came over to my table for a tête-à-tête. Maybe she was digging at Pete. Perhaps she was truly lonely. Whatever the reason, she left with me.

Even so, nothing happened. We merely drank the dawn in, telling our life stories—with, no doubt, some selective editing on each side— and listened to my car radio throb ballads and love songs. Only I got further exposed to whatever contagious germ she carried and broke out in a record case of the malady. I had it bad, and it got worse. Soon there were other nights and other happenings, and among them sweet joys that no callow sophomore knows about.

And after that promising beginning she reunited with Pete. Up to a point. There's no use to stall about the way it was, or try to gloss over it. The plain-vanilla fact is that Pete Winston and I got to engaging in a sort of personal mathematics, in that we divided Roxie's favors.

So I sat and thought about all that, and dwelled on how I felt about her leaving him again. And wasn't sure. How do you judge a splendid misery? What's the balancing point between pleasure and pain? Is the fragrance of the rose worth the sting of the thorn?

After a long silence, Roxie's voice brought me back from the land of ether dreams.

"Don't you have anything to say about it?"

"I guess so. But I'm trying to think what. 'Congratulations' doesn't sound exactly proper. 'I hope you'll be very happy' is a little trite. And I can't honestly go on about how I'm sorry. I'm not. I think," I said slowly, "a decision is beginning to form. And I think I'm beginning to like the idea. Why don't you come over here? I bet you would find me of right friendly persuasion."

"Will you be good to me?"

"Yessum."

"Real good?"

"Very good. The best, is all."

"Promise?"

"Anything. Only you had better get on over here before we get any older. I'm past my prime as it is."

"Give me a half," she said. "I'll be there in a half."

"Come on," I said, "before it gets cold."

"You're good for me," she said. "You really are."

"I've been trying to tell you. Hurry on over."

"Jim. Jim, I think I may love you a little."

What do you say when somebody gives you the world?

Later on, as they say in the books, she said I had been good to her. Very, very good, indeed.

She lay beside me, curved and soft and warm, the heat of it gone now, the great need fulfilled. The thin sheet over her breasts lifted with the rise and fall of deep breathing, the rhythm constant, her features in easy repose as if she had come to some pleasant accommodation of all inner conflicts.

Roxie could do that. She could swap all the passions, cry and tremble and feel the earth move, then sigh one vast explosion of contentment and slip away to slumber, in peaceful truce with turmoil. And I would stay rigid beside her, shaken to the taproots, chain smoking, and fumbling with the enigma.

Did the Pyramids still stand?

A man—I thought—a mere man, possessed of face moles and cavities and all the ancestral fears, had no business sliding around in the hip boots of God. He should be content to stumble along barefoot on the sands, making small tracks, walking in the low places. But someone or something would come along to loom over his world like a mighty mountain, and he would try to climb it, to scale its peak, to conquer it in hip boots.

So I dwelled in frightful shadows on the outer fringe of sunshine, while Roxie sweetly slept with one soft hand lightly at home on my chest, fearful of the future even as her touch begat immediate promise and hope. Goddammit, why wasn't the present moment enough? Moments after we had been as close as Creation, why did my nagging hounds of worry bark unease?

The unvarnished hell of it was (and maybe the perverted truth and the mystic charm of it was) that I never knew when it would be my turn to collect bounty from her riches. I didn't know from one soul kiss to the next whether I would be hand-fondled on the neck hairs and called sweet names in the velvet cushion of night, or turned away from the warm door of promise like a peddler of some inferior face powder. Well, maybe Pete didn't, either. Maybe we were brothers under the sheets. And *he* had a certificate over which, in the long ago, some priestly being had mumbled holy decrees against any man putting asunder. But the mumbled decree had been offered up long ago, so long ago the ink had faded from the certificate, and the union sanctioned by the paper with all the fancy scrolls and the flowing signature on it had come slightly apart at the seams.

I don't profess to know the whole of their troubles, for as you might surmise I got exposed largely to Roxie's view of the puzzle. I had heard how Pete Winston in his youth had been the white hope of the nightclub comics and had been right up there elbowing for attention with the best of them. Oh, he had never rivaled Skelton or Berle, but he'd made the Sullivan Show a couple of times, and for a bit—before he discovered Roberta Peters—Walter Winchell had been enamored of his wit. For a while his world was full of puffed promise. Only it got deflated. It went stale, all that good promise, because Pete fell in love. And what he fell in love with did not come wrapped in skirts and ribbons, but came in small, powdery packages that sold for prices higher than a cat's back, and the needle did not come with it free, nor the eyedropper. Yeah, Pete was sniffing something, and it wasn't honest snuff. He was riding a wild horse named heroin.

Roxie had married him when all that promise was glowing, and, no doubt, their mutual *I do's* had a sincere ring when uttered. It wasn't long, though, until the magic fled. And after a while he lost his good bookings. Then he lost even the one-nighters, doing blue jokes for the Heavy Equipment Salesmen convened in flea-bag hotel ballrooms at uncharted villages, and next he lost his personal balance to the extent he got sent off for the first time to take the cure. There was, in accord with the curse, a second time and a few times after that.

And if Roxie didn't show the patience of Job when that worthy was most severely tried by an experimenting Lord, she came within a gnat's eye. Whatever she might have done later, she can't be faulted for the way she stuck with him through that private purgatory some men seemed destined to wreak on themselves. She held Pete when he had the quaking rigors and she fed him soup, and she mopped up what resulted when he couldn't keep it down. She went to him in the lonely terror of night while he screamed at weird hallucinations. She spent her Sundays looking at him through meshed wire, encouraging him, telling him lies when the truth wouldn't help him. He would get out, only to start the cycle again. And one day when they hauled him back to that gray place where they parcel out the cures, Roxie came to the end of her rope. She packed her things, and she cut out.

She tried a cure of her own. Repeated doses. But the balm was merely soothing at the moment. The particular cure didn't take on her, any better than Pete's had on him. Periodically Pete settled down to fight the good fight. He started to regain some of what he had lost. Not all, because all that ripping around had strained the basic fabric. He got back some of his bookings. He even got some of Roxie back.

But, like I said, not all.

I didn't have her all, either. Or, more accurately, some days I seemed to have everything a man can wish from sweet woman in this earth-bound life, and on other days I was pure pauper. So I knew only to expect the unexpected. One night I would be entwined in warm arms, sweet breath fluttering in my ears, riding the crest of the ninth wave, seeing the blinding flashes like it is when that fortunate blend of chemistry and sensual appreciation and timing all conspire to make love the greatest boon to mankind since somebody stumbled from a cave and came up with the first coal of fire. We wallowed in a terrestrial paradise, and if you don't think it can happen like that then I feel very sorry for you.

For it would be like this.

It would be Roxie, warm and God-close, the world shut out of the scheme while our little universe ticked its own time, with all the little gasps and shudders and whispers dropped in the right places. It would be too much to miss and too big to share. And later, in that warm afterglow, Roxie saying in a soft sigh, "My lover. My one and only lover."

Which, I could not help thinking through the mist of bliss, was a slight exaggeration. Because, otherwise, what did that make Pete? And the others, from whom she had sought her cure? It was just one of those things you try not to think about. Like funerals in childhood.

But dammit, you can't stone truth from the streets. So I would think of the dark blot even as we traded tender touches on the pale edge of dawn. It would be there to rankle even as we shuddered our shared ecstasy, whispering, "Let's do this forever." It would rub raw against the heart even as she gasped, and said, "It's only heaven." And gave careless tongue to the intimate words of love. Oh, the honeysap would always rise. The honeysap would rise and give the grip of robust thrills, but it would bring some mingled joyful sorrow. Because there was always the other thing. Like the haunts of children, it was more terrible in its own special hours. But it was always there.

All our time together wasn't spent in the hay. Hell, anybody can work up a pretty good case of the hots on a regular basis just by depending on biology and giving free rein to inhibitions. But there was more to it than that with Roxie. In flashes and spurts during her periodic shuckings of Pete we shared a lot of discoveries. We took midnight strolls in the rain and found a cozy little offbeat Italian restaurant where the pizza was crazy and there was wine to match. We brought in the dawn digging the sounds of Lester Young, Count Basie, Louie Armstrong: The Pres, The Count, and The King. We became addicted to a theater specializing in works of the old master comics: Chaplin, Keaton, Laurel and Hardy, the Keystone Cops. We drove to the coast and gave lazy hours on sandy beaches to soaking up sun and feeling the warm wash of salt water. We developed our own private language, our own little inside jokes. We laughed a lot together, and it was good.

But about the time I would begin to think it couldn't get any better and would start to push the dark forms of old, retroactive jealousies aside, it would go sour. For maybe five minutes after we had threshed our runaway passions to a slow walk, she would lie in bed coolly eying the ceiling, smoking a cigarette in those sudden birdlike puffs of motion while the surging fever in her blood calmed down to norm, and she would say with shattering directness, "Jim, don't ever believe anything I tell you for more than two hours. It's easy to get carried away." And maybe a day later she would say with the cold mien of a hair-curlered housewife turning away the Fuller brush man, "I don't need this. I don't want this kind of hang-up with you."

Once, after I had not seen her for weeks, she sat on my bed pulling on her stockings and preparing to leave my apartment. Her twin gold-enrods of sensuality stretched out alternately while silk was pulled over spots my lips had so recently explored, and she said with a remote aloofness chilling to the blood, "Thanks, Sport. I guess I was a little overdue."

I lashed out. Wanting, I suppose, to give her reciprocal bruises. "Goddammit," I said. And my voice quivered. "Goddammit, if that's all it means, why don't you just pick up some horny bastard in a bar?"

"It's neater this way," she said, evenly.

"Listen, doesn't it mean anything that I *love* you?"

"Love!" she said. "How can you people offer your love and take it back so easily?"

"Speak in the singular," I said. "I haven't played Indian giver."

"Not yet. The time hasn't come. But it will. It always does."

"What have I got to gain," I demanded, "by playing funny games with you? Is it so goddamn impossible to believe a man can fall in love?"

"No," she said. "But after a while it's difficult to believe they can *stay* in love. And I have the scars to prove it."

"If you want to compare scars from this little relationship," I said, "I'll show you ten to one. All right, so somebody gave you a rough time. What's that got to do with me?"

"Not just one somebody," she said, stepping into her skirt and tugging at the zipper. "Several somebodies. Pete, first. Pete, who I married when I was green as a gourd and"—she twisted her lips in a bitter smile, putting a little something extra into her battle with the skirt fixtures—"hot as a popgun. And thought I knew it all. Thought we had the greatest love together since the commodity had been discovered. Thought we had invented it." She finished with the skirt and began hooking her bra. "Except," she said in a flat voice, "after a while I found Pete didn't look at it that way. He played around."

"Hell," I said. "He played around. Most men do."

"But their women," she said with sparks in her eyes, "are supposed to wait home with their hands folded."

"The rules seem a little one way."

"Well, I'm no goddamn Madonna. I happen to dig sex, and if that makes me some kind of freak, then I'm sorry. But it took me a long time to admit that. I thought I had to be in *love*, so it would be respectable. So I conveniently fell in love a few times."

"You don't have to say all this. It doesn't make any difference with me."

"A few years ago," she said, ignoring my noble lie, "there was this businessman who fell in love with me. He flipped. Couldn't-live-without-me bit. Butter-wouldn't-melt, and so forth. Well, it got to me. Pete was in one of those very bad times . . . driving me out of my head. I *needed* somebody. I was tired. I needed somebody to look after me. I'd had my fill of being the strong girl. Of having to pick my husband up and brush him off and pay the bills. Even if Pete was the sweetest, best guy in the world when . . . well, when he didn't have his troubles." She moved to a wall mirror, running a comb through rich, dark brown hair. "Then after a while," she said, "Pete couldn't play around any more. He lost his stroke. He became . . . impotent." She sought my eyes in the mirror. I reclined on the bed, smoking. Letting her cough up what choked her.

"So I started meeting this fellow. I met him everywhere. Atlantic City. The Kentucky Derby. Washington. New York. We even took a cruise to the Caribbean together. And all I heard was the same old record: 'I love you, I love you, I love you.' Like the needle had stuck. After a while I made a decision. To give up Pete, because I just couldn't *take it* any more. I talked myself into loving this man. And I think I really did. So I told him I loved him. But I wanted to be honest. I wanted him to come in with his eyes wide open. And that's when I told him about the others. Everything. You know what happened?"

"He went around the world in eighty days," I said. "In a balloon. He fell out over the Virgin Islands and the natives crowned him King of Celibate Ways, and he lived to a ripe age in chastity. Goddammit, how do *I* know what happened?"

"It ought to be obvious to you. He had second thoughts about his unmatched love. He wrote me a twenty-four-word note saying he was going back to his wife and kids. They always do in the end." She pulled the comb through her hair with a vicious jerk. "Two years," she said. "Two years, and I got a twenty-four-word note. A word a month."

"Come here," I said.

She obediently turned and came to the edge of the bed, the comb jumping nervously in her right hand. She stayed just out of reach.

"In case you haven't noticed," I said, "I'm not carrying that fellow's burdens. I'm not playing Mickey Mouse games, and if you'll just say the word I'm here for the long haul. I want it all. Home and hearthside and crabgrass. Only I just want it with you."

"Yeah," she said. "You want it so much you suggest I pick up men in bars."

"Dammit—"

"My former gentleman," she said, "came to a club where I was singing. That's how I met him. So I guess you might say when it comes to picking up men in bars, I'm already an old China hand."

"Roxie. . . ."

"Forget it," she said in a flat, defeated voice. "On the record I'm flattered by your proposal of marriage. If that's what it was. So your obligation's over. You don't owe me a dime. Just relax and bang around with Lulu and—"

I reached for her. She fought like the proverbial wildcat. She was all teeth and elbows and snarls. I heard the skirt rip, and one of the stockings go, and she clipped me a good one under the chin. But after a while she moaned and began to use her energies in more satisfactory ways. "Goddamn you," she panted. "Goddamn you. . . ." Soon she was the aggressor.

And I dug it. It turned me on. We were setting a record for enjoying high pleasures, and we got to doing nip-ups of the type Grandmaw is professed not to have known about. We moved away from plain vanilla and got to doing the biological equivalent of Howard Johnson's ice cream, so to speak. You know, twenty-seven wonderful varieties. If you have ever found yourself in that kind of circumstance, you know how a high-spirited boy can get his enthusiasm waxed. Which I did, breathing to her when we came to brief pause, "Did anybody ever do that particular kind of love thing for you before, Miz Lady?"

"Yes," she said. "And it was not my businessman friend."

"Well," I said, "ask a silly question. . . ."

"Lots of times," she said, making herself unnecessarily clear, her voice harsh and grating. "He did it for me lots of times."

"Goddamn you," I said. And started, under the spur of her goading, to top the previous act. I suggested another type of mattress high jinks, only I did it by action and not words. And thought I had the show stopped. So after some pleasurable time had flitted by, after we had climbed the hills and descended into the valleys, I caught my breath and said, "And who did *that* for you?"

She named the fellow.

I looked at her. A long and level study. She held the gaze, unafraid, unblinking.

"Aren't you going to call me a bitch?"

"No," I said. "I had hoped to be a little more original."

"I might not feel quite so much like one if you would," she said. Then: "I'm not ashamed, Jim. Right now I'm . . . well, I regret it. I don't think I'd do it again. But I'm not ashamed."

"You don't have to be," I said.

I jumped from our place of recent splendors and prowled the room, cracking knuckles and grinding teeth. I had a little speech to make and it needed to come out right. Hell, it *had* to come out right. After a while, I said, "Maybe this satisfies some masochistic need, I don't know. Maybe *I'm* some special kind of freak. But if a woman means anything more to me than a passing stranger on a train . . . well, I want to know all about her. Every little detail. Whether as a little girl she played dolls or climbed trees. What she likes for breakfast. Her favorite books. Where she was on days of special significance to me, and what she was doing. And"—I said after a delayed count—"with whom."

"All right," she said. As if maybe I had asked for the next waltz. "All right. Bring me a cigarette."

With her head on my chest, moving now and again to draw on the smoke, she told me. Yeah, she told me to the very last in number. Names, dates, and places, sparing not even the clinical details in a brutal, compulsive honesty that must have acted as a strange cathartic. She spoke as if reciting very commonplace facts about some absent third person, baring the bones of her soul. When she had it all out, she slept.

"The bastards," the Governor said in a gutty rumble. He belched his breakfast cantaloupe, twisting his lips in distaste, and squinted through his reading glasses at the newspaper. The newspaper made crinkling sounds as Cullie Blanton manipulated it to avoid the taxpayers' coffee cup resting on the marble-topped table. "So they finally found 'em a third man," he said. "Less'n forty-eight hours before the filin' deadline, too. The bastards."

"More like an eighth or ninth man," I said. "Already about six others in it besides you and the general. Before Poppa Posey stuck his hand in."

The Governor peeped over the rim of his spectacles. "Hell," he said, "wasn't any third man among those other six nobodies. Pig farmers and used-car salesmen and an eye doctor. And some nutty schoolteacher gonna make the world over without usin' clay. They couldn't of put us in a run-off using them. Why, those pirates wouldn't get as many votes as the Elder Zion seekin' office against Nasser."

"Poppa Posey's likely to get some. He always has."

"Tell me somethin' I don't know by heart," the Governor grumbled. He held the paper in one hand, moving it away from the big bulk encased in green silk pajamas, shaking it lightly for emphasis. "How come you didn't tell me about this?"

"A man can't tell what he doesn't know."

"Hell of a note," the Governor groused. "I got more paid spies than that goddamn C.I. and A. outfit up there in Washington. I spend a fortune in wiretaps and allegedly got a boatload of stool pigeons in ever' county just tremblin' to tattle on folks. And *still* don't know what's goin' on in mah home precincts." He poured coffee from the cup into the saucer, blew three mighty puffs, and gulped it down. Caught in the act, he grinned sheepishly. "Emily Post don't like it," he said, "and my good wife didn't either, God rest her soul. But goddamn and hell. Coffee just *tastes* better saucered and blowed!"

"How much money you reckon changed hands?" I asked him.

Cullie Blanton pursed his lips and pulled on his nose as aids to the thought processes. "Enough," he said after a bit. "Poppa Posey don't work cheap. He probably held a gun on 'em."

Now if you happen to be a bit backward about the finer subtleties of

claybog politics, you might wonder about the omnipresent "theys" the
Governor and I bandied about that morning on his sun porch. You
might also wonder about the reference to the third man, and who
Poppa Posey was, and why the "theys" had laid on him gold. And for
what dark purpose.

The "theys" included the wire pullers and king makers and fat cats
palpitating to cremate Cullie Blanton in the public furnace, who had
lined up behind Bayonet Bill Wooster as the most available instrument of their desires. The third-man was a stalking-horse candidate.
One who could whittle and chop on the front runner in the race
(which Cullie Blanton obviously was when the perfidy was plotted)
and who could attract enough votes to fall short of victory, but still
throw the thing into a run-off. Where anything can happen.

Anything can happen in a run-off election for a lot of reasons. The
first of which is that the folks are wearied of politics after six months of
mud slinging and verbal jousting and hoo-haw, and so thirty days later
when the run-off comes around they may be more disinclined to trouble themselves at the polls. And the second of which is that most of the
local races are decided at the grass roots in the first primary, when
everybody and his dog turns out to exercise the franchise because
Uncle Charlie, who is averse by nature to working for a living and
much prefers to strike poses in the mufti of high officialdom, is hell-bent
on being High Sheriff, and Cousin Alfred (who maybe is a cripple or
has a glass eye) is taken with the thought of parlaying public sympathy
for the afflicted into something better than he has ever known, and
therefore is trying to make it as Justice of the Peace. When the respective fates of Uncle Charlie and Cousin Alfred have been resolved for
good or ill, it seems a little irksome to trek into voting stations again
just to place a common X by the name of some remote god who holds
sway in distant temples as far removed as the Governor's Mansion.

So with a smaller turnout a man like Cullie Blanton, who has drawn
his base strength from the masses given to voting for kinfolks and
neighbors, suddenly becomes more vulnerable. Especially if the third
man and the more minor candidates, who picked up isolated votes here
and there for assorted reasons, unite against him. Which they will do if
the price is right, and somebody usually makes sure it is.

That takes care of the mechanics. Poppa Posey was the most perfect
third man in the world, that's all. For Poppa Posey was once a front
runner of the first water. Poppa Posey was, in fact, governor of the
state for a couple of terms long before Cullie Blanton came to the

public favor. He talked of slaking the common folks' thirst, but never got around to carrying any water for them. Even so, he missed being a United States Senator only by the margin of God's will, which turned out to be less than five thousand votes, when the heavens opened up on Election Day to flood the back roads over which the Posey lovers had to negotiate their way to polling places.

Poppa never got over the celestial trick. He never became reconciled to the notion that God had a legitimate political interest in our state. So Poppa had withdrawn to a cabin high in his native hills, to shake his fist at enemies on high, and to raise hound dogs. Now and again, though, if the price should be right, Poppa would slip down out of the hills to cry his ancient nostrums in election years.

Enough time had passed so that Poppa couldn't have legged himself into major office even if Deity had switched sides, but he still had a dedicated following of old-timers and ignoramuses in the swamps and hills who would back him against Matthew, Mark, Luke, and John. And without inquiring into the party affiliations of the latter four saints. So Poppa was in a good position to do commerce.

"Bound to hurt us," the Governor said from a pall of gloom. "Me and Poppa, we root in the same wallows. We're after the same slop."

"Damn him," I said. "He's got one foot in the grave and lives like a miser up there in the hills. He got his pockets lined when he was governor. He won't spend thirty cents a week, and he's bound to die rich. He didn't have any reason to get in this race."

"Boy," the Governor said, "some folks collect stamps and some folks collect frozen butterflies. Poppa Posey collects money. It is just in his craw." He had another go at the coffee. Then he folded his eyeglasses and dropped them in his pajama-top pocket, taking it slow and easy. When he had performed the ritual he said, "That's why we're gonna offer him bounty, too. We're gonna buy the old buzzard. Or try."

"It looks to me," I said with a nod toward the newspaper now folded by the Governor's cup, "that he's already been bought."

"Nope. He's just rented hisself out, probably. We might be able to persuade Poppa we can give him a better lease for his talents. You'll be leaving in about an hour to take him his contract. Or less, if you get high behind. They'll print the goddamn ballot in just three days, and I don't want Poppa's name on it."

"Me?" I asked. "Why me?"

"Boy," the Governor said, fixing me with the All-Seeing eye. "There's a burr under your saddle. What is it?"

"No burr," I said. "I reckon I'm just not in the mood for a payoff today."

"*Get* in the mood," the Governor ordered flatly. He gazed at me through the curling smoke. "Two things a man can't hide," he said. "A twitch to seek high office and a twitch for some particular woman. And I don't recall seein' you make announcement for public post."

I didn't have any answer for that one. The All-Seeing orb hadn't lost its vision. "She'll be here when you get back," the Governor said confidently.

I sighed. "You sure have a way of making it sound simple."

"Starts out simple," the Governor said. "Like everything else in life. Only man is so simple he has to complex things all up. You take man out of life, and you have removed all the complexities." Divested of the philosophy, Cullie Blanton sat back serenely in his chair. I waited for instructions about how to handle Poppa Posey. When the information wasn't forthcoming, I said, "How much do I offer Poppa?"

"Dicker with him," the Governor said. "Start low and keep goin' until his eyes get greedy and start to glitter. Then stop right there."

"That all the advice you got?"

"No," Cullie Blanton said. And looked at the invisible something that always seemed to attract his attention. "No, there's one more thing. Don't let that ole sumbitch get you in a blackjack game, for he will sprout aces out of his ears."

That morning when I had come slowly awake, groping for her warmth, there was only the emptiness beside me. The emptiness of where she had been. There was a note on the pillow, written in lipstick, the paper pinned to the pillowcase with a safety pin. *I shall return. Rox.* Three red X's signified a like number of kisses.

After leaving the Governor, I returned to my apartment to throw a few things in an overnight bag, and crawled into the nearest thing I could approximate to a mountaineer's uniform: a faded old checked sports shirt, khaki trousers, my most decrepit pair of brown shoes, appropriately scuffed. I would go to Poppa Posey dressed for the part.

I wrote a note to Roxie, scooped up Poontang under one arm, and made it to the lobby. There I left the note and a dollar bill with the switchboard girl, along with instructions the note should be sent by cab to Roxie's address. What the note said was: *General MacArthur. HST was crazy to fire you. Gone to make black magic for Cullie. I*

*have thought of a new way to make beautiful music. Looking forward
to the duet. Love and stuff. Jimbo.*

Poontang deposited at Happyland Animal Home, I stopped at a
service station and, while an obese attendant with grossly dirty fingernails gave my car a reluctant lick and a promise, I stepped into a pay
telephone booth to worry the Governor with a couple of final questions. When I returned to the car, the attendant was giving the hard-
eye to the Blanton-for-Governor sticker gleaming from the bumper.

"I reckon," I boomed with fraternal cheer, "you're gonna vote for
Governor Blanton, too." And favored the fat fellow with my simpleton
grin.

"Hell," he said with a sneer, while his dirty fingernails poked in the
change belt to bring equality to our transaction. "Hell, them politicians is just like brands of beer. They all claim to be the best, but your
piss don't look no different after you make your choice."

"Well," I said, "all's not gold that glitters."

I started the motor and eased into the street. With luck, I could be
jawing with Poppa by suppertime.

THE SUN had two hours of life left before it would expire behind sharp razorback ridges when the convertible rounded a horseshoe curve and flushed out Red Hill, which was the name of the incorporated blight said to be nearest Poppa Posey's modest diggings in the woods.

Red Hill wasn't any more than I'd expected. It was a watch-fob town, tiny enough to put in your pocket, with a rusting water tower and about six blocks of crumbling sidewalk just short of grass bursting through its cracks. A miserly clutter of violated buildings cringed at the base of a hill that wasn't red at all, but blazed greenly with the full dress of summer.

I pulled into the lone service station, parking under a flaking portico, waiting respectfully while the grizzled old bandit inside peered through flyspecked plate glass trying to determine if my trade would be worth the bother. While he judged the contest I looked over the town. Which consumed about forty seconds, for it was all laid out in front of my eyes and offered no distractions.

The old bandit hobbled out the door, sighing as if the Lord had sent me to test him. We traded howdys. Then we eyed each other in the manner of combatants in a cockfight, and after two or three centuries had whizzed by he reached a shrewd conclusion. Through a lip-bulge of snuff he said, "You wanten gas?" I ratified the suspicion. The old nester jake-legged it around the rear of my car, propelling his heft along by gusty sighs with each suffering step. Honest to Jesus, the gasoline was stored in an old hand pump. One of those antique types shaped like an inverted Coke bottle, or maybe more like a thick-stemmed lollipop, with a latticework of mesh wire ringing the crowning ball. The local citizen rocked with the motion of pumping. I got out to stretch muscles cramped by long miles, and he made a big show of ignoring my inspection.

I nodded toward the hand pump, my voice equating it with the Boer War. "Don't see those much any more," I said.

"Ever' day," he said. "I see this 'un ever' day."

The way I scored it, he took an early lead. I consulted my strategy and decided to try the direct approach.

"Hear tell," I said, scuffing the dirt with a practiced toe, "my good friend Poppa Posey lives in these parts."

"I speck you know what you talken about," the old man said. "You and him bein' such good fren's."

So the city slickers were down 2 to 0.

After some of the agony had passed, I made an offering of intelligence. "Look's like Poppa's running for governor."

"She-it," the old man said, splitting a syllable. "Poppa ain't even runnen for the county line. Poppa's just setten up there on his front porch counten his money. Hit's the dudes and big shots doen all the runnen 'round. Maken fools of they sefs. Poppa's setten and laffen and rocken."

"Just suppose," I said, "a man wanted to go running up there so he could be judged a fool, and give Poppa the chance to bust a gut laughing at him. How you reckon a dude like that would go about it?"

The local boy got sullen. He did not find favor with smart alecks who came tooling up in fancy cars and flashed their unstained teeth and made sport of the natives. The field of his face reddened under a crop of whisker stubble as he wound up the pumping, and he spoke in numbers. "Three sixty-fie," he said, quoting from the pump meter.

I stood my ground. The old man shuffled his brogans and shifted his snuff. "Three dollar sixty-fie," he repeated for clarity.

"How," I asked softly, "you reckon a man would go about it?"

"Hit ain't hard to find," ole whiskers said grudgingly. When I didn't make any moves toward my long green, he forfeited the match. "Go on down the slab," he said, "for nigh to nine mile. Snake off on that side the slab"—he gestured to the right, jerking a thumb—"where you come on a dirt road past a cross. Keep on goen on the dirt road for three winden mile."

"You mentioned a cross on the slab," I said.

He nodded confirmation. "Jesus cross. Put up by the Campbellites." When I didn't react, he added, "They putten 'em everwhurs. Wanten folks to git saved. Plagen the land with 'em."

I nodded pleasantly, jingling coins. The old man hated me out of his pig eyes, wondering how many words I would demand in exchange for three sixty-fie rightfully his.

"Up the slab for nine mile. Snake off and three winden mile." And when the repeated instructions didn't part a fool from his money, old whiskers came to terms of unconditional surrender. He made a vague gesture toward the Blanton-for-Governor sticker on my rear bumper. "Hit's no worry," he said. "Poppa cain't git hit. Too ole and wore out. He's jes maken money."

"Well," I said, "that's the American way." The old man averted his pig eyes and shifted snuff. And all at once I felt a revulsion for the bully boy I had become. Goddammit, what made a man grow hateful? What kind of profit could be shown by baiting an old nester whose feet hurt and who only wanted night to advance so he could get home to empty his bladder and put his head on a pillow?

I handed over a five-dollar bill. "Keep the change," I mumbled. And now it was me doing the eye shifting.

The old man snatched the bill and hobbled inside to his cane-bottomed chair, stiff-necked and trembling, choked on his legacy of inherited hate for the suspect stranger who was of different breed. And that little financial apology I had tossed in wouldn't change what burned darkly in him. He wasn't going to sell me any soothing salve to smear on my conscience. Nosir, not for a little old piddling dollar thirty-fie.

On up the slab, the old man had said. *Fer nigh on to nine mile.* The hills were sprouting taller now, on the verge of blossoming into a harvest of mountains, rising on each side. The countryside looked all soft and green and gentle. But it was wild and mean, hiding its traps behind a curtain of green.

Out there in the woods and on the razorback ridges and in the tangled convolutions of grass and bramble bushes lurked a peck of trouble for the tenderfoot. Black bears and coyotes and javelina hogs so mean they scared rattlesnakes. The sun would drill through foliage to parboil the brain, and moss-infested streams pollute you with typhoid fever, while strange serpents slithered through stands of poison ivy. The woods were plain bad-natured. It was not a great place to take the kiddos, unless you didn't want the little darlings to come back.

Up ahead was the Jesus cross. Fifteen feet high and cut from crude lumber over which the aroused Campbellites had sloshed a coating of prayed-over whitewash, it told in blood-red letters how:

```
        S
        A
        V
        E
    J E S U S
        A
        V
        E
        S
```

I eased up on the throttle, and a couple of hundred yards past the paid commercial turned the convertible off the slab. The shock absorbers got a workout from the potholes and chugbogs in the uncharted path, and I marveled at how smart a governor Poppa Posey had been. Too smart to hand his opponent a burning issue of how he had used the tax dollars to pave himself a sweet road up three miles of jagged hillside. He would bounce up to his cabin on weekends in the finest automobile taxpayers could provide him for that day. With a chauffeur at the wheel and maybe a fine blonde at his side. Oh yes, surely a fine blonde by his side, for I had boned up on political history in my native state and the pertinent information had not come from textbooks. So Poppa would jostle along over the old dirt road with his kidneys recording the shocks, while his pockets bulged with booty from the state treasury and get credit, because of the punishment to his kidneys, for being an honest man.

Well, I had known I wasn't being sent to deal with any animal of common stripe when Cullie handed me the hunting permit. Which is why I had paused on the outskirts of Capitol City to telephone the Mansion and pop a couple of key questions to the game warden. The Governor had brought his grace to the telephone making smacking sounds. Eating, it turned out, apple-goddam-pie-and-ice-cream.

"Suppose," I had suggested, "Poppa won't play. Suppose I can't buy him."

"Suppose," Cullie Blanton said, "Hell ain't hot." He chewed pie, gulping. "Poppa Posey would go at public auction," he advised. "All you got to do is settle the price."

"Just in case," I hedged. "In case Poppa got took down with a dose of religion or sprouted new morals, what we got to threaten him with?"

The line hummed while I listened to the Governor eat apple-goddam-pie-and-ice-cream. "Boy," he said, "if you happened to be a light bulb you wouldn't throw enough shine to radiate a clothes closet.

How the billy-goat hell you gonna threaten a man who is eighty-one years old, and has seen it all and had some of it?"

"I hoped you'd know."

"I know everything worth knowin'," the Governor said with due modesty, "but you keep bringing things up would put a strain on the prophets. Hell, that old man is past all hope and carin'. He's got one foot in the grave and the other at the mortuary. He ain't likely to change in his last days."

"Unless," I said, "he gets second thoughts about his immortal soul."

"Poppa Posey's idea of how to untangle that snarl," Cullie Blanton said, "would be to offer Saint Peter a cut of the proceeds. You bring back what you're goin' after. For this thing has passed the point of spoof and games . . . you had your radio on?"

"No," I said. And got a sinking feeling in the gut.

"Our great senior Senator hauled off up there in Washington not an hour ago and declared a pronouncement. He laid heavy blessin's on that goddamn general."

"Muley Pool endorsed Wooster?"

"Precisely that," the Governor said. "Muley took the position I am a nigger lover without peer. In statesmanlike language of course."

"Jesus! What you doing about it?"

"Prayin' to my Savior," the Governor said blandly, "that Muley dies in his sleep. And startin' rumors he has left his wife and lost his mind."

I said, "You don't seem too shook up about it."

"Boy," the Governor said, "if it would undo the foul deed, I would run tremblin' and nekkid through Saint Patrick's Cathedral. But Muley is one those rare fellows I can't lay the deadwood on. He got to Washington without me, and I never could find a way to call him back."

"All this doesn't give me any new confidence about approaching Poppa. You know how close he's always been to Muley."

"As close," Cullie Blanton admitted, "as runaway niggers. But you got money in your pockets. Money has unraveled many a love match."

The hound dogs bayed like they'd got the scent of fox. And the fox was me. Poppa Posey had preserved the privacy of a fifty-yard stretch of rocks and jutting stumps and mudbogs fronting his shack by throwing up a barbed-wire fence. It wasn't enough fence to keep anybody out who might really be hell-bent on getting in. Just three sagging strands of rusty wire nailed by those old U-shaped metal staples to a few scattered cedar posts from which dead bark peeled and drooped without splendor. But it was enough fence to prevent the passage of automobiles. So I parked the convertible, gazing up the steep incline toward the cabin. There was Poppa, making immediate prophet of the old geezer who presided over the hand-operated gasoline pump down in Red Hill. Setten and rocken.

While I scuffed up the incline the hounds gave concert. They made wide circles, a few of the bolder ones leaping down the incline on direct course. There was a prickly feeling along my backbone, for personally my platform is very anti-dog, but I plodded on toward the shack. Poppa didn't lift voice or a finger to call off the dogs. A dozen yards from my goal one of the hounds stood his ground, baying as if he'd treed the biggest coon in the hollow. When I was within striking distance, heart pounding until it had the feel of jungle drums, I reached out to give the hound a fleeting pat on the head, mumbling the inanities men use when communicating with animals and children. The hound gave an uncertain yelp or two, then backed off meekly to accuse me with sad eyes of having exposed him as a fraud.

"Good way to draw back a nub," Poppa called from the porch. "Reachin' fer a strange dog."

"Naw," I said. "Naw, he didn't have nothing in his throat. If he was gonna bite me, he'd of growled some."

A grudging look of respect came into Poppa's eyes. *So he ain't all dude,* the look said. *So he knows somethin' about hound dogs.*

"He wouldn't of waited until I reached for him," I said. "He'd of come on the bounding jump and took me six paces back." Poppa waited, his face impassive. "He ain't the lead hound," I said. "The others didn't follow him. He was just showin' out some. Just barkin' for the record."

While Poppa visited me with his rheumy old orbs, I gave the long stare back to him. And I can't say the sight was inspirational. Poppa Posey's frame had shrunk. There wasn't any meat to speak of on his tall frame, and his neck wallowed in the collar of a sun-faded blue denim shirt. His legs stuck up like pipestems from a pair of sockless brogans, the little flash of flesh between the brogans and the bottoms of his khaki pants was as white as the underbelly of fish. The white flesh of the legs made a notable contrast with the burnt-orange hue of his face, lashed by the weather of eighty-one seasons. Time had been eating on the face. All the padded flesh was gone, just skin stretched

tight over bones, and the skin crinkling enough for dry parchment.
Above the face was a wild mop of dingy-yellow hair, tangled and uncombed. "You must of come a fer piece," the old man said, "to lecture
me about my houn' dogs."

"Far enough," I said, "to work up a thirst."

"Hep yourself." Poppa nodded toward a galvanized bucket swinging
from a wire, and the wire was looped around a support beam on the
porch roof. A hollowed gourd dipper rested on a wall peg. I took the
dipper from the peg, brought up water tasting of cistern depths, and
drank. Letting some of the water spill down my shirt front, I turned
windward, tugging the shirt in a series of rapid motions.

"Farm boy," Poppa judged flatly. "Or was, once."

"Yep," I said. "I've made it up the turnrow."

"Seen you take the fence," Poppa nodded. As if that settled something. As if that explained all inner workings of the universe. We
watched the hounds sniff and mill about the yard. "That fence,"
Poppa said with a gesture toward the barbed wire. "You oughta see
some of 'em try to take that fence. It affords vast amusement, and don't
cost me nothin'." He brought up a chortle, ending in a slight whinny.
"Some of 'em try to wiggle under it, and end up rippin' open they
fancy coats and maybe a slice of backbone. Or would, if they had backbones. Some try to ooch betwixt the top strand and that second one,
and would wind up deballed if I didn't crip down and set 'em free."
He laughed, viewing again the old scenes. "Coon-ass show. Them
jumpin' around with they balls hung up, and the houn's after 'em."

I grinned. So the old man wanted to talk. Hell, there was no pre-
mium on my time.

"You now," Poppa said, "you taken that fence like you owned it.
Grabbed them three strands and pressed 'em together, and give a little
hop. A little spring." He sat and thought about my fence-hopping
technique, nodding approval. After a moment he turned his head to
favor me with a direct look for the first time since I'd passed initial
inspection. "Where was it you made it up the turnrow?"

"Callahan County," I said.

"Good country," Poppa judged. "Raise cotton?"

"Cotton on purpose," I said. "And rattlesnakes and cockleburs and
Johnson grass by the mysterious will of God."

"I don't suppose," he said as he shifted his pipestem legs, "you come
up here to sell me a bale of that cotton you growed down there in Callahan County?"

"Naw," I said. "I'm plumb out the cotton business. Snake business, too."

The old man birthed a silent laugh. He said, "Yeah, I seen your hands. Soft and white as a girl's. Face a little peaked, too. And them clothes. You've lost the feel for them clothes. You'd feel better in one them button-down collars. With a tie swingin' and tappin' you on the belly button." He smiled at some private joke. "Callahan County," he said. "Carried it ever' time I run for office."

"Time was," I said, "when you carried near-about all the counties, Governor Posey."

He screwed his wasted body around in the rocking chair, running the old eyes up and down me. *"Governor Posey,"* he said. "Well, now. I reckon that's the tipoff. Some feller comes stumblin' up that rise and braves the houn' dogs and calls me Governor Posey, why he just naturally wants somethin'. What is it you want, son?"

"I want to talk politics," I said.

"Awright. Start talkin'."

Through the trees, down past my idle car and the barbed-wire strands, I could see the winding dirt road. The red-clay strip stood out starkly in the gilded profusion of trees all around. In the valley there was a carpet of wild grass greener than dye, and above the valley the razorback ridges. And above the ridges a sky blue enough to give a man the weeps. The late sun touched up the glint of rocks, melding orange gold on the blanket of restful green. Soon the sun would lock up for the day, and the land would be swallowed by shadows. *Beautiful,* I thought. *Beautiful beyond any crying of it.*

And I had an old man to bribe.

I sat on the board steps, resting my back against a roof-support pole, half facing the old man and half facing the landscape. A couple of the hounds sniffed at my feet. "Restful here," I sighed. "Peaceful. A man would hate to leave it. A man would lose something, going away."

Poppa's eyes rounded in innocence. "Why, son," he said. "Don't leave, then. Stay long as you like. Take supper."

"I meant you, Mister Posey."

"I ain't about to leave," he said flatly.

"Except that you're running for governor."

"Shit," he said, chortling. "I ain't runnin' for governor. I'm runnin' for money."

"Well," I said, "you putting it like that short-circuits a lot of jaw wagging. Let's me and you talk about money."

"You're Cullie's man," he said. It was a pure statement, none of the tenuousness of inquiry fouling its bloodline.

"I reckon I know him."

"Yeah, I would so surmise. Wondered how long it'd take ole Cullie. To get a man up here." Then: "Your mama give you a name?"

"Yessir," I said. And called it.

"Nice and mannerly," Poppa Posey said. "Calls an old man 'Mister' and says 'Yessir' like a garrison soldier. Knows a little bit about houn' dogs, and how to cool hissef off with cistern water and take a bob-wire fence. Ready to sit here and jaw until the moon's high, or jump right down in the dirt. Got patience or cheek, whichever it takes . . . looks like Cullie knowed his man."

"He makes it his business to know men," I said.

"Cullie tell you how to deal with me?"

"He said don't do any dealing," I said. "When it comes to cards. Seems like you got a way of sprouting aces."

The old man threw back his head and howled mirth at the sky. His pale eyes watered, and he gasped for breath. When he had it under control, he leaned toward me with his eyes full of mischief. "He tole you right," he said. "For I am the cheatinest old bastard with cards in my hand ever roamed the hills. You gimme a decka cards, and I will cheat you. Widder woman or lumberjack. It is pure scandalous." He rationed himself another chuckle. "What kinda price Cullie put on my honesty?"

"He left it flexible," I said. And then, "I don't suppose you're itching bad to say how big a bundle the Wooster bunch laid on you?"

"Piddlin' sum," he said, spitting a stream into the powdered dust of the yard. "Miserly amount. Shames a man to sell that cheap."

"Running for governor," I said, "that's hard work. And getting harder. Nowadays, you got to stew and sweat in the glare of all those television lights 'til you damn near go blind. You got to stand up before a bunch of reporters with smart mouths and answer fool questions. You got to plod up and down the streets and flush folks outta stores to squeeze their hands. Crowds don't turn out for speechifying any more. They've got television and air-conditioned cars and dollars to spend. You got to near bust a gut to get to the folks. A man doing all that hard work, he ought not work cheap."

The old man's voice crackled with dry irony. "Maybe," he said, "all us politicians ought to form us a labor union."

"A man don't have to run," I said. "A man could sit here and rock and count money. A man might rock here all summer, running his hands through dollar bills. Five thousand of 'em."

A look of genuine pain crossed the old man's face. "Son," he said, "you been raised too mannerly to insult your elders that-a-way. Your ole mama would be mortified."

"How much better you reckon Mama would feel," I inquired, "if I raised it to ten thousand?"

"It might perk your mama up. But it don't move me much."

"Twelve," I said. "And that's high dollar."

"No," the old man said. And did not prevaricate over the decision. He stared into space. "You a little late," he said. "Two year ago, a year mebbe, we could of done commerce at twelve. But not now." He turned to me, a strangely soft smile on his old lips. "How long you lived, son?" When I told him, he said, "I got purt' near a half-century on you. I wallow in the wisdom of years. So twelve won't do it. Nor fifteen. Not even twenty thousand the greenest bills you could pilfer from the tax box. That surprise you?"

"Some," I admitted.

"Then you better grab what you wanta preserve," he said, "for this next oughta stagger you. I have gone and got me some honest convictions in my old age." He laughed, and the laugh turned into a cough, and the cough grew so violent that veins hammered at the edge of the dingy-yellow hair, and the old face turned crimson. "Water," he said, making a fluttery motion toward the bucket.

When he had tilted the gourd dipper a few times, hawking his throat and clearing up troublesome juices, he leaned against the rocker and closed his eyes.

"This nigger business," he said. "Cullie won't do much about it."

"He'll do all he can. He'll be able to do as much as Wooster. And be less likely to let the state go to hell in a fast freight while doing it."

"No," Poppa disputed. "No. Oh, Cullie'll hoot and dance some for local consumption. He'll put on a show for the folks, and it will be a better show than you can find in most whisky-and-trombone towns. But it won't mean nothin'. He's too soft on the question."

"You got a strange notion of what's soft," I said, a trifle sharply. "The graveyards are full of bones Cullie snapped. More than anybody since Huey, I expect."

"Yeah," the old man nodded. "Cullie is a bone snapper. *If* you cross him when he's atter his way and has got a ghost of gettin' it. But Cullie has got some peculiar ideas about justice. He is fool enough to think folks got justice *comin'* to 'em. He is crazy enough to think God meant it that-a-way, when he could dispel the fool notion by lookin' around him at cripples and idiots and blind folks and fires in orphans' homes. Time was, ole Cullie toted water for the poor folks. Now it's the niggers. Cullie, he has a bad habit of bleedin' from the heart. He is a queer animal. He is half tiger and half pussycat." My host had more to say. It was in his manner. I waited.

Poppa opened his eyes. "Money, it ain't ever'thing. It is right close to it, but it ain't ever'thing. I was a long time gettin' to that notion, but now I am there and there I am stayin'. This old shack"—he turned in his rocker and looked the cabin over, as if maybe he had never had the opportunity to inspect it before—"it could be fancier than a New Orleans whore house. That roof could be sterlin' silver instead of rusty tin. Them floors could be covered with ten-dollar bills in place of pine boards, and I could have me a privy with gold-plate fixtures. Once, it was in my bones to do it. Yeah, I was goin' to have me a show place here would put the king's palace to shame. I couldn't do it when I was governor. For it wasn't good pollyticks. So I left it be, exceptin' I snuck in some indoor plumbin' and 'lectric lights. But I promised myself when I got free from public office, why I would fair build me a birdhouse here. But I ain't. You know why?"

"No," I said.

"Because," he said, "all at once I liked it this-a-way. With iron bedstids and tin on the roof that leaks some when it rains and pine boards wore smooth by walkin' feet. Because it was somethin' of the *old* days. It was somethin' hadn't changed. Somethin' I could count on stayin' the way I remembered it."

"No," I said. "It's changed. Even if you don't take notice of the changes. The sun beats down on it, and the rains lash it, and it changes. It decays by the hour. And one day it will fall down of its own internal stresses. One day it will be a heap of worm-eaten lumber and twisted tin, and the rats will come. Unless it is shored up in the weak places." Poppa Posey gazed across the valley at the ridges, lost in some private vision. "The same is true of man," I said, "and all his institutions."

"Too many changes," the old man mumbled. "The fools got bombs can blow the whole show up. Some bearded little barefooted demagogue can make hissef a revolution in the cane fields and the whole world trembles. Machines doin' work man was cut out to do, and man has got no choice but to set on his butt and wring his hands. There is way too much hocus-pocus. There is way too much change." He stood from the rocking chair, stuffed his hands in the back pockets of faded britches, and regarded the hounds. "You, Claudius," he called gently to one. "You foul-breathed sunnuvabitch. You ain't even good fer fish bait." Claudius wagged his tail and looked ecstatic. " *'Slanders, sir,'* " the old man roared. " *'For the satirical rogue says here that old men have gray beards, that their faces are wrinkled, their eyes purging thick amber and plum-tree gum, and that they have a plentiful lack of wit, together with most weak hams.'* " All his native accent had dropped away.

"Hamlet," I said.

"Hamlet," the old man agreed. "You spen' a lifetime," he said, "bein' taught how niggers are hewers of wood and drawers of water. Hell, even the Holy Scripture ratifies the teachin'. You git taught how they are like little children and got a natural sense of rhythm, and will screw a snake if somebody will hold its head, and how they had druther steal a watermelon than to set at the quick right hand of God. You look around you, and see 'em workin' in the canebrakes and cuttin' on one another with knives on Sattidy night and playin' the happy fool. And the old lessons seem most likely true." Poppa Posey raised his head and his eyes caught an angry glint from the fading sun. "Then you git ole," he said in a near-whisper. "You git ole, and all at once they change up the goddamn rules on you. They cry to you 'bout brotherhood and equality. Yeah, they tell you it is in the nature of niggers to quote Shakespeare and to marry up with blondes. And how it is our bounden duty to hep 'em do it. Well, I am just one those old men Hamlet spoke on. Yeah, my face is wrinkled and my eyes purge thick amber and plum-tree gum." He stooped, reaching from the porch, taking in one blue-veined hand a parcel of yard dirt, and he sifted it slowly through stiff fingers. "The earth," he said. "The earth will git you back. When you come my age it won't wait. The earth comes lookin' fer you. And no man ever drew air could satisfactorily hide." He stood, throwing the handful of dirt away, rejecting it in one sudden motion. "Well, I can't hide from it but I can be true to its order. I can leave the ole earth the same I found it. I don't have to spen' my last days tryin' to change it up."

"Don't you think Cullie feels some of what you say?"

"Not enough," he said. "Not *near* enough. So I made me a promise to mysef a week ago. I made me a promise to make one more race. To offer my tired bones up to the folks one more time. And it is a offerin' of sacrifice, for like Hamlet said of old men, I got 'a plentiful lack of wit, together with most weak hams.' Yeah, but wit enough and hams enough to stagger before the people and pull down the wool just one more time."

"You can't win," I said.

"Hell," he snorted, "you think I figger to win? You think I am in the goddamn race because I got it in my craw to hear the high cheers and ride my ass around in a big limousine agin? I had my fill of it. All of it. Creepin' Jesuses comin' in with they hands out and cryin' to me of sin. I have supped aplenty of bein' at the mercy of ever' sunnuvabitch has got the price of a postal stamp, and stirs off his ass ever' two years when he gets a twitch to play God, purgin' his hates by strikin' a line through some ambitious feller's name. And calls it Democracy, and feels pious about it. Listen"—he stabbed a finger at me, a quaking, righteous finger confident it pointed the way to truth—"listen, I mighta took a few things from the people wasn't exactly mine by contract. But the sunnuvabitches got no worse than fair swap. For ever' dime I took from them, they got two nickels and change from me. Yeah, they will sap you with their wants and demands, the people." He folded his arms and stuck his chin out. "Hell," he said, "I thought there was any danger of my winnin', I'd go in that shack and take down the ole .410. I'd put it against my chin and dispatch my brains to the ceilin'."

Poppa addressed the rocking chair carefully, as if determined not to spook it, easing himself down. He started a gentle rocking motion: rocking the anger out of his face, rocking in celebration of a serenity known only to the old and the doomed. "I fooled 'em," he grinned. And the grin was wicked in its victory. "Yeah," he said, flashing the wanton grin. "Yeah, I was edgin' up to runnin' as a matter of personal principle. About to turn honest in my ole age. To fight change. To help stop Cullie. Then they come up here bearin' they gifts and whisperin' they honeycomb lies in my ears with they jowls shakin' over the sport, and they eyes showin' mischief. So I taken the sunnuvabitches' money. And tried hard not to laugh in they faces. For it was a joke. And the joke was on them."

I stirred away from the support post.

"Well," I said, "you will pardon me for not busting anything loose laughing with you. I don't reckon Cullie will raise my pay any."

"Tough tiddy," the old man said. "Spen' less money." He paused. "A man," he said, "has got to learn to accommodate hissef to circumstance."

He left it there, rocking his great satisfaction, at peace with himself. An ancient Pharaoh, dim of eye, tired in the joints, waiting for the earth to find him. We were of different ages. Dammit, why should I want to lean across the abyss to touch his withered soul? And say, *It's all right, old man. It's all right.* Yet, I knew in the moment a strange kinship stirring in the blood. We would clutch and grab each other, sobbing sectional sorrows, bound together by romantic memories of Lee's Lost Cause and three-cent cotton, bemoaning carnage at Richmond and Shiloh, twitching the agony of some common loss. But the moment passed. Goddammit, he had got his and had spent it where the lights were bright, and sniffed his share of lilacs. Hell, why didn't I fold my tent and leave the old fool to the wicked worms that worked his mind?

Which I did. After long silence. When the old man's chest rose and fell, and his breath came steady and whistled through dry nostrils, I slipped off the porch and marched through neutral moonbeams down the slope.

"Get me the nigger," the Governor said.

He issued the order as casually as he might have instructed me to fetch his coat or slosh another three fingers of bourbon into his glass.

I suppose I stared at the Governor as if taking account of ghosts, for his eyes glittered a little and he set his jaw. "Goddammit," he growled, "I didn't ask you to make rain or hoot like a witch doctor. I tell you to bring me one mortal out of the many inhabitin' this earth, and you go slack along the jawline." The Governor ran a hand towel over his face, blotted at his neck. The towel came away almost as soggy as if fished from a river.

"Davenport?" I gaped.

"Naw," Cullie Blanton said, his voice dripping malice. "Sammy Davis, Junior. What I need is a one-eyed nigger can do the tap dance."

I groaned inwardly and forced my mind to grapple with the proposition while watching beads of sweat ball up on the Governor's body, and feeling warm droplets course down my own flushed carcass. The Governor grumbled faintly, adjusted a silver knob until steam hissed through the fogged-up room like a den of aroused serpents. Within a couple of minutes, through the thick towel protecting skinny shanks, I felt the wooden boards respond to new jolts of heat.

"Chief," I gasped, "is there anything in my contract says I have to bake here 'til Christmas?"

"Boy," Cullie Blanton said, "I am just gettin' you acclimated to the kinda weather you'll most likely experience in the afterlife." He swabbed at his face again, opening and closing his mouth like a fish marooned on dry beach, gasping some painful delight. Just before I would have fainted the Governor rose in naked splendor and pushed out of the little glassed-in cubicle, your present hero hard on his heels. We plunged into a couple of cold showers, the Governor splashing and grunting happily, somehow remindful of a great whale at play.

The gym in the basement of the Mansion was Cullie's great passion, second only to the mystic ritual of politics. He had drawn up the plans with loving care, providing the steam room, a paddle-ball court, a lone basketball goal, badminton facilities. He had hatched the whole project, and when the newspapers waxed indignant over the luxury, Cullie had defended it in a voice chocked with righteousness and piety. He had even taken to television in defense of his project: "Man's body," he had thundered, "is the sacred temple wherein God deposits the immortal soul, and man has a duty unto his God to keep that temple fit and tuned and clean." He had invoked the memory of Theodore Roosevelt and Charles Atlas and Samson himself, burning with intensity. It was one of the few times I had found him wholly without humor, either public or private.

From the first, Cullie brooked no nonsense about his Anointed Temple of the Flesh. He came to it each day the sun dawned, unless he happened to be on the road, which meant I spent half my time trying to avoid the rigors of keeping him company. On this day, I had most miserably failed.

Cullie Blanton came snorting and bellowing from the shower, streaming little puddles on the tile floor. "Melacadies!" he thundered. The houseboy quickly put aside a lurid paperback novel and approached the Governor, towel in hand. He gave the gubernatorial presence a vigorous toweling, while Cullie obediently lifted arms and hiked legs in proper order. They carried out the ritual flawlessly. It was rather like seeing two dancers who had worked in perfect synchronization for a very long time. Completing my own drying-off process, I crawled into a pair of clean white shorts and got a cigarette going. Cullie motioned me to pull up a footstool, and I perched on it while the Governor stretched his nude form on a narrow table. Melacadies, his chocolate face a total blank, began to pound on the Governor's bulk as if kneading bread dough. His client sighed and grunted huge satisfaction. After a while, the massive head cradled on folded arms, Cullie turned his gaze sideways to me.

"What about it? Think you can do it?"

"Hell," I said. "I guess so."

"He can't come to me," the Governor said. "Goddamn newspaper boys get wind of it, I'd be up stink creek without a paddle. And I can't go to him, for it would give him too much advantage. There is a lot to be said for psychology. Too bad the psychologists keep screwin' it up." He broke off the thought and tossed his masseur a quick order: "Work the kinks outta my back, Melacadies. I'm knotted up worse'n the rope of a tenderfoot Scout. Pound me some."

"You think it's wise?" I asked.

"Hell," he said, his eyes popping surprise. "Why not? Best way I know to get kinks out."

"Not that," I said. "I mean this Davenport business."

"Now if I did not decree it wise and judicious," the Governor snapped peevishly, "would I tell you to get me the nigger?" Melacadies presented an unreadable face. His hands did not falter at their task.

"So be it," I said. "But I don't like the notion."

The Governor's voice quivered with the beat of Melacadies' busy hands. "Goin' to that blackbird hat-in-hand," he said, "ain't exactly my idea of high pleasure. But I got no choice. You know how things been goin'."

"Yeah," I said.

For things were not going as we would have willed. Things were about as smooth as corncobs when applied as toilet tissue.

There was Poppa Posey. Who had come down out of the lonesome hills to run his race. No doubt a sightless half-wit could have perceived that Poppa wasn't running to win, for he avoided any town big enough to display one of those little signs on the outskirts boasting of *Public Water Supply Approved*. He was strictly the candidate of the bush apes, haranguing the ignoramuses at branch heads and creek forks; and the disciples who turned out to hear him dispense old Gospel talked of ancient droughts and home cures applied against their limitless ailments ("Put a cow-chip poltice on hit—hit draws out bad blood") and their aging children ("Dan'el, he got a good job workin' fer wages in the broom facktry") and how to make gooseberry pie. Poppa was a stalking horse, pure and simple. But you never would have picked up on that fact by reading what passed for newspapers in our state. The fearless crusaders of the press played Poppa's candidacy as straight as the Pope plays High Mass. And while the newspapers played it straight, Poppa played it cute. He would slouch on a flat-bed truck or maybe under some shade-breeding oak, and he would wall his eyes at the heavens and forgive folks their past sins. Foremost of which, the way Poppa presented it, was having voted for Cullie Blanton. He would get the old nesters swinging and swaying until it sounded like the Hallelujah chorus.

"The Bible," he would thunder dramatically, "the Bible tells us we got to be without sin to cast the firs' stone."

"A-men," the disciples would rumble.

"Well, I reckon under that edict I ain't in no shape to go around throwin' rocks. For I have *sinned!*"

"No," they would cry, disputing the confession. "No!"

"Oh, yes. Oh yes, I have sore sinned even as *you* have sinned. Fer like you I have been deceived by the serpent's tongue. Yeah, I have tuned mah ears to the sweet lies Cullie Blanton put upon his lips, and come rushin' outta the hills to bless him with mah vote." And he would throw back his head while his Adam's apple bobbled at the gawkers, and he would cry skyward, "Forgive us for what we done!"

"Oh, Father," some poke-bonneted crone, sucking snuff from the end of a masticated twig, would cry in honest agony, "forgive us for what we have did!"

"In beggin' forgiveness of his Father the chile must *repent!*" the old fraud would sing from the stump.

And they would ratify the Gospel: "A-men, Poppa!"

He would tune his voice to pain. It hurts me worse than it hurts you, the tone would say. Spare the rod and spoil the child, it would say. And in that voice he would damn Cullie with faint praise.

"Oh, Cullie wasn't such a bad feller once." And he would hold out his hands, palms extended flatly to the crowd as if to ward off protests. "Oh, he added a piddlin' little to old-age pensions and he got the young 'uns a few new books to read in they schoolhouses. I'll give the ole devil his due. Yessir, Cullie done that." Then his face would harden and the fury jump in his eyes. "But that was so long ago man hath no memory to tell him when. That was before Cullie's heart got so hard a cat couldn't scratch it! That was before all he got inter-rested in was goen to his fancy clubs and silk-sheet brothels and turnin' his ears to a buncha collidge perfessors fer namby-pamby advice!"

"Tell it like it is, Poppa!"

"Oh yes, I'll tell it like it is. And it's like the good Gospel forewarns: 'They have sown the wind and they shall reap the whirlwind!' Great is truth and mighty above all things!"

And they would stir under the stars or the parching sun, shrieking their absolutes.

"Ye cannot serve God and Mammon!" the old man would shout.

"Put no false gods afore me," somebody would sing out.

"Does addin' a few piddlin' pennies to old-age pensions so long ago a elephant can't recollect it—does that give Cullie Blanton eny earthly right ta make yore little blue-eyed boys and blonde-headed girls go ta school with a buncha dad-blamed hankerchief-headed *blue gums?*"

"No!" they would hoot in frenzy.

"Didja ever see a red bird in a *blue bird's nest?*"

"No!" they would sing in some frantic joy.

"You want a chocolate chile callin' you granpappy or granmammy? That whatcha want?"

And they would roar their defiance. "No! No! No!"

"That's the way we headin'," he would shout, "unless we stan' together and stop it! For Cullie Blanton, *he* ain't doin' nothing."

"God have mercy on the white man!" some old nester would quaver.

"God have mercy on the white man," Poppa would echo, "and God have mercy on the backslidin' Governor of this here state. We have got to take up the cross!"

Poppa would grab a Coke bottle and pour over his handkerchief, bathing his face and neck in the sticky solution, and he would flash a grin. "Hot," he would judge. "But no hotter'n we gonna make it for Cullie Blanton come Election Day. Air you with me?"

"Yeah," they would cry. "We with you, Poppa!"

"Repent! Cast down wickedness! The day of judgment is at han'!"

I reckon you get the idea. And if you don't think it can happen like that, you don't dig camp-meeting psychology. For that's the way it was.

So I sat and thought about the fantastic medicine show Poppa was putting on in the boondocks and I thought of Bayonet Bill Wooster. Who, for every two dozen backwoods freaks Poppa drew at the creek forks, would pack three or four hundred trembling lunatics into some flag-draped hall, there to inspect endless Communist conspiracies: fluoridation of drinking water, Federal aid to schools, the United Nations, galloping Socialism, Reds and perverts in the State Department; an endless goulash stirred up in Moscow. The prime ingredient of which was mixing of the races.

Yeah, I thought of all that. And of the night-riding Klansmen who kept stirring up crappy little incidents, and of the Attorney General in Washington who felt called upon to fan the flames by proclaiming threats and ultimatums. And of the suave national news boys, in search of headlines, who kept goading the President into statements not exactly calculated to sooth the situation. Of leakage of the official secret of how Cullie and Lieutenant Governor Stanley Dutton had encountered trouble in their political paradise, and how some dark feud was simmering in the Governor's official family.

So I knew how things were going, all right.

I stirred on the stool and Cullie opened one eye.

"I reckon," I said, "you want to talk Davenport out of entering the university."

"Boy, sometimes you are so bright I consider cancellin' all the electricity in this place."

"Bright enough," I said, "to know the chore won't be easy . . . you think you can persuade him?"

"When a man goes fishin'," the Governor said blandly, "he don't generally have a previous understandin' with the fish. All he can do is bait the hook and throw it in the water. Listen . . . get me everything on that nigger. I wanta know more about him than his ole black mama knows, or is likely to find out." He flopped over on his backside, eying the ceiling as if expecting assault from high station. Melacadies, stoic and apparently without present spirit, kneaded the great king about the abdomen muscles. "Set it up at a neutral site," the Governor said, his voice quivery from the pounding. "Make it hush-hush. I want the same kinda silence you get in family circles when company comes and Baby Sister is great with child in the absence of matrimony. He can bring one witness, and I'll bring you. That's the ground rules the goddamn game."

"When you want all this done?"

"I want to see that boy one week from this day. And I want the skids plentifully greased in the meantime. And I *don't* want you goin' within fifty miles of that blackbird. Tap one your bleedin'-heart buddies for the high honor." Cullie Blanton wallowed in contentment, listening to the slapping sounds Melacadies made on his flesh. "Melacadies," he said, "how'd you cotton to servin' five to fifteen years in the penitentiary?"

That broke the sure rhythm of the pounding hands. "Suh?" Melacadies asked in disbelief and bewilderment. "*Suh?*"

"I think," the Governor said, dryly, "you got the question."

"Why . . . ah wouldn't like it. No suh! . . . Ah don't think ah'd be a-tall satisfied down there!"

"To be sure," the Governor observed solemnly, "there are more pleasant places. Now I'm makin' you a promise and it is not one I am likely to break. And the promise is this: I hear so much as one god-damn whisper about the chin music I been makin' here today, you are as good as locked up. I don't care if the whisper comes from backstairs gossip or is written by Almighty God in His sure hand among the stars. Either way, you are evermore a troubled Nigra."

"Ah didn't hear *nothin'*," Melacadies said with passion. "Ah ain't eben *seen* you in two weeks!"

"You," the Governor said, "got the makin's of a very bright boy."

"Ain't heard a *sound*," Melacadies said, grinning grotesquely. "No suh, got something in mah ears wont' let sound *pass!* Deef as Aunt Annie! Couldn't hear a *tree* fall!" He appeared on the verge of a soft-shoe shuffle. Cullie Blanton judged him with level eyes. "Don't overdo it," he advised. "Don't hand me too much that Stepin Fetchit busi-ness." Melacadies looked abashed, his act exposed to a harsh critic. The Governor had gone hard in the eyes. The boy bent to vigorous massag-ing of the Governor's thick torso. "Alcohol rubdown," Cullie said, after a bit. He closed his eyes while Melacadies moved in a nervous jerk toward a small steel cabinet. "Jim, get somebody to handle the thing don't want to make goddamn history. Don't get it bollixed up, for Jesus' sweet sake. Get me somebody plays bass." The Governor sighed and stretched his kinks while Melacadies applied the soothing alcohol in great, circular swabs. Cullie Blanton gave me a fierce, direct grin. "Goddam, Jim! Good as this feels, you oughta be ashamed to waste it internally."

The spot was perfect. The white house nestled in the protective cover of a clump of tall pines, well-kept but not ostentatious, a coating of year-old paint giving it sort of stolid Rotarian respectability. The house was maybe two hundred yards off the slab where tires swished in the aftermath of one of those sudden summer showers that stop as abruptly as they begin.

We had encountered a series of showers on the drive down from Capitol City: now a torrent, then nothing, then the cycle repeated, like the tears of a flighty child turned on and off at will. We had made good time on the hundred-mile drive, Cullie Blanton faintly griping and scowling on the seat beside me while we bored through the night to our secret rendezvous, having taken the precaution of staging a little drama in the Mansion before departing.

The drama featured Governor Blanton in the starring role, with your obedient servant heading the supporting cast. The bit players, who were not aware the drama was going on, were the Capitol correspondents for the two major news services. Watching them at their ease, I had the notion the competing wire services had purposefully assigned physical opposites to their respective beats, so as to avoid confusion. Associated Press was a lean drink of water with teeth protruding enough to shame Bugs Bunny, and above the teeth a highly waxed mustache, and above that a pompadour of pomaded silver hair. He engaged in much limp crossing of ungainly legs while sipping daintily at white wine. United Press International was a chunky soul with jowls running considerably to chubbiness and a mowed crop of black hair bristling in some mysterious anger. When he approached his bourbon and branch water it was with no-nonsense gusto and two hands.

The two had been invited in for drinks, a buffet-style dinner, and friendly ruffling of cards. There was nothing about the arrangement to excite suspicion. Cullie frequently played host to working newsmen, sometimes in intimate groups and at other times in howling bunches and clusters. The idea on this chosen evening was to present the Governor at home in social circumstance, apparently untroubled by anything more serious than the luck of the draw. Later on, if allegations should be made to the effect that Cullie Blanton had been skulking around in the dark, intent on private deals with a certain celebrated gentleman of color, the two wire-service reporters would be perfect witnesses to the obvious lie.

Watching Cullie's performance that evening, I could not discern any hint of the big-game safari staring him in the face. He played his usual dashing game of five-card stud and draw poker, taking fantastic chances and like as not being blessed with fantastic luck, now and again raking in a pot with fiendish glee that tipped off losers to the fact he had run a bluff. I had always noticed that the Governor much preferred buying a pot to winning one, and on this night he seemed no different. He made the usual small talk, speaking with apparent candor, safe in the knowledge he was off the record with the news boys. "Yeah," he would say, "that sophomore quarterback at state is gonna make 'em forget Harry Gilmer, for he can evermore throw that goddamn ball." And he would say, "This is a lie if you repeat it, but a bird tells me our state senator from Ogleetree County is thinkin' of offering his high talents for state treasurer next time out." And, "You boys seen that strawberry blonde ole Henry Muggins hired? She has got boobies enough to make a man quit home." Through the performance A.P. simpered and sipped, paying a modicum of attention to the game, while U.P.I. bet his cards as if trying to raise rent money.

Along about a quarter of midnight, Cullie pushed back from the poker table and made a show of counting his chips. "I sure hate to quit winner," he said, "but it's near time for my beauty rest."

"Yeah," I said. "You've got to be up to enlighten that group of business and professional ladies at seven o'clock. That's when the breakfast starts."

The Governor frowned, still fingering the chips. "Count your blessin's," he said to the two reporters. "How'd you like to be up hootin' wisdom and platitudes about equal rights for women to a buncha frustrated frumps six-seven hours from now?" The reporters mumbled appropriate sympathies. "Goddam," Cullie Blanton said, "the women got ninety-seven per cent of the money and *all* the pussy and now they want equal rights!"

Fifteen minutes later Cullie Blanton stepped swiftly from blue-black shadows at the rear of the Mansion to climb into my convertible, and we eased through the Capitol grounds, mighty oak trees humped and huddled against the dark backdrop of sky, to begin our journey.

The practiced ease exhibited by the Governor during our little drama quickly fell away. All through the ride he fumed and fretted over my not turning up anything of a derogatory nature on Hamilton Davenport. He cursed and railed at traffic not moving fast enough to suit his fancy. He griped and growled at the rain, peering through the moisture-dotted windshield as if faced with some complex navigational problem in heavy fog. He asked me a series of nagging questions to which he already had answers.

"You think Dallas goddamn Johnson covered his tracks?" he growled.

"Yeah," I said. "Yeah, he was right careful."

"Whose place is it we're usin' for the meetin'?"

"Dallas' campaign manager for that county," I said.

"It safe?"

"It's off the road," I said for maybe the fifty-first time, "in a clump of pines. The campaign manager's taken his family on a little trip. The front door's unlocked and a light left on."

"What time Dallas tell that blackbird to be there?"

"Midnight," I said. "With instructions to wait until we show."

"He knows to bring just one man?"

"He knows," I sighed.

"Goddammit," the Governor said, "they sure picked 'em a winner. Why couldn't that blackbird have been caught up sometime on a morals charge or abandoned a batch of debts someplace?"

9

HE HAD TRIED every act in his repertoire. He had come on jocular and voluble, spinning yarns, grinning his trained glee, eyes twinkling fellowship and fun, the huge head inclined now, then ducking to register some sly, left-handed humor while he peered from under the frosty eyebrows like a little boy who has been naughty and caught at it, and is trying to clown himself past the threat of discipline. He had boomed and hoo-hawed and exuded camaraderie, until he became a travesty on himself, using the broad gestures, striking the cardboard poses so much a part of Cullie Blanton the public man; employing the technique that maybe could thaw icebergs and cause stone figures to weep.

And got nowhere.

The two men sat across from us, wrapped in an ethereal dignity, watching the show dispassionately, as if perhaps they had paid to see high drama and had been served up low comedy in its stead. So they would suffer the lesser act, but damned if they would applaud it. They sat and sipped slowly at their drinks the way a reforming drunk might carefully count his beers, determined to make no misstep, no commitment that might suck them out of position.

Cullie couldn't get his finger on what was wrong. Who had short-circuited the wires? Why wouldn't the ice melt and the statues weep? Hell, hadn't he moved the multitudes and turned water into wine? He sucked his lower lip and the little gears and wheels meshed in his head. Goddammit, what was wrong with these pirates? Why couldn't he reach them? Watching him, I was reminded of the aging matinee idol whose name no longer made it in lights, and who spends his days going from casting department to backstage door, singing of old glories with Fay Wray and Billie Burke and Gloria Swanson.

That's when I knew.

That's when I got staggered by the blinding light, and the light portended Truth and Truth was this: the times had passed Cullie

Blanton by. He was as outdated as buggy whips. It wasn't enough any-
more to give the people bread and circuses. Their coats were buttoned
over full bellies and they had seen the show. This was the age of what
the liberal pols called the New Freedom, and it would not be bought
off with cake and ale or hoary jokes.

The two fellows turning deaf ears and untouched hearts to the Governor's patented performance were in wild pursuit of some caroming
dream, and nothing would rest in them until they had grabbed it by
the vitals.

There came a moment when Cullie knew his show was sham. He
worried his earlobe, tapped one foot in a jerky dance while the other
remained disapprovingly stationary. And in the moment he surrendered old ghosts. He jettisoned useless baggage, pushed back his
drink and dropped the bogus cheer and all that insane grinning, and
he gave them as good as he got out of the eyes. And he said, "All right,
enough of the claptrap. Let's hull down to the bare bones. . . ."

We beat day back to Capitol City with a good hour to spare, and the
air carried a sharp predawn chill in it. Later on, when the sun's fireball
hung high and blistering, a vaporlike steam would rise from grass plots
and trees and little puddles deposited by nocturnal rains. Government
clerks would stew in their white collars, and merchants along the Drag
would crinkle eyes against the white glare of sidewalks and drip sweat
on idle counters while silently railing at the elements for putting such
an anti-business face on the day. It would be a scorcher, all right.

But now it was cool in that hour said to be the blackest before dawn,
and light poles cast weird shadows about the capitol grounds. I eased
the convertible by the massive sandstone statehouse, circled under
overhanging tree branches that dripped and sprayed the last tears of
rain, and came to halt in the dark void behind the Mansion. When I
killed the motor and the lights, we were swallowed by the pitch.

Cullie Blanton shifted on the seat, the first sign in more than an
hour that he might still be possessed of operable chemicals. He had
said little during the long ride back from our hush-hush rendezvous,
just staring googly-eyed and abstracted down the slab, stroking his jawline now and again, nodding his head silently as if to ratify that yes,
yes, that certainly was a goddamn road ahead, lots of road. . . .

Maybe he had been running over in his mind how cool a cat Hamilton Davenport had proved to be. It was almost as if the N.A.A.C.P.

had prayed to God for a duplicate of Harry Belafonte, and He had honored their petition. Davenport didn't have the blue-black shine of the Pullman porter nor the sickly freckles-on-mustard hue of the near-white, but was a fine, honest chocolate brown like icing on cake. His eyes had been neither insolent nor fearful, and he rode easily in his chair so that you knew he had control of his spirit and was not the type to beat on a tambourine and curse evil. He fit none of the old molds. You couldn't put him in the shuffling shoes of the grinning Uncle Tom any more than you could imagine him with the padded shoulders and finky goatee of the bop hipster; and looking at him there in the road-side farmhouse I had tagged him as the New Breed.

Cullie had leaned forward from the bulky old divan, placing his drink on a heavy, dark-stained coffee table, cocking the white head to give Davenport his perfected inspection from crown of head to ball of foot.

"Boy," the Governor had said, "I've come here to strike an accommodation. Where do we start?"

"I am twenty-nine years old," Ham Davenport said, without flickering a face tic. "We start by not calling me 'Boy.' "

Cullie had struggled with his color, but the color prevailed and the color was red. The flush won out over his neck and, having conquered that territory, advanced on his face. No doubt he had been as angry at himself for the blunder as resentful at being so bluntly put down. But the Governor tried to recover, stretching a small grin. "Hell," he had said, "let's don't start this thing tryin' to find somethin' to sandpaper our hearts. I call Jim here"—and he had nodded his head leftward toward me—"the same thing. And he's so old he's catchin' up to Methuselah."

"The day my father died," Davenport said in that same level voice, "I was told by a banker and a police chief and a minister that he was sure a good *boy*. My father lived to be sixty-four years old."

"All right," Cullie Blanton said. "I made a mistake. I'm a creature of habit, and habit dies hard. You want me to call you Mister Davenport or Doctor Davenport or Ivan-the-goddamn-Terrible, it is all the same to me. I'm here to reach compromise."

The Negro had permitted himself a humorless grin. "Just call me plain Davenport," he said. "That's *my* compromise."

The moon-faced young lawyer crossed stumpy legs, nudging a brief case with the polished point of his shoe. He ran a hand through the bristle of cropped blond hair as if the gesture might be frequently made. He said, "I imagine we have more serious subjects on the agenda, Governor. So any time you want to proceed. . . ."

"No," Cullie Blanton had said. "No, maybe we oughta stir this sensitivity about name-callin' up some. Maybe there is a point to the parable." The Governor had reached for his drink and robbed it of three hearty swigs. We waited in expectation of some weighty pronouncement as Cullie returned the drink to its old station and leaned back against the couch, resting spread-eagled arms in crucifixion posture along the top.

"Nigger," he said, flatly.

I thought the young lawyer would come unglued. His facial features jerked in approximation of spasm, and then he went into an instant trance. Ham Davenport didn't flinch. His eyes burned into Cullie Blanton's.

"Spade," the Governor said.

"Hey!" the lawyer protested, jerking out of his trance. "Hey!"

"Coon," Cullie said. He grinned, dropping his head to peer up from under the crop of eyebrows. And when he spoke again it was to whisper. "Burrhead," he said softly. "Goddamn watermelon-eatin' *jigaboo!*"

The lawyer couldn't get through hey-ing. "Hey," he said, as if his voice protested at what his ears told him. "Hey, now. . . ."

"Easy," Ham Davenport said, reaching out a restraining hand. His eyes, bright and alert, never left Cullie Blanton. And when he spoke his voice matched the crooning, whispery timber the Governor had introduced into his own speech. "I know what the Governor's doing," he said in the singsong croon. He locked eyes with the Governor for a long moment. "He's seeing if I can take it," the Negro said with a little smile. "And I am telling him. Yeah, Governor. Yeah, I can take it." After their eyes had done more battle, the Negro made a short, scornful sound free of mirth. "Hell," he said, the little laugh grating on the brain. "I ought to be able to take it. I've had a lifetime of practice."

Cullie Blanton twirled the highball in his hand. He said, "All those ugly words I used. They'll be shouted at you from faces twisted in hate until the faces will look like ugliness drenched in sheep-dip. And the words will be spat at you like gobs of phlegm."

Davenport treated us to another stubby burst of the bitter laugh. He said, "You think it will be the first time?"

"No," the Governor said. "But I didn't figure to be the first person ever called you 'Boy,' either."

"I don't expect it easy," Davenport said calmly. "I've been trained for this. For two months I had my face slapped and my hair pulled and all the names shouted at me. I was spit on, and not just with words. They gave me a worse time than the Army did."

"There's a hell of a difference in mock war and real battles," the Governor said. "That's why a general can't always tell who'll be his hero." He peered over the rim of his glass, paused. "Or," he finished, "his coward."

Ham Davenport employed stabbing, agitated motions to crush a cigarette in a glass ashtray shaped like a star. He said, "Governor, don't forget I grew up down here. I've climbed old Yessuh Mountain and danced the dance of shame. I tell you every day was a battle, *white man!*"

He had exploded the last two words. He'd hissed them between his teeth, and their serpentine sound coiled in the air. After a moment, Governor Blanton crossed his feet and grinned. "Hell," he said, "sounds to me like bein' colored's a lot like bein' in politics."

Davenport stood and stalked around the dim farmhouse parlor, casting a giant shadow of himself on one wall, prowling, possessed of the same driving energy I knew so well in the Governor. "Every day was a battle," he said, as though discoursing to himself. "It was a battle just to get up out of the shucks and leave the shack and go out there in that white world."

The Governor nodded great understanding. He said, "Some days the only reason I get up is a fear of dyin' in bed."

"I used to wake up with feet in my face," Hamilton Davenport said. "Sleeping nine to a cabin, and rain dripping through cracks big enough for mockingbirds to fly through and the cabin on the edge of a swamp. Breakfast might be a little bit of fatback with thickening gravy, and I'd go to the fields hungry enough to eat what the mules dropped."

"Hell," the Governor said, "you want to tell poor-boy stories, I got some to tell when my turn comes."

"You can't tell me what it's like to be black. You want to hear, Governor?"

"It's your story," Cullie Blanton said.

Hamilton Davenport measured the Governor in a direct way, frankly staring. When he had apparently resolved something of which the rest of us were unaware, he said, "Being black's like nothing else in the world." He mulled on the proposition, running it through the gears of his mind, shaping his thoughts before putting them on view. After a bit, he said, "When I was thirteen a drunk white man came to the Flats one night and offered me a dollar to fix it up so he could screw my older sister. Less than a month later that same man sentenced an uncle of mine to six months on the chain gang for stealing a two-dollar ham from a grocery store."

"The world," Cullie Blanton said flatly, "is fulla sonsofbitches."

"It is." The Negro dipped into his drink. "And most of them seem to have passed my way. I was too little to remember it, but a goddamn cracker yelled an obscenity at my mother once. When my older brother threw rocks at his truck he had to be rushed out of town in the dark of night. And my father had to apologize to that cracker and his drunk friends when they came back likkered up the next night. He had to grin and sing and dance. They made him sing 'Old Black Joe' and 'Dixie' and do what they called a 'jig step.' " Ham Davenport grinned, but there was nothing funny about the grin, just a taut stretching of flesh. "A *jig* step," he repeated. "And he kept grinning like it pleasured him the most, because he didn't want to die."

Cullie frowned at his glass, swirling its contents.

"When I was seventeen," Hamilton Davenport said, "I went to a two-bit shoot-'em-up movie one night and sat in the Jim Crow balcony, and on the way home I had the hard luck to pass a store window somebody had heaved a brick through. And I was in jail three weeks. Without a lawyer, without going before a judge, without making a telephone call. I got hosed down and beat with nightsticks because I wouldn't confess. I guess I would have in time, only they caught some poor bastard throwing a brick through another window and he copped out on the job I'd been arrested for."

Hamilton Davenport stretched to his full height, his face lined and old for his years. He had about him the look of a man who has been flimflammed at a carnival, but knows he can't do a thing about it, because the carnies had the foresight to lay gifts on the sheriff.

The Negro said, "I grew up and all my friends grew up without mothers because ours had to nurse some white kid and clean for its parents, to help put meat on our table. When my old man brought home his pay check it might be the last one, because you let business slump a dime's worth and the Negro's the first to be fired. The county put up an honor roll of servicemen on the courthouse lawn during the war against Germany and Japan, and when the Negro community peti-

tioned to have the names of our people added to it, the county commissioners offered to put one down in the Flats. But they wouldn't
put it on the courthouse lawn."

"If it was all that bad," the Governor said suddenly, "why didn't
you stay in that college out West?"

"Because," the Negro spat, as if he had rehearsed for the question,
"it was *out West!*" He turned his back, and shrugged his shoulders.
Then he spun to face the Governor. "Jesus," he said. "Jesus! You . . .
you people just don't *understand!* There have been pressures put on
me—"

He whirled now to face his attorney. "Tell him, Robbie. Didn't they
put pressures on me? Didn't they try to con me into giving this up?"
When the lawyer had confirmed by nod, he swung around to face Cullie Blanton again. "One of the reasons I kept hearing was because you
love this state so much and don't want to see it ripped and gutted. 'It's
his home,' those tame Negroes and the 'good' whites kept saying to me.
'It's his home, and he loves it!' Dammit, it's *my* home too. Can't you
people understand that?"

"Sure," Cullie Blanton said agreeably. "*I* understand it." He cocked
his head to the right, gazing up at Davenport. "Jim here, *he* probably
understands it. But we're in a minority, son. You think that goddamn
Marine general who's blattin' how he'll bar you in the doorway—you
think *he* might understand it?"

Then, "And I'm not sure you do."

"A man," the Governor said, "does the best he can with what he's
got. I don't claim to have any brotherhood trophy comin' from you
people. But I've done the best I could with what I had."

"It's not enough," Hamilton Davenport said evenly. "I still can't go
in a café and get a bite to eat when I'm hungry, unless I go to the back
door with my hat in my hand and pay two prices for whatever swill
some cracker cook wants to throw at me. And then eat it sitting by a
garbage can swarmed by blowflies. My bladder can be so full it's killing
me but I can't walk into just anybody's store or service station to empty
it. My tongue can be swelling from thirst, and I might have to walk a
mile to find a place I even dare ask for water . . . Governor, did you
have children?"

"We were never blessed," Cullie Blanton said shortly, dipping into
his drink.

"Well . . . sometimes I've thought it might be better if I hadn't had any. You try to explain to your kids why they can't sit down in a restaurant and eat with other people even if they've got the money. Or why they can't wait in a certain waiting room when they've paid white prices for a ticket, or can't go to the bathroom; and why they've always got to smile and be agreeable and admit they're wrong a thousand times when they *know* by God's name and logic they're *right*."

Cullie Blanton loosed a great sigh. "I don't say it's perfect."

Ham Davenport released another burst of his burp-gun laugh. *"No,"* he said, "it most certainly is not perfect, Governor." His laugh became helpless, and he shrugged as if to surrender something. "Before I could read," he said, "I learned it wasn't perfect. When my father and mother taught me I must *never never* put my hands on a little white girl or even *look* at a white girl or talk sassy to any white person, I don't suppose I exactly understood the reasons. I just knew that something bad might happen. Hell, *would* happen. The hardest licks I got from my father was to teach me that lesson. But I had to learn it to save my life. So I would agree that it isn't exactly perfect."

"It's gonna take a while," the Governor said, "to make things much better. Longer than I'm gonna live. You, too, maybe."

"Maybe," Ham Davenport agreed. "But I decided in Korea to come home and fight the best battle. I decided it one night when I walked up on the C.P. tent and heard the C.O. talking with my platoon leader about sending out a night patrol. It was right after the Chinese Reds had come across the Yalu. Nobody knew where they came from or how many they might be.

"I'd been out on patrols," he said. "I hadn't done anything heroic. Just crawled out there in no man's land fumbling around in the dark with all the other guys, as scared as anybody else and wanting to live as much as the rest. Red or yellow, black or white. . . . So these guys were batting their gums in the C.P. tent about who to send, and my platoon leader called off a few names. When he said 'Davenport,' the C.O. said, 'The spade?' And the platoon leader said, 'Yeah, the spade.' And the C.O. said, 'Better not. Hell, you get that jig out there and let one those chinks blow a bugle or start ringing their bells, and we'll be lucky if the boog don't stampede the whole goddamn regiment.' Yeah, and they laughed and I didn't get sent on that patrol. And you know what? I was *elated* about it, and ashamed at the same time because I didn't want to go . . . but not for that reason. Hell yes, I had been scared on those patrols! Show me anybody with good sense that wasn't scared half witless. But I had been out there and fought back the fear and beat it. Only nobody noticed. They still had me down as a type. Jig. Boog. Spade. Fear and voodoo, Governor. They looked at me and saw black skin and fear and tribal dances."

Hamilton Davenport made for the highboy where the drink mixings waited. He turned to the Governor with a mock smile. "Mix yew a drank, suh?" he asked in broad parody. "Shine yew shoes, suh? Lawdy Lawd, y'all need the best cotton-choppin' nigger in tha fiel's, Boss?"

"Don't play the fool with me," the Governor said, shortly.

The Negro laughed. He said, "Governor, I've got to get it all out of my system tonight. Come tomorrow morning I go back playing straight and chasing the dream. You don't see it, maybe. But *I* do. You read much, Governor?"

"Election returns and the Bible," Cullie Blanton said.

Davenport took a sip of his drink and grinned. The lawyer had stirred uneasily and muttered something to his ward. "I'm all right," the Negro said with a wave of his hand. He turned back to face the Governor, who had started to twist and squirm impatiently on the couch. "Couple of years ago in Texas," Ham Davenport said, "a fellow wrote a piece about the New Negro. He said if you call him 'nigger' when he shines your shoes in a barber shop he'll never show up for work there again. The word has spread, the fellow wrote. The shine boy has the dream, too." He gazed across vast visions, smiling dreamily. "The shine boy has the dream," he repeated softly. "Well, I got the dream. I was going to get me the best education money could buy and come back here as sort of . . . of a combination Kingfish and Dr. Ralph Bunche. So I went West and worked for six years, and saved my money. I parked cars and delivered messages and swept floors. I finished high school at night and then pieced together two years of college. Hell, I even took elocution lessons." He chuckled. "Elocution lessons! That's a kick, isn't it? Got rid mah fiel'-han' accent." He cracked his knuckles, grinning broadly. Then the grin went away. He said, "So I came home to be a leader. You imagine that? And couldn't get a job emptying slop jars, unless I went into my shuffle and called everybody 'Boss.' *Elocution* lessons, for Christ sakes!"

The young lawyer cleared his throat. He said, "Ham, why don't we let the Governor put his . . . ah . . . proposition?"

"I know what he wants," the Negro said. "He wants me to postpone entering the university. A year, probably. Or at least until he's got his election laid by." When the Governor didn't answer he said, "Right?"

"Why no," Cullie Blanton said. "I rode all this way just to hear an inspirin' speech."

Ham Davenport had dipped into the whisky again, but he came out quickly. Grinning, he said, "Don't begrudge me my speech, Governor. It was the only chance I'll have to make a speech like that. Tomorrow I go back to looking solemn, and present my polished image to all the folks out there in television land."

"Governor . . . ?" The lawyer waited with his eyebrows raised.

"Don't seem to be much point in goin' through the motions," the Governor said.

"Aw," Hamilton Davenport said. "Now, you wouldn't want to deprive me of being asked, would you?"

Cullie's laugh was a mixture of bile and vinegar. He said, "Hell, why not? Okay . . . how about it?"

"No," Hamilton Davenport said.

"You're not even interested in hearin' the proposition?"

"Sorry."

The Governor moved his head in a series of little affirmative nods. He drained the last of his bourbon and water off slivers of ice, plunked the glass down, and rose all in one quick, liquid motion. "Let's haul ass, Jim," he said. At the door he wheeled around so abruptly I had to side-straddle and hop to avoid bowling him over. The Governor engaged in one final study of Hamilton Davenport.

"Boy," he said, "I feel for you but I can't reach you. I wish you had some notion of how it is to be in my shoes."

"Governor, I wish *you* had some notion of what it's like to be in my skin."

After a long moment, Hamilton Davenport raised his glass in mock salute. Only there was nothing mocking in his eyes. He gave the Governor a look tinged with some new respect, and maybe there was a little compassion mingled with it. "Maybe," he said, so low I couldn't be certain he had said it. Until, that is, Cullie Blanton let a smile tug at one corner of the wide mouth and echoed it in flat tones. "Maybe."

Then he turned and plunged from the house.

Cullie Blanton had nodded to reaffirm the existence of the road: *yes, yes, that was a road all right, it sure enough was, lots of goddamn road.* He looked down the slab at the beam of light we were always chasing but could never quite catch, and after he had watched the uneven

contest for ten miles or so he said, "That is one tough nigger." Two
miles more through the ink, and he said, "And he had better stay
tough, for he will have need of the commodity." Another half-dozen
miles, and he said, "All this tearin' around in the rain and the dark
just to get lectured by a nigger's been off to U.C.L. and A."

The Governor nodded at the highway for another dozen miles and
then he laughed shortly and said, "Life! You know what it's all about,
Jim? You know what life is?"

"No," I said. "Listen, what was all that 'maybe' business you two
gave each other there at the end?"

"Goddammit!" the Governor said in instant rage, his head turning
quickly toward me in the night. "Goddammit, it was just words, that's
all. Just *words!* I asked did you know what *life* is?"

"No," I sighed. Except, I thought, it is an acre of Hell from my vantage point. But I just said, "No."

"I do," the Governor said, smugly. Another three miles, and he said,
"The nigger, he knows." And after enough fence posts had whizzed by
to satisfy the Governor's sense of timing, he said, "Life, it is just a
kiddies' playground." He let me struggle with the puzzle while the car
flashed down the slab, leaning a little to the right because of the middle hump, and then said, "Yeah, it is all just a bunch of goddamn
swings and seesaws. And now and again a few long slides."

At the Mansion he said, "Come on in. Let's figger what we can pick
up from the ruins and shambles."

It was what I expected, for knowledge had come upon me that politicians cannot abide the thought of being alone. You'd think with all
the jam and crush of public posing and pumping hands they would
yearn for the solitude of distant monasteries, but loneliness to them
is a fear worse than nameless. Maybe they can't afford to risk the adventure of themselves. So I crawled from the car and dutifully followed the Governor's looming bulk into the center shadows.

After the Governor had fumbled our way into the Mansion, he said,
"Jim, put us on some coffee while I freshen up. And see can you lay
hand on some cantaloupe." He clattered through the darkened Mansion, signifying by grunt when he bumped into the taxpayers' furni-
ture, while I bustled about the kitchen making like a Japanese houseboy.

Sitting to sip the coffee, I felt the urge to make a speech. It was an
old habit of mine, a secret sin, the petcock on the pressure cooker. Oh, I

seldom made the speeches save in my own pleasing company, but they were all the more enjoyable for all of that. So I clanked down the coffee cup and lifted voice and eye: "Fellah ogres, visiting fools, and wicked wisemen: I stan' before you most proudly and all hung up. For I stan' here uncorrupted by the muck and mire of the years, and human in mah passions. Yas. An' ah have skated aroun' the periphery of greatness without fallin' in wunst! Whut's more, have glimpsed green visions and have seen heathen armies fall nekkid on the plain. Yas, ah yas. And more. Have gazed on hallucinatory splendor and know of instant mirth. Ah say to yew! Ah say, it is all jus' a buncha swangs and seesaws! And humphety-dumpety sat on a wall and got a great fall, while I have personally and in high sadness genuflected in manner most fine at the graves of princes and kings and heroes. Give me yore tard, yore poor! Hut sut ralson on the rilleraw, mah fren's. Yas, appease the dragons and a bralla bralla suet! Keep scufflin' and eat bran flakes. An' than' kew!"

A voice behind me said, "You can't for hell's sakes explain what that was all about, can you?" Cullie Blanton stood in the doorway, a very perplexed public man, plug-in telephone gripped in one huge hand, flapping about in loose silk robe of rainbow hues.

"I will have to think about it," I said, "for the longest time."

The Governor grunted and padded to the table. He plugged in the telephone and placed it within easy reach. He eyed the coffee as if he expected it to boil with strange poisons and leaned across as though to sniff my breath. He said, "You find any cantaloupe?"

"No."

Which was the truth, as far as it went.

"Goddamn that Nettie," the Governor said with feeling. "Sometimes I think she's in the hire the goddamn Republicans." He stretched his feet under the table, sighing. He sampled the coffee and made a face. "Good thing you're not a woman," he said, "unless you happen to be a demon in bed. For you'd never make it on your cookin'."

The Governor wrapped lower limbs around the wooden legs of the high stool on which he perched at the table, worrying down a slug of coffee. "Nettie," he said. "She's always feedin' me eggs and goddamn sweet potatoes. When I was a kid and you couldn't pick up a quarter in the backwoods even if it rained dollar bills, everybody raised chickens and sweet potatoes. Glutted the market. You couldn't of sold a wagonload of eggs for the price of the axle grease went on the wheels. And the yams. Hell, even the hogs turned up their snouts at the yams. So *we* had to eat 'em. I ain't been able to look head-on at a goddamn egg or yam since."

I said, "You always pack away about forty pounds of sweet potatoes at the Yam Festival."

The Governor grunted, sucking up coffee like a waterspout might be at play in the cup. "Boy," he said, "a political man will eat somethin' tastes a lot worse than yams to tie down a few votes." He dialed a number on the telephone, looking up at me sourly. "Hallucinatory splendor and instant mirth!" he said with a negative motion of the great head. "Jesus!"

I sat thinking how grateful I was for not being home, what with Cullie pawing the telephone and posing his jaw for a workout. There is something about the sound of a telephone in the dark of night that conjures up visions of dead sons and delinquent daughters . . . crashes on the highway and fatal abortions . . . bankruptcy and pronouncements of wars and old enemies rescued from ancient deaths.

The Governor was squawking into the phone. "This Hedy Lamarr?" he boomed. "Red Grange . . . Kaiser Bill, maybe?" He grinned in an evil way. "Henry," he said chidingly, "you don't have any more sensa humor than ole Tom Dewey did. How the hell you figger to get to be President the United States without a sensa humor? . . . Listen, I need to make chin music with you. You get over here for breakfast?" Cullie Blanton tweaked an ear and tugged at his nose in a quick one-two motion. "Fahn! Jes' fahn! Make it in 'bout an hour, then. . . ." The fun faded from the Governor's face and he scowled, his features slate gray and lined. "Yeah, I got the rumble. You hold 'em off? . . . You *got* to hold, Henry. I struck out on that little mission I was tellin' you about, and if those seg bills got called . . ." He trailed into monosyllabic grunts and closing hoo-haw and in due course banged up the telephone. He sat looking across at me, frowning. "Henry's havin' trouble keepin' those seg bills bottled up. You reckon it'd do any good for me to address a joint session?"

I stirred on the hot seat, uneasy. "Might just fan the flames."

The Governor fretted, cocking a head to the early bustle of the city coming alive under the transfusion of a new day, hunting for wisdom in common sights and sounds. "Hell," he said uncertainly. "Hell . . . I just can't stand around waitin' for somebody to hand me the pearl. They're closin' in on me from all sides. That goddamn general . . . Poppa Posey . . . the nigger . . . goddamn legislature. . . ."

"Talk to Henry," I suggested. "See if he thinks you'd show any profit addressing those jackdaws. Personally, I think it's a waste of prime time."

"You know a better way?"

"Maybe. I think maybe you ought to trot out your tent and put on a road show."

"I got the same notion," the Governor said. He sighed, "Though," he admitted, "my bones swell at the thought of it." He engaged himself in silent debate. Then he reached some quick point of decision. "Set it up," he said. "Let's take a swing along the coast and then cross over to the brush country. Get the city dudes and country boys both. And I want bands playin' and folks throwin' roses and palm leaves. Hell, I might even ride into town on a jackass and wearin' a white robe. And tell our county men I want *people,* by God. Live warm bodies, and I don't care if they have to shanghai winos outta beer halls. And *don't* for Jesus' sakes have 'em puttin' me in some big, drafty hall you couldn't fill up if the attraction was the twelve Disciples playin' the United Nations in ice hockey, with a free fish fry on the side."

"When you want to start this safari?"

The Governor communed with himself, chewing his cheeks. He said, "Three, four days. Take about a week for the kinda swing I wanta make."

"Christ," I said. "We do more road time than a bus driver."

"The folks want to be *loved,*" the Governor said. "They wanta have their hands pumped and their elbows kneaded and be told how they are the power under the hood. The folks want their pols to come a-courtin'."

"Yeah," I said. "Hooray for the folks."

"I got to bring 'em the Gospel. I got to save their souls from false gods."

"Well," I said, "you seem to be a few sermons behind. Wooster and Poppa Posey, they're preaching hard Scripture and taking up collections and may be converting a lot of your flock to heathen ways."

The Governor wallowed coffee in his mouth and swallowed, nodding. "All that might be true," he said. "But church ain't over till they sing."

I stopped off to tell Roxie the road show would go out. Do not think I own backward hormones when I tell you we talked and talked. There is simply something about a warm bed which brings out the verbosity in Roxie.

About Pete Winston, first. Who was hung up in the worst way and who was on a very sad kick lately, staying as high as Mount Rushmore and possessed of as many stone eyes. About Cullie's confab with Ham Davenport, and of the tinderbox that was the legislature. About my going away. Which I brought up in gentle fashion, turning slightly to face her so that our bodies touched lightly at breastbones and knees. I kissed her to silence, and said, "That's not exactly one for the road. But it's close to it."

She propped up on an elbow, frowning. "What does that mean?"

"I have felt the blood," I said, "and have got to move. Down the road a piece. Though the notion grieves me bad."

"Goddammit," she said. "Politics. Where to this time?"

"Up and down and all around. See the local lions and mudbog Mikados. Huddle with rainmakers and palm readers."

"For how long?"

"Three big nights three," I said.

"I hate it," she said. "I *despise* it. Damn politicians, anyway. They go around promising this, that, and the other thing, but they're all just alike. So it really makes no difference."

"No," I said. "Sometimes it makes a difference. And this is one of the times."

"They're fools," she judged stubbornly. "All of them."

"Yep," I said. "They're fools, all right. Only there is a grand difference between Our fool and Their fool. Our fool, he may not be possessed of the most tender sensibilities and is no doubt capable of using the wrong fork. But now and again he stirs off his duff and does something that needs doing. While Their fool is a throwback to the age of dinosaurs. He not only opposes fire and the wheel, he wants to move us back into caves."

"I don't see that kind of difference," she said. "Your fool and Their fool seem to whistle the same tune."

"Music hath charms," I quoted, "to sooth the savage beast. And the beast is the folks. You think Cullie's got a chance to be reelected by prancing around in front of the folks and singing about how red and yellow, black and white, they are precious in his sight?"

Roxie wrinkled her snub nose. "So why all the noise? Why don't people just leave each other alone and . . . and let everybody swing?"

"Now there is something I hadn't thought of," I said. "I will recommend that very thing to the Governor."

"Oh, Jim. I just don't see it. All this aggravation!"

"That," I said, "is because you have been off to New York City and have eaten of kosher food and saw colored folks taking sociology courses at N.Y.U. Now us cornbread types, we ain't blinded by the artifices. We know how important it is to guard old hates for ourselves and our posterity."

"You Southerners," Roxie said.

"If it ever gets out how the Governor's top wiper has got for a lover a Yankee by birth, and who sings with dance bands besides. . . ."

She smiled. "I won't admit it," she said. She leaned down and nuzzled me most pleasurably about the neck. "I'll say I hardly know you."

"Knowing you would do all that for me," I said, "makes me feel good all over."

Roxie did something most artful with her hands.

"And does *that* make you feel good all over?"

"Ah. . . ."

"And this?"

"Baby," I said, "that makes me feel so good I can't decide whether to clap hands or throw money."

After that we didn't talk for a while.

There was a time when I had puffed with importance at being Cullie Blanton's advance man out in the boondocks, likening it to walking on water or at least building the Taj Mahal by hand on weekends. But the fact is, I had found glamor where glamor was not. For all the job required was patience and a paucity of bed rest, with a smattering of whisky drinking in the cluttered offices of lawyers, shopkeepers and weekly-newspaper editors who had become local cheerleaders for Cullie, leading the unwashed in shouted huzzas when it became necessary to rally troops against the foe. Maybe some of them wanted a little business thrown their way, but most of the local leaders got their jollies simply from being known as an intimate of the Governor, from being allowed to call him by his first name (and have the favor returned in kind), and from the annual barbecue and whisky drink he threw in their honor. Or even from such a simple thing as having their egos buttered now and again by the Governor's traveling emissary. So if a man had to roll a few flattering words over his tongue in order to oil a few pussel-guts who had nose warts and smelly breath and some kind of left-handed ambition beating in their breastbones, I could do the job.

Coming on the series of little towns where the mischief waited to be done was like seeing an old movie again and again. As if some giant hand had reached down and plucked one flawed and seedy miniature metropolis from the claybogs or marshlands and plopped it down at intervals along the highway. You would look at The Farmers' State Bank done squat and red-bricked on the main drag, the Elite Café where local gentry queued up at noon to smack their lips over the Blue Plate Special (sixty cents with coffee, tea, or milk), the rusting water tower, and get a fleeting glimpse of the old nesters with turkey necks whittling on benches fronting the courthouse square, and you would know by some dark instinct where to go to mail a letter or buy a block of ice.

You would round a curve and see the local library sitting quietly, as if it hoped not to attract attention, on a street walking the thin line between residential and commercial, and you would know that some round-eyed boy sought escape from his daily woof by delving in the pages of dog-eared books and dreaming of glory to be his. You would know that behind cheap chintz curtains in houses of cracker-box construction men worried over meeting their car payments and whether they would Get Ahead before they got cancer, and you would know that their women wrung hands over the plight of unmarried daughters whose coupling chances faded with each day, or over their own tardy menstrual cycles, or over whether they would be judged worthy of invitation from the local social lioness on the occasion of her next bridge game. So they would all be there in the little towns. Men, women, and children, stirred by their private devils and supping on their solitary fears.

I came into the little towns and looked upon the commonness, and did my mischief. I rented halls and auditoriums and arranged for Cullie to exhibit his person on courthouse lawns. I hired bands who could play hoedown music full of the gusty thump-thump of guitars and the high whine of fiddles, and I arranged for preachers to pray pious prayers over the assemblies. I greased and exhorted the grass-roots precinct workers, who would carry signs or faithfully whoop on cue, and came the proper time I closeted myself with the local pharaoh and after oiling him with words of high praise I gave unto him an ear.

And what I heard would have clabbered fresh milk.

The first to sour what was in the churn was an old judge with a puckered mouth and a heart hard enough to be used as a flintstone. One look at the old blackguard and you knew he would thumb through his dusty tomes in search of precedent to excuse whatever harsh punishment he might levy against one who stood at harvest of the wages of sin. The old judge had twitched to go to Congress in his youth, but the fates had decreed it not. The fates had put his young wife aboard a spirited steed and then had promptly bucked her off so that her spine slammed hard against the frozen ground on a cold winter morning, and the old judge (who was then a young judge, and who was from the bench merciful when it attended his large ambitions) spent a few hard hours praying to God that his bride not die. God granted his petition, and the judge gave up tobacco to show his appreciation to Deity. But it turned out the judge didn't pray for the right thing. He somehow forgot to pray for his wife's eventual recovery, and Deity didn't see fit to amend the petition without due cause. The young wife turned old in a hurry, bound to her bed and a wheel chair, and the flush left her cheeks. She grew hollow of cheek and brittle of bone, and gave herself to long fits of weeping. The judge found it in his heart to bear his burden uncomplaining.

He held the slim hope that someday his wife would rise from her bed and walk, and that forthwith he would rise from his low station to that of statesman in Washington. So he kept cheerful countenance and emptied her bedpans and spoke pious words, and everybody said what a brick the judge was in his trial and how the Lord had tested him severely and could not find him wanting. But the everybodys who said it couldn't see the judge pump acid in his soul. In the privacy of darkness he switched his prayer around by 360 degrees, asking God to take his wife and give her a home On High where the angels could attend her while he attended his own biting ambitions. But God Almighty saw no profit in the transaction and stuck to the original bargain. So the judge got old and grew sullen in his ways.

The old judge slouched across from me in his creaking swivel chair, cigarette ashes in little mounds and heaps on the desk cluttered by yellow law books and curling papers, his black suit hosting a crop of flaking dandruff. He puckered up the withered mouth until it looked as if he'd been sprinkled with alum. And gave the gathered mouth a sardonic twist, and said, "The Governor, if he's a prayin' man, he'd better rip off his most pious."

And I said, "If you were in the Governor's shoes, what would you pray for?"

And he said, "An early death and a place in glory."

And I said, "Is it that bad?"

And he said, "Hell, I've been watching this business more years than you got hairs on your head. It's as bad as you can get it."

And I said, "Well, what can we do to change it?"

The old judge favored me with a wicked smile and pronounced the sentence. "Buy some boats," he said. "Yeah, and when you get the boats, load them with niggers until the white folks turn handsprings, and then ship all the niggers to Afiker. That's the only answer to the riddle."

He's just down on life, I told myself. The old judge, he's just emptied too many bed pans.

But the young lawyer in the next town, who looked as if he might be president of the local Jaycees, and was, and who you knew lived in a rambling ranch-style house on the good edge of town and cut up at gin rummy at The Club on Saturday night and lifted voice in song in front of Presbyterian altars on the Lord's morning, crooned me the same dismal lullaby. Oh, he rendered it slow and without relish and there was inbred caution in his eyes, for he was the kind who comes upon early understanding that you don't get the crown by sticking your neck in the noose. He smiled, and let a pensive look take him, and he suffered respectfully around the eyes. Then he said apologetically, as if breaking news of a death in the family, "The younger people, they don't have the Blanton voting habit. You can't arouse them like you can the old folks because they don't remember the Depression and they don't feel any debt to the Governor for his social legislation."

"Then they've got midget memories," I said. "If it hadn't been for Cullie, they might be working in sweatshops or selling apples."

The young lawyer spread his hands helplessly, as if to show he had exhausted his resources in ill-fated causes. "They've kept some of the old traditions," he hinted.

"The wrong ones," I said. "Goddammit, they seem to do it by instinct."

He drew on a menthol cigarette and furrowed his smooth brow. "Right now," he said, "this situation about the Nigra going to the university has everybody uneasy. They're thinking about how many Nigras might be in the university when their little Johnny gets of college age. They don't howl about it like their elders, but they whisper a lot."

"How do you evaluate the Governor's chances?"

Discomfort camped in the young lawyer's face. He offered a silent prayer for deliverance from the moment, for predictions have a way of coming back on lonely nights to haunt the erring seer. "It could be marginal," he offered as a compromise.

"Cut the crap," I said. "Can Cullie take your county?"

He swallowed stagnant juices and gazed through the ceiling at the moon. "Right now," he said, "as of the moment, you understand . . . not saying things won't change. . . ."

"I guess I get the idea," I said.

And when he stood mute, I prompted him.

"You think we got the chance of a snowball in Hell?"

"There's always a chance," he said. "We might show them something yet."

"Sure we will," I said. "For the show is on the boards and we have got the star under contract."

The sign poked up from a matted clump of Johnson grass, and love vine climbed out of the tangle to cling to the base, and what the sun-faded letters said was NIMROD. *Pop. 1741.*

Cullie Blanton winked at the sign like it might be an old friend with whom he was in league for mischief, and he tossed the great head and brought up an honest laugh.

"Hell," he said, "they don't have seventeen hundred and forty-one people in this burg even if you count the cemetery and all in it."

Henry Muggins stretched his diminutive legs on the floor boards. He said, "Looks like the whole town oughta be buried."

"It's dead and don't know it," the Governor said. "Anybody who has come of age and kept his right mind has left it on schedule for the last twenty years."

"I hope you won't put that in your speech," I said.

"Boy," the Governor rumbled, "I will make the yahoos think this is Paradise lost and I have found it."

Our caravan rolled past a defunct service station with old posters advertising gas and oil curling on broken peninsulas of plate glass, and by a rusting cotton gin surrounded by careless weeds. Bo eased the limousine into the burg's short stretch of street, and above the street was a hanging banner, and on the banner in red, white, and blue letters large enough to smite the blind was what passed for the town's official greeting: WELCOME HOME, CULLIE.

A likeness of the Governor grinned down at us from the red-brick façade of The Farmers' State Bank, the meaty lips stretched over enough canvas to drape a wagon frame, and under the graven image the assurance that HE'LL NEVER SELL YOU OUT. Cullie eyeballed the trappings and let his gaze float to the platform draped with bunting on the open space of the courthouse lawn, where he would soon stand obliquely facing the Confederate soldier whose stone countenance commanded the square, and he said, "Right nice spontaneous outpouring of affection."

"Yeah," I said. "That little spontaneous outpouring of affection set us back about four hundred bills. Not counting the big feed to come."

"Some folks," the Governor grumbled, "seem to get a kick outta unmaskin' Santa Claus. All mah spoiled illusions. . . ."

A little coterie of local nabobs stood stiffly near the platform, nervously fluttering their hands and pasting their cowlicks down with spittle. They broke into an excited babble complete with broad gestures when some alert soul among them put the finger on our caravan.

The Governor said, "We're early, Bo. Tool on around the square and stop at the barbershop. Down there by the hotel."

Bo guided the limousine to the appointed place, nudging against the cracked concrete curb, and the half-dozen cars carrying reporters, photographers, and captive legislators trotted out to witness the kickoff of the Governor's campaign in the stomping grounds of his lost youth backed and hauled as they jockeyed for choice parking position.

The Governor flashed me a quick glance, "You think the picture takin' went off all right?"

"Couldn't beat it with a stick," I said. "Great man returns to humble beginnings. Tranfuses his spirit from the blood of boyhood. That's strong gargle."

Cullie Blanton grunted approval and bounded from the car, blinking in the mid-morning sunlight, running his eyes up and down the sidewalks starting to dot with folks. He favored the world with his professional grin.

A balding jerk of beef with stained teeth gaped at us from a bench in front of the barbershop, and snapped erect. His hands spasmed in empty air, and his Adam's apple bobbed like cork on water.

"God's sakes," he choked out. "God's sakes, that you, Cullie?"

Cullie Blanton stopped on the sidewalk, hands on hips, grinning. "You expectin' one the Apostles, maybe?"

The skinny jerk of beef made spluttering denial of the contention. "I'm Andy Potter, Cullie."

"God's mule," the Governor said. "You think I don't recollect mah own kind, Andy? You think I could forget a pan like that?"

Chuckles emitted from the gathering crowd, and the string bean with stained teeth wallowed in his private heaven. He bobbed his head in ecstasy and did a little unconscious shuffle step on the sidewalk. He gazed into the crowd, beaming broadly. "Knowed the Governor since we was boys," he announced.

"Yeah," the Governor grinned. "Yeah, me and Andy was hell on bullfrogs any time we could lay hands on a slingshot."

"Just like he always was," the string bean proclaimed.

"Hell," the Governor said. "Ain't nobody like he always was. What happened to that crop of hair you used to grow, the cows eat it?"

The crowd whooped and the string bean brushed his bald pate, too happy to form words.

"You gonna make a speech?" somebody called out.

"Try and stop me," the Governor said. "You think I drove all the way from Capitol City just to look at Andy Potter's bald dome?" There was much chortling and slapping of backs, while Andy devoured his hero with a lap dog's look of trust. "Yeah," Cullie Blanton said. "Yeah, I am goin' to make a speech. Only I'm gonna wait until you git your gizzards full of barbecue and catfish and until cold sody water sloshes around your innards so that you puff like a toad. Hell, you think I'm gonna waste my words of wisdom on a passel of folks got nothin' but vittels on the brain and growls in the guts?"

Through the laughter an old man yelled, "You been out to the home place yet?"

"Yeah," the Governor said. "Yeah, I been out there."

"How'd it look to you?" the old geezer inquired.

"Like some mortals I know," the Governor said. "Old and wore out and like it's passed too much water." While the crowd hooted and danced in glee, Cullie grinned at his interrogator. "Lord's sakes, Talmage, don't you never intend to give up the ghost?"

"Naw," the old nester grinned. "I made me a pact with Jesus."

"I hope," the Governor said, "it's good until after the election."

"If it is, I might vote for 'tother feller."

"You might come down with boils, too," Cullie Blanton shot back. He eyed the crowd while the knee-slappers did their bit, and he said, "I hope the rest of you got better memories than Talmage. I hope you remember how hard it is to wean a bull calf, and how I went up there to Capitol City and jerked the public tit out of their mouths and turned 'em out to forage."

"What you done for us lately?" somebody called.

"Stepped on a tumblebug," the Governor grinned. Then, "You know how long it took me to git in from the home place today over that slab I built?"

"Fifteen minutes," somebody guessed.

"Eight," the Governor said. "Eight minutes, and I've spent half a day under the boilin' sun clankin' over that old road when it wasn't any more than a hog wallow. And you got slabs like that runnin' to ever' place in this county. Ain't that pure as Gospel? Well, ain't it?" And when their huzzahs had affirmed truth, the Governor turned toward the old nester tagged as Talmage. "And you talk about votin' for 'tother fellow. Jesus! Don't you like yourself?"

"Aw," somebody called, "Talmage, he's just talken to hear his head rattle."

A young dandy with pomaded hair and an officious air pushed into the inner circle, groping for the Governor's hand. After he had pumped it enough to draw up a keg of water from pure stone, he made noises about the official welcoming committee awaiting His Excellency's pleasure on the platform. Cullie Blanton turned, squinting through the sunlight, to regard the official party.

"You go tell ole Monk Mawson," he said, "that I'll be over there after I git a hair trim. Hell, it's early yet. Tell Monk to have another slug of fruit-jar whisky and sweat under the sun a while. It'll be good for his skin pores."

The young man coughed discreetly. "Mister Harry Clark is mayor now," he said. "He's heading the delegation."

The Governor's eyes popped surprise. "What the hell happened to ole Monk? Somebody catch him with his fingers in the till?"

The fop with pomaded hair, who looked like the local high school speech teacher but turned out to be the band director, gave out with a few more of the covering coughs. Then he said, "Mister Mawson passed on almost two years ago."

A shadow crossed the Governor's face. "Monk?" he said. "Monk Mawson . . . dead?" He whirled to face me. "How the hell come nobody told me that?"

There was an uncomfortable silence; then one of the nesters in the front row offered up wisdom. He said, "You sent a spray of flowers and a tellygram. I seen the bouquet myself. And they read the tellygram over the remains."

The Governor tried manfully to recover lost ground. He said, "Sometimes the mind won't hold too much sorrow. Sometimes it will spit out what hurts it to remember." He shook his head in sadness. "Ole Monk Mawson," he muttered. "Why I remember the times we roamed these woods and. . . ." His voice trailed off and he corralled old visions. "What possible use could Jesus have had for ole Monk Mawson?" he demanded of nobody in particular. His head came up and he put the grin back on, and said, "Hell, let's don't cry over spilt milk. Ole Monk, he'd want us to have another slug and sing a round of 'Seein' Nellie Home.' You give ole Monk his due cracks at the jug, and he would sing that song as sure as God made Chinamen."

"And the Devil made niggers," somebody yelled.

"Hell," somebody else offered. "Even the Devil wouldn't do that. Niggers must of sprung from apes."

The Governor ignored the sallies. He told the pomaded one to express his greetings to the official committee, and said he would be along when he had his hair trim. He turned back to face the barbershop, put an arm around the spindly shoulders of Henry Muggins, and said, "I want you to know my good friend Henry Muggins. Henry, he don't look like much stuffin's but he's Speaker of the House and when I have to bust nuts it is Henry who hands me the hammer." When the crowd had nodded and mumbled its welcome the Governor said, "Y'all stay around and jaw with Henry if you like. I'm gonna let ole Whitey Vinson chop on my scalp some. He's been botchin' my hair for forty years." The Governor stopped and looked around him, faint puzzlement crinkling between the eyes. "Where the hell *is* ole Whitey? He makin' so much money he can afford to give the cold shoulder to his governor?"

From the crashing silence I knew something was amiss. But the Governor, caught up in homecoming, missed the signal. "Whitey!" he yelled toward the shop. "Whitey! You ole butcher! You in there?"

"Naw," the string bean named Andy Potter said. He shuffled his feet in agony. "Naw, he ain't in there."

"Well, where the hell is he?"

There was a little more of the silence. And Cullie said, "Cat got your tongue?"

Then somebody in the crowd said, "He's the same place Monk Mawson is."

The silence grew, and Cullie turned in it, his face old and all the joy gone from his eyes. "Dead," he said flatly. He let his eyes rove along the sidewalks, and across the square, and he turned to inspect carefully his own giant image posed over the bank building as if he might be deciding whether to favor the fellow with his vote. "All gone," he said. "Jesus. All the old ones gone."

We had repaired to the Governor's little pea-patch farm for the weekend to lick our wounds and succor our souls—both kinds. After five days of the slab connecting all the Nimrods to each other, the Governor had blurted, "Jim, how'd you like a little outin' this weekend? Seek a few country pleasures . . . ?"

"Always look forward to it," I said, thinking: *the way I look forward to typhoid fever.*

"Fahn, jus' fahn," the Governor had said, flashing teeth. "We'll retreat inta the rollin' hills and commune with God's own bountiful blessin's of nature. Refurbish our immortal souls."

So we went tooling along the broad highway yet again, bouncing over back roads leading up to the pea-patch farm, looking for all the world like a safari of winners from second-rate quiz shows: our cars laden with electric fry pans, silk pajamas, a few bottles of choice sour-mash bourbon, prime beefsteaks, smoked oysters, an ice-making machine—any creature comfort happening to pleasure the Governor's mind.

Generally, Cullie Blanton invited a few pols up to the farm. (It was a good place, he said, to put axle grease on their political wagons.) He might summon some common garden-variety legislators to play the role of court jesters, and they would come, too—for they had by-God better. He might ask an old crony along, like Speaker Muggins, or some tame newspapermen. And a couple of captive staffers would be brought in to pissant toddies or place phone calls when the Governor's restless juices started to flow. There was always Bo, who drove, and who was pressed into service as combination cook and bottle washer if Melacadies didn't merit weekend punishment. And there was always lucky me.

On this particular weekend the Governor had disdained the hangers-on, newspapermen, and clowns-at-court. Only three great nature lovers wended their way back into the woods: Bo, the Great Man, and your present hero. We arrived at the little pea-patch farm about sundown on Friday, and after we'd done violence to some prime beef, we had

twitched our toes on the front porch and yawned up at God. We
crawled early into sheets, logged by the pure, thin country air and
lulled by chirping crickets.

Saturday wasn't so bad, if you have the stomach for clattering over
all passable paths crisscrossing three hundred sixty acres, and inspecting barbed-wire fences while keeping your suede shoes out of fresh cow
chips. The Governor was in his benevolent country-squire mood,
whooping at plowed ground and praising wild flowers. There had been
plenty of cold beer iced down in a metal milk can like the farmers cart
to market full of old Bossie's juice, and the beer had helped anesthetize
my bucolic pain.

Saturday night, while everybody else swarmed out of the hills to
stomp their feet to fiddles down at the community center and carve
each other up with their Barlows when likker got confused with personal honor, we settled down to more serious toe twitching. The Governor gazed on his sock feet as if studying some way to improve his
technique, while I presided as sole sitting judge. Along about nine
o'clock his head began to nod against his thick chest and he jerked it
up suddenly, stiffly, as if afraid his cane-bottomed chair might run off
the road. On what I'd counted as the eighty-third nod the Governor
padded into the old house, yawning unconditional surrender to Mor-
pheus' sweet arms.

By Sunday morning I was ready to dynamite the church of my
choice just for the sound of the boom. The Governor had slept late,
and on arising tucked away all the flapjacks Bo could mangle in the
electric fry pan. Then, patting his belly in reward for the manful way
it had taken its punishment, the Governor began to plow through a
brief case stuffed with paper work.

He said, "You want some flapjacks, Jim?"

"No," I said.

"Bo, fix him a stack."

"No," I said again. "I had coffee. And some juice."

"Hundred proof most likely," the Governor said, rummaging in the
brief case.

"No. Orange juice."

"*Sissy* goddamn breakfast," the Governor boomed. "We got a big
week ahead. Bo, stir him up somethin' will stick to his ribs." Bo's oxlike face struggled to comprehend the conflict. When he'd figured out
who was boss he reached for the batter bowl.

After the forced feeding I wandered among the chinaberry trees in the yard, listening to a mockingbird, searching the sky hopefully for a tornado or the Second Coming. When the telephone jangled inside the old cabin, I moved toward it on the run, determined to talk to somebody even if it proved to be a wrong number. Bo met me in the gloomy knotty-pine hall, jerking a thumb toward an old antique wall phone I knew to be a disguised modern job with jazzed-up innards that had set the Governor back two bills. After a concert of humming telephone wires, Zero Phillips mumbled in my ear.

The Governor's laconic aide said, "I wouldn't have called, only I got some very bad news."

I said, "Zero, you got a special talent for it. Any of your ancestors on the *Titanic?*" After the wires had hummed a couple of eternities, I said, "You want to leave that bad news general, or make it specific?"

"The morning papers are out."

I waited, and there was the hum of wires. Along about the middle of the fifth symphony, I said, "Well, that's real bad news, all right. Sure thank you for calling. You think we ought to request Federal troops?"

"*The Avenger,*" Zero said. "It endorsed the Governor for reelection. On the front page."

I made a flat whistle, then broke the Sabbath with pithy expletives.

"They laid it on heavy," Zero mourned. "Called the Governor the greatest friend they've had since Franklin D. Roosevelt." I figured Zero would save the worst for last, his sense of drama dictating it. He didn't disappoint. "Worse thing's how they called it the way it *is.* Said the Governor's *got* to hoot and dance for local consumption—but in the end will help that black boy get in the university."

"Father, forgive them. . . ."

"It reads like the Governor had signed a secret pact with Martin Luther King. Whole editorial sounds like the other side wrote it."

"Hell," I said, "they probably did. They paid for it." To anybody raised in the rickets-and-boll-weevil South, the thing was as familiar as Moon Pies and Ara-Cee Cola. *The Avenger,* as the more clever may have wigged out, is a newspaper. And that's not all. It's a Negro newspaper—the biggest of its kind in our state, and the most cussed. For it often had the pure-dee audacity to imply the Negro isn't exactly overjoyed in his Stepin Fetchit role, to hint that he may not be a plumb damn fool about watermelon or have a natural sense of rhythm.

Still, *The Avenger* was often a happy convenience. It was something all pols must have around: a whipping boy, a straw man to flog. Let a cornpone pol worth the elastic in his red galluses face a tough election, and he would take the stump to cry how *The Avenger* was the willing tool of Thurgood Marshall, the Pope of Rome, Organized Jewry, the Kremlin, and Jimmy Hoffa. Nobody with a nominal sum of their marbles coveted an endorsement by such a sheet—and for a long time nobody got one. Then somebody with a nose for commerce got struck with a profitable notion. If endorsement by *The Avenger* was such a cross to carry, how did you load the burden on the other fellow's back?

You did not do it, it turned out, by hydraulic lifts. You did it by application of long green. You bought your opponent an endorsement calculated to cause him blushes. Then you trotted out the endorsement to show how your opponent was doing ugly behind the barn with insidious forces God had no doubt thought up just ahead of serpents. You rolled up the endorsement and hit the endorsed over the head. You bashed in his brains.

The bidding got spirited. *The Avenger*'s publisher, like a lot of his white colleagues, proved to be a mathematician first and an idealist second. He could always determine the highest price. Now Zero was telling me, in his fashion, the Wooster forces had met the price.

Zero said, "I didn't think they'd dare. It's a damn double cross."

"So it's a double cross. You think they invented it?"

"But the Governor passed that *special bill* for them! He gave them a tax break on some quasi-legal corporation they'd formed. It was . . . well, pretty raw. All our tax experts advised against it. It was a malodorous boondoggle."

"Before you get too far into the self-righteous bit . . . you remember how that particular bill got to be law, Zero?"

"No. . . ."

"It was a little business transaction between our great leader and a free, enlightened press," I said. "It was in payment for an endorsement of one of the Governor's opponents four years ago." The wires hummed while Zero's memory dealt him powerful pokes about the conscience. Before I hung up I said, "Hurts, don't it?"

The Governor was reigning over his rumpled bed midst a profusion of papers. He spoke from around a lemon drop. "Jim, loan me some brains. This here"—and he waved an engrossed bill—"is that farm-to-market road bill Speedy Sparks whooped through the other day. For Kerrilee County. It makes nearly eighty miles of blacktop road. But—"

"Boss, Zero just called. He said—"

"But," the Governor continued, "I've looked at the map. And it wouldn't take more than forty, fifty goddamn miles at most to accomplish the same objective. *If*, that is, Speedy's real concern is paved roads." He chewed on a pencil, frowning. "Ole Speedy's bill winds that road around like a snake. Pure-dee waste of money."

"Then veto it. Zero said—"

"Not that cut and dried," the Governor muttered. "Speedy Sparks, he's a good man. He's got good instincts. He pops it to the rich folks, and does his damage in the poor folks' name. I like ole Speedy. He's got somethin' in his head besides gourd seed."

"Then give him his road," I said, impatiently. "Zero called—"

"If that road winds for eighty-odd miles because somebody didn't do his homework—well, that's a waste, all right. On the other hand, if that eighty-odd miles happens to be less than accidental because old Speedy's got a relative or pal in the pavin' business—well, that's a greater waste still. For it would corrupt a good man."

"Either way, it's a waste. Zero—"

"But there's a third possibility. Suppose ole Speedy is just featherin' his political nest—not paddin' his pocketbook? Suppose he's figgered out that paved roads runnin' by all those farms would increase the land value. Which, in turn, would cause the farmers to think kindly of him and to vote for him until they got too old to vote—and then teach their *children* to do it?"

I said, "That justify the waste of money?"

"It might," the Governor said, nodding. "Looked at the right way, it might not be a waste. More of a good investment, maybe. Speedy's got a tough row to hoe in that district. If he can hang on to his seat he might get to be Speaker of the House, one day. Maybe even governor, after they've scattered my dust and voted appropriations to build my goddamn statue. And Speedy would do a lot for the folks." Cullie Blanton's big hand worried his upper lip. "It'd be cheap at the price," he said. "Boostin' somebody like Speedy up to where he'd do some good."

"Then," I said, "it boils down to judgment. You think Speedy'd steal?"

"Boy," he said, "*ever'body* will steal. What you got to worry about's whether the stealin' makes sense." He placed the bill on the edge of the bed. "First thing tomorrow get Speedy for me. I'll check his pulse."

I said, "Provided I can get it out—congratulations. You just got endorsed. By *The Avenger*. And on the very front page."

The Governor's head snapped up from his sheaf of papers. "Bad?"
"Compared to you," I said, "F.D.R. was the Grand Kleagle of the Klan."

"Hell and goddamn," the Governor breathed. "The time I've lost in wooing. . . ." Amidst new and greater oaths he said, "At least I hope they got a good price. I hope they didn't sell me out cheap."

Cullie Blanton rose from the bed and stalked to a window. His view took in a sagging chicken house, and beyond the chicken house a mound of hay. "Goddammit," he said, and his jaws knotted. "Goddammit, how you gonna help the buggers when they won't help themselves? Sometimes I feel like chunkin' the whole kit and caboodle."

"Well, this makes it official. You're the certified boogy man now, Governor. You're the black man's choice and the white man's burden."

The Governor said, "I *knew* Wooster's bunch would put in a bid. But that darky publisher, he sent me word he wouldn't sell. He sent me word he was committed to this thing heart and goddamn soul. I guess he forgot to commit his pocketbook." Cullie Blanton accused the distant cow pens of some vague indiscretion. "I got careless," he said. "I shoulda had foresight to go to him in sweetness and reason, and threaten to by-God *ruin* him if he sold me."

With a misplaced attempt at levity I said, "At least we'll get the Negro vote."

The Governor lip-farted. He said, "That's about as helpful as leprosy."

And I knew what he meant. Anybody who had reached school age would have known what he meant. The old statistics were there in my head. We had a million Negroes in our state. But only forty-six thousand were qualified to vote, and it wasn't getting any better. And wouldn't for a long time. For the poll tax was there to stop them, and the buck-six-bits it cost. If that wasn't enough to do it, there was the state literacy test, on the books since the end of Reconstruction, which I doubt even the Governor and I could have passed by pooling our brains or writing half the answers on our shirt cuffs. Even if the forty-odd thousand showed up to vote for Cullie Blanton to the last man, it wouldn't be a drop in the bucket.

I said, "What can we do about it?"

"Tell the truth," the Governor said. "Drastic remedy, but it might just work. Hoot and howl how the other side bought 'em off."

I said, "You think the peckerwoods will buy it?"

"Hell, I dunno. It's all we can do. Maybe the goddamn truth will confuse 'em enough we'll get away with it." The Governor wandered about patting his pockets in fruitless search of a cigarette. When I had supplied it and fired it he drew in a deep, shuddering poke. Exhaling, he said, "One of these years all that will be changed. One of these years the Nigra will be commonplace in our colleges, and eatin' in our restaurants, and joinin' up in our clubs. And they'll come boilin' out of the brush and out of our factories to vote in wholesale lots. But don't hold your breath till it happens. For it won't happen in the time of our bones."

I could hear Bo banging pots and pans preparatory to spoiling the noon meal, while the Governor sucked at his cigarette. After a bit I said, "And in the meantime?"

"In the meantime," the Governor said, "I reckon us one-gallus politicians got to declare a moratorium on goddamn statesmanship and go around yellin' a certain amount of nigger. . . ."

10

THE GOVERNOR said, "Jim. Mah shoes."

So I got up from the leather couch and carried my form over proudly, and I pulled off the Governor's shoes.

He grunted as they came free, two short explosions. He rubbed the ball of one foot, kneading it in slow circles. Then he propped his feet on a leather-covered stool and let his toes stir in their new freedom. For a moment he measured me and Speaker Muggins, as if trying to fit us for pine boxes. "You ever know me to run from a fight?"

The Speaker stirred uneasily under the "politicians' wallpaper"— the grinning mugs of folk heroes who grimaced at us from framed positions on the walls: postured statesmen, movie stars, old soldiers running to medals, men who had knocked home runs for pay.

"Well, I am in a fight," the Governor said. "And I am not runnin'." Cullie Blanton swung his eyes around and it was like doing business with the business end of a shotgun. The man behind the shotgun said, "Henry, I wanta address a joint session tomorrow."

"*Tomorrow?*" The Speaker wanted the folly reaffirmed. "Tomorrow?"

"Tomorrow noon," the Governor said. "I am goin' to knock all those fool segregation bills in the head. Yeah, like I had done it with a poleax."

Henry Muggins had no words fitting to the occasion. So he just bugged his eyes and emitted a long, low whistle. Finally I shook free of my trauma. "Hell," I said, "you can't do that."

"Hide and watch me."

I said, "Goddammit, we've worked ourselves to the bone hauling you around this state trying to perfume you up so you'll smell pleasing to the electorate. And now you go and jump in sheep-dip. Out of some strange twitch to be noble."

The Governor looked at me like maybe I had lent on usury. He said,

"Nobility's got no more to do with it than you have got to do with the Miss America contest. I am goin' to do it for the good reason I *got* to do it." The Speaker stared at him, faintly awed. Cullie Blanton seemed not to notice. He said, "If that buncha stumble bums ram their seg bills through, I am done the same as burnt meat. The President'll send in troops and declare martial law. That your idea of what we need to win an election?"

Henry Muggins said, "Might reach some accommodation. With the President."

The Governor snorted. "You think the President's gonna sit on his hands until his rump grows knuckles while those cornpone cavemen over there"—and he made a sweeping gesture toward the capitol—"whoop through laws puttin' a goddamn nightly curfew on Nigras? You think with all those Yankee pols yellin' for scalps the President can afford the luxury of lookin' the other way while those swamp boobs over there"—he jerked his head—"twist the laws around so our schools become some kind of hybrid private institutes supported by public funds? You think he'll hold still for voter qualifications to be toughed-up until a bluegum couldn't get a poll tax even if he happened to be rich as goose fat . . . or maybe had enough brains to rent out?"

"You put a hard question," the Speaker confessed.

"Hell, Henry, you don't have to be smart enough to read in the dark to come with the answer."

I said, "Boss, what makes you think the folks will buy it?"

The Governor cut the shotgun eyes at me. "The road show we just come off of. Mah crowds were good. They still clapped at the right placcs and turned on tears when the script called for it."

"On the road," I said, "you avoided the Mau Mau question like the pox. This time you'll be trying to sell the folks merchandise they've never bought down here."

"Boy," the Governor said, "I could sell the folks life insurance on the Rosenbergs."

I said, "Suppose the legislature balks?"

"When a mule balks," the Governor said, "you bust his ass. Anybody don't vote with me, I'll go to his home district and tell the folks how their public man's taken to eatin' Russian fish eggs, marcellin' his hair, and talkin' with a lisp. Henry . . . what you think?"

Henry Muggins unhappily pondered the proposition while I silently screamed at him to respond in the negative. After he had agonized with himself, he said that yes, he thought the Governor could do it.

Cullie Blanton rewarded his old friend with a dazzling smile. I gave
the Speaker a look of reproach, answered by a shrug of puny shoulders
that seemed to ask why should a man piss into a hurricane?

"Boss," I said, "I don't think you can do it."

Cullie Blanton turned his head abruptly, as if somebody had just set
off a dynamite cap in his presence. Coldly, he said, "Speak your piece."

"Number one. I disagree about the crowd reaction. I tried to tell
you out on the road, but you were too carried away to listen. They gave
you the big cheer in your home town, and you kept hearing it the rest
of the trip. But what you heard was an echo. Oh, you're a brand-name,
Governor, and so they gave you your due. But I don't think their hearts
were in it. I didn't see anybody jumping up and down." I paused, but
the cold eyes didn't flicker. "Number two. You didn't talk about the
boog thing—but *they* did. Out on the crowd fringes they were grum-
bling about 'this here nigger business' and asking themselves, what's
Cullie going to do about it? Nobody told them the answer."

"Any more?"

"Number three. Those opinion polls we got a couple of days ago
showed Poppa Posey picking up ground. He—"

"Poppa Posey! That old clown couldn't win with a fix on."

"That old clown's siphoning off votes. And the votes that old fraud
is siphoning off come out of *your* political gas tank—not Wooster's."

"You about through playin' Walter Lippman?"

"Not entirely. Number four is the Wooster campaign. It's been
wised up. Somebody's coached the general in the fine art of greasing
the folks. They've taught him better than to go stiff-necking through
the crowds with his nose turned up like he was sniffing dirty feet.
Somebody had him get rid of those fanatics who wouldn't reveal his
campaign schedule to the press for fear of violating some obscure
'security arrangement,' for God's sakes. They persuaded the general
you can't run for public office in secret."

The Governor's only comment was a frown. He tapped a foot impatiently. I said, "If you try to hatchet those seg bills, you'll go it alone.
Our two U.S. Senators will jump on you with both feet—and except
for ole Ed Gobert, so will the whole Congressional delegation. And our
state's attorney general, whose ambition is beginning to show on his
sleeve, may get to seeing himself as a future governor—and use you to
get there. And think how the newspapers will turn you over live coals
on a slow spit."

Cullie Blanton said, "You must think I'm crazy as ole Hitler. The newspapers, our Senators, all those Congressmen—hell, they've never been in my corner. As for Poppa Posey and that nutty general, I'll take the play away from 'em. It's the kinda thing will cause the folks at the creek forks to bang their knees and say, 'By gum, ole Cullie tole 'em, didn't he?' For in spite of the lack of faith in me *some people* seem to have put on display lately"—and the shotgun eyes bored in on me—"I know I can get my message over to that legislature without soundin' like I'm for mixed marriages and chocolate drops. I'm gonna put this thing in such a way can't anybody—Wooster nor Poppa Posey nor a convention of Baptist preachers—fight me without castin' their lot with rabble rousers and infidels."

I said, "Would you mind explaining how?"

"I sure would," the Governor said, cheerfully, "until the proper time." He turned to the Speaker, who sat with a long-suffering air about him. "Noon tomorrow, Henry. And I want those brush apes sittin' in their seats like good little boys, and with their hair combed."

Cullie Blanton jerked around to face me. "At the hazard," he said, "of offendin' one of the Free World's greatest political analysts, I got to set you straight on what happened durin' our little road show. While you mooned around the malcontents on the edge of the crowds, you musta forgot to look up near the platform where the *folks* gathered. Why, little ole ladies cried and told me how they prayed to their Lord for me at night—and the snuff dippers lined up ten deep to wring mah goddamn hand!"

When I left the Governor's office he was pointing out bruises to Speaker Muggins—evidence, he said, of how the folks had nearly squeezed him to goddamn death in their love.

The visitors' galleries were jammed a good hour before the Governor claimed the podium. Something about a joint session puts a special crinkle in the air. Legislators scrambled for seats where their likenesses would be easily picked up by TV cameras. Zero Phillips jangled around the crowded press table near the front of the chamber. Now and then a newspaperman would pluck peevishly at his skinny elbow, and the lanky Zero would go into a shrugging, flapping soft-shoe dance of personal regrets.

Hell, I was no different from the rest of them. I was in the chamber before it had half filled, gawking. I exchanged a little light banter with some early-bird legislators, and shuffled around wishing time to pass. The thing now rested with God and Cullie Blanton. The Governor's speech—worked at and rewritten and sworn over through the dark of night, christened in coffee and bourbon and fizz waters said to cure heartburn—was neatly mimeographed and locked in Cullie Blanton's private office safe.

Zero disengaged himself from a griping newsman and ambled my way. He said, "My press relations could stand a little repair."

"They bugging you because you won't release the speech?"

"Not won't," Zero said. "*Can't*. Wish I knew the Governor's reason for guarding it like gold. No disrespect intended, Jim—but I don't think it's that hot a speech."

When Cullie Blanton came stalking down center aisle he was all crackle and business. There was none of the mane tossing and grinning of the campaign trail, none of the old winking and rubber-facing that he often used to tell legislators he knew the joke was on somebody, and the somebody wasn't him. The members and state officials rose in the Presence as was custom, the black robes of the state Supreme Court justices rustling a bit when they settled back. The Governor's ovation was restrained—to put it mildly.

Speaker Muggins droned through the necessary introduction of the Great Man. The Governor accepted dutiful applause, shuffling papers at the podium while photographers got in their last-second licks. He gave the assembly a moment for final throat clearings and ritual coughs, and when his head came up Cullie Blanton cocked it, as if listening for some celestial signal. It was hard to say whether he heard it, but after a while he held the pages of his speech up in full view. His eyes studied the huge fist that held the orderly sheaf of papers.

The Governor said, "As speeches go, I reckon this is a purty good one. A lot of hard work was put in on it, and some of it was mine." He posed with the speech above his head, scowling slightly when some of the photographers violated House rules by firing their flashguns after a speech had started.

"I worked harder on this speech than the one I gave when I graduated high school. The top member of the class got to show off by speakin' at the graduation. And I won." Then he grinned, his first departure from sobersides demeanor. "I wouldn't want anybody to be overly impressed by the fact I qualified," he said. "We only had three in the class. One was a blind boy, and our little one-room schoolhouse didn't have too many books in Braille. One was a poor boy hated school so bad he only came to the schoolhouse on cold days 'cause he was too lazy to cut firewood at home. And the other one, the *smart* one who got to make the speech"—the Governor's eyes twinkled merrily—"was such a durn fool he wound up in pollyticks."

While the chuckles died away Cullie brought his speech down and placed it on the podium. He frowned down, rapping knuckles in measured strokes against the papers. "The speech won't do. Oh, it's got all the magic words in it. Justice. Democracy. States' rights. Responsibility. Freedom. It even manages to brag on me a little bit without makin' it sound like I invented gunpowder. It quotes the Bible where it should, and it's even got some lines my college-boy speech writer assures me come from a poet by the name of"—and here the Governor made a show of shuffling through his notes—"Geoffrey Chaucer. This speech"—he thumped it once more—"tells how I've labored to build you folks roads and highways and good schools for your kiddies. How I raised your pensions, and shoved some your tax burdens off on the fat boys, and it brags on you for havin' sense enough to elect me several times. It compares you august members of the legislature to Winston Churchill, and the Englishman comes out loser. I reckon it's a document could serve as a model of its kind. But then, it don't say anything you don't know by heart. . . ."

Down at the press table Zero Phillips offered a series of shoulder shrugs to his agitated wards, who muttered frantically while they dived for papers and pencils. A restless rustle swept the galleries. On the floor, experienced old pols shuffled uneasily in the presence of the unconventional.

The crazy Governor said, "I am goin' to do somethin' certain candidates offerin' themselves for high positions consider fatal as snake bite. I am goin' to stand up here and talk sense. Plain gumption. No fancy words to dress the speech up in. It's high time the truth got told. Some of you won't like it any more than the castor oil your mamas forced down your throats when you had the bellyache. But like your mama reached for castor oil because it was *needed,* I'm gonna reach up and take down a whole jug of one hunnert-proof, uncut, bottled-in-bond truth. The kinda truth no *good* man ever gagged on."

The Governor blinked, pulled at his nose, stared at the television cameras as if he'd just discovered them. "There's some," he said, "would have you drink rotgut. Rotgut'll make you go blind, cause your innards to boil and your feet to stumble. It'll make you see things that ain't there. It'll make you fight your own people." After a pause for effect, he leaned across the podium and put the question straight: "That what you want?

"No," the Governor supplied. "You don't want that. And *I* don't want it. You want to be clear in the head and in charge of all your limbs. So have a little swig of pure, uncut truth. Try a little of my bottled-in-bond."

Behind the podium and six paces to the right stood Bo Steiner, his trooper's face showing puzzlement at why the Governor chose to talk about drinking whisky. Bo's brains were having trouble handling what his ears picked up, so he could merely stare numbly at unrevealed menaces in the crowd.

He said, "A century ago our granddaddies took up arms. They fought at Fort Sumter and Shiloh and Manassas—at Gettysburg and Richmond and Atlanta. They ran through shot and shell at almost ever' spot the creek forked or grass grew under dew. They fought for a cause they had faith in—a cause that even today can send chills up my spine when I hear the old songs and see visions of old warriors."

An abrupt, automatic-reflex cheer went up for The Cause. Then the applause faltered and faded in uncertainty when Cullie Blanton held up a stopping hand.

"But that cause," the Governor crooned, his voice so low and hoarse everyone leaned in to hear, "that cause is dead." Then he stood on tiptoe and roared it up from the whisper, lashing them with it, knocking them off the edges of their seats and back against their spines. "*Dead, dead, dead!*"

There was a great, involuntary sucking in of air throughout the chamber. Mutters and growls and whispers followed. I thought, *Now you've done it. You've gone and kicked Jeff Davis in the nuts.*

The Governor brought his voice back to normal. He said, "Death is a painful thing. Especially to the mourners left behind. But there comes a time to dry old tears and bury the dead. And get on with God's prime business of livin'. So let's bury our dead. And that ole cause we've loved . . . friends, it's dead. It lies mortally stricken." Having ratified the heresy, he paused ever so slightly. Then, "All my life I've worshipped at the feet of old Confederate soldiers—just as you, and your daddies before you, did. And nobody gets more pure pleasure than ole Cullie Blanton when the sap of spring commences to rise and we turn out all over our beloved Dixie to reenact the old battles against the Yankee invader. Oh, it's enough to make the step

quicken and the blood boil. The beauty of it! The pageantry! The romance! All that marching of strong-limbed young men . . . all the rattle of sabers and the boom of cannons . . . all the white horses loping
by. Yes, it is beautiful! My, and how stirrin'! Oh, and so upliftin'!" He
let them shift with the doubt of where he was taking them. Then he
said, his voice flat and metallic hard, "And it is all bosh. It is pie in the
sky, and the truth ain't in it. It won't come out in the wash."

The sharp, hissing intakes of breath again.

The Governor plunged on. "It is false, because no blood runs red
from the broken veins of men when we bugle up the old glories! It is
false, because no horses spill their innards on the ground, and no
homes are burned and pillaged—no torch set to the grain! It is false,
because when the show is over no mothers take their children by the
hand to make the sad, slow walk to the graveyard! It is false, because
when the show is over our young warriors don't set in belly-deep bogs
eatin' maggots in their stew. It is false, because our play soldiers rush
off the field for a glass of lemonade, a shower bath, and pizza-pie
wedges in a air-conditioned picture show!" In pain and puzzlement the
Governor asked, "Didja ever see a single solitary *one* of those re-created
battles where the South didn't *win?* Didja ever see one whur the Yankees didn't flee in terror?" He let them think about all the bosh they
had seen under the label of history, let it soak in. Then he asked in soft,
cat-walking tones, "Did the South win the war? Did it? Hah? Is the capitol at Montgomery?"

The Governor said conversationally, "No, the South did not win the
war. The South did not win with Robert E. Lee, nor Jefferson Davis,
nor ole Jubilee Early. It didn't win with Stonewall Jackson, nor with
Nathan Bedford Forrest gettin' there 'fustest with the mostest.' It
didn't win even with—presumin' we *had* it—the blessin' of Almighty
God."

Cullie Blanton inspected the audience below the podium and un-
seen thousands massed in front of their magic tubes. He said, "You are
good folks. I like to think I'm a good man. But are we wiser than
ole Jeff? Can we win battles General Lee lost? Are we stronger than the
Army of the Confederacy? I don't flatter myself by presumin' to succeed
whur better men have failed. It's like a friend of mine—ole Earl Long
over there in Louisiana—said a while back. Earl said, 'Whatta we
gonna do now? Da Feds have got da bomb.' "

Down on the floor legislators swapped secret looks affirming suspected gubernatorial madness. The gallery owls grew angry faces. Through it all, Cullie Blanton seemed about as sensitive as the workings of a two-bit wristwatch.

He said, "The war's over. And if you gentlemen down there on the floor"—he made a vague, sweeping gesture—"where I once served with the same problems, the same ambitions, and the same high hopes you feel stirrin' your innards today, if you good gentlemen pass a bunch of hard-line bills, you've plunged us back into the war. And it is a war that *we just can't win!*"

On the floor somebody yelled, "Quitter!" A mumble of assent from legislators and spectators mingled in the tight air.

The Governor's eyes were hard marbles. He rasped it out: "Was Lee a quitter at Appomattox Courthouse? You think he had a *choice?*" It stilled them. "Like it or not, *I'm* your general. If you pass those bills been dropped in the hopper the last few days, you've tied your general's hands. Yeah, you've handed over his sword, and you've robbed him of his bargainin' power. We'll be lucky to keep our horses for spring plowin'. For the Federals got the bomb. The Supreme Court"—the Governor suffered in what passed for patience a rolling, round chorus of boos—"the Supreme Court has ruled against us. The Congress has voted against us. The Justice Department's against us. The national news outlets have propagandized against us. The President of the United States—well, I don't want to speak harsh of him. He's the leader of the Free World and everybody's devilin' him. But I think we all understand *he* won't hold with us in the long run. But that don't mean we got to be ground down to dust. I don't think the President the United States wants that, nor the Congress wants it."

Like a shot, a leather-lungs exploded in the galleries: "What *do* they want? To put the South in chains?"

And near the husky, well-dressed man who had yelled from the gallery to my left, a little ole woman with her hair bandannaed like Aunt Jemima shook her fist, screeching, "Ne' mind all that windbaggin'. How about them *niggers?*"

Speaker Muggins was at the podium before the hubbub could rise. He crashed the gavel down. His voice was strong, though full of trebles: "Sergeant at arms! Remove those people!" His face was wizened and red as he banged the gavel again and again. Page boys and capitol cops began to tug the demonstrators into the halls. The old woman screamed and clawed all the way. When her shouts were only an echo the Speaker said, "We will *not* tolerate further incidents. You are here as guests. You will either conduct yourselves as ladies and gentlemen or take your leave." Most of the galleries sat sheepishly under the lecture, though a scattered few tromped out, muttering defiance. Some newsmen broke from their table to pursue the malcontents.

Governor Blanton moved behind the podium, rolling his eyes to the vacant seats of the expelled demonstrators. "My departed friend up there," he said dryly, "raised the question of puttin' the South in chains. My good folks, our beloved South *is* in chains. Tied hand and foot. Reconstruction. A terrible time. Reconstruction brought the chains—and oh! it was Hell, right enough. We suffered, and of mercy there was none. God grant it never happen again. But Reconstruction was a long time ago. Yet, we keep on wearin' our chains—white as well as black, friends. *White* as well as *black*. How long we gotta languish in the foul dungeons of ignorance and fear and suspicion? How long we gonna be jailers to ourselves? How long we gonna stay bound to the dark burdens of the past?"

The Governor's breath came in ragged jerks. He gripped the podium, leaning in like a Baptist preacher. He said, "We got a choice. We can stay in chains until Stone Mountain sinks a thousand feet below sea level, or we can shuck 'em free. You men down there"—the Governor addressed the lawmakers—"can help the chains fall free, or you can tighten 'em. If you pass all those bills you're just pullin' the chains tighter. You put me in a pinch with the President, and you bite into the flesh of every man, woman, and child in the South. For if you pass those bills you're beggin' for trouble. Those bills are nothin' but a red flag in the face of the bull. The courts will knock 'em down in quickstep. The Justice Department will send in gas and guns and bayonets. Troops will camp in our cities."

Again the ripple of mutters and hushed oaths in the chamber. A woman to my right hissed to her companion, "That cowardly ole thang! Why don't he stan'up and be counted?" A very obnoxious state Senator made a big thing of clomping ponderously off the floor. At the chamber door he turned to hold his nose. A few colleagues and gallery birds tittered appreciatively.

Cullie Blanton said, "Let there be no mistake how I feel in mah heart. I take a back seat to no man drawin' air when it comes to reverence for this state. For this is *my* land. I was born unto it, and one day my bones will rest in its clay. I have slept under the wide sky of this state, and scratched a livin' from its precious dirt. Yeah, and I have watered this land of ours—with my sweat, and with my tears. And if there was *any* way it would help us to victory, I would water this soil with the last of my blood!"

The Governor stood in a sea of throbbing silence, letting it wash over him in soundless waves, and I saw his gripping knuckles whiten on the podium.

"I'm not promisin' you there's any way to victory. No, for I'm stingy with my promises and some say a fanatic about keepin' 'em. Maybe . . . just maybe . . . there *is* a way our people can come through the rigors. If there is a way, the road to it ain't smooth and paved like the superhighways we've built together. No, the road is rocky and there are serpents in the ditch. We'll need patience. We'll need to help each other, like neighbor flocked in to help neighbor when this land was bein' carved from raw wilderness. We'll need a higher type of courage, my friends, than night riders will ever know. We'll need men! Men unafraid! Yes, and men who won't be stampeded into turnin' against their brothers or into blame placin' and hate, nor riots in the street."

The Governor stepped away from the podium. He stretched his arms out beseechingly. He said, "Help me. Trust me as you have in older times. Give me time. Time to talk reason with the President, to fight this thing in the courts. . . . Back off from all those inflammatory bills. Give me . . . give the *people* . . . give your state and your hearts a coolin'-off period, and I'll give you the best that's in me."

Cullie Blanton dropped his arms. He said, "There was a man named Moses. A leader of men. And like all leaders he came upon a time of peril. A time when his weary people, deviled by plagues and famines and swarms of locust, rebelled and knew wicked ways. This Moses went into the mountains, and on Mount Sinai came to him the mighty voice of God, terrible in the stillness. And God laid down His law—the Ten Commandments. Ten. Just ten. Ten simple, clear, plain laws without whereases and whyfors and sobeits. And yet, here we are, two thousand years later—still passin' laws. Tryin' to enforce the simple, wunnerful will of God. I don't know how many laws we've passed. Ten million, maybe. A billion, for all I know. And now, are we gonna add six more to the burden—when all they'll do is throw fuel on the fire?

"If you gentlemen of this body love this state the way I do, you don't want to see it pulled apart, invaded, and ground under the Federal boot. So I'm talkin' to you now as Moses talked to his people when he went unto them and told them of God's laws. And knowin' in despair his people had come to slothful ways of the flesh and the spirit, he told them they'd have to choose who they'd serve. The true and livin' God on the one hand . . . or the false gods on the other. And I say to you now, even as Moses said unto his people: choose you this day whom you will serve. . . ."

The Governor stood at the microphone for one slow spin of eternity, eye to eye with every man not blind. Then he said, "I have told you the truth. And the truth shall make you free."

With that he plunged off the Speaker's platform and was halfway up the aisle before anybody could get demesmerized enough to start applause. If somebody had started applause, the Governor might have made it. He might have pulled it off. And if Hardtimes Hanson hadn't been such a die-hard he felt a need to confront the Governor in mid-aisle, Cullie might have pulled it off. But as it turned out, Hardtimes did intercept him and he did start jawing with the Governor—who had been followed up the aisle by the television cameras. Nobody knew what Hardtimes Hanson said to spark the exchange, but everybody knew (or soon would) what the Governor said as his part of the piece. For somebody—whether by accident or from sheer cussedness or through an improvident act of Allah—turned on one of the floor microphones not four feet from where the Governor stood. And Cullie Blanton, lean-ing in to answer Hardtimes Hanson, mouthed right into the micro-phone he presumed to be dead. His words leaped out to God and ev-erybody: ". . . if you let that Sweet Jesus talk fool you, you redneck sonofabitch!"

His eyes were bloodshot and mean. The white hair was a tousled tangle tempting to homeless rats, and when I came near the Governor his breath smelled like a wino's blanket. The evening papers lay twisted and soiled around his feet. Cullie Blanton sprawled across his bed, his feet making restless twitches among the discarded papers, a tic working overtime just under his left eye.

"You been to the circus?"

I nodded. For I had been to the circus, all right. Our claybog states-men, after the Governor's extraordinary oratorical performance, had stayed on in overtime session. Now, long past midnight, they were still at it. The bills Cullie Blanton had gone before them to burn dead had risen from the pyre and—slowed only by choice denouncements of leg-islators anxious to get on record against the Governor himself—were being whooped through by the numbers.

Cullie Blanton said, "Goddammit. You'd think I was the first gover-nor ever used a cuss word."

"You probably are," I said. "On television."

He banged his hand down on the round night stand, causing the Jack Daniels and a soft-drink bottle to jump in concert. "I *had* 'em, Jim. I could *feel* it up there. By God, I had snared the impossible and had it in my fist—then I threw it away."

"How'd it happen? How'd you let Hardtimes get under your skin that way?"

"How do wars start?" the Governor asked, irritably. He eyed the balled-up newspapers on the floor, twisting his lips. "Those sanctimonious bastards! You think Hardtimes Hanson didn't have qualifications enough to *stack up* as a sonofabitch!"

I said, "It's the particular kind of s.o.b. you called him that split the fabric." For the newspapers were crying foul: BLANTON SLURS 'REDNECKS', and GOVERNOR CALLS SENATOR REDNECK S.O.B., and, in an evening tabloid, CULLIE FIDDLES WHILE REDNECKS BURN. A couple of our magnolia-garden newspapers had rushed front-page editorials into print, demanding the Governor apologize for use of what one tabbed "a snide, demeaning term favored by carpetbaggers, Yankee propagandists, and fuzzy-minded Harvard professors." One had printed a black-bordered box containing numerous Cullie Blanton quotes borrowing heavily from the Bible, topping it with a black overline set in quotes: ". . . *if you let that Sweet Jesus talk fool you. . . .*"

The Governor raved on. "They want to make goddamn morality the issue, I'm ready. You know of anybody else ever left the Governor's Mansion without linin' their pockets? I haven't stole so much as a streetcar token from 'em. *You* know that."

"Yes," I said. "*I* know that."

"All those pirates in the legislature," the Governor grumbled. "Standing up over there cryin' crocodile tears about me cussin' a little bit. Why, dammit, I don't know a one of 'em hasn't grabbed some pleasures between the sheets. You ever know me to go around hustlin' skirts?"

"Not exactly hustling," I said. "Though one time at that governors' convention in New Orleans, I *did* wonder a little bit about you and that proxy blonde newshen you disappeared with for a couple of hours. The one who had green-painted toenails and bazooms like a milk cow."

Cullie Blanton's face colored. He said, "Well, you keep on wonderin'. I ain't been a philanderer. Maybe I just never had *time* to be.

Seemed like there was always somethin' else around to claim my energies. Maybe I'm what experts of the behaviorial sciences call goddamn
power-driven. But I never wasted myself in a series of tawdry back-street
romances, and that's more than can be said for all those pious pirates
puttin' me down." The Governor slanted the Jack Daniel's bottle into
his water glass. He took a snort, wiped his mouth, and said, "I gave 'em
good counsel. I pushed a bill through so they could draw enough salary
to keep honest. I've supped with 'em and wept with 'em when they
buried their dead. I've bragged on 'em in their districts and posed for
goddamn pictures with 'em, and made 'em look smart in front of their
folks."

And he was right—as far as he went.

But the Governor didn't look at the tarnished side of the coin. Yeah,
he had done all he said. But he had stepped on their toes, too. He had
cracked their bones when they were stubborn, bullyragged them to get
his way. He had swaggered through their ranks, slashing and striking
out at all who stood in his path, and never mind their bruises. He had
brought in a lobby-control law tough enough to rob cash from their
pockets. He'd made it difficult to sell votes on the market by whipping
them into line on key measures. He'd held such a tight rein on patronage legislators couldn't indulge in the time-honored custom of reward-
ing favored friends and relatives with cushy state jobs. He had, in short,
stomped on their sand castles and clobbered their milk by stripping
them of dignity and back-handing their egos. I sat marveling at the
blind spot in Cullie Blanton that kept him from seeing the obvious:
Nobody is so dead as a dead king.

I said, "Well, don't expect to win any popularity contests over there.
Hardtimes and some of his friends are making noise about impeaching
you."

The Governor waved the irritation away and expelled air in an
honest belch. "Pap, stuff, and bullshit," he said, delicately. "They're
just makin' senseless chin music. I've read the constitution. No *way*
they can impeach me." His eyes took on a bright glitter. "They try
anything like that, I'll splinter their limbs. And it will be more fun
than Christmas."

I picked my words carefully. "Times change," I said. "They might
not be as easy to crack as they once were."

The Governor lurched to his feet, waving the whisky bottle like a
baton. "Listen," he said, and the whisky was thick in his throat, "listen,

some things don't change. You take a bunch of pirates got sawdust for brains and lilies for livers and they're stuck with their afflictions until they lie safe in the grave."

"Maybe so. But all those sawdust brains and lily livers have found enough spunk tonight to whip those seg bills through." That gave him a little jolt back toward reality. "The first one passed ninety-two to nineteen. The second one passed ninety-four to sixteen, with one abstaining. The third one passed ninety-eight to thirteen, and the fourth —well, when I left it was already seventy-odd to six."

The shock of it seemed to numb the Governor. His eyes dulled and he swayed before me in his sock feet, suddenly drunk from the new knowledge as much as from the bottle. "Christ," he said, rocking in some private gale. "Things . . . got outta hand. It . . . ain't as much fun as it usta be." His knees sagged, and the Governor plopped down on the bed. He didn't notice when the Jack Daniel's bottle squirted away to clomp on the floor. Cullie Blanton stared at his knees as if wondering why they'd collapsed.

Thickly, he said, "Jim, help me to the shower. And order me some black coffee. A little food."

"Maybe if you took a nap. . . ."

"Time for sleepin's long passed. I got . . . thangs ta do." When I hesitated he said, "Goddammit, drunk or sober I'm boss hand around here." So I helped the boss man to the shower.

11

CULLIE BLANTON.

All through those weeks of high-voltage tension the Governor prowled the darkened Mansion: a fleshy ghost, scowling, gesturing as he spilled nocturnal goddamns and Christ Jesuses into the telephone.

By day he would scuffle about on urgent errands. He would grab the telephone to bedevil high places in Washington. "Goddammit," he would belch, banging up the phone, "those Washington warblers got no *clue* how it is down here on thorny limbs. All they think about's *their* pretty painted birdhouse." Then he would rub his weary eyes, and maybe stifle a yawn. "Hell," he would say, "hell, they don't have to sweat. For they have got the power." He would give me a look from his burning eyes, and he would say, "Yeah, power. And power is what makes the buggy run."

He called in the nervous university officials for private confabs. Their eyes carried pain at the wonderment of why a sweet and merciful Lord would choose their time and place to shake up the rules of His settled world.

"Listen," he said, striding among them like a great war lord among his councilors at home-camp fires, "Listen, all you great minds got to come down from ivory towers long enough to deal with beasts at the gates. Dammit, you made one iota of preparation over there?"

And Dr. Campbell, the university president, would pucker around the mouth in prim hint of disapproval. He would move his pot belly while lights picked out bald spots hidden under scruffy strands of meticulously placed hair, and he would clear his throat and say, "Governor, we think it's best to follow a normal course of activity. Adopt a routine, business-as-usual stance so that—"

"Jesus in the foothills!" Cullie Blanton said. "You think it was business as usual at the Chicago fire?"

231

"Governor, we feel—"

"You feel like you can stay above the battle," the Governor said. "You feel like you can keep your hands out of what makes perfume sell. Well, guess again. For it is ever'man's fight, and I need the brains and bodies of ever'body you got over there. From your doctors of goddamn philosophy down to the lowest creature swabs the commodes."

Doctor Campbell fingered a gold key looped on a vest of wan gray. He said, "I don't know . . . the regents . . . improper utilization of. . . ."

"The *regents!*" Cullie Blanton snorted. "How you think you get to *be* a goddamn regent? You're lookin' at the man *makes* regents. And what I make I can break."

There was a huddle with the chief Federal marshal dispatched from Washington. The marshal reeked of some special strength inside his thickening body. He might have been a construction foreman or a small-town superintendent of parks, except that his eyes told of having looked on man in the execution of high folly. A well-chewed cigar poked from his shanty-Irish face, and his rumpled suit might have been picked up at a fire sale. When he spoke to the Governor it was not with the language of diplomats.

"How I feel about this thing's not an issue," he said, his jaws agitating the cigar stub. "I'm here to do my job. You can make it easier, or hard. But the job will get done."

"I reckon I know the speech," Cullie Blanton said. "I've made it a few times myself. What I can give you, you got."

The marshal nodded matter-of-fact acceptance. "Best thing you can do is be ready. If you give the O.K. I'll work with the head of your state police on crowd control, riot control, all that. Main thing is to have your troopers briefed and well equipped."

"You just say what they need."

"Billy clubs," the marshal said. "Tear-gas bombs. Riot guns. Gas masks." He spat out a soggy fragment of the cigar. "Patience, too," he said, "but not so much it gets in the way. They've got to know when to call and when to bluff."

"I'll furnish the cards," the Governor said. "You teach the players how to deal 'em." He leaned across the desk, catching his weight on crossed forearms, his face sober in its pose. "Marshal, I don't intend to have this thing busted open by the picayune jealousies of police-barracks politics. My boys'll be under hard orders to work with you fellows hand-and-goddamn-glove. The first one screws up's gonna be rendered down for lard and object lesson. Anybody gets outta line, you yell for me. But there is one thing. . . ."

The marshal clomped the cigar and waited for Cullie Blanton to reveal the one thing. The Governor stood, prowling the office which held for him no secret footpaths. He said, "There's somethin' about a badge or a pistol makes smaller the man the longer he carries it. Most of the troopers I got have been totin' sidearms and wearin' badges a long time. Small-town cops, deputy sheriffs, constables. Most of 'em grew up where the Nigra gets tossed in jail for common drunkenness or gets the piss-elm club laid on for not goin' to the back of the bus. Or maybe lynched for whistlin' at the wrong time. And some of 'em are just plain goddamn mean." The Governor looked directly into the marshal's eyes. "I got a few new boys who been to college, and a few more managed to pass a six-weeks G-man course. But mainly, I got a bunch of old pistol toters from the days when I needed nut busters to run this state. I don't apologize for it. I just regret it."

"Governor, my boys can get along with all kinds."

"Tell your boys not to get pushy," the Governor said. "Some my troopers kinda soured on the idea of bodyguardin' a boog. They got no stomach for blackbird pie. It's all they can do not to gag on the dish, and to tell the truth I'm not exactly smackin' *my* lips over it. But by God, we'll get it down and keep it on our stomachs. You just see your boys don't make it stick in our craws so it comes spewin' back up."

So the rules got laid down and the battle lines formed. Each day the Governor seemed to tighten up more. He began to sneak looks at the clock, cursing it for quick gobbles of precious time. A haggard thing came to camp in the once-fleshy folds of his face, and his hands palsied in quick rigors he tried to hide by steadying them against his coffee cup or by tight gripping of the telephone.

"This thing," I said one night as we left the Mansion for an eighty-mile ride to a campaign supper, "is draining away too much of your battery juice. Better slow down."

"Can't ease up on the hairpin turns," the Governor said wearily. "That's where the goddamn race is won." He slumped against the car door.

"It's too much," I protested. "The Davenport hassle . . . this hysterical campaign . . . all the mystic rituals of officialdom. Goddammit, you could lay the burden down any time you get weary. You think you have to be governor in order to sleep in silk pajamas or have your carcass hauled around in a black limousine?"

The Governor's grunt was beyond translation.

I said, "Half the corporations in this state would weigh you down with gold if you'd pretend to practice law for them. They might hate your guts but they'd love your connections."

"Man don't live by bread alone," he said.

So the farce continued. Cullie Blanton played his public role in time of special stresses until the stresses seemed not to be: now cheerful and crazily smiling on the hustings, pressing the arms and hands and elbows of a steady stream of callers come to wring special favor from the state. There was low, ironic comedy in the official buffoonery that ate of his time while our world gathered itself together to explode.

Like the morning the delegation of Junior Granddaughters of Confederate Captains came to call. They came bearing some scroll said to be historic for the Governor to accept amidst popping flashbulbs.

"Ah'm honored," he had said. "And you fahn ladies can rest assured this document will be cherished long after this moment has flown away upon the wings of tahm." They had sighed over the poetry while the Governor paused for effect, then turned to pinpoint with dramatic finger a stingy bare space on his overburdened walls. "That spot of honor," he said, "that spot raght there—raght by mah favorite portrait of General Robert E. Lee and by that mounted scrap of lead they dug out of mah grandpappy after the Battle of Shiloh—that spot is reserved for this document which means so much to you, and to me, and to all whose roots are bedded in sacred Southern soil . . ."

For long minutes he pulsated with the flow of old history, extravagant claims for the land and its fruits. Then he shifted gears. He said, "Now I wanta mind the manners mah mama taught me. I wanta give *you* a little somethin'." And he had beamed on their delighted little titters, their weak, fluttering protests, their coos and gasps and twitchings under flattery too obvious to fool a mountain goat. "Yes, ma'ms," he boomed, "I wanta give you somethin' from this soil we share. A token gift, true. Not worth much on the scales by which man weighs his gold, but more priceless than rare rubies to me. Because it represents God's slow, gentle rain upon His earth and the benevolent blessin' of His warm sun, and the bendin' of man's muscle to honest labors of the land. What I'm givin' you is a bushel of cling peaches grown on mah own little ole wore-out dirt farm up in the hills. Jim, get these nice ladies that bushel mah peaches I picked for 'em."

So I got the peaches, while the ladies twitched and fluttered in the grip of sweet ecstasy, and somebody popped a flashbulb to freeze the moment for generations yet unborn to trouble.

After the perfumed and powdered Granddaughters had taken gushing leave, I said, "How much longer you think you can get away with it?"

The Governor turned a bland face from paper shuffling. "Get away with what?"

"You know what. Hell, you didn't grow those peaches."

For they had, I knew, been wished upon him an hour earlier by representatives of the Peach Growers' Association, who came with hair slicked down and silk neckties appropriate to the honors. And who, in return, got gifted with a sack of peanuts "from mah own little mule-and-hookworm patch up in the hills"—which, naturally, had been laid on the Governor, to the winking of flashbulbs, by delegates from the Peanut Producers' Association.

The Governor might have grinned, though I couldn't be sure. "So I didn't grow 'em. Hell, I might have. If I hadn't had to spend all my time receiving delegations of alligator trappers, or Descendants of the Unmarried Mothers of the Blackfeet Wars."

"I hope they don't catch you at the trick."

"Boy," he said, "without I sign a confession drawn in the precious blood of the Lamb, nobody will believe the deception. People take as Gospel what they wanta hear."

"But about that slug up there"—and I motioned to the wall— "from your ole granddaddy's heroic flesh. Don't you think you ought to pick out one particular battle and stick with it? Today it was Shiloh. Yesterday it was Bull Run. Last week I think it was Cumberland Gap."

"Good idea," the Governor said, nodding judiciously. "Which you like best . . . Gettysburg, or the Battle of New Orleans?"

Henry Muggins.

He would sit, in those last weeks before the ball of yarn unraveled, manufacturing brow wrinkles and plucking at loathsome neckties. His face got to be strange territory for smiles.

The knowledge that he exercised nothing more than a shadow of control over the pussguts and corporate tools who assumed the people's power was, for Henry, a painful cut. He couldn't be blamed. For before Cullie started suffering serious slippage, back in the days when he steam-rolled opposition and bulldozed obstacles aside without shrug or penance, Henry Muggins was to the legislator what the Pope is to the parish priest. Cullie himself had said it: "When I hafta bust nuts it is Henry hands me the hammer." And it was Henry, with the advice and consent of the Governor, who had the power to control coveted committee assignments, docket bills on the House calendar, make leaders of men by the employment of but a few of his rationed words, or dash dreams by the same monosyllables.

But now the Speaker sat stuffed with glooms, the memory of high times behind him, hunched over a marble-topped table held up by twisted metal legs. I joined him in the silent sniffing of honest smells: the musty fragrance of cardboard containers holding patent medicines, the sulphur-and-molasses reek from the pharmacist's dark cubbyhole, fresh coffee burbling at low, hot-plate simmer in a plexiglass pot. The drugstore was so dated raised lettering on a front door of frosted glass spelled out ORRS CONFECTIONARY, and in smaller letters *Pharmaceuticals*. There was even a little cluster of bells over the door to announce by jingles its openings and closings. It was one of those few quiet places left in this world of hurry and glitter. You couldn't buy redwood picnic benches there large enough to accommodate the Last Supper, nor electric lawn mowers with multiple gears, nor three-speed records of some chorus of former weight-lifters offering off-key grunts to the accompaniment of somebody who played piano by weight. The Speaker liked the place.

Henry Muggins poured double cream into his coffee, stirred sugar in slow. He said, "It's been a bust."

"Goddammit," I said, "can you believe it?"

"Yeah," he said. "I saw it happen." The Speaker lifted his coffee cup and trickled tan liquid into his saucer. He blew on it in gentle ripples.

I said, "I remember when we asked a hundred and nineteen House members to endorse Cullie. Only two refused."

"And they didn't come back," the Speaker said. He smiled at the recollection of old vengeance gained. After a cautious test sip from the saucer, he said, "Cullie went stompin' through their districts. Blew 'em up. Accused 'em of everything but golden deeds." Henry Muggins paused for breath. "Folks bought it," he finished.

"Nobody's buying much now," I said. "Those headlines blaring how we couldn't muster even two dozen signatures for Cullie's endorsement petition won't help business any. I wish I had my hands on the cut-throat who leaked it to the newspaper boys."

"My fault," the Speaker said, staring into his coffee cup. "I let the petition be circulated. Didn't have my finger on the pulse."

"Hell," I said, "you can't take the blame. It's just—"

"Blame belongs to me. Shoulda known the temper of the House." Henry Muggins' scrawny frame seemed to shrink in defense against unknown dangers. He sipped at the coffee, and his sucking sounds mingled with the soft jingle of the front-door bells. "My daddy," he said, "ran his farm till he was past eighty. Grubbed stumps. Plowed. Did the milking." The Speaker fished in his pockets, then spread a handful of coins over his open palm. "Momma lived to be damn near as old. But her last twenty years she wasn't much good for work. Wore out early." Rising, he dropped a nickel and two pennies as tip. "I reckon," Henry Muggins said, "I take after her."

Poppa Posey.

The unwashed prophet high-tailed it through the boondocks, a couple of his choice hounds trailing him to podiums where he flashed backwoods brilliance. The forces who had prodded Poppa into the race had invested in P.R. men wise and slick. The wirephoto services carried pictures of Poppa and his hounds which popped out on front pages. The hounds were trucked from town to town in accommodations approximating silk, built into the rear of a battered and bannered pickup truck. Just before Poppa's little caravan would come on the next way station he would transfer into the pickup's cab and crawl behind the wheel. The late-model car in which he had been chauffeured would zip on down the road so its three occupants could start innocent-appearing conversations with nesters gathered for Poppa's appearance. By the time the old fraud jolted into the hamlet the seeds of sly mutinies had been planted against Cullie's rule. All the yokels saw was Poppa taking stiff-jointed leave of the old pickup, going around to let his faithful companions bound tail-wagging to his side. He would lean over them, the hounds licking his hands, the old man muttering over them (maybe cussing them for bad breath or maybe quoting Shakespeare), and the hounds would sniff their way with him to the podium.

"Thet ole houn' dawg," he would cry, pointing one skinny old arm, "thet ole houn' dawg may look dumb and half blind and plumb off his feed. Like I look to you, mebbe. Like the desperate bandits runnin' this state fast to ruin are whisperin' about me in they high fear. But thet ole houn' dawg—he ain't so dumb he don't know when somebody's sneakin'

up on mah place to make mischief under cover of dark. And he ain't
so blind he don't see tha mischief tha prowler's tryin' to make. And he
ain't so off his feed he can't git on his two hine legs and bark about it."
   Then Poppa would draw back the withered arm pointing at the
wise old hound, and he would give the gawking nesters a minute to
mull it over in their slow brains before hitting them with it. "A man
can learn a lot from thet ole houn' dawg," he would say, fierce and
glaring under the wide brim of his cotton-chopper's straw hat. "And I
learned it. I learned who it is sneakin' up. And the name of the robber
is an evil thang on mah lips." And he would twist it off, spitting the
name, his face contorted and vile: *"Cullie Blanton!"*
   He would let the explosive roar of it echo and sink in. Then he
would lower his voice a few ranges. "Cullie Blanton . . . Judas Iscariot . . . Benedict Arnold. . . ." He would raise his eyes to Heaven
and emit personal roar to God. *"Sold out! Sold out, O God and coun-*
trymen! Sold out by one among us!" Then he would lean into them,
the old eyes like hot coals sizzling in snow, whooping and coughing of
evil in Cullie Blanton's heart, holding rank sins of the Governor up to
public mirror, swearing war eternal on Yankee agitators and uppity
niggers and all things putrid to the Southern soul.
   Poppa Posey, I knew, was eating too much of our lunch. But how to
get his hand out of the lunchbox, I knew not.

   Bayonet Bill Wooster.
   The mad general rode the highways at the head of his bully army.
His show took on all the marks of Hollywood. And not very good Hollywood at that. It shouldn't have fooled anyone aware of a world beyond the hills. But the hokum wasn't directed at the most sophisticated
of audiences. It was piped to citizens whose men of cloth thundered at
them each Sunday about the wages of Sin, at men and women who had
been nurtured in childhood on old myths, at office clerks and house-
wifely matrons and balding shopkeepers to whom a trip to Atlanta to
watch the university play Georgia Tech represented a bold adventure
into outer darkness.
   Billboards hosted General Wooster's image in living color and bigger than life, sprouting along the highways. If you turned on the television set Wooster's likeness jumped from a film clip, to yodel of
conspiracies dark and deep. You couldn't open your mailbox without
finding a fistful of tracts depicting the former Marine in his military

regalia, as if he meant to drive the Imperial Army of Japan off the mainland with a single fixed bayonet and volunteer help. His clipped voice railed forth from the radio, martial music heralding the line he was about to lay down, polishing up the visions of old glories: *From the halls of Mon-te-zoom-a to tha shores of Trip-o-lee.* . . .

The Wooster campaign got cuter. With Poppa Posey taking pains to inform the folks of how Cullie Blanton was the world's champion mixer of races, the general found time to expose new Communist conspiracies. Governor Blanton's past success in building hospitals for the mentally ill was cited as evidence of a plot to have committed for lunacy all who opposed his policies. Textbooks in the schools which made even slightly favorable references to the United Nations or reciprocal trade were said to be the works of bearded left-wing authors who owed allegiance to no less than Lenin; the Governor was charged with permitting (if not encouraging) their use to brainwash innocent waifs at captive lecture. Low-rent housing projects, to which Cullie Blanton had always pointed with pride, became a detriment after a blitz campaign compared them with communal housing in Russia and not-so-subtle photographs dwelled on those projects set aside for Negroes. Hell, even the state prison farm, where produce was grown by prisoners for their own consumption, was held out as the model for Castro's land-reform program in Cuba. Farmers were told how the Governor and his official lackeys and cronies ate of the produce while the farmers' own commodities rotted in the fields.

There was even mass circulation of what had been carefully labeled "a genuine composite photo" seeming to depict Cullie Blanton in the smiling company of Earl Warren and Martin Luther King. The nesters and yahoos, however, missed the little subtlety of language. They took the "genuine composite photo" for truth caught on film as reliable as that in the family box Brownie.

The booming martial music, the flags, the doctored tracts, the posturing of Wooster as superpatriot and grand warrior, the sly digs at Cullie Blanton's having failed to march into battle under arms and national standard, the hysterical oratory—it was like something put on as farce to parody another age. But it wasn't another age, nor was it meant as parody. I would stew in nocturnal juices, wondering how much of the madness Wooster himself believed. How much of it was bile pumped by a misguided heart, and how much was hokum for consumption by main-street yokels and cow-pasture seers?

Hell, the question was moot. It didn't matter. What mattered was how much of the poison would pollute the state's bloodstream.

Enough, I reckoned in my sheets. Too much for comfort.

Stanley Dutton.

The fellow who pined for the love of all men. Who coveted the Good Life, and who couldn't have told a pickpocket from the Sainted Host. Who had learned a great deal of what there was in books, but who knew nothing of what happened in the streets.

Stanley Dutton, the world's only lieutenant governor kept under lock and key, and who came into my office one day with his forehead worried. He was trailed by the trooper with the scrawny arms and the killer eyes.

Stanley shifted from one leg to another while his creased hat turned circles, and finally he spat out the thing gagging him. He motioned his handsome head toward the sorry hunk of clay stuck to his shadow, the hunk of clay standing with fixed sneer while he pared yellowed fingernails with the unsanitary blade of a five-and-dime frog sticker. He said, "Jim, could you talk the Governor into reconsidering my having a . . . a bodyguard?"

"You know the Governor," I said. "He couldn't be talked into a lifeboat when the ship's sinking, if he had his mind set the other way."

"It's getting on my nerves," the Lieutenant Governor said in a blurt. Then he looked abashed at his boldness. "Having him around . . . my wife, she can't stand much more of it. She's giving me a fit." He tried a grin, which didn't come off. "You know how women are," he said in apology.

I looked over at the tawdry replica of man made in His image. At the sneer, and at the frog sticker at its dirty work under the thick, yellow fingernails. The tawdry replica grinned at me. It was a dirty grin, like some fellow might give you the day after you'd gotten fool-drunk with him and participated in a gang-bang of the town floozie. Without taking my eyes off the trooper I said, "I can't blame you, Stanley. Or your wife. It must be like carrying a rattlesnake in your coin purse."

That wiped the grin off the trooper. His mouth turned down. The frog sticker made a sharp, snapping sound as the blade clicked, and for a moment I had the chilling notion the snap had been wished for my vitals.

"Justa minnet," the trooper said, his face inflamed. "I don't—"

"One thing you don't," I said, measuring the words carefully, "is give me any lip of any kind. Another thing you don't is stand in my office picking filth from under your goddamn nails. And you don't foul the air in here with your uninvited presence. Wait outside the door."

His face was red enough to burn asbestos, and he looked eager for mayhem. He said, "The Governor put me on this job and—"

"And the Governor put me on *this* job," I said, icicles hanging on the words, "which has varied duties. Among them the busting of nuts when people grow too big for their britches. Yours seem to be hanging a little loose on you." The trooper begat evil in small, flecked eyes. "Out in the hall," I said, biting it off.

It was the kind of language the breed understands. At the click of the door Stanley Dutton sprang forward to wring my hand as if it had just come dripping from the wash and he had to make it ready for the clothesline.

"Don't go getting all cheered up," I said, rescuing my hand from the wringer. "That little rebellion there—hell, it might *sound* impressive. But it just flushed my bile sac. Cullie won't hear to calling off his bird dog, Stanley."

"I can't take much more of it," Stanley Dutton said. "I'm telling you for true, Jim. I just can't *take* it any more."

"You'll take it," I said. "For you will consider the source of the gift."

It seemed a safe prophecy at the time.

12

THE GOVERNOR was one mad whirl of motion. He busied his digits at intercom buttons, fled to wide windows where he mumbled at the street scene below, let his gaze wander just behind treetops to the fringe of State University's sodded campus. He scurried behind his mahogany desk to pick up the telephone, dropped it back in the cradle unused. Then he stood with the massive head cocked slightly upward as if to spy on the ceiling, breathing aimless goddamns.

Clearly it was no day to be in the Presence. But as if sensing my thought to slip away, Cullie Blanton brought his eyes down from the ceiling and fixed me to my spot. "Day like this," he snorted, "and they don't have any goddamn coffee here." He poked at the intercom apparatus until a faint, whispery echo told he had made contact with the outside world.

". . . Yessir? . . . sir . . . ?"

"This Ella Lu?"

"No sir. . . ."

The Governor twitched during the wait. When no sounds were forthcoming he said in heavy tones, "Would it ruin the game if you said who it *is?*" The young lady gave her name in uncertain timbre.

"Where's Ella Lu?"

"She . . . I think she . . . went out for coffee."

Cullie Blanton rolled his eyes. He said, "Jesus alone in the garden had nothin' on me . . . Listen, unless he's gone off down the street to enroll in college, send Melacadies in. With some goddamn coffee."

Then he descended upon a television set built into a recess in the mahogany bookcases, fiddling with the dial. Theme music from a midmorning soap opera piped into the oval study. Cullie Blanton glared as a tearful actress and her long-haired romantic clutched at each other on the shining screen, their profiles giving the poor slobs out there in television land assurances that The Beautiful People, too, know heart-ache. Fade-out, and an announcer flashed capped teeth to exclaim over the wonders of some cleansing powder.

"World crackin' at the seams," the Governor growled, "and they got nothin' to do but hawk detergents and paste for our molars." He faced me, screwing his features into varied poses of anxiety. "What's goin' on down there, Jim?"

"Not much. Looks pretty calm."

The Governor steamed across the rug and dropped anchor at my shoulder, gazing down. Troopers in their mustard-hued finery, khaki-clad marshals wearing burnt-orange helmet liners dotted streets run-ning round and about the capitol building and university grounds. Working in pairs, a trooper and a marshal would occasionally move into the nearly deserted streets to stop a cruising car, poking their heads inside to speak to the occupants. A few cars were passed through to the campus, most turned back. The rejected were escorted away by motorcycle cops, appearing, from the point where the Governor and I looked on, to be rolling without sound.

"Good work," Cullie grunted when a crimp-fendered flivver had been routed away. "We keep the troublemakers off campus, we don't run the risk of mob rule."

"There's one troublemaker you'll have hell's own time keeping away."

Cullie Blanton's eyes took on worry. He said, "I got ever'body with passable sight lookin' for him. But no trace."

"He'll show," I said. "He got more publicity on his promise of show-ing up today than Christ is likely to get the second time around."

"Only Wooster's return is more immediate," the Governor said, chewing his lip. "One thing I am *not* goin' to do. And that is make the mistake of givin' that goddamn general a heel-coolin' in the jail cell he deserves. For that'd be piss on his paddle."

Melacadies came bearing gift of coffee, rattling cups. Cullie lunged for the tray and sucked eagerly at a cup rim. He made a satisfied sigh. "Pour Jim some."

"Not for me," I said.

"Pour Jim some," the Governor repeated, his tone unchanging. So Melacadies poured, and I prepared to drink.

Zero Phillips materialized in the doorway of the study, lank bones rattling in yards of trouser leg, a cadaverous apparition hosting the soft eyes of a trusting Saint Bernard. Cullie raised an inquisitive eyebrow.

"Sure is hell," Zero volunteered by way of preamble, "tryin' to keep the news boys entertained."

"Dance 'em a soft-shoe," the Governor said.

Zero shifted clanking bones. He said, "They're all up in the air about when the Nigra will show up. To register."

"Tough tiddy," the Governor said. He went back into his cup. When Zero continued his slow shuffle in the doorway, the Governor came out of the china to say, "Tell those hunt-and-peckers that particular mystery is deep and eternal."

Zero withdrew in abject misery. I said, "Aren't you afraid all this hush-hush business will get the reporters' bowels in an uproar? Censorship . . . managed news."

"Those pirates ain't tremblin' to compare me favorably with major prophets even if I hand out scoops on a silver platter. Besides, lettin' people know the exact moment the boog will make his appearance makes no more sense than a man with hemorrhoids ridin' in a rodeo. If that goddamn general don't know, he ain't as likely to have a chance to bump bellies with him at the door."

I said, "No doubt you know what you're doing. But I can't see it would hurt for the newspaper boys to have a few minutes advance notice."

"They won't need it," the Governor said, shoving his cup under the spout which had appeared magically in Melacadies' hand. He carefully paced his swallows from the cup, as if to draw maximum sustenance from the shallow depths. "He'll be pretty hard to miss. Unless they happen to be color blind."

By the time the noon whistle hooted mournfully in some far-off reach of Capitol City, tension was thick enough to spread on toast. The Governor reflected the mood. He prowled without ceasing, boomed into the phone, drummed on his desk top. He doodled on a white pad. He monitored the radio, agitated the television set in a vain effort to learn something of Bayonet Bill Wooster's whereabouts.

"Goddammit," Cullie Blanton said, pitching his pencil on the pad among the doodles, "it is all this crashin' silence puts a man on edge."

I said, "Maybe I could find out something from the newspaper boys. We're not exactly overburdened with information here." I hoped to escape the oval study and the feeling of being caged with a very cross bear.

The Governor silently debated whether he could risk facing himself alone. "All right," he said grudgingly. "But watch your tongue. And stay off television. Don't go scarin' little kiddies waitin' for the Popeye cartoons."

I left the Governor bent to doodling, making my way to the Mansion's front lobby, where Zero had uneasy charge of a pack of bitching, pacing, rumor-birthing newsmen. The main force fell on my person with wild cries, braying questions that I parried with shrugs and negative shakings of the head. Zero sagged gratefully against a supporting wall and cast eyes skyward.

"Okay," I yelled above the babble, "let's don't get anybody hurt. One at a time."

"Has the Governor got a statement?" somebody called.

"No statement," I said. And kept pushing.

"Will he have one?"

"I really don't know."

"Aw come on . . . will he be at the university when the Nigra registers?"

"He's the Governor," I said. "Not the registrar." I had been hemmed in, encircled, the escape route closed off.

"Does he intend to call out the Guard?"

"You think the National Guard's needed?" I parried. "Have you seen how calm it is out there?"

"Yeah," said a dour head from the *Morning Call*, "but how calm's it gonna be when the jig shows up? And General Wooster?" He gave me a look at his perpetual sneer. I knew the fellow to be very bad news—one of those reporters who sees it his role to throw the public man on spears.

"I'm not in the predicting business," I said.

The *Morning Call* man wouldn't let it go. He flashed the sneer and looked among his fellows in the craft for backing. "You think the general can stop the boog, or you think he can't?"

"I don't think anything about the general," I said—and after a pause, "that's fit to print."

"You don't know much of anything do you?" *Morning Call* hooted.

"Not really. It's just I sometimes seem smart compared to the company I'm in."

Then, before they could recover enough to elect a lynch-mob captain and send somebody for rope, I pushed through the reporters and made for the door, leaving behind a swelling chorus of gripes and curses.

Dallas Johnson peered through the smoky gloom of The Tavern, his face elongated and cheerless. His beer glass had made a series of wet, interlocking circles on the mutilated surface of pine table top. Claybog statesmen had for generations in the fullness of their cups carved out dreams, advertised passions, attended bloated ambitions: *Rep. Bob Wheeler, '46 . . . Hon. D. Kennard is a horse's ass . . . L. Gilbert, future Gov . . . No $ales Tax on the People's Bread. . . .*

The Honorable Johnson, manifesting signs of lightheadedness and temporary palsy of hand, scuffed his feet in green-dyed sawdust and leaned across old, burning messages preserved in clear varnish. He said, "I feel it in my bones, and it will happen. We fight at the wrong times," Dallas intoned. "Fort Sumter . . . Little Rock . . . Oxford. It's some heavy fever in the blood. Some perverted image of grinning darkies strumming happy banjos under sweet magnolia blossoms. . . ."

"That your reelection speech?"

Dallas Johnson hoisted his schooner, grinning like a jackal. "Mah fren's, ah say tew *yew!* Dew yew seriously take unto heart the a-the-*istic* doctrines of those who would drive the ghost from mah political body . . . ? Dew you really believe your great grandpappy drug his knuckles in buffalo grass an' come as a tadpole from tha sea?"

A sleazy gent in ash-strewn trousers and a frayed high-school-letterman's jacket of ancient vintage regarded Dallas Johnson from the safety of a three-legged bar stool, his eyes altogether alarmed. Dallas brought his beer down from its high station, traded his grotesque grin for a frown. "I know how to *rouse* the boobs," he said, "but I don't know how to calm them. It's a lost art. Like blacksmithing or soothsaying."

"If there's trouble," I said, "we're ready for it. Cullie's called out a hundred troopers. You could drag race clear across the state today and not get a ticket. And the Feds sent in fifty marshals. They're pretty tough boys."

"I guess tough is what it takes," Dallas said dully. "Might maketh right."

I said, "You red-hots oughta make up your mind. You rail about the

Governor sitting on his hands. Then you recoil like you've found a snake in your boot if he uses muscle to get something done."

Dallas confessed to his beer. He said, "I guess I'm as big a hypocrite as the next man. I get visions of running the world like it was the Southern Pacific Railroad and I had fee-simple title to the rails. Then some crisis comes along and my bunghole falls out. It's . . . not that I'm *afraid*, you understand. It's just I get to seeing two goddamn *sides* to everything."

The waitress paused at our station, brushing back a strand of rebellious hair. She had a faint mustache of sweat beads and gave off an odor which might have been slightly toxic. Her hands hovered over the squarish, thick-cut beer mugs. "Say," she blurted, "ya'll with the government?"

"Myself," I said, "I just came in to fix the pinball machines."

"We don't have no pinball machines," she said in obvious relish. "The goddern government passed some fool law you can't have pinball machines." She gave us the hard eye. "Ya'll have anythang to do with that law?"

"Not me," I said quickly. "And as for Representative Johnson— well, I don't intend to rat on a buddy."

"Oh thanks, buddy," Dallas said. The waitress propped her hands on the pine-board table top, leaned into Dallas Johnson's face with her neck cords straining. "Caused our biness to fall off twenny, thirty bucks a day," she said in strangled tones. "Whyn't you big shots use your time keepin' the damn niggers outta our schools instead of messin' with honest biness folks?"

Dallas made a hopeless, palms-up gesture. His look appealed to me for help.

I said, "Yes, Representative Johnson. I was about to ask that very question myself."

"And that ain't all," the waitress said, her voice strident. "Why, they got ever' cop in the state over there today helpin' that damn spade force hissef on our biggest collidge. They got collidges of they own we built for 'em. Whyn't they use 'em? Huh?"

"It's a very complicated subject," Dallas said, sighing.

"Why, you could rob and rape in the streets and git away with it, for all the cops lined up over there playin' wet nurse to that nigger. Usin' *my* taxes doin' it. If we let the black sonsabitches go to school with us it won't be five years till they'll be marryin' us."

"They'll be mighty sorry," Dallas said, weary and dejected.

The waitress reddened. Her eyes bulged. "Whatta you mean?"

"I mean," Dallas Johnson said, forcing a little steel into his voice, "that I would like to have a little less conversation and a little more beer." The waitress flounced off, clinking glasses, heels biting angrily into the floor.

Dallas rounded his shoulders, head in hands. "Jesus H. Kee-rist," he mourned. "You know anybody wants to buy one slightly tarnished, cracked, and upside-down goddamn world? *Cheap?*"

Zero came flapping down the walk to meet me as I approached the Mansion. "You better shake a leg," he advised. "He's having an absolute conniption."

I gazed across the terraced grounds at saplings and rose gardens and rock-lined walks. Overhead the sky was blue enough to love.

"What's the matter?" I asked.

"I think he's given his sanity unconditional release," Zero said. "He told me to leak out word slyly that he's headed for some secret rendezvous. '*Goddamn* secret,' he said. The idea was to make the news boys think it's with Davenport. And they bit."

"Where is this alleged rendezvous?"

"Damn if I know. But you're supposed to drive him there. He said get your car and come to the east side entrance. By the greenhouse." Zero paused, torn and troubled. "What's our crazed king up to?" He fled up the walk.

When the Governor climbed with artful grunts into my car his look laid down Alamo siege. He said, "You damn near ruint my show, pullin' your Houdini act." He mined an ear with a wooden kitchen match. "Go out the east gate," he said. "Gun the motor some. Like one them hot-rodders trying to dig out. Only don't go so fast we can't get caught." We came down the winding road to the designated gate in a great spraying of gravel. A knot of reporters stationed near the white sentry box broke into babbles and gestures, sprinting for cars in convenient appointments.

Cullie Blanton ducked his head to shield a broad grin. "Catfish takin' the bait," he said, vastly pleased. "Turn left. Time yourself so we don't cool our heels at red lights."

In the rear-view mirror I spotted cars shooting out of all exits opening from the Mansion and capitol grounds. The earth seemed to belch speeding vehicles driven by species of wild tribes: mobile television trucks, sedans hired by Yankee reporters from distant cities, our own coon-dog press boys rattling along fearfully in wheezing jitneys whose parts would be retired ahead of their mortgages.

The Governor bubbled and boiled mirth. He said, "Hell, it is like dynamitin' little fish. And them so all-fired smart with their college diplomas and flitty tattersall vests."

I said, "Not that I don't enjoy a good chase. But it might help if I knew the route. I wouldn't mention it, except I'm driving."

"We're goin' to see Bertha."

"*Bertha?*"

"Bertha," he repeated, reaffirming it by nod. His darting eyes checked our pursuers in the rear-view glass. I tooled through the business district's wide streets and leveled down on the south side of town. We bumped across railroad tracks and on by a Mexican cemetery with graves sadly furbished by bits of colored glass, wilted flowers, crumbling wreaths. The caravan zipped by one of civilization's higher crimes: a modern shopping center. The place was a tangle of garish lights, tubes, signs setting value on barbecue grills, clothes direct-from-the-factory-to-you, kumquats.

We left the outskirts of the city. The air freshened. I sent the convertible up a little rise and by a cold-springs swimming pool, cutting through a park measured for softball and pitch-and-putt golf. The Governor twisted in the car seat, grinning. His eyes took in the fantastic string of vehicles bouncing wildly behind.

"God Almighty," he beamed. "We got ever'body with us but Huntley and Brinkley."

I said, "In case you're hot to explain this little sojourn, I could probably find time to listen."

"You as suspicious as those pirates behind us," the Governor said. "All I'm gonna do is visit Bertha."

All right. So we would visit Bertha. Though I couldn't imagine how she could be of assistance in the moment, her grinning skull rotting as it did in death's final shroud, and her bones maybe worked by worms. Bertha was the Governor's wife, who had been a long time dead.

We bumped across a wooden bridge and turned down a narrow lane guarded by well-spaced oaks. At the end of the lane was Bertha, stretched in final rest where fine old trees shut out the sun, and the hint of rain in the air brought a wild-flower fragrance to the shaded little plot she had chosen one bright summer afternoon as her final repository of bones. She had been in the full bloom of health then, though the brood-stock ripeness of the figure that had stirred fluids in a younger Cullie Blanton had gone out of control so that she was made of many corseted bulges and multiple chins giving off faint aroma of face powder.

The Governor, then vital and bombastic in his second term, had whooped raw jest at his wife's discovery of "the sweetest little cemetery," where she wanted to rest until Gabriel's horn tooted. She had implored Cullie to come with her to the site of discovery. He had begged off by reasons of eggs to lay and chicks to hatch, swatting her affectionately across a great expanse of thonged-and-tied buttocks.

Less than four months later the Governor saw the site for the first time—from a mat of bogus grass dyed richer than nature could have done the job, his eyes dulled and uncomprehending while he blinked on walled banks of flowers and peered into the final, awful hole. Men of high station had groped for his hand, mumbled vague words meant to be comforting. He had looked at them in shocked disbelief, as if they made horrid mistakes of identity; he simply could not accept the fact of Bertha's death. She was of his plan, and no mere God would dare rip his plan asunder. But she was dead, and Deity had not seen fit to take her in ennobling ways: she had fatally choked on a fish bone while taking Friday lunch at a Catholic orphanage. The man of cloth who wished her soul Godspeed at the bier had tried to repair the ghastly joke played by the Reaper of Souls, unctuously crediting her with saving some motherless child from the fatal portion by taking it herself.

We turned under a stone arch presided over by two grotesque, carved angels guarding the ends of a sign: REST HAVEN. "Jim," the Governor said, "hold those pirates off. I don't want 'em in here stumblin' over graves and bawling fool questions." Cullie Blanton climbed from the car. He frowned when I banged my door shut, as if I had disturbed the dead. Threading his way between stone markers, he carefully watched his feet.

The posse members arrived at the stone arch in a braking of tires and acceleration of curses. Several of the reporters eyed the carved angels with deep distrust. I stood just inside the cemetery gates, holding up my hands to implore silence, a buffer between the trampling herd and His Excellency. They came with brayings.

I said, "The Governor is visiting his wife's grave. It's a private moment, gentlemen."

"What's the goddamn *story?*"

"No story," I said. "Governor Blanton comes here quite often to
meditate and pray."

Somebody Up There sounded a warning. Lightning crackled, illuminating distant thunderclouds. The newsmen gaped incredulously at
the Governor. He stood alone midst profusion of tombstones, ruddy
and robust among cold, pale markers, his hand on the marble monument over his wife's grave as if bracing it against gale winds. As he held
the pose I found myself wondering how much of it was for real, how
much for show? Or did *he* know? Had there come a day back there in
all the wild exhortations, synthetic cheers, routine exhaustions, public
brags, whoopla and shouting, when he no longer could separate the
flesh-and-blood Cullie Blanton from Cullie Blanton the stump-water
legend?

"He's supposed to be meeting Davenport," one of the visiting Yankees shouted.

I said, "Yeah and right after that he's boxing flyweight in the Olym-
pic trials."

The *Morning Call* reporter fashioned an accusation. "He just came
here to throw us off. He detoured here after he spied us following
him."

I said, "It's not exactly like you were hard to spot. It looked like the
Oklahoma Land Rush. But you're wrong. The Governor puzzled all
the way out here over why you followed him."

"Then why in hell didn't you stop and tell us he was just going to
. . . to visit his wife's grave?"

"Would it have turned you back?" I demanded. Risking ruin by
Heavenly bolts, I said, "The Governor is an old-fashioned man. Maybe
he clings to values you'd term outmoded. But coming here gives him
strength." Cullie Blanton had dropped to his knees, head bowed in
an attitude of prayer. The reporters goggled, uncertain whether to
throw stones or remove their hats. The A.P. man gathered all available wits and wrung from them a suggestion: "Let us talk to him."

"Not here. He made it plain this is private."

Morning Call said, "Private, hell. This is a two-bit show if I ever saw
one."

I said, "All right. You play it that way. You go to your typewriter
and cut the Governor a new one for the high treason of visiting his
wife's grave. If your editor thinks that's the way to win an election, you
grab it and run with it."

"Nobody's gonna do that," A.P. said. "But we would like to ask him a few questions."

"Try me," I said. "I'll pass the questions on—if you'll give your bond not to come clomping across the cemetery."

They groused about it, but ultimately I turned toward the Governor armed with inquiry. As I approached through paths among the dead, he rose from his prayerful posture. He leaned forward to ogle the legend on Bertha's marker as if unable to accept the final grief it told. I stood back at distance hoped to be respectful. Cullie Blanton sensed my presence. Without turning around he said, "She was my great anchor. The calm captain in stormy seas. She'd know just what to say to comfort me durin' this goddamn—" He broke off, turning, grinning ruefully. "She never approved of my salty language," he confessed. "Remember, Jim?"

"I remember."

"She'd say, 'Cullie, I swear the Lord is goin' to strike you mute and I wouldn't blame Him.'" The Governor gazed on the flattened mound. "She was a grand woman," he said. "She loved her God."

I cleared my throat. "Boss, the reporters have some questions. They want me to pop 'em to you."

The Governor rested his hand on the marker. I shifted weight from foot to foot while his mind dwelled in lost years. No doubt he was refurbishing memories: conjuring up visions of a wife who was a saint in church, a comfort in the home, a demon in bed.

Suddenly the Governor turned to me. "What those pirates want to know?"

"About Davenport. You're supposed to be meeting him. They've compiled—"

"Should have brought some roses," the Governor broke in. "Make a note to get some out here tonight . . . in the mornin', maybe. Bertha, she was partial to roses. Before she made that rose garden wasn't nothin' there but brambles. . . ." He trailed off, raising his eyes to mine. "And don't send any those skimpy roses sell for thirteen dollars a dozen in the shops. Send a fresh armload from that garden of hers at the Mansion."

"Okay," I said.

"Write it down."

So I took a small notebook from my coat pocket and wrote: *Bertha roses.* "Now," I said, "about those questions—"

"She always wanted a child," the Governor said, abruptly. His fingers made plucking motions at his chin, soothing some old ache. He let his eyes wander toward the reporters.

"Governor, those guys are—" Then I whirled to see what had happened at the stone arch fronting the cemetery, warned by a flicker in Cullie Blanton's eyes. The reporters were running in circular patterns, scrambling toward their cars, twisting radio dials, shouting.

"What the hell happened?" I asked.

" 'Let them that are in the midst of it depart out,' " the Governor quoted. " 'Take heed that ye be not deceived.' " His smile was sly and secret. "Boy, I wouldn't be surprised if they've found the gentleman of African descent in the woodpile."

Snatches of shouted oaths reached us: ". . . about ten minutes ago yeah, Davenport . . . *registered* . . . *whaaat?* . . . Goddammit . . . He musta slipped through the basement. Nobody *saw* him. . . ."

They departed in a revving of motors and a wild spinning of tires. One or two of the scribes looked back uncertainly as if to quiz the Governor, but Cullie spun quickly to posture again beside his loved one's tomb. I saw his shoulders shake as he surrendered to an invasion of chuckles. "Boy," he said, "you are witnessin' a pluperfect case of lockin' the barn door after the horse has got out." The last reporters jumped into cars ripping off from the scene. Sensing the all-clear, Cullie Blanton dropped his poses and turned, hands on hips, grinning as he watched the hasty departure.

I said, "You don't exactly seem bowled over by the news."

The Governor raised an eyebrow. "You reckon our Creator was surprised when the world got itself made?" He chuckled. The chuckle turned to a mild laugh, and the laugh to a hearty booming. He tossed the great head, one arm thrown around my shoulders, roaring at the swollen, bruise-colored sky. We moved through the cemetery like two dawn revelers, the Governor's whooping tugging at my nerve roots. Behind us, the first patter of raindrops fell on Bertha's grave.

Cullie Blanton seemed immune to slings and arrows being sent his way over the airwaves. Between the electronic beeps, bells, and sirens so much in fashion in the age of frantic radio, announcers poured out the skeleton story: *First Negro admitted to university* . . . (beep, ding-a-ling, whurrr) . . . *spokesman for Wooster accuses Governor of unconditional surrender* . . . (beep, wheep, bong).

The Governor was a mute, morose bulk beside me. All the insane glee and pious proclamations of the cemetery scene had been left behind with the dust of the interred. The show was over, the star off the boards, brooding in his dressing room and drained of higher emotions. The only thing he had said was, "Drive slow." After a couple of creeping miles I said, "Maybe we ought to hurry back to the Mansion." The Governor amputated the suggestion with one word. "No."

"It must be hell among the yearlings," I said. "Zero could probably use some help."

The Governor said, "Suppose you just operate the vehicle and leave the high strategy to wiser minds." Then, to soften the blow, he said, "I need some thinkin' time. Can't think back at the Mansion with ever'body jumpin' through their butts."

Well, if the Governor needed any food for thought the radio was a good provider. The newsmen had recovered enough to start rounding up Cullie's foes in front of microphones, and there wasn't any shortage of yahoos willing to exercise their jawbones A state senator known to have more prices on his official wares than a mail-order catalogue put the Governor down as a bargain-basement buy.

"That senator," I said, "is the biggest crook in the legislature. Which puts him on the chart somewhere between Al Capone and Billy the Kid."

"He is so crooked," the Governor agreed, "that you can't show any profit tellin' it on him." Cullie Blanton stared out the window, sorrowing over men too amoral to be fair game for blackmail.

Poppa Posey's wheezing invectives rode with us down rain-flushed streets. He tagged the Governor "a undigestible lump in the belly of the people," which lump, he predicted, would soon be spewed out. He alluded to Biblical admonitions against plowing oxen and lions in common yolk. He managed to misquote Scripture, anthropology textbooks, and Cullie Blanton all in one slumgullion-stew sentence.

"Ole Poppa," the Governor said with the half-twist of a smile on his lips. "He is the Rembrandt of artful liars."

"That doesn't make it right," I said. "Poppa's been on the hot seat. He knows there are some things no politician can control."

"Boy," the Governor said, "you have got some peculiar notion that folks are wedded to what is *right*. Well, shuck yourself of the fable. For the great American hero is the fellow who comes up a goddamn success, and never mind the route he traveled gettin' there. Mankind," he said sadly, "has come and spoilt the earth for weeds and serpents." And after a moment, "God's damn lucky," the Governor said. "He don't have to stand for reelection on His record."

I said, "Changing the subject slightly from God to you, how'd you sneak Davenport into the Administration Building?"

"Candy from a baby woulda been harder," the Governor said, with a satisfied smile. "Long as a nigger's hewin' wood or drawin' water he stays invisible." I waited for the Governor to wring maximum mirth from his low-boiling pot of private chuckles. "Had four Nigras in coveralls," he said. "They carried a desk in the side door leadin' to the auditorium. *Our* boog, he had a-holt of a back leg. With the bulk of the desk hidin' his face. After he got inside, all he had to do was strip his coveralls and march in his Sunday-go-to-meetin' best to one those little classrooms where they cut up the insides of frogs. Registrar was waitin' with the papers filled out."

"Who arranged it to coincide with this little outing?"

"Your very best buddy at grog and gals," the Governor grinned. "Your fellow lecher and bleedin'-heart liberal. Dallas Johnson."

"Damn him," I said, feeling foolish and grossly betrayed. "I lifted a couple of beers with Dallas just before this milk run. He didn't give me a clue."

"That's why he got picked for the chore," the Governor said. "Dallas, he is old-fashioned enough to think when a man gives his word it still *means* somethin'. He's got so much integrity he has dizzy spells. And he don't insist on havin' his name put up in sky writin' ever'time he empties a spittoon." When I accepted the verdict in silence, the Governor said hurriedly, "Not sayin' *you* do, unnerstan'. But you're hot as a diamond thief. All the press boys know I don't generally move so much as my bowels without you're standin' by with toilet tissues. That's why you made the perfect decoy for this little goose chase." Cullie Blanton sniffed a wrapped cigar in visible satisfaction at his own cunning.

I said, "I can't figure Wooster missing his chance. He should have hit that campus at sun-up. When he realizes how he's botched it after making all those public brags, he'll do something desperate."

Cullie Blanton's facial flesh shifted like melting wax, then hardened into contours of gloom. He said, "Goddammit, why don't you hire out to deliver singin' death messages? I think you'd get your kicks. . . ." The Governor expelled a harsh gust of laughter, startling in its origin. He said, "Who am I kiddin'? You remember what I said back there . . . about how Bertha would know what to say to comfort me?"

"I remember."

"Well, that is purely what the bats leave in the cave. She wouldn't have the foggiest notion what to say, for she didn't know the difference between an Act of Congress and the Book of Job." He twisted in the car seat, full of some mysterious anger. "You know what she'd be doin' if she was here while all this brouhaha's goin' on?"

"No."

"She'd be givin' me unshirted hell about *small* things," the Governor said peevishly. "Yeah, frettin' me to the bughouse. Tryin' to stuff me with warm milk and choky cheese sandwiches or naggin' me to come early to bed. With things bustin' open at the seams she'd be wheedlin' me for fifty dollars to give some beggar had an addle-brained scheme to open a school teaches proper table manners to whores and hobos." The Governor made frightful faces at the road, grinding his teeth. A mile of the grinding and he said, "You get old, and you try to fool yourself. Hell, *she* couldn't help me. Nobody can." We were back in the jungle of neon tubes, surrounded by unmatched bargains in garments and foodstuffs, threatened by low down payments and easy credit terms. "You go ahead and send Bertha her roses," the Governor said in curiously soft tones. The tones you might use in the nursery when the baby has just dropped into fretful sleep after a bout with colic. "Hell, she's got a right to her roses. . . ."

I had one of my very own home-cooked dinners at my apartment. My specialty. Grilled-cheese sandwich, potato chips, glass of milk. While I gummed the cheese, the cycloptic television set traded stares with me. A review of Cullie Blanton's public life was being offered up on a local channel, the announcer's voice hushed with that Jesus-in-the-vestry solemnity, as if drumming the Governor's body to some immediate political crypt. As the old news film clips unraveled on the screen I saw a Jim Clayton with hideously wide neckties, double-breasted suits, hair down to the belly button, attending a younger Cullie Blanton.

The young man who was the old me grinned and fingered a forgotten pompadour lost to Time while the Governor laid crown on a beauty queen. He drummed a table in ill-concealed boredom as the great man railed of the people's needs to the convening session of a new Legislature. He stood appropriately sad-eyed beside the Governor at the casket of a predecessor Cullie Blanton had held in contempt and had reviled on the stump. He scrambled into an early-vintage limousine to join the Governor in riding off to deal with some dimly remembered crisis.

Newscasters dealt in verbal witchcraft. General Wooster, though still among the missing, was reliably reported to be massing supporters at some unspecified site for a march on the capitol. Six minutes later he was just as reliably reported to be halfway across the state in seclusion with key advisors deep in pine-tree country. Hamilton Davenport was said to be lost in textbooks under guard of Federal marshals in a room outfitted with a small desk and G.I. cot in one of the buildings outside the regular dormitories. One newscast had it the Administration Building, another the fieldhouse where basketball games were played.

Governor Blanton, an announcer said, had been visiting his late wife's burial site at the moment the university's first Negro student was admitted. The Governor had reportedly supped on Oysters Rockefeller and gone early to bed. I winced. The fable of what exotics the Governor had allegedly put on his tongue at table, and his going supinely to bed while the very shadows gorged on some dark fear, more than offset the Christian charity of his trek to Bertha's tomb.

So I telephoned Zero at the Mansion. He came on soaked in melancholy, mournfully reporting an influx of cars bearing out-of-county license plates: the rural rabble come to defend gates of the city against invading hoards of outside agitators. Three groups of milling students had been dispersed to classrooms, their leaders booked for creating a disturbance. Floodlights played on the campus grounds, recording eerie shadows. One had been shattered by stones belched up from the darkness. The news boys, Zero said, were driving him beyond the fringe of sanity.

"You better get image conscious over there," I said, "for the television boys have got Our Fearless Leader blowing Z's in the sack. And with his belly full of Oysters Rockefeller. Hell, they'd just as well accuse him of dining on chocolate-covered ants."

Zero groaned. After he had cursed his vocation he said, "There is only one speck of truth in all that. The Governor had a slight headache and is grabbing a quick cat nap."

"Well, you'd better get him on his feet and in view of the news boys. And don't, for Christ sakes, let 'em see him in those silk pajamas, for the boys are seeking new ways to shaft him. If they've just got to see him dressed for beddy-bye, see if you can find an old-fashioned night-shirt would hit him about the ankles."

Zero said, "You think maybe we'll wake up and find all this is a dream?"

"Or a nightmare," I said. "Listen . . . get His Nibs outta the sack.

Feed him some fried possum. Pose him with a hound dog, Miss Dixie
Darling, his grandpappy's Confederate flag. Have him turn water into
wine. Get pictures if possible."

Zero named the King of the Jews and hung up.

13

POONTANG HAD BEEN FED, watered, and bedded when the doorbell rang. Roxie's brown eyes were murky and burdened, though she flashed a quick, red smile.

I said, "We're too broke to buy any. But come in, Miss, and show us your samples."

"The fuzz stopped me three times near the capitol. Are the gypsies in town, or something?"

"You're lucky. There's a seven-state alarm out for you. Why, I could be locked up for harboring a wanted person. Why didn't you answer my calls, Rox?"

"I tried." She treated me to a nervous flutter of white gloves. "Several times. You were always . . . out."

"Yeah, I was out. Looking for you. You want to talk about it?"

"What I want is a drink."

"Vodka stinger do?"

"Please. Jim . . . is it going to be all right?"

"Sure. It's eighty-proof Smirnoff's."

"No," she said, her frown deepened. "I mean all this carrying on at the university. Will there be trouble?"

She had followed me into the kitchen while I clanked out ice trays and bottles. "Yeah," I said. "What is it Cullie says? . . . 'for man is born unto trouble, as the sparks fly upward.' "

"You have a lot of faith in people, don't you?"

"Hunny, whut these ole eyes 'uve *seen*." I handed her the drink. "For instance, I see you have something to tell your ole Uncle now. So spill it."

The brown eyes rounded. "Tell you what?"

"You can knock off the Orphan Annie bit with the eyes. Cough it up."

Roxie moved ahead of me into the living room. "I was away for a couple of days. The beach."

"Yeah. I called The Sailfish. Probably not over . . . oh, three or four hundred times."

"The weather was perfectly lovely," she said, the words tumbling out. "The sun was just right for tanning, and there was a soft breeze. Not too *much* breeze. Just enough to make you feel . . . you know, cool . . . and yet not. . . ." She trailed off, and I let it simmer.

Finally, I said, "That takes care of the weather. You wanta talk about Red China for a while?"

She sighed. Her shoulders sagged in surrender to some great weight. "I had it all wigged out, Jim. Exactly how I'd say it. I even wrote you a mental letter. But of course . . . you can't mail a mental letter."

"Of course."

Roxie sat. There was a rustle of silk and a flash of bronze as she crossed her legs. She said, "It sounds so melodramatic. But . . . Jim, I can't see you any more."

I waited for something to hit me and hurt. But nothing happened. There was no pain. Goddammit, it wasn't fair. There ought to be a rule when they cut your heart out they've got to let you bleed. There should be some great sadness. Some final loss beyond inventory. But there was just Roxie sitting there with her fine legs crossed, the vodka poised at lips I'd kissed, and the lips saying: *Good-bye, Ole Pal.*

"Doris Day," I said.

"What?"

"Doris Day," I repeated. And so help me, I laughed. "You're Doris, and I'm ole funny-face Jack Carson, who wears his heart on his sleeve. And you have come to tell me—ole lovable egg-on-his-face Jack Carson, who has held your hand and bought your twin nephews cowboy suits, that 'we can only be friends.' For Rock Hudson has come back into the picture, swearing not to dump basketball games or vote Socialist-Labor or whatever it was bugged you in the first place." I was seized with new fits of mirth, holding my sides and leaning against the bed's headboard for support. "Who'd ever thought," I gasped, "that I'd wind up being a regular Jack-goddamn-Carson, hah?"

Her eyes registered indignation. I wasn't following the script. I was supposed to cry or tremble or maybe threaten her with slow death. But I stood against the headboard, gasping and wheezing some awful mirth.

"I'm sorry," I said. "It isn't *funny*, of course. It's just—oh, hell, it *is* funny. Only the joke's on me." I managed to shut the insane laughter off, wiping my eyes with a white handkerchief. I said, "Is it Pete?"

"Yes," she said. And brought her chin up to show defiance. "He's my husband, Jim. He needs me."

"Well, as far as I'm concerned he's got clear title. Now don't get mad! Roxie, I dig you. But Baby, I guess I'm just plain tired. I don't have the stomach or the heart or whatever it takes for the kind of roller-coaster romance you seem to specialize in. Oh, I don't say I wasn't warned. The first night I met you, you said you'd drive me crazy. Make me a basket case, wasn't it? Well . . . you could. I guess for a while you *did*. But there'll be no total and permanent disability, Roxie. And to tell you the truth, I feel some vague surge of relief. Some great lifting of weights."

She said, "Pete's in a bad way. The doctors say he may not make it for . . . well, very long." For a second she twisted her lips. "You see, *he* hasn't got the heart for it, either." Then she bit a trembling lip. "I'm sorry for that crack. Pete's really . . . sick. He's past helping himself."

"So the good wife returneth," I said. "Exit, Jack Carson."

Roxie rose with a tremulous smile. She placed the vodka glass on a table. "And exit," she said, "Doris Day. I'll find my way out, thanks."

I said, "Good-bye, Baby."

Only by then there was only Poontang to hear it.

It could not have been love, I muttered to the expanse of rolling capitol grounds below Cullie Blanton's office windows. Something was happening down there in the shadows. A scurrying about of vague forms, a rumble of engines and gears, a quick deployment of men and machines. There drifted up the uneasy sense of some carefully controlled urgency.

No, I said in sober soliloquy to dear-heart Jim Clayton, it most assuredly could not have been love. For love was but another of man's self-serving myths. Spotlights bathed the university campus in stabbing swabs, and in the beacon's brilliance crouched long, stalking shadows. There was a sudden scuffle under a cluster of mimosa trees; a violent balling-up of forms, floating shouts, a dispersal of dark, kicking ghosts. In the eerie wash of streetlights a knot of troopers hustled two struggling bodies toward a state-police car. Through the open windows came catcalls of students bunched in their dorm windows.

Behind me the Governor dispatched curses to his Commandant of State Troopers. He said, "Goddammit, a buncha pimply faced schoolboys and they are makin' you look like Keystone Cops." Cullie Blanton suffered what was no doubt a passionate explanation from the other end of the phone, drumming his desk top with a pencil. "Listen," he growled, "the President sent word not one hour ago that if this thing blows to kingdom come he'll nationalize the Guard. If that happens I know some gun-totin' pussguts will be elbowin' senior winos outta bread lines tomorrow." He took a deep breath. "You get that bunch wavin' Confederate flags outta the dorm windows, and throwin' shower clogs? Well, you tell your damn bullies to be mighty careful how they treat that flag. Men died for that flag, and the first lead-foot gets his picture snapped lettin' it trail in the dust will be handed over to the mob."

I stood looking down at the restless campus, thinking how what masquerades for love is merely an extension of ids and egos. Love *me,* we plead in agony. Be *my* love. *I* cannot live without you.

The Governor said, "Unless you are constitutionally opposed to earnin' your salary, we might engage in conference."

I turned from the window. His face was a thoughtful mask. He said, "If you wanted to trot out somebody could make those college kids listen to 'em—somebody not a bloated politician or fuzzy-brained prof —who would it be?"

"Somebody in show biz, maybe. One of those rock-and-roll idols with tight pants and uncombed sideburns."

Cullie Blanton made an impatient gesture. "Naw, I mean somebody who's one of 'em. Somebody on campus."

"How about the student-body president?"

"No," the Governor said. "For he is a politician in his own right, and so suspect of playin' footsie with the authorities. What's the biggest thing on campus? What makes the wheels go 'round?"

"Sex," I said. "With drinking a poor second. And losing ground in the stretch."

"No doubt they are high art forms and have their partisans," the Governor admitted, "but they don't fill a fifty-thousand-seat stadium ever' Saturday afternoon." He leaned back in his chair, altogether smug.

I said, "Football. I would have thought of it, only I got dropped on my head in infancy."

"Football," the Governor repeated. "Who's the football-playingest sonofabitch they got over there?"

"A young man by the name of R. R. Novak," I said, "who for the last two years has led the Dixie Conference in yards gained and touch-downs scored."

"Get me that Novak person," he said.

"Mister R. R. Novak," I said, "also leads the Dixie Conference, and maybe the Western World, in quizzes flunked, young ladies forcibly violated, and assorted hushed-up scandals. It is said by intimates his initials stand for Rockhead and Rotgut—for reasons you might find consistent with logic."

"Goddammit, he—"

"Also, he is a damnyankee from some coal-mining paradise in Penn-sylvania. Also, he is congenitally incapable of utterances shorn of base language. So if you are thinking of him in terms of somebody to plead with the students for good conduct, you would do well to surrender the thought."

"They must have somebody over there," the Governor fretted. "It ain't a one-man team. We give 'em fifty-odd scholarships to buy beef ever' year."

"For moving pianos or staging street muggings," I said, "you'll find no superior specimens at any accredited university. But for more gentle persuasions, I personally would recommend the Cosa Nostra."

"Goddamn and hell," Cullie Blanton said. "I am caught in the snares of many fowlers." Slumped in the leather chair he raked stubby fingers through his crop of whitening hair. Then, choking back a weary yawn, he stood to stretch his arms in a giant Y. Posed on tiptoe, the living Y flexed back muscles, gulped hugely for air, did an awkward shimmy shake. Abruptly, the arms fell away and the rumpled fellow who stood where the Y had been said, "You my talent scout. Rustle me up a football hero not at the moment featured on FBI posters, and who has got enough Confederate kin to retake Richmond. A girl, too. Yeah, one those campus cuties with the sweet face of an angel and the boobs of a carney stripper. I reckon you can make the selection, you bein' the lady-killer type."

I said, "I wish to announce my retirement from that particular field."

Cullie's shrewd eyes judged me. He said, "I figured that was what all your deep sighin' and shallow thinkin' was about. That songbird trill you a sour tune?"

"The cranberry waltz. Clinkers all the way through."

"Not to make light of your burden," the Governor said, "but unless you can cry on the run we don't have time for proper grief."

"Hell," I said, a little stiffly, "I didn't expect a proclamation of mourning."

He shook his head, a wry smile hovering about the wide mouth. "Vanity, vanity. . . ." Abruptly he came back to his own bed of coals. "Bring those clean-cut types to me for the layin' on of hands. Time you get back I'll trot out incense to burn and goose grease to smear. Practice my goddamn smile." The Governor practiced his goddamn smile. I turned to go. But his mind, which I knew to bound about like mountain goats, jumped back across the abyss to a prior ledge: "And don't worry about your love life. We get this election laid by, I'll pop for a free week, two weeks, anywhere you want to go. Hell, a month . . . New Orleans . . . Acapulco . . . Paris-goddamn-France, even."

"Sound's swell," I said. In tones you'd use to welcome diphtheria.

"Feast your flesh on new delights." The Governor warmed to the subject. "Tumble in the sands with some hot-breathed Mex gal . . . pass the night with one those French courtesans. *That* oughta repair your busted innards. It will beat heart surgery by the Mayo brothers. You like the idea? . . . hah?"

"Ducky," I said.

"I might even send along that simpleton who thinks he is lieutenant governor," Cullie Blanton boomed. "To brush cracker crumbs outta your bed and mend the douche bag when it busts. And Bo, he can chauffeur you around and keep you in protection against social diseases."

"Boss," I said, "you are an incurable romantic."

"It will be my ruination," the Governor agreed, nodding solemnly. I left him to the creation of great sucking sounds, a lemon drop bulging one fleshy cheek.

When I came from Cullie Blanton's inner office that night under orders to secure prize flesh from the campus, there was a gathering in the anteroom where visitors customarily cooled heels until the Great Man could ration them time. But the outer door, leading into the marble hall, was slammed shut with that look of being buttressed against invader hordes, and the hall was dark beyond.

It was not exactly a festive occasion. The two primary delegates present looked as if perhaps they had come together for the purpose of declaring bankrupt a family enterprise founded in ancient blood. Zero Phillips presided over an ash-strewn desk, hangdog face taking mournful notice of a clutter of coffee cartons half full of dregs blacker than midnight in a coal mine. Dallas Johnson slouched in a straight-back chair, a flush on the face half hidden in cupped hands, his person giving off faint aroma of whisky. Now and again Zero would dip into one of the coffee cartons, and come out of the waxed cardboard making bad faces. Behind a corner desk the Governor's blonde receptionist pushed buttons and dialed digits, causing miracles.

Zero nodded toward the door just closed behind me. He said, "What's been going on in the nutcracker's suite?"

"Just the normal thrombosis," I said. "Nothing to startle your average attendant in the violent ward."

Dallas Johnson poked into a coat pocket and the gesture produced a wad of yellow Western Union messages. He dipped into another pocket and produced what remained of a pint of bourbon. It only took him a split second to reach divvy of the spoils. He kept the bottle for himself; the telegrams he thrust toward me.

He said, "Read 'em and weep. If you got enough stomach." Then he uncapped his jug and showed how very much stomach he had.

I riffled through the telegrams, handing them back with the old saw about how he obviously liked what he'd been drinking better than what he'd been reading.

"I'm readin' more and enjoyin' it less," Dallas Johnson admitted. He stuffed the telegrams back in his pocket. "These just a few of the rotten apples in the barrel. More where these came from."

I said, "No doubt your perfidy has been discovered. About how you helped guide our most celebrated student into university portals. And hoodwinked the folks, doing it."

"It's gettin' more coverage than the invasion of Normandy," the young legislator mourned. "Disk jockeys stoppin' Roy Acuff records to tell it."

"How'd it get to be public knowledge?"

"Hell," he said, with a vague hand wave. "You know how those things are. They're borne on the wind."

"He's getting censured," Zero offered.

Dallas Johnson affirmed the censure by nod. He said, "I got a Democratic chairman in one my counties been after my hide. Wouldn't back his shiftless son-in-law for appointment. As state director of public works. Fellow named Harris. You remember?"

"I remember," I said. "From Lawton County. And his outstanding qualification was that he'd gone bust some five times in the contracting business. On his daddy-in-law's money."

"Wished we'd whooped that no-account boy's appointment through with a rollin' of drums and muted giggles," Dallas said. "If we hadn't been so damn noble, his old-man-in-law wouldn't be callin' all mah district chairmen together to drink mah blood."

"Maybe the censure resolution won't pass," I said.

Dallas Johnson birthed an inelegant lip-fart. He said, "And maybe Jesus Christ was a Fuller Brush man. Yeah, it will pass. And I will have to go home and practice the law. For my election is the same as lost."

I said, "If I had your money I wouldn't be digging around in peanut politics anyway. I'd get me a fine blonde and quit home. I'd go to some island paradise where the gals give Scotch and soda from their breastworks and have problems about nymphomania."

"Can't do it," Dallas said. "Family tradition . . . the useful life . . . old urges beatin' in the blood." He tasted the bottle. "I sure hate to practice the law. Not sure I remember how. . . ."

The blonde secretary said, "Zero, you want to speak to McFarland? Of the *Herald?*"

"Not even to the Pope of Rome," Zero said. He tested another carton of reject coffee. The girl turned her head with a fine swish of hair, the better to spiel polished lies into the mouthpiece.

"Always hate to break up a good party," I said, "but God Junior in there"—and nodded toward the door shutting out Cullie Blanton's private prowling from the outer world—"decrees it thus." Then I had a thought of how to short-circuit some of the business at hand. So when the blonde got her lie told sufficiently to break the connection with grace, I said, "Ella Lu, get President Campbell for me. At the university."

When the good doctor heard my request he did not set any indoor records for joy supreme. He divested himself of a little speech which, in honor of the earned letters behind his name, was permitted to continue for almost thirty seconds. Then I said, "Doc, it may be shocking to you. But to me it's just another in a long line of jobs. So unless you want to explain *personally* to the Governor how his so-called request, which is not a request at all but a goddamn *order,* is outside the pale. . . ."

You could almost hear the struggle over the wire. The doctor of many letters weighed his sense of honest outrage against the pension soon to be his provided he didn't run afoul of high places. The matter was weighed on fixed scales, really. You don't get three chins, a pompous air, the trappings of goodly position, and a belly so bloated your Phi Bete key will hardly stretch across your good gray vest, by leading insurrection. His voice was easy when he said, "When will you require them, Mr. Clayton?"

"Fifteen minutes," I said. "On the dot. Your office." I hung up on the president of one of the nation's largest universities, who maybe stood looking at his shoes; stood under the fine crystal chandelier swinging from the ceiling and no doubt wondered if all the brain-grinding hours at books had been for the purpose of being ragged one day by the wiper for a mad mudbog mikado.

Dr. Campbell was waiting for me in the main hall of the Administration Building, his schoolmaster's mouth pursed in the same expression of distaste with which he no doubt greeted students who stood in the shadow of scholastic probation. The hall was gloomy, with a dull, yellow light in which university lackeys scurried about on mysterious errands with that sense of self-importance impending disaster can bring to the fringe witness.

The doctor was a tall man whose head was balding in circular pattern. You could envision him at a convention of morticians in Atlantic City. He would be the one with the fastidiously clean fingernails and the grimly pious pucker about the schoolmaster's mouth, which would deepen when one of the boys told an off-color joke. The boys would call him Soupy, of course (as did his students behind his back), and would struggle to teach him the secret handclasp. But at some point a small-town practitioner of the embalming arts, who would be carrying more drink than a prohibition rumrunner, would berate him as a supercilious sonofabitch who would choke on the vagrant thought of fun. And the loaded embalmer would be right.

Bo clattered into the building a few seconds behind me, gasping and laboring under the Governor's order to keep me in plain sight at all times. At the sight of the trooper, Dr. Campbell's mouth puckered. The doctor touched my hand lightly in a darting motion, and I gathered that in his mind we had just shaken hands.

He said, "Miss Prescott and Mr. Clampett are in two-oh-three." Then he stood back as if the transmission of such intelligence entitled him to retire from the field.

"You and me for two-oh-three, Doctor."

Dr. Campbell reddened but he turned to push his dropped little pot of a stomach down the hall. I followed, Bo steamboat-whistling through his nose as he plowed along in our slipstream. We turned left, clomped up a flight of concrete stairs, then made a hard right to two-oh-three. The doctor frowned at the sight of the closed door. He hesitated before laying soft white knuckles against it in a smart rap calculated to give anyone inside ample opportunity to quit whatever they were doing in the event what they were doing turned out to be of a private nature.

Once we'd gained admission, I had a notion the good doctor had acted wisely. Miss Prescott was one of those sun-streaked blondes with breastworks enough to cause commotion any time she might choose to pass by the Old Soldiers' Home, and she had one of those pert noses turned up ever-so-slightly. She also had a warm, spreading flush on her face and reason to be resettling her blouse tail into a checked skirt. Mr. Clampett, the subsidized athletic scholar, was putting his best drama into appearing innocent of recent perfidy. But his oxlike face made him a bad actor. I wondered if these two young animals had known each other before the authorities had thoughtlessly shut them together in common pen.

Dr. Campbell made a grimace which probably registered on his brain as a smile, proceeding to stumble through a tangle of introductions, complicated by Miss Prescott's contortions attendant to the stuffing-in of blouse. She had the full attention of all witnesses, Bo in his single-minded way attaining perhaps the deepest degree of concentration.

Mr. Clampett, who did not get his name in headlines as regularly as the young men of flashing feet and touchdowns, was nevertheless a handy young man to have on your side in games of mayhem. His bridgework bore suggestion of repeated repair, and there was something in the bullish face that told of being stepped on each Saturday afternoon. He was about the size of a healthy gorilla, which is approximately the size of a Dixie Conference starting left tackle, which in turn was what Mr. Clampett was by profession. He had about him the look of needing private tutors so as to stay eligible for each Saturday's work; and above the slab of face his hair had retreated enough to isolate a small widow's peak. Mr. Clampett would not, I hoped, prove a stubborn man: he had too much chin.

Miss Prescott, in addition to being generously endowed in areas bespeaking woman, was the owner of a well-coached Sweet Sue smile. But she did not, in my flash opinion, sound true chords. There was something in her bearing which suggested visions of roadhouse whisky, or running off to California with her best friend's husband.

I said, "Miss Prescott . . . Mr. Clampett . . . the Governor has asked to see you. I wonder if you'd mind accompanying me back to the capitol?"

The muscular gridder came up off the back of his neck from the chair in which he'd lounged. His number fourteens hit the floor in twin booms. "The Governor? Ole Cullie need my advice on how to run things? Or he want somebody killed?" Mr. Clampett brayed a rough explosion of mirth in deference to what he thought was wit. Dr. Campbell's lips thinned out in manifestation of authority. "William," he said, "this is a *most* serious matter."

"The Governor," I said, beaming my old poolhall Lothario smile full upon Sweet Sue, "feels you might be of some service to the university."

Sweet Sue said she did declare. Her posture portended pleasure. Mr. Clampett, however, had in his muscular mind immediate returns on his investment.

"For room and board and a lousy hunnert-twenty-fie buck a month laundry money," he said by way of preamble, "what is it I got to do besides git myself crippled ever' Sarday, practically?"

Dr. Campbell made of his mouth an inverted horseshoe. *"William!"* he managed to choke out.

"Willyum-my-rumble-seat," the gladiator of grid wars said, huffy. "Hell, I played halfa last season shot fulla Novocain, and my knee throbbin' fit to bust ever' goddamn step."

Dr. Campbell drew himself up and sucked hard at the dropped pot belly, calling from within the stern voice of Jesus-in-the-foothills. "You will," he ordered, "cease such profanity!"

"Balls," one of the Leaders Of Tomorrow said.

Gently, so as not to spook the creature, I took Dr. Campbell by the arm. In lock step we made for a water cooler in a distant corner. After verifying the suspicion of pulse in his form I whispered, "Doctor, you gave me a sow's ear for the Governor's silk purse. You have, in fact, procured something wholly swine, and from the muddiest part of the wallow." I made him gift of paper cup, filched from wall container. "You take this," I said in the same low hiss, "and quaff hearty of juice from that cooler. And by your God and by your school colors, you drink until I am through housebreaking your ape. Even if it bloats that pot you're pushing."

The next ministration was to Bo. Who got invited out in the hall through jerk of my head.

"Bo," I said, "you stand guard here. If so much as the spooked spirit of Solomon singing songs slips by, forget about payday."

"That guy," Bo coughed out. He dug a thumb toward the classroom, swallowing. "That guy . . . he don't . . . talkin' dirty like that."

"He's common as duck droppings," I said. "But I'll set it straight. You just insure my privacy."

Bo struggled at squaring weight-rounded shoulders, one thick hand plucking at his holster.

Back with the wild ones, I exhumed the ghosts of dead charms. I said, "Miss Prescott, you've heard how Pretty is as Pretty does. I've got a notion you'll make the Governor proud. And he doesn't forget his friends."

She showed me how her little pink tongue would look passing slowly along a moist upper lip. "Ah sut-an-ly wood lak to help," she cooed. And you could see the honeydew drip sweetly from the vine. "If ah knew jus' *ha*-ya. . . ."

I said, "Maybe you can help merely by standing by. In case you're needed. And if you *are* needed . . . well, the Governor wanted somebody like you and Bill Clampett here. Somebody respected. Popular on the campus. Looked up to."

"To do whut?" the physical culturist asked the pale green ceiling.

"I'll lay my cards on the table," I said. "We've had a few incidents tonight. In the event there's any spreading of the . . . well . . . unrest, about the new student—the Nigra student"—and I gave it the very careful pronunciation used by Southern ladies and gentlemen in the presence of visiting Yankee journalists—"Governor Blanton would like for you to make . . . ah . . . conciliatory statements to the student body."

Big Bill Clampett came up from his chair the way he sprang across the scrimmage line on his very best Saturdays.

He said, "Hold on, now. I don't dog-rob for no damn nigger."

I said, "Bill, you've got it in you to be a leader of men. I know personally a lot of your teammates preferred you for captain this year to the fellow who—"

"You can knock off the grease job. I don't claim to of got in this here school because my brain was needed. But I got sense enough to know what'd happen if I commence pimpin' for that jigaboo the Supreme Court sent down here. Why, I'd be a marked man ever' time we lined up for a kickoff. I'd—" He turned to his companion. "You goin' along with this thang?"

"Way-yull . . . ah'd lak to know moah about it."

"I can tell you this about it," Clampett said, his voice rising. "You go along with that nigger, you through at this here school. You let these nigger lovers con you and—"

"Clampett," I said, trying to sound like Dumbo Allison, our walking mountain of a football coach, "you're a free agent. But you knock off the crap. Miss Prescott's got a mind of her—"

"Lissen," he said, "you come 'round here tryin' to sucker us inta a goddamn trap play and—"

"I'm not trying to sucker-punch anybody," I said sharply. "The Governor's given his word—"

"The Governor's hind tit," he sneered, advancing.

"Sit down," I said. Trying for the Alan Ladd fog-and-steel effect.

"Make me," he said. "You and that two-bit politician—"

"That two-bit politician has got a trooper out there in the hall, who in turn has got a gun and a near-crazy desire to test its metal against your head." One of the Dixie Conference's outstanding young behemoths slowed down to let his brain tug at the problem. Which was: how hard, relatively, was his head compared to a swinging pistol powered by two hundred and fifty pounds of aroused trooper?

He said, "Well . . . awright . . . but I be damn if I'll play the Governor's game. Count me out."

"Dealer's choice," I said. And to the campus cutie, "How about you? Ready for the Governor?"

Her red, red smile said yes she was ready. Very ready, indeed.

He stood outside the emergency-room door, his face so white freckles normally dormant under his skin stood out almost in bas-relief. The shock of white hair, ruffled, wild, on end, seemed stiff and of itself. His eyes burned. "How'd it happen?" he asked for maybe the twentieth time since the limousine had pulled into the hospital's curving drive behind wailing motorcyles. "Sweet Jesus H. Christ, Jim! How'd it *happen?*"

There was something quivering in my inner box of nerves. *The glitter. The glitter of fluorescent lights, bathing the marble halls of Cullie Blanton's prized healing temple in a bluish glow.* I tried to hang on to the lights, to focus on them, so that the quiver wouldn't come bursting through my skin where all could see it.

Cullie Blanton stared down the hall bathed in false blue light, his eyes X-raying the two troopers posted at its far end to block off traffic. He said again, "How'd it happen?"

I said, "I've told you the best I can. For God's sakes, Cullie!"

"Tell me again," he said, toneless. "For I have got to know. All of it." He sent his eyes to the closed door behind which men in white masks were trying with steel and drugs to snatch something back from an unknown place.

"And get it right," he said, softly.

So I told it again.

We had come promenading down steps leading from the second flight, Bo's bulk leading the way, Sweet Sue twitching her assets ahead of my pleasured eye, Dr. Campbell shambling behind like a dog at heel.

The athletic specimen had taken ungracious leave ten minutes earlier. I had invested the time since his departure in flattering handy information out of Sweet Sue—which Cullie Blanton might somehow grind fine as grist in his personal mill. The idea was to unearth any smelly secrets the young lady might harbor beneath a perfumed façade, which might tend to disqualify her as a gentle Southern lady: old abortions, family lunacy, blood ties with Yankee carpetbaggers, recorded kleptomania. She seemed to come clean in the quick wash. Sweet Sue was the daughter of a Local Success: a merchant of good Main Street number, an active Rotarian, a bestower of small gifts upon his Alma Mater, a Saturday-night three-bourbon man at the club, a Sunday Methodist who sang with neither special piety nor tune, a twenty-eight-year husband to the same woman. Sweet Sue had managed to finish high school in the upper half of her class; had been a leggy cheerleader known for superior cartwheels, addiction to Farley Granger movies, copping local beauty baubles, and for sweetly flaring nostrils exhibited in amateur theatricals. She was fourth-generation South, and her speech was hominy grits and redeye gravy heated over soft, whispering flame.

I had also tried to infuse some lost spine into the dazed doctor of letters. Though my other patient under treatment of flattery had responded quickly and well, the doctor's infusion had been less of a success. So when we encountered Bad News at the bottom of the stairway, in the form of a gesturing slab of hypertension who in rational moments had taught Accounting II, Dr. Campbell was not the man most capable of leadership.

"Doctor," the twitching member who taught Accounting II said, "I was just going for you. There's . . . out there. . . ." And he waved a thumb behind him at some vague menace. "We thought . . . you should know. . . ."

"Spit it out," I said.

He shied at the lash of my voice, saying, "Students. A great number. They're . . . excited. Quite . . . unruly." He was walking backward at a rapid clip while we advanced on him, the thumb wagging, his steps half spastic. Dr. Campbell did not seem to hear. Accounting II fumbled ineffectively at the doctor's elbow in a series of pointless little plucking motions.

We turned down the hall, and there was the sound. It was not yet ugly. Raucous, maybe. A bit of derision in it, but something of adventure, of spirited fun, too. At the end of the sidewalk leading away from the Administration Building a goodly number of students had collected, their focal point my convertible and Bo's trooper car.

I said, "How the devil did they collect out there?"

"Amazing," the twitching unit gasped. "All at once . . . from nowhere . . . by the time we saw them . . . didn't know if Dr. Campbell wished to be interrupted. . . ." The doctor stood in the doorway, numbly taking account of the collected students, his expression faintly surprised, as if caught unaware by nocturnal frontstoop carolers. There were a few catcalls and whoops making reference to "Soupy." Two or three troopers had moved from stations inside the building to positions halfway down the walk.

Somebody in the crowd yelled, "She's with 'em. That's her."

Sweet Sue ran the tongue over her lip, and I took her by the elbow. "Listen," I said. "There's nothing to be afraid of. It's just a bunch of kids. You see them every day." She nodded, the tongue working in rapid darts at the lip. I said, "We'll walk straight to the trooper's car. You get in the back, and I'll get in with you. Everything's cool." Again the vague nod, and I said, "The Governor. He's waiting for you. He's counting on you."

"We'd better call those marshals," the fellow with the nervous thumb said. "We'd better get them here before somebody out there—"

I said, "Dammit, get off the panic button!" The agitated one nursed an abrupt silence. Dr. Campbell appeared to be counting the crowd by fractions. I took the university's top dog by the arm. "We're going out there in a minute, Doctor Campbell. You walk with us. You get in the car next to Bo, up front. And pull yourself together. You're the big man here, so act like it. Bo, lead the way."

Bo bolted through the door, his pace quicker than I would have liked, but the moment to slow him down had passed. I took Sweet Sue by the arm and gave Doctor Campbell what I fervently hoped was an imperceptible nudge. As we started down the steps to the walk (or maybe it was as Bo thundered out ahead of us; it was a split-second thing) the cry blossomed forth, suddenly strident, rising, a high-pitched threat of roar. The posted trio of troopers stirred uneasily, and Bo's pace seemed to quicken. Sweet Sue's firm flesh trembled under my touch. I said, "Easy does it. We're cool." I smiled at her reassuringly, and with the smile (it seems now) a quick, fearful silence fell. A blanket of the whole absence of noise: thick and suffocating. It was, in its way, more frightening than the cut-off roar; there was something flesh-prickling about how the silence came where should have been the echo of the roar. Down the walk, our shoes tapping time in the silence, I could hear Sweet Sue's breathing, shallow and forced. We walked through the eternity of flickering lights and the bombardment of silence.

It came.

It was born of the shocking silence, a bastard sound, deformed and ugly, sired by hate and bred of evil.

"*Don't go with them nigger lovers!*"

The soft arm under my hand turned to convulsing stone. Sweet Sue jerked from my grasp and began to stumble forward. She took three or four off-balance steps, going for a header, just as Bo turned by instinct to see her flight. He grabbed for her, the instinct at work, intending, I guess, to break her fall. And break it he did. But the sudden shock of stopping her full, free-falling weight as he pivoted caused Bo to lose whatever sense of balance his bulk held.

"*He pushed her! That fat cop—*"

The roar.

When it hit, when it washed over us, a wave of shock and fury, Bo was standing over Sweet Sue's form in an ungainly tangle of legs and elbows. "Get up," I yelled, "for Christ sakes, get up! Smile! Smile!"

The roar came up to peak, then started down, and some of what I yelled echoed over the lower regions of the scale.

Bo jerked Sweet Sue to her feet, the sudden bunching of muscles almost popping her neck, and the roar came again.

Sweet Sue panicked.

Her red mouth flew open and the tawny hair whipped around her face, full of honest terror and maybe some strange, malevolent joy, and her neck corded with the screaming: "I won't help a black nigger! I won't help a black nig—"

Explosion. Doomsday in Hell.

She bolted as if to flee into the crowd, screaming soundlessly into the deafening commotion, but when she reached the limits of Bo's reach her arm almost tore from its socket. A surge in the mob, and they were nearly upon us. I sprang forward as Bo released the girl, saw his hand snake toward the revolver.

"Don't, Bo! For God's—"

They hit Bo in a body, a flying wedge of them, too many for numbers, knocking the girl back into him. She spun around, a puppet gone out of control, her eyes widening with the new shock, propelled smack into Bo's protruding belly, and the force of weight behind her felled the trooper as if by sledge.

It was while he was going back that the revolver cleared the holster, and that the booming sound turned chaos into nightmare. The rounded lead slug ripped into her vitals with only the tight jersey blouse to deter it, and I caught a horrible glimpse of her terribly dumb expression at the instant her flesh ripped and rippled. And then on the sidewalk there was the dark liquid, the molasses ooze of it making blots, and the sudden stain spilling onto the clean, clipped grass. Then came the silence that will take the earth when all life has left it.

Bo offered a short, gurgling prayer. He said, "Jesus! Jesus! Jesus!"

Later, I would read that death came only thirty-seven minutes from the time her torn body was hauled at frantic step into the emergency room.

Cullie Blanton was pacing the corridor, wearing a wild face, when the moment came sufficient to the purposes of careful physicians. I guess we both knew from the instant the hospital's chief surgeon came in slow motion from the emergency room. The doctor was a tall ghost gowned in white, his facial mask swinging free from one side.

He said, "I'm sorry, Governor. There was no hope."

"No hope?" the Governor said. "Sure, there's hope! Goddammit, there has *got* to be hope. You got to—"

I said, "Easy, Governor." And moved forward to put a hand on his arm. Cullie Blanton shrugged the hand away. He said, "Goddammit, this is the finest hospital money can put up, and ever'thing in it. I carved this hospital out of goddamn rock and foot-draggin' legislators. I gave you air-locks and miracle drugs and ever'thing a doctor needs—"

"For God's sakes, Cullie!" I tugged on his lapels, shaking him from some desperate, unsuspected coil of strength until he broke my grip in struggle. The Governor grabbed himself inside. He mumbled apology, straightening his coat where my hands had gathered it in rude bunches. "Ever'thing you need," he said tiredly. "Except the one great gift. The secret of life."

The chief surgeon pretended not to have noticed our little tugging match. In a cool, antiseptic tone he said, "The pupils were dilated when the subject arrived. Respiratory efforts were extremely agonal. There was no discernible pulse, nor did electric impulses register any meaningful heartbeat. If you'd like, we can prepare a briefing. . . ." Then the antiseptic tone changed, the voice thickened with a touch of passion: "Dammit, you never adjust to it. Especially in the young ones! You never get—" The Governor patted the doctor's arm in an awkward, forgiving motion. Abruptly, Cullie Blanton turned to take the marble corridor in long, hasty steps.

Dogtrotting behind him, I heard him utter one short, broken word. He brought it up as if he'd pulled the name hand-over-hand from the deepest mires of private grief, until the hands blistered and the blisters broke open in the hauling.

What he said was: "Bo!"

14

THERE WOULD BE TIME, and yet more reason, to agonize for Bo. But not at that moment, when Cullie Blanton's churning legs chewed up huge distances across marble bathed in bluish lights. For on that night, almost from the moment we emerged from the antiseptic corridor to clatter down into the waiting limousine, there were simply too many brush fires to permit excessive weeping in Bo's name.

At the limousine the Governor pulled up short, his eyes flickering over the lean trooper who stood holding open the door that had so many times felt the heavy touch of Bo's thumb. The trooper had one of those elongated, slightly evil faces you see among the hard-bitten sons of the soil. For a moment, it appeared the Governor would say something to the trooper. He opened his mouth, then snapped it shut unused. He plunged into the limousine and wallowed in the leather of the back seat. His face was pained and scowling.

I said, "Boss, is there anything I can do?"

"Yeah," he said, curling his mouth so it drooped at the corners. "Raise that girl from the dead." The trooper pulled the car away from the hospital, stark and sepulchral in the light of heaven's soft moon, while the Governor stared into the night to spy on its larger mysteries.

Well, I had worked my share of the miracles. But the Governor's order was a little larger than anything I carried in stock. Lena Ruth Prescott. Who had won her last beauty contest. Who was safe forever from the risk of running off with her best friend's hubby. Who would get no chance to charm the Governor and thus polish her own cup. Bo had delivered her from all that. And Bo, who sat now under barracks-arrest at trooper headquarters, no doubt twisting the big hands and with a dazed look on his dumb-ox face, was almost an incidental problem. He became, for the moment, merely an object to curse in vexation and helpless rage.

Cullie Blanton said, "If the sunnuvabitch had kept his hands off the goddamn gun. . . ." The Governor twisted in the seat, fingering his big nose.

"You'll have to make a statement about it," I said.

The Governor snorted. "You think it's likely to put the Holy Ghost back in that poor girl?"

"No," I said. "But you know the rules of the game."

"Write it up," the Governor said shortly. "How I'm prostrate with grief . . . how that girl's gone to bring sparkle to the Heavenly host of angels . . . sit at the Right Hand in Glory. . . ."

I said, "What about Bo?"

The Governor pinched his nose. He said, "Say I'm callin' a board of inquiry. Promise swift justice with neither a whitewash nor a lynchin'. And blame the goddamn mob, some. Quote me about how the fear-mongers and haters have got new blood on their hands."

"They'll be screaming for Bo's scalp," I said. And when he didn't answer, "You thinking about giving it to them?"

He swiveled his neck and the big head came around to give me a clear look into eyes dark and smoldering. Anger was in them, and a hate of the moment, and a kind of cold, dry-ice heat. He said, "God-dammit, clean the wax outta your ears. I said neither a whitewash nor a lynchin'." After a moment he said, "Think me up some respectable names can serve on that board. Business executive or two. A Baptist preacher, but not one those brimstone types wants to gouge out an eye for an eye. A doctor, if you can find one has got any human juices." He blinked, thinking. Then: "Couple of lawyers, maybe. But not any young fire-eaters who'd use the thing as a springboard to run for god-damn office. Old, dry-bones type lawyers with high-button shoes and faces look like blueprints for living. . . ."

I said, "How about Henry Muggins?"

Cullie Blanton mulled it over. He said, "Henry'd be a stabilizin' influence. But I can't run the risk. Henry's too close to me, and every-body knows it. The thing can't look like it's stacked." The two-way radio was crackling with action, had been emitting a series of squawked orders in low undertones beneath our conversational level. The Governor leaned forward. He said, "Turn that thing up, Troop." We listened while a series of commands burbled out of the radio. There seemed to be a concerted dispersal of men and machines to some place repeatedly described as station seven. Blanton said, "Troop, hand me that doodad."

The trooper took the radio speaker from its U-shaped metal hook and handed it back, the rubbery cord curled like small pigtails. "Punch the button down ta talk, suh," the trooper said.

Cullie Blanton poked the button. He held the microphone almost against his lips. He said, "Unit one to unit two." Almost immediately the high, nasal whine of the Commandant of Troopers came from the receiver. "Unit two to unit one. Yessir?"

"What's goin' on at station seven, and where is it?"

"Unit two to unit one. Sir, the ten-twenty of station seven is the—"

The Governor pushed vigorously at his talk button. In violation of all Federal Communication Commission Talmuds he said, "Goddammit, quit talkin' like a cop. Where the hell is station seven in plain English?"

"Unit two to—yessir! It's the fieldhouse and gym. On campus. There's been a build-up of people over there. We're sending in more men to disperse the crowd, sir."

The Governor swore softly. He said, "Word's got out where the jig's billeted." Into the microphone he rasped, "Lissen, you boys break that crowd up and don't fool around doin' it. They give you any trouble, go into riot control formation and push 'em back. But I don't want your boys breakin' any heads open just to hear brains rattle. You got that?"

"Yessir."

"How many folks gathered over there?"

"Ah . . . sir, four or five hundred at least. And growing."

Cullie Blanton poked the button again, his eyes almost crossed as he viewed the microphone in close proximity to the end of his big nose. He said, "They raisin' any cain?"

"No violence yet, sir. But they're in a wild mood. The ah . . . General Wooster . . . he's . . . ."

"What about that pirate?" the Governor spat.

"He's on campus, sir. The students have been ah . . . rallying around him. He's more or less directing—"

"Jesus H. Kee-rist!" the Governor exploded into the mike. "How the hell did he get through your men?"

"Sir, right after the ah . . . unfortunate accident . . . the young lady . . . during all that confusion, the general . . . he—"

"Now you get this," the Governor said, his meaty lips moving rapidly almost against the microphone. "We have got a bear by the tail. I don't want a hand laid on that Wooster person without it's a absogoddamn-lute necessity. We've had one fatal shootin' tonight and that's one over the bag limit. You workin' close with the Feds?"

"Yessir. Chief U.S. Marshal and his deputies are in station seven with . . . with the subject Davenport. We—"

"Awright. Now, if that Wooster does anything endangerin' the peace, *really* endangerin' it, and has got to be removed from the campus or anything . . . if that happens, I want one of the *Feds* to do the removin'. Not our troopers. You unnerstan'?"

"Yessir."

"And keep everybody's trigger fingers loose, for God's sakes. I don't want any shootin' gallery over there. If there *is* any shootin', the shots better be discharged in the air. Not down low, where it might cause a goddamn ricochet and hit somebody. You got it?"

"Yessir . . . sir—just a moment, sir." The Governor frowned, fidgeting while he waited. When the Commandant came back on there was a visible tremble in his nasal voice, and his whine was higher pitched. He said, "Governor, word of the girl's death has just reached the campus. The mob's getting ugly. They've started throwing rocks and bottles at the fieldhouse. There's a big bonfire burning and—"

The Governor cut in to still the rising, near-panicky whine. In a suddenly calm, resonant voice he said into the microphone, "Boys, hell has popped and you're on the front burner. Break up that mob, and break it up *now!*" He tossed the microphone into the front seat and leaned forward. "Kick this thing in the ass, Troop," he said.

If you read the newspapers or saw the film clips, I guess you remember what happened that night. What happened was one of those secret shames in the family of man, only the secret got out. Somebody rattled the skeleton in the closet, and the closet was opened so the whole world saw hidden bones.

Within an hour after we piled into the Governor's study at the Mansion, the campus was in chaos. The mob grew, feeding on itself. Folks seemed to come out of the woodwork like worms: rednecks and students and keepers of small shops, unruly and inflamed, crying their passions in magnolia accents, and as bent on mischief as the hordes of Genghis Khan. Roving bands plundered and destroyed. Groups circled around burning pyres of lumber ripped from a few wooden structures on the grounds, piles of textbooks, old clothes, anything fire could consume. The flames flickered on their mad faces, and in the light you could see hate and fear and hysteria. In the Mansion, with windows open, we could hear laughter of the meaner sort, bursts of wild singing, harsh tinkles of broken glass.

Through the long night Cullie Blanton sat at council with his chieftains. It was as if he had ringed himself with old cronies as arms against the dark moment, the way a crowned head whose army was in revolt might call favorites of the palace guard around him in the castle under siege. It was as if, somehow, the Governor feared to face himself alone.

There was Henry Muggins, incongruously elfin in the overstuffed chair he always chose as if perversely to accentuate his stingy proportions. There was Dallas Johnson, chiseled features pale and peaked under stress. From time to time, there was Zero Phillips, his face impassive as he brought word of new disaster; and there was the chocolate-hued Melacadies, with his silver coffee pot, seemingly unmindful of the bombast roar around him.

"Fire in a cedar thicket," the Governor grumbled. "You drench out one blaze and another 'un crops up." He took hold of one set of balled fingers with the other and bore down, as if putting pressure to Christmas nuts. At each cracking, Speaker Muggins gave a slight, almost imperceptible wince.

The Governor spun around, answering the buzzing summons of his squawk box. He poked at a series of buttons, faintly swearing, until Ella Lu's voice in mid-sentence told him he had at last made appropriate selection.

"What?" he said. "Who?"

". . . from the *White* House?" Ella Lu was saying in the honeyed drawl, ending each statement with the rising, slightly querulous inflection that turned each statement into a half-question. "A Mistah *Ward?*"

"Goddammit," the Governor growled aggrieved. "How about the big cheese hisself? He down with lockjaw?"

". . . said tha President wasn't a-*vail*-able? Said he'd—"

Cullie Blanton cursed and switched from intercom to the outside telephone. He said, "Who's this again?" He listened. Then: "Yeah. I'm gonna put you on broadcast. Got some my advisors in here. That awright with you? Fahn." He flicked a switch and the slight hum of the telephone wires, many times magnified, came through a small portable speaker.

"Lissen," the Governor said, "we got more troubles here than a dog has got fleas. Any chance of talkin' with the Big Man?" He strummed impatiently on the desk top while the White House aide explained the difficulties of such an arrangement but provided profuse assurances of how the President was being kept advised up to the minute.

"I sure hope he is," the Governor said, gloomily. "You got authority to make decisions yourself?"

The aide made cautious admittance to a certain amount of the commodity.

The Governor said, "What I need is somebody can talk sense to your U.S. marshal. I need his boys out there to help disperse that crowd we got, but he won't play ball. He's got all his deputies pulled back into the fieldhouse guardin' the boog—that Davenport fellow, I mean. You the boy can change that marshal's mind?"

The White House staffer said the Attorney General would be immediately apprised of the situation, since the Attorney General would have to make any decision involving change of strategy.

Cullie Blanton gritted his teeth and made fantastic facial grimaces. He reached deep inside himself for control, and when he had it in grip he said, "Who is it can release some the National Guard to me? They layin' around in their tents four or five miles from the goddamn action . . . no good on their asses."

The faceless voice said how the National Guard was on stand-by alert. Its use would be coordinated through the President, the Attorney General, and General Such-and-So, if conditions worsened.

"Look," the Governor said, fatigue thick in his words, "I guess you doin' the best you can. But we don't exactly have time to submit this thing to the U.N. for arbitration. It seems like the President and the Attorney General and maybe ever'body down to and includin' the First Deputy Under Secretary of Trivia and Bullcorn is all-time bein' *immediately apprised* or kept in constant goddamn *touch* or stand-by-alerted or some such. But dammit, nobody's *doin'* anything." The White House aide made soothing sounds, though a coolness of manner crept into his tone. But at length he promised to take counsel with the President and call back.

"Do that," the Governor said. "I need some those Guardsmen and a few deputy marshals, if we got any hopes of controllin' that mob." The Governor banged up the phone and propelled his bulk to the wide windows overlooking the capitol grounds. He said, "They ain't plumb out of hand yet. But we don't have great gobs of time. That goddamn pensioned-off Marine keeps up his harangues down there. . . ."

Speaker Muggins winced at another pop of knuckles. He stirred, clearing his throat. "Maybe you better have him arrested."

"I can't," the Governor said. "He ain't broke the law yet, Henry. Can't arrest him for speechifyin'."

"You can for inciting a riot," I said.

The Governor tossed me a baleful glare. "I'll let you know when we got us a riot," he said. "You makin' any headway gettin' that dead girl's poppa on the phone for me?" I told him a relative who had answered said the girl's parents were en route to an airport for a flight to Capitol City. He swore a quick oath. Then: "Find out when and where the funeral is. Send the biggest goddamn floral wreath money can buy, and with my name on in unblushin' letters. Pick out some Scripture to quote on it, too." He raised a quizzical eyebrow at Zero Phillips, who had just walked in the door wearing a look of faint regret at the experience of life.

"Boss," Zero said, "the news boys are having conniptions. I know you're busy but—"

"Naw," the Governor said. "Been wonderin' what to do with myself. A slow night like this."

"Well. . . ." Zero stood, a dejected spectacle.

I said, "It might not hurt if you'd spare them a minute."

"And it might not hurt," he said, "if you'd rest your jawbone a minute."

"Hell," I said, angry, "the other side's getting *their* story told."

The Governor's look was level and cold. "You think it's a publicity contest?"

"No. But I think we're giving them damn near a monopoly on the news. And I don't think that's wise."

"*Wise!*" the Governor hissed. He repeated it, softly. "Wise! Sweet Jesus. . . ." He laughed, or it went down on his books as laughter. "Come over here," he said. Clipping the words. And with one darting motion of the hand and a half-skip on the carpet he had reached for my coat lapel and had it in the grasp of his huge hand. He propelled me across the expanse of carpet until we stood by the wide windows. "Look down there," he commanded. "You see that? Goddammit, you see it?" His face had flooded with crimson and his eyes bugged until I thought they'd jump from their sockets and come whistling toward my own. "Goddammit, three thousand people down there gone crazy! Settin' fires and howlin' at the moon and some of 'em throwin' rocks." He twisted my coat lapel under the strong hand; the grip was like death.

"Let go my coat," I said, struggling.

But he seemed not to hear. The hand did not relax and the eyes did not go back in their sockets. He said, "There is a goddamn *madman*

down there, a madman wants the seat I set in and this state in his grip
so bad he'll do anything to git his hooks on it, includin' the drawin' of
blood." And he gave me another twist of the coat. "There is a girl with
silk hair layin' cold on a slab, and the girl is ripped open from belly
button to backbone. And they're tryin' to put her blood on me!"

"Let me go," I said. "Dammit, Cullie—"

"There is Bo Steiner," he said, twisting my coat into a wad and
beginning to rock my whole body in slow, controlled motions, the eyes
burning into me. "Bo, the poor dumb sonnuvabitch, settin' somewhere
with death in his eyes and fear in his heart, and no goddamn brains in
his head to help him." I had given up the struggle to break free of his
grip. I settled for bracing against the slow, terrible shaking and the
force of steel. "There is the President," Cullie Blanton said, the eyes
wild and burning, "and the Attorney-goddamn-General, and U.S. marshals till we're standin' ass-deep in 'em, and *nobody* is givin' me one
flyspeck of help! And you"—he paused, gulped for breath—"*you* think
I got nothin' to do but trade tittle-tattle with a buncha boozy reporters
wouldn't know the truth if it flew by on buzzard's wings and with
cowbells on." He released me suddenly, his grip going as I reached
the rearward peak of my orbit, so that I stumbled and caught myself
against the windowsill. "*Wise,*" he said. "Sweet Jesus, all *that* and you
presume to lecture me on what's wise!"

When I could risk voice, I said, "Okay, Governor. I rumpled you at
the hospital. I guess this makes us even."

But he was still back in the other thing, looking on it with smoking
eyes, so mad his lips turned blue. He could not get away from the word
that had triggered the explosion. "Wise!" he said, spitting the word
like a gob that belonged in a snuff-stained cuspidor.

And just as Melacadies slid into the room under burden of a new
tray, the Governor spat the real thing after the word. The deposit
plopped wetly on the taxpayers' fine carpet. *Plop!* Melacadies flickered
a glance toward what Cullie Blanton had dumped on the carpet, then
shucked his burden and whipped a white towel from underneath a
starched mess coat. He approached the gob, and his knee was almost
touching the carpet, the white towel poised, when the Governor
stopped him.

"Let it alone!" Cullie Blanton boomed.

I said, "God's sakes, Governor—"

"Yeah, let it alone," he thundered, "for it may represent this world's
last speck of truth." He stood over the gob, a man gone mad, his eyes

malevolent. "Yeah, you see it as filth," he raged, "but I swear by God's many and repeated mistakes it is more of cleanliness than the dirty ways of His creation. Yeah, that right there"—and his huge hands jerked in a spasm of vicious pointing—"which I brought up from my innards has got more wisdom in it than is stored in all of mankind's brains. And you know why?" He pivoted, a thick, wheeling motion, searching our faces. "You know why? Hah? Because it is *real*. It is just a gob of mucous matter with germs in it. And thus does it become pure *truth* and *wisdom!*" He eased the voice down from a roar, and suddenly his expression became beatified. "It don't hate," he said, dreamily. "Neither does it falsely love. . . ."

Dallas Johnson moaned softly. Zero studied indoor stars. Melacadies kept his face carefully clean of expression as he rose from his kneeling position. We froze in tableau, and there was only the Governor's ragged breathing to give the still scene life.

After the same amount of time it took to build the Pyramids, Henry Muggins stirred in his chair. He permitted his head the stingiest nod toward a mahogany sideboard playing host to a bottle of Jack Daniels and assorted mixes. "Melacadies," the Speaker drawled, "bring us a little snort of that phlegm-cutter. I reckon we can use all the truth and wisdom we got."

His scrawny chest gurgled. His mouth puckered.

Henry Muggins spat full upon the floor.

Cullie Blanton sagged against the executive desk, holding his sides, shaken by mirth. "Melacadies," he gasped between whoops, "get over here and clean up this mess. You think you workin' a pigsty?"

The Speaker had known exactly how to snap Cullie Blanton back to sanity—how to appeal to his sense of the absurd, so that he would crawl out of the pit of self-pity. He knew that his old friend was bone-tired in all the secret places, and wanted nothing so much as to sit on the bench and blow a while. But the moment wouldn't permit rest. So over the quick snorts of phlegm-cutter served up by Melacadies' brown hand the Speaker (who was, I knew, himself almost past the point of dropsy) worked at fanning the flickering flame. And Cullie responded. For at last somebody had found him on his island.

There was good color on the Governor's cheeks. He belted down his drink, grinning. He said, "Boys, I am back on the holy road." He snapped his fingers and magically appeared therein a cigarette. From out of the smoke he said, "I nearly forgot the lesson. But by the ancient ethic, I have got the lesson relearned. You know your Bible, Henry?"

Henry Muggins grunted. He said, "When I was a kid our house burned, and the Bible with it." The Speaker paused to draw breath. "We never had to buy another 'un," he said. "I just wrote us one from memory."

"Then I reckon," the Governor grinned, "you know about Daniel. There was Daniel," the Governor said, "who got cast into the den of lions. There was nobody to help him. Just poor ole skin-and-bones Daniel flappin' about in some kind of tattered smock. And, a-course, the goddamn lions. Next mornin'—what happened next mornin', Henry?"

" 'No manner of hurt was found upon him,' " quoth the Speaker.

"History is about to get repeated," the Governor said. "Out there" —and he waved toward the wide windows—"out there's the goddamn lions. You're *lookin'* at Daniel."

"Rest of it," the Speaker said, "goes: 'because he believed in his God.' "

I said, "Boss, the way I remember the legend Daniel had foresight enough to put the fix in with Deity. You got the same kind of prior agreement?"

"Not in writin'," the Governor admitted. He clenched one hairy fist above his head. "But I got me some mean troopers, and I got a gutful of do-nothin'-ism. So I'm goin' out there and slap the lions in the snoot. Includin' that seagoin' bellhop."

Dallas Johnson said, "I wouldn't, Governor." He held his Jack Daniels under his nose as if it might be smelling salts. His voice came out quavery and he kept his pale features carefully turned away from the spot where the Governor had deposited Truth and Wisdom.

The Speaker nodded concurrence. "Too dangerous," he said. "The girl's death and all."

"That's the main reason I got to do it," the Governor said flatly. He began to roam the office, long arms swinging free, a fierce light in his eyes like the old warrior who hears distant trumpets calling him to joys of battle. He said, "Jim, get me a half-dozen troopers. Good, tough boys with matchin' nerves. Get me one those bullhorn doodads you can hold in your hand and speechify through. I want a pair of galluses. Like ole Gene Talmadge used to wear down in Georgia. The snappin' kind. Melacadies can get 'em from my closet." The Governor's mind was racing and he crisscrossed the oval study in bursts of energy and nerves. "I want the official standard-bearer of our troopers marchin' out ahead of me by about ten steps, and him carryin' the state flag. With white boots and gloves and scarf on. And three minutes on the goddamn nose before we start the march, I want the crowd told on those bullhorn gadgets that their Governor's comin' out. Get whoever makes the announcement to go through all that 'His Excellency' horseshit like on formal occasions. We got to impress 'em with the trappin's of authority. . . ."

I said, "I hope you don't intend to wander around in the mob bellowing over that amplifier."

"I'm tellin' my wants," the Governor snapped. "I want ten troopers posted around the marble steps and porch of that big science buildin'. The one near the fieldhouse. And I *don't* want folks chased out of that area with bayonets in their asses."

Henry Muggins said, "Cullie, that crowd—"

"That crowd," the Governor said, "is a goddamn *mob*. It's got to respect me the minute my foot hits the ground. If I go skulkin' along scared to death and with my bullies holdin' 'em back with guns, we're beat before we start."

I said, "You're running a risk. Think about it."

"I have, and the debate's over. Listen, get somebody to make the announcement I'm comin' has got a strong voice. Somebody sounds like he's got *balls!* And those six troopers comin' over—when I go through the crowd I want those troopers near enough to be noticed but *not* steppin' on my heels. Not circled up close like they're marchin' me off to be shot." He dismissed me by hand signal. I jumped for the telephone. Cullie Blanton smiled as Dallas sniffed at his brimming shot glass of bourbon. He said, "You got your innards under control enough to keep it down?" Then he leaned over the puny form of Henry Muggins huddled in the leather chair, and he grabbed one of the parchment-thin, slender hands in his own brute ham. "Thanks, Henry," he said softly. "You give me somethin' back."

"Try to hang on to it," the Speaker said gruffly.

They fell back as the flag-bearing trooper cut through them, stiff-legging it toward the rising marble steps of the science building, and Cullie Blanton churned through the opened corridor in his splay-toed walk. His bearing was that of a man who knew where he was going and saw no reason to tarry for chatter. Trailing the Governor, I chanced quick peeks into the crowd. The folks had that hungry look. You've seen it in the faces of ragged men huddled in front of the unemployment office. The state's six escorting gunmen, fanned out at a discreet distance from the Governor's form, darted uneasy looks at random spots in the crowd. And the crowd was restless. Now and again from the distant fringes somebody would catcall or imitate a hoot owl. There must have been three thousand folks on the campus, milling and shuffling.

The Governor mounted the steps in solemn cadence. He flicked his right hand lightly to acknowledge salutes from ten troopers posted in a semicircle at the top of the steps. Then he turned to take the slate-gray bullhorn from me. The bullhorn hung loosely at his side, held in the left hand, and with his right hand the Governor unbuttoned his suit coat and flipped the coat open. He stood with a thumb hooked into the red galluses, stretching the elastic in a series of short tests. He looked out over the crowd, looked above it, as if to survey a distant fold of mountains. He let his gaze drop down to the crowd. There was a faintly astonished expression on his rugged face. Like maybe he'd presumed himself alone, and wondered where the folks had come from and why all the upturned faces. He smiled once. Just a bare flicker. It could have been at some private joke, or at the sudden sighting of an old friend.

Cullie Blanton's left hand came up, and with the left hand the bullhorn. He tilted the bullhorn slightly upward and settled it back near his fleshy lips.

He said, "I am your Governor. And you are my people." He paused while the metallic echo of his voice floated in the night. As if awaiting challenge to personal duel. The silence rendered no clear-cut verdict. He said, "Our common bond is the uncommon soil of this state where we stand. And this"—and he half-turned to face the object—"is our flag. *Our* flag." He let it soak in and they waited him out. "I was born to this soil, and under these colors. So was my father, and my father's father and his father before him. I say the thing as a boast. For there is a fierce pride among our people, and it is a pride won in toil and tears and time." There was the beginning of a smattering of applause. An automatic reflex. Such as might be triggered when the local Congressman makes his expected declaration of patriotism at the annual Americanism Day festival. But the Governor killed the applause before it could either grow or drop dead of natural causes.

He stilled the applause by an outstretched motion of his right hand, letting the folks have a look at his open palm, and he said, "I didn't come here lookin' for hand claps. Naw, nor to make brags on you as favored creatures." The wind walked softly in the night, its steps echoing from the metal bullhorn as faint ringing. "I reckon," the Governor said easily, "when God looks down on our mudbogs He must see we got nose warts and secret sins like ever'body else." His chin was thrust out and for a fleet moment a suggestion, the merest hint, of some wintry humor ghosted his features. "So forget about the soft soap," he said. "Forget about the fakery. Enough witch doctors been tryin' to peddle those stale wares without me lookin' to do business in the same ole line."

From the crowd a lone shout fired like a raucous arrow: "Whad you come lookin' to do, then?"

"To talk horse sense," the Governor shot back. "You too much a jackass to qualify?"

The cold, metallic shock of it numbed them. Cullie Blanton rained more verbal blows while their senses were still fossilized in the rock of their disbelief. For they had expected to be begged for their charity, only to feel the hot tail of the wasp. He said, "I'm goin' to give it to you without fluff or flavorin'. I'm goin' to give it to you without sugar-coatin' it and without buckets of honey to wash the pill down. For it is a time to take up truth and put down fables." The crowd muttered and milled at the rebuff. They had been robbed of their expected bounty of goose grease and honey. They had been served bitter alms.

The Governor said, "Yeah, this is my motherland, and I love her well. Whatever she is I have helped make her, for good or evil. She is neither as good as we claim her to be, nor as evil as other men have told you. She is work-worn now, and tired. But she is not yet used up."

Cullie Blanton juggled the bullhorn from hand to hand as he shucked his coat. I moved forward to take the garment and he grunted thanks. He said, "I have been as good a son to this mother earth as I knew how. But she is the mother of many. She cannot suckle only me. I cannot claim all her favors nor change all her ways. Not by gnashing of teeth nor by shedding of tear nor by rule of mob. Nor can you." He let the words sing for a moment. Then, softly, he repeated the message. "Nor can you."

He paused, one hand plucking at the galluses, scowling like a drill sergeant. A mingling of childish deference and hostility seemed to reach out of the crowd toward him, but he did not flinch. He said, "You have named me to a job, and I am goin' to *do* the job. Maintain law and order in this state; protect its property and its citizens. You

think that means you? Hah? Do you? No," he said. "It does *not* mean
you. It does not mean you, for at the moment you are not citizens but
a mob! Yeah, a mob. Roll it on your tongues! Taste the dirt in the
word, and the bile and the shame of it. A *mob!*" And the word was a
roar, carrying in it all the ugliness that he claimed. "A mob," he said,
coming down off the roar, "convened for mischief and played for fools."

He judged them with the fierce, nonyielding eye of the eagle. They
looked up at the angry eagle on its perch. The eagle said, "No man is
big enough to laugh at the law. Not you, not me, not some self-
anointed superpatriot, not even the President of the United States.
God knows *I* don't hold with everything put on the books. But if I
find a law contrary to my likin' I have the right to change it if I can.
But to change it through the courts and through the ballot box."

The Governor half turned again, to indicate the flag. "I said this is
our flag. And it is. But it's just *one* of our flags. We have another. The
stars and bars. Old Glory. We are under its law. We have fought for it
and we will not fight *against* it now. We have spilled blood for it and I
am here to say that no blood is gonna be spilled falsely in its name!"
He let the angry words lash them.

He said, "We came out of our hills and off our farms nearly a hunnert years ago to fight against Old Glory. We took up arms and shot
men marchin' under her stars and bars. *And . . . it . . . was . . . a
. . . mistake!*" The Governor threw the five words at the crowd like
hot coals, a spaced interval between each chunk of fire, and he hit the
target. There was a wave of angry muttering and catcalls; a growing
harvest of jeers. The troopers shifted nervously. "Yeah," he roared, "a
mistake! A mistake paid for in blood, and in Southern pride and in
the lyin' fallow of our burnt fields! Paid for, beginning with Fort
Sumter and paid again and again through the last hunnert years. And
still there are jackals and false prophets who come brayin' for the old
debt to be paid through the time of our children and our children's
children. *My God,* do they want to bankrupt us *forever?* I say we've
paid enough! I say we end the debt tonight! Here, at this place! On
the campus of this great university and with the gone ghosts of old
soldiers beggin' us not to repeat their mistakes!"

He flicked his head to put the strand of thick hair back where it
belonged. He said, "We have paid again tonight on that old debt. A
lovely young girl lies forever stilled, her dreams but dust and ashes.
And though I would trade my remainin' days in exchange for the
breath that went out of her body, there is no way to strike the bar-

gain. For the business is fatally done. There is the girl cold on the slab, and there is an honest man who gave the people of this state many years of sweat, and the man sits dumb with grief. He sits under stern guard of those so recently his comrades. He is a good man, as his unintended victim was a good girl, and I weep for them in equal measure —the girl on her slab, and the man in his private Hell. How did it happen?"

In the silence, Cullie Blanton lowered his voice. He said, "I am goin' to tell you who the culprit is. Yeah, I am goin' to name the real honest-to-Jesus killer of that girl. And it was not Bo Steiner. No, it was not the trooper. It was not one man alone who caused the deed. It was many men. A gang, you might say. One of the gang members was an old thug who deals in bitter potions. He travels the world. He is ever'where men presume they are different or better than somebody else. He is out there now, wearin' his false face and singin' his siren's song and he is travelin' under a phony name. But his real name is Hate."

The Governor's lips turned down at the corners. Little sprays of spittle splayed onto the bullhorn. He said, "Hate has a buddy. The buddy deals in lynchin' and night-ridin' and floggin'. In burnin' crosses and prayin' in ways to sicken the gut of The Maker. And the buddy's name is a four-letter word, too. You spell it f-e-a-r. Yeah, and another member of the black gang is named Lie. And there's Meanness and Vanity and Ambition. Oh, don't think I've named all the killers. There's at least one more member of the foul gang. Maybe the most violent. Maybe the lowest of the low. A Mister Mob. M-o-b. You ever heard of him?" They sucked in breath in one huge, collective gasp. It was like a whole town had been kicked in the vitals, that gasp.

Cullie Blanton allowed the horror of their guilt to quiver in the air. Then he spoke in a low croon. "That girl," he said. "She was on the way to my office when . . . what happened happened. She was actin' out of the goodness of a pure heart, and a mind as free of ugliness as her face was free of it. She was comin' to my office to ask what she could do to help. She had volunteered to come back here and try to talk sense to you. To reason with you. To ask you in the name of all that's precious for just one small favor. Well, she can't ask you now. She can't beg you in a voice as sweet as any angel's to put aside your old hates. She's beyond it. Beyond relief of tears, or reach of hurt. You've done all you can to her."

Down in the crowd, open-faced crew-cut boys blinked and thick-necked men stood with bowed heads. A few people started edging away from the base of the steps, as though to seek a hiding place further back in the crowd.

"Father, forgive them," the Governor said in a near-whisper. The near-whisper roared and rumbled from the speaker in hoarse gusts. He said, "You're not bad folks. I have eaten at your tables and walked in your paths." After a moment, he said, "Go home. I ask it in the name of that poor dead girl. Go home and ask your God. . . ." He broke off the thought and his voice went dead, flat. "Just go on home," he said. "In the name of Christ, go home."

He turned his back on them and walked in measured steps toward the door leading into the science building, the flickering lights picking up silver in his hair.

He's done it, I thought. *The old fox has done it!*

Then it happened.

One voice out of the night and out of the crowd. One word. Screamed. One ballbat swung against the nerve ends.

"Judas!"

The Governor whirled, the bullhorn coming up before him like a weapon, to stare into the crowd.

To stare on the contorted facial features of Bayonet Bill Wooster, who stood at the base of the steps. The general's accusing finger, pinning the Governor against the backdrop of white marble.

"Yes, *Judas!*" the general screamed. "Judas who has betrayed us and has tried to put the blood on our *hands.*" The general hopped up three of the steps in a little motion, and turned to face the crowd.

"Ask him where the trooper is who shot that girl! Go on, ask him! He sits under guard, does he? That's what you heard with your own ears. But it's a lie, as all you've just been told is a lie. The trooper's *escaped.* The killer's *free!*"

A gasp, an ugly swell.

"Escaped!" the general screamed. "And from where? From the headquarters where he sat guarded by his *friends!* Oh, isn't that convenient —to be guarded for the crime of murder by your friends?"

The ugly swell, rising.

"It's a lie," Cullie Blanton rasped into the foghorn.

The general crouched on the steps, turned in profile to the crowd and to Cullie, his head swiveling like something on a stick. "Did they furnish him a getaway car?" he screeched. "Will the state pay for the

gasoline? Did they spirit him off as part of a plot to draw the wool over
your eyes and save their sorry skins?"

"Don't listen to him! It's a trick—"

The crowd clamored, surged toward us. The troopers behind the
Governor moved forward. He spun, grabbed the leader by the arm and
forced him back. The Governor barked an oath. The swell rose.

"Yeah, it's a trick," the general was screaming from the steps.
Screaming while the head swiveled on the neck, the eyes alternating
between Cullie Blanton at the top of the steps and the surging crowd
below. "But *we* didn't play the trick. *We* didn't turn the killer free!
We didn't call out force against the people. *We* didn't put their necks
into the tightening noose of Federal power. *We* didn't sell out to the
one-worlders and the pinkos and the N.A.A.C.P.! *We* didn't kill the
girl—"

The rest of it was lost in the roar, but he had said enough. A swarm
of toughs came clattering up the steps, hoarse shouts bulging cords in
their necks. The troopers bounded down to meet the danger. There
was a flailing of arms and elbows, a tangle of legs, and then a great
crashing down of struggling forms. There was all that, in a twinkling,
and there was the roar below us again, and the lights flickering over
the unreal scene, highlighting the nightmare. A surge in the crowd
now, and more of them up the steps. A bottle whizzed by my head and
broke on the porch, sending up sprays of glass, and one of the troopers
shoved me toward the Governor, bellowing orders to get inside the
science building. The flash of a club raised in the air as a couple of
the toughs broke through, a deadly whistle as the club came down,
and the sickening sound of flesh broken open. Blood. Seeming to well
up from the stone. Splattering the porch, dotting the steps, and then
we were inside the building and two troopers feverishly bolting the
door, drawing guns, the Governor's face a white blob of dough, and
in the dough two eyes gone lifeless and staring, and outside the roar.

The National Guard got there in time to save the Governor from
the jaws of the lions, and to save Ham Davenport from the same savage
mauling. But nobody could save the peace.

Maybe you saw the newspaper pictures of cars overturned and burning. Or newsreel shots of the mob surging on the fieldhouse in a vain
effort to drag the Negro out and do him final honors at the end of a
rope. Maybe you remember how they came howling with clubs and
bottles and shotguns, and how on each side heads were broken open

and limbs gashed by pellets and splinters of glass. It took the Guard to turn the trick. It took bayonet points and tear gas well into the morning to put the mutiny down. The campus still bears the physical scars of it in seared embers and in grass blistered by the gas.

Bo had escaped, all right. So the general didn't involve himself in trickery to trigger the thing. But there was some trickery involved. For when Bo (under loose guard because he seemed to his comrades the same ole Bo, so dumb and harmless, who had run into a little bad luck) simply slipped out of the trooper station and let the night swallow him up, word went out on police radio. Trooper Shivers, guarding the Lieutenant Governor, was among those who got flashed the word. Naturally, the word was heard by Stanley Dutton. Who, you will remember, was at the end of his rope. Who had sat manufacturing bile over the low way he had been treated. Who, it turned out later, resolved something within himself, and whatever it was he resolved got acted upon by the simple process of going to the telephone. Where he flashed news of the escape to the Wooster camp.

So Stanley Dutton was the Judas.

Stanley Dutton, the harmless simpleton of whom we had no fear. And he had used brains we did not know he had to carry off the deception. He had gone to the phone, mumbling to Shivers about checking for news of Bo's apprehension, and he had said into the phone, "This is Stanley Dutton, Lieutenant Governor. We just got the flash on police radio about that trooper escaping. Bo Steiner. The one who shot the girl. Any news yet? . . . Well, I hadn't heard anything except the first flash ten minutes ago. Let me know if anything comes in." He gave the number where he might be reached, to make it look good at his end, and he hung up.

But of course it was not Stanley Dutton who got reached with news. It was Bayonet Bill Wooster, who had withdrawn into the shadows of the university grounds until he could see how Cullie Blanton would make out with the crowd.

So Stanley Dutton, harmless, empty-headed, who wanted the world to love him, calmly sat down after he had ignited the dynamite and engaged his guard at cards. The one deception of his life was done.

They did not catch Bo. They did not have to. He walked a mile maybe, with God knows what thoughts spilling and whirling in his thick head, and then he stripped off his uniform. He folded the mustard-hued pants neatly, as he had been taught to do in the long-ago days of rookie training school, and neatly he placed on the pants his badge and assorted identification papers. He did not add his shirt to the orderly pile. The shirt he took and tied into knots. One end he secured firmly to an oak tree he had climbed, and the other he carefully put around his neck. He did his work well, for when they found the beef swinging that was once Bo Steiner it took four men and three minutes to cut him down.

15

THE GOVERNOR seemed to be doing everything in slow motion. Very carefully he pulled his remaining shoe off and permitted it to thump to the floor beside its mate. He leaned against the headboard of his king-sized bed, shooting a glance at his jeweled wristwatch.

"Boys," he said, "I reckon they have named the baby."

Henry Muggins stirred his puny bones on a footstool he had chosen. His slumping posture and low station reminded me of a homeless waif waiting on the curbstone, hoping an unattached daddy would happen by. The Speaker verified the time by slow inspection of his pocket watch, studying the numbers, as though he'd just discovered them. He said, "Be another hour before we get any returns. And just scattered ones then."

Cullie Blanton unbuttoned his shirt collar and slowly relieved his neck of a bright blue knit tie. In the dusk his eyes appeared dark and thoughtful. "Henry, you reckon we pulled it off? You think I'll lead the ticket?"

The Speaker seemed discomfited by the question. "Damfino," he said. He produced a kitchen match from his pocket and methodically began to pick his teeth.

Election Day must be like that day when the condemned man awakens to his final sunrise. There is a feeling of dread about it, a heavy burden attached to each fleeting minute, and yet there is some secret relief that no matter what happens the old and special terror of the long wait will be ended.

"Thank Christ it didn't rain," the Governor said. "Folks can get in from outta the mudbogs and brush. And that'll mean Blanton votes." Cullie Blanton stretched his legs, crossing them on the bed. "Hell, I wouldn't even mind if that general person led the ticket over me by four, five thousand votes. Make my troops work harder in the second primary. Way I figger it, Poppa Posey'll come in with about seventy-five thousand votes for third. And after that the ribbon clerks and feather merchants will be strung out with just barely enough to count."

The Speaker said, "Poppa's hound dogs may get him more votes than any seventy-five thousand."

"Hah!" the Governor said. "That old ghost? He gets over seventy-five thou his wicked heart can't stand the strain." Cullie Blanton turned his head to where I sat squirming in a padded chair. He said, "God's sakes, will you quit that fidgeting around?" Then he proceeded to out-fidget me on the best day I ever had.

I looked at the Governor and thought of the weeks since that night when the lions had roamed the streets, and of the eternity the short span had covered.

The day they'd buried Sweet Sue, the graveyard in her little home town swarmed with newsmen and television crews. Student demonstrators lined the approach road to the cemetery, standing in a sullen silence, turning their black-draped backs one by one on the Governor's limousine as it brought him to the discharge of his duty. They lowered Sweet Sue away with appropriate wails, Cullie Blanton standing wan and mute by the yawning cavern, the girl's father cutting him with sharp looks over the remains. When the Governor approached the father after the unleashing of the last pious prayer, the old boy took a page from the demonstrators' book. He turned his back on the Governor.

So it was no real shock when—a week later—the man who had sired Sweet Sue let go with a blue blast at the Governor. He had done the thing from a public platform. The platform hosted Confederate flags, a larger-than-life photo of the late Sweet Sue, and it also hosted Bayonet Wooster. It was the general who spoke at great length of Sweet Sue's joy in Heaven until you would have thought he'd read the personal report of God Almighty himself.

Nor did we make a profit when they buried poor Bo. The Governor had stood as if anchored in stone, no emotion visible save for periodic flexing of jaw muscles, while around the cemetery a hundred state troops posed solemnly in their dress blues and the departmental bugle corps piped Bo off to the Pearly Gates. Yeah, the Governor had accorded Bo Steiner a formal state funeral with all the trappings—and the newspapers flayed him to the core for it. The way it appeared in print, Cullie Blanton had heaped all available honors on a cold-blooded killer.

By this time the newspapers were taking a solid one-way view of the whole shebang. They found little wrong in General Wooster inciting a riot, but picked the Governor's bones clean for the same sin. According to popular published versions, Cullie Blanton had foolishly gone before an assembly of peaceful people to enrage them with insults against the sacred ghosts of their granddaddies.

The newspapers bannered a story about how Hamilton Davenport had been court-martialed in the Army for insubordination. The details were skimpy enough, but you could almost hear the grumbles of "uppity nigger" over breakfast eggs. When the slow truth got out, it developed Davenport had been given a week's company punishment for being caught on pass in Seoul out of uniform—meaning he wasn't wearing his GI hat.

There came a spate of stories of how Yankee-born paratroopers, moved in to replace native National Guardsmen, had searched the brassieres of sweet Dixie Darling coeds on the guise of looking for hidden weapons. Official denials were drowned out by Baptist preachers glad to have new grist for God's mills. Yarns were put in print about Hamilton Davenport failing his courses, or being on the verge of failing them, and everybody adept at reading between the lines knew this proved the black man didn't have brains to equal what Deity had bestowed on monkeys or mules. There were pictures of Davenport being escorted to class by Federal marshals under arms—the pictures appearing alongside stories telling how his education was costing the taxpayers two million or three million or maybe ten million dollars, depending on who had done the arithmetic. Any acid comments Bill Wooster or Poppa Posey made were writ large and often. Hell, they could have quit the campaign in favor of a fishing holiday. Because the thing was running on its own momentum.

The Governor worked goddamn hard. He was up every morning with the chickens and flashing down the slab to call on the folks, standing in the sun to howl at them until his skin leathered. His voice became a rattling rasp from the thick chest, as he whooped of the price of cotton, of forgotten floods, of the bountiful blessings brought the state through the fortunate partnership of God and Blanton, Ltd. Sometimes the folks stood rapt and reverent as in the old days and were free with their cheers. But at other times they would squirm like a rube who has paid his dollar to see the hootchy-kootchy dance, only to find the midway shill had talked him into mock shows. Then you know they had one thing on the brain. And the one thing was black and wool-headed. So, knowing it, the Governor would approach the subject. He would go as far as he could—and the pure hell of it was, sometimes it seemed too far and sometimes not far enough. For one crowd would be sullen and silent, another raucous and cold, still another thoughtful, and maybe some of the people would nod to show the Governor wise. But you never knew. It kept you off balance.

Now it was Election Day and the Governor fidgeted on the bed. He said, "Jim, you got ever'thing set up in mah study?"

"Everything. Pencils and pads. Extra phones. Booze. Coffee and sandwiches. Tally boards, and election records going back to ancient Greece."

"Let's go over there, then."

The Governor pulled on his shoes, faintly grunting. He knotted the bright blue tie loosely around his neck, patted his pockets, and glanced around the bedroom as if suspecting a recent run by burglars. Down the hall, and he said, "Reckon Aunt Lizzie Qualls will be the first to call in?"

"She always is."

Cullie Blanton chuckled. He said, "Ole Aunt Lizzie. She gets her kicks bein' the first of mah precinct leaders to call in. She don't have but thirty-odd votes in her whole precinct. But she rounds 'em up and votes 'em early so she can call soon as the law allows the polls to close."

Speaker Muggins grinned. He said, "I recollect. Always insists on reporting to you direct."

"Godamighty yes," the Governor said. "One year I was out of pocket and she wouldn't give the results to anybody else. Staff spent twenny minutes huntin' me so we could coax the figgers out of her." Thinking of Aunt Lizzie's adulation made the Governor feel good. He slouched along the hall thinking about it, grinning. He said, "Last election I got thirty-two out of thirty-four votes down in Aunt Lizzie's territory. But you think it satisfied her? She was mad as a wet hen when she called in and hadda report two that got away. She said, 'Governor, I done everything but give bribes or vote *dead men* tryin' to carry it a hunnert per cent for you.'"

"Got to have those folks," the Speaker said. "Wasn't for a few dedicated fanatics. . . ."

"And the pure pleasure of it," Cullie Blanton said, "is they don't *want* a damn thing from you. Most folks are grabbers. Grabbin' for a contract to make 'em money, or a job for Uncle Misfit. The goddamn *moon,* even. But the Aunt Lizzies—all they want is to feel like they got a friend, and be patted on the back once in a while."

We came to the Governor's outer offices. He blinked at the secretaries standing by to man telephones. The radio and TV people would have the results, sure. But the network of Blanton men in every county would run hours ahead of them gathering results and would flash the results over the phone. The girls would tabulate the returns, posting them and sending in quick reports to the Governor's private chambers, and if any of our people at the grass roots smelled something rotten in Denmark (or, more accurately, in their particular precincts) we could get a trooper on the way to impound the ballots for investigation.

The Governor eyed the huge board carefully lined and ruled into columns fit for posting the votes by counties. He grinned at the secretaries and moved among them, murmuring thanks and God-bless-yous to their profuse good wishes. When the ritual was attended to he led the Speaker and me into his study, with Zero Phillips joining the procession from behind. Melacadies padded in to attend to coffee chores. The Governor stirred sugar in slow circles, grunting over his cup. We accepted his silence as cue to our own conduct. Long minutes departed our lives while the Governor fiddled with the dial of a portable radio. Newscasters spoke of a record vote around the state. Cullie Blanton welcomed the news with a grin. "More the merrier," he said. "Higher the vote goes, higher my percentage goes. That's goddamn *history.*"

After a while, I said, "You want me to turn on the television?"

"Too early," the Governor said. "Give it another half hour."

Cullie seemed less troubled by tension than the rest of us. He pawed through papers on his desk, peering over his reading glasses, rousing himself only to exchange hoo-haws when Dallas Johnson joined the inner circle. Speaker Muggins whistled some tuneless ditty from between his bogus teeth, Dallas and I engaged in muted small talk, and Zero slapped a pencil against a notebook until the Governor turned a frown on the sound. Dallas was launching into a dispirited story about one of his earlier campaigns for office when the Governor's intercom sounded.

Cullie Blanton listened, grinned, and said, "Put her on." He punched another button, saying, "It's Aunt Lizzie. I put it on broadcast so you-all can hear." Into the phone he thundered, "Aunt Lizzie? That you?"

"Howdy, Governor. Yep, it's me awright." Her voice came quavering and full of the backwoods out of the loudspeaker. You knew it was the voice of a snuff-dip Lamb's Blood Christian.

"Fahn, Aunt Lizzie. You know any secrets?"

The old woman giggled. "Wal, I just *mought* know wunner-tew."

The Governor chuckled. He said, "Never have any doubts about *your* territory, Aunt Lizzie. With you doin' my legwork I don't believe the Messiah hisself could beat me. Not with you around to bad-mouth him."

Aunt Lizzie professed shock at the blasphemy through an intake of breath. While the rest of us squirmed, the Governor chuckled and said, "You got the mournful numbers?" He poised a pen over a small white pad.

"Yessir, here goes. Fer Wooster . . . five votes."

"Wooster, five votes," the Governor repeated, writing.

"Posey," the old woman said—milking it—"thirteen votes."

The Governor frowned as he repeated.

"Blanton"—and the old woman waited—"*fifteen votes!* I knew you'd beat that ole fake. Some of 'em down here said you wouldn't. But I said, 'Why, that ole goat Poppa Posey never seen the *day* he could beat Cullie Blanton in *my* precinct—even with his houn'dogs.' And sure 'nuff!"

"I'm much obliged, Aunt Lizzie," the Governor mouthed, automatically.

"I could skin that ole Grannie Mobley alive," the voice on the speaker said. "Silly ole fool! She said she was gonna switch off of you and vote for that dern Poppa Posey. But I fixed *her* red wagon! She taken sick and I seen to it she didn't get one them absentee ballots! I kept puttin' her off and makin' excuses until it was too late—*then* I sent her one. Lordy, by then I woulda give her a *tubful* of 'em!" Aunt Lizzie chortled over her contribution to good government, much pleased with herself.

"Well now, you take care of yourself, Aunt Lizzie," the Governor said. "I sure thank you for callin'. You got in first again. Much obliged." He hung up on her closing whoops and titters. Then he looked across the large and silent room at me. "Jim, what's the least number of votes I ever got down there before?"

I had already turned to the proper page in the thick, black loose-leaf notebook that was our master file. I ran my finger down columns smudged with the ink of years. "Four years ago you beat Bosh Pritchard down there twenty-one to thirteen. And your margin over him there was about . . . uh . . . ten per cent higher than you ran state-wide."

The Governor chewed on his cheeks. He said, "Loosen your ties and open your dinner buckets, boys. Looks like we're in for a long night of it."

But it was not, as it turned out, a long night. At least the part of it that was meaningful. The slow trickle of returns told the same story: Cullie Blanton winning this precinct by a hair, losing that one by a smaller margin, first to Poppa Posey and then General Wooster. The girls bringing in the returns agonized and cheered by turns. Their cheers were wasted—but they didn't have the message yet. All they saw was that the Governor had a lead on the board; sometimes a little bigger than it was five minutes before, sometimes a little smaller. But inside the Governor's office those of us who sat as reigning experts weren't fooled. The dice would not, we knew, come up with Cullie Blanton's point this night. No, the Governor would crap out. For the returns coming in were from bedrock Cullie Blanton country; from the boondocks and creek forks and pine thickets near his boyhood home country. When the towns and cities came in, Cullie would be a gone goose unless ancient voting patterns did an about-face. And we knew they wouldn't. But, knowing it, we avoided the subject and each other's eyes.

An hour. And the first big crack in the dam. Bill Wooster carried one of the seaport cities by thirty-eight hundred votes. Cullie Blanton was behind on the big board now, and the riddle began to come clear to the secretaries. Their eyes carried a new, puzzled hurt. Fifteen minutes later DeKalb County went to Wooster by eleven hundred votes. Then on short notice a new disaster: Peachtree County, deep in the boondocks, and always one of the Governor's strongholds among the larger counties, had gone to General Wooster by an amazing four-thousand-vote margin! Poppa Posey had been a fair second. The Governor trailed badly. The secretary who brought the fatal figures was pale. She relayed the slip of paper to me as if it burned, then turned to hide trembling lips.

When I handed the paper to Cullie he studied it, grunted once as if somebody had poked him in the ribs with an ax handle, and silently passed it to the Speaker. Henry Muggins took a brief glimpse and passed the pain to Zero Phillips. Zero handed it poker-faced to Dallas Johnson. Whereupon Dallas swore a blue streak.

Cullie Blanton said, "Well, the horse has kicked the barn door down."

"Goddamn," Dallas Johnson breathed.

The Governor said, "Jim, start writin' me up a purty little speech concedin' to Wooster. I'd do my own, but"—he grinned a twisted grin —"I ain't had much practice at the thing."

"It's too early. Hell, you might come back! Maybe—"

"Maybe Judge Crater might come back, too," the Governor snapped. Then, softer, "Write it out, Jimbo. Play the game."

Forty minutes later, there was no doubt. We gloomed in front of the TV set while a Wooster spokesman claimed victory. He was flushed and sweating, the lights reflecting off his bald dome as he bawled of the great victory for God and Country. Cameras panned over the frantic crowd in the campaign headquarters, catching the zealots in high glee. They danced, pounded backs, waved Confederate flags.

Cullie Blanton watched it unblinking. Then he said, "There's nothin' like it. I'm glad I hadda chance to know how good it can be."

Henry Muggins lunged from his chair and turned off the set. His little prune-wrinkled face was screwed up to avoid what I thought to be tears.

The Governor said, "Call one the girls, Jim. I'll dictate a telegram to that pirate. Zero, you call the news boys and tell 'em I'll be at our downtown headquarters in twenny, twenny-five minutes."

"Goddammit," I said. "You don't have to go on television and eat crow. You don't have to smile at the bastards any longer. You can tell 'em where to kiss."

"Jim!" he said, with something like bemused humor. "Jim!"

"You don't have to do it for the sonsofbitches," I insisted.

"No," he said. "I'll go. Hell, I went when I won, didn't I?"

That cracked me up. I bowed my head and let the hot scald come down. The Governor put one fumbling hand on my shoulder. He said, "Save your tears for the future, Boy. The past has been watered well enough."

I saw him one last time.

It was only hours after election returns made of Cullie Blanton a virgin loser at the only game he knew. The sun was making ironic dawn from its easterly fixations. *Goddammit,* I thought as I scanned the heavens, *it's not right.* There should have been holocaust among the stars, a crashing together of planets, blood flecks on the clouds to record our disaster. But there was only the fresh sun. What a world. You lose your love, then you lose your job, and the sun comes up.

Away from the Mansion, down the gentle slope behind me, the city made its gurgling wake-up sounds. The air was tangy with the special spices of Indian summer. There would be a smoky haze on the fields come dusk, and in the fields the uncorruptible scent of earth freshly turned. Warm wisps of fog would settle in swamp bottoms ghostly under a yellow Yokum's moon. It would be a good night to run hounds.

But I would not be running hounds that night. Though I would be running. For I had come to decisions leading West in the long, painful hours between the time Cullie Blanton had tossed in the towel and the time that I stood, drained and wrung out like limp garments from the wash, on the state's manicured lawn, where I searched for signs of our disaster in skyward stations. Yeah, I would be running—but *away* from the hounds. Away from those hairy hounds of horror Cullie had rumbled of way back there. I would be running, with anxiety in my innards and faithful Poontang at my side, my few worldly riches lashed round and about.

I would put my life in the souped-up convertible and would go, a latter-day pioneer, following grizzled wagonmasters west. Braving the frontier dangers of my age; exhaust fumes, neon villages, speed traps, hitchhikers who would turn killer for the price of gumdrops. And like the rest of Jehovah's foolish mortals would go lickety-splitting down the slab, as if maybe the dizzy motion had some meaning.

So I stood on the lawn, weaving slightly and not in full control of inner quakes. I focused on the Mansion to still my jitters. I felt a reverence for the place. Hell, you can't spend eight of your rationed years *any* place without wanting to take something of it away when the bugle blows charge. What I wanted to take away was the look, the feel of the place. The solid, clean, white bulk of its lines. The soft aura of faint decay told in paint just beginning to flake, the revelation of hidden flaws. The ripe, mystical, Old South flavor of its mimosa trees, arched weeping willows, grassy turf spongy with earthworms. I wanted to take with me the memories of good times, gay times, times of camaraderie felt in the sweet surge of power. Yes, take even the Governor's mad hoots and outrageous histrionics.

I wondered what the old stud in the Mansion would be doing in his misery. Prowling, maybe. Jangling in the never ends. Half-numbed with shock. Taking his chosen poison from the bottle—straight and uncut, like deep-dip Baptists take their theology. Muttering vengeance against all who had wired his private world for detonation.

I glared at the sun's sinful exhibition of itself and thought of Cullie Blanton drunk in the Mansion. I said, "Poor ole sonofabitch." Well, I had to go in there and knock the poor old sonofabitch a little further back on his keester. For the fluttering thing would not keep inside me.

Cullie Blanton was in the kitchen. He was freshly showered, his cheeks scraped clean of growth. His shirt bore the markings of fresh laundry, the starched cuffs turned back to expose whorls of white hair on the forearms. The Governor was perched on a high-backed wooden chair in the copper glitter and tile shine of Nettie's cookhouse. Coffee perked on the stove.

He was eating apple-pie-and-peach-goddamn-ice-cream.

The Governor didn't notice me frozen in the doorway. He shoveled in goodies, and between elbow bends monitored a portable radio telling of his demise. For all his detached air he might have been giving judicious ear to the piping of some light opera. But his nerves must have been coiled, for when he caught a glimpse of me his body gave one huge jerk and he damn near lost the ice-cream bowl to breakage.

"Jesus in the foothills," he grumbled. "You grow up with Apaches, creepin' around like that? Man as short on friends as I am has got to keep his eyes on the door. Carry a gun, maybe . . . you want some this good pie and ice cream?"

I said, "I don't seem to have much appetite." I reached across the small, round table to get a coffee cup. He caught a whiff of my all-night breath, crossing his eyes like somebody had staggered him with a hickory stick. "Godamighty," he said, "you don't have much appetite for anything *I'd* eat, I tell you that." While I poured coffee the Governor dipped a nod toward the prattling radio. He said, "They got me down by over two hunnert thousand votes, and the margin risin'. And Poppa Posey's crowdin' me for the suspect honor of second place." Cullie Blanton wiped his mouth with the corner of a silk handkerchief. "Don't do much for a man's ego. Gettin' beat by a madman and crowded for leftovers by a foul-smellin' old ghost."

"You don't seem very shook up about it."

"It hurts." And pain was in his saying of it. "But I reckon ole Adlai spoke for all us losers the second time Ike whopped him. Adlai said it hurt too much to laugh but he was too old to cry."

I said, "No reason to stall about what I've got to say, Cullie. I'm going away. Cutting out."

Cullie Blanton poured himself a cup of coffee. He blew into the steaming liquid with gusts approaching miniature tornadoes. When he had satisfied himself the act was safe he took an experimental sip from the cup. Then he said, "I never had any practice closin' down a operation like this. Guess I could use a hand. *Somebody's* gotta hang on till help comes."

"Well, the somebody is not me. I don't owe the blind robbers of this state as much as two minutes."

"No, you sure don't."

"I'm not obliged to keep a caretaker government for the bastards until—"

"You're not obliged to anybody," the Governor cut in. "You don't owe the folks a dime or me a minute."

"—until the nuts and kooks they've elected take over."

"Nobody's holdin' you, Jim. It's still a free country."

"Yeah, a free country. And I'm free to go anywhere in it, or *away* from any part of it. And you can bet your sweet, defeated Democratic ass that's what I'm going to do. I'm sick of it, Cullie. Sick of the stink of its unwashed rabble and its hateful pussguts, and jackals who'd sell their votes or their sainted mothers for the same cheap price."

"We changed that a little," the Governor said.

"But not enough. For they are in the saddle, and comes January you'll be gone. Dammit, the legislature will be full of the same ole pickpockets and con men. They'll team up with the maniacs who go around preaching hate in the name of Jesus Christ, and nobody will *do* anything about it. You think that general can stop 'em? Or anybody can?"

"No," he said. "*I* couldn't stop 'em. And I'm about the best goddamn man in the business."

"They can have it," I said. "I leave this state to the buzzards and worms. Welcome to it."

"Boy," he said, "no doubt the place could stand fumigation. But we don't own a monopoly in sonsabitches. The world market's glutted with 'em." He dived into his coffee cup. Then: "You couldn't stand it until we wind things up?"

"I'm sorry, Cullie. It won't wait."

"You headin' west?"

"Yeah," I said, surprised. "How'd you know?"

"Boy," he said—his smile carrying some secret, sad wisdom—"it is one those things the stork tells you. You are born knowin' it. For west is where you go when the spooks are restless. It's where the grass is greener and the promise fresh. It's where you go to pick up the pieces when the bubble goes bust. It's where the sun goes down."

I said, "You told me something once. About the hairy hounds of horror. Remember?"

"Most likely I won't remember tonight what I said this mornin'."

"Well, you said something about how a man is chased by the hairy hounds of horror. From the swaddling cloth of the cradle to the dark folds of the shroud. Hoping—you said—hoping he won't be bayed down and treed."

The Governor chuckled into his coffee cup. "I think I stole that somewhere. I think maybe ole Huey Long said it first."

"I won't quarrel over its origin. But it's true."

"You want some more coffee?" he asked abruptly. When I shook my head in the negative he moved in a concert of stretching arms and stifled yawns. Then he cast a sharp glance. "You think there was any way I could have won the thing?"

"No," I said.

"Me neither. I just got in the way of goddamn history, that's all . . . how you fixed for money, Jim?"

"I'll get along. I had a few dollars socked away in the mattress."

"You can stay on the payroll till they run me off," he said. "You got it comin'. Might need a little Christmas money."

"I can't leave an address. I don't know exactly where I'm going."

"Drop me a line when you get settled," he said. "Checks don't spoil."

Standing there, something swelling and throbbing inside, something knotty and choking and threatening, I said, "Governor, I want you to know . . . well, of all the men—"

But he stopped me, putting one hand straight out and the palm flat and open, like a traffic cop. "Hell," he said, "save it. You might need to write it in a speech some day. If you're ever crazy enough to get back in politics." He grinned, poking the huge right hand across the table. And I stood gripping it, taking a final look at the mudbog Buddha who had come out of the barren hills to do the things he had dreamed of doing. And I thought: *He's luckier than most. He's done what he set out to do.* Cullie Blanton said, "Boy, we been through a lot of stuff together."

"Yeah," I said, forcing the word out from around a spreading lump in the chest.

"One thing about it," he said. "We got more of the stuff on them than they ever threw on us. Think of it that way."

I let go of the hand then. I said, "Good-bye, Cullie."

"Hell," he said, "come up to my little pea-patch farm in the spring. We ain't fished that creek for mudcats in so long I bet it's crawlin' with 'em."

"I'll do that," I said, swinging away.

The Governor said, "So long, Jim."

And just before I reached the door and the blessed privacy of the hall beyond, he said, "Stay ahead of the hounds, Boy."

That's the story, or as much of it as I lived. Like I said in the beginning, it was all just a bunch of hoo-hawing around. The historians haven't yet managed to slice it up carefully and put it in place like bacon frying in the pan, with every fatty curl and lean streak neatly in place. But they will, in time. That's why I wanted to tell it first—before they could sugar-cure it.

From reports I've heard, General Wooster discovered the same thing Father Divine found many years before him: that being God ain't no bed of roses. For Hamilton Davenport stayed in the university, and next fall two more of his race will enter. A couple of junior colleges in my old state have admitted Negro students, and if you read the papers you know there's a big drive on now to register Negro voters there. They'll do it, too. Oh, they've been met with fire hoses and police dogs and mean-eyed sheriffs who wear buttons saying "Never." A civil-rights worker got shot from ambush and the jury let the killer go, and Bayonet Bill Wooster has cock-a-doodled his hate and nonsense through the hills and piney woods. But in the end, it will all come to the same. For he's finding the same thing Cullie Blanton found: you can't get in the way of goddamn history.

Maybe that creek on Cullie Blanton's pea-patch farm is still crawling with mudcats. Or maybe he pulled them out one by one at the end of a bamboo pole. If he did, he did it without any help from me.

I've been in this place two years now, and if you date it back to the day I left him there in Nettie's kitchen, I spent another two years getting here. I got here the only way you get to a place like this—by a very hard route, where the scenery is ugly and the comforts are few. The landmarks along the way were very commonplace. Nameless towns and cities, jails, flophouses, and bars. Empty bottles enough to stretch from here to wherever the hounds started gaining on me. Aches in the gut and vomit on the shoes and hallucinations in the lonely pit of night. All that was part of it. For I did not, despite Cullie Blanton's last instructions, stay ahead of the hounds.

I am going home soon. Or to put it more accurately, I'm going out of this place. Not back to the land of my birth. For it is strange to me now, and still in upheaval. And I don't have left what it takes to struggle with the birthing of revolution again. I'm not enough midwife for the task, that's all.

It's been peaceful here of late. The sun has been good to me, and I've grown some flowers in a window box. My nerve ends have mended, and I've dried out. Getting this story down has been a great relief, too. Like an honest belch of gas with no worry over offending somebody's drawing-room etiquette. So the doctors say I'm cured, or what passes for it. Every day I tell myself I *am* cured. Maybe, if I say it long enough, one day I will be.

So I will go out to seek something of my past. I have her letters here in a neat stack—the months of them, dating back to that first one a year ago telling me of Pete's death and going up through the last one the postman left three days ago. I read it again this morning, and the reading of it was good. It offered me the one thing necessary to any man. Hope.

You can't be afraid, the purple ink put down on parchment said. *Maybe we'll both find the love we've needed. But first we must find tolerance, and patience to rekindle the love. And then enough forgiveness to make the love grow. We must forget the old mistakes, Jim, and learn to live with what you once called "the dark rustle of old, personal ghosts." If you think you can do that . . . if you want to try . . . well, I'll meet you when you're ready.*

Tomorrow I go—seeking recovery of the ancient loss.

ABOUT THE AUTHOR

A native of Putnam, Texas, Larry L. King is the author of thirteen books and seven stage plays as well as television documentaries, screenplays short stories and hundreds of magazine essays. He has been a Nieman Fellow at Harvard, a Communications Fellow at Duke, and has held an endowed chair at Princeton.

King's honors include the Stanley Walker Journalism Award, the Helen Hayes and Molly Goldwater awards as a playwright, a television "Emmy" and nominations for a Broadway "Tony" and a National Book Award.

King is best known for *The Best Little Whorehouse in Texas*. His stage plays also include *The Dead Presidents' Club*, *The Night Hank Williams Died*, and *The Golden Shadows Old West Museum*. His most recent book is *Larry L. King: A Writer's Life in Letters, Or, Reflections in a Bloodshot Eye*.